They Knew W

Jack Bauer and Pete N...
surprise, drawing their ha...
the professionals they were...

There was a stall for several heartbeats as the store's front door, sealed for months, balked at Jack's efforts to open it. Jack put a shoulder to it, popping it open and rushing outside, crouching low and dodging to the left. Pete followed, breaking right.

They knew what had to be done. The situation was unexpected, the solution simple.

Paz was necessary, a living link not only to the machinations of the Venezuelan spy apparatus he headed, but also possibly to the elusive and much-wanted General Beltran, himself the key to uncovering a subversive communist Cuban network that had been operating in the United States for decades.

Putting the would-be assassins in the expendable column.

The chunky guy caught a glimpse of the CTU agents coming, his eyebrows rising in surprise over the top of his sunglasses. He shot at Pete, missed.

Pete fired back, scoring. The chunky guy's knees buckled and he slid down the side of the truck, leaving a bloody smear to mark his descent. He sprawled on the street, motionless.

Herm the driver turned toward Jack, the two throwing down on each other at the same time. Jack fired first, pumping two slugs into the driver's middle, all but cutting him in two.

24 DECLASSIFIED Books
From HarperEntertainment

STORM FORCE
CHAOS THEORY
VANISHING POINT
CAT'S CLAW
TROJAN HORSE
VETO POWER
OPERATION HELL GATE

Coming Soon

COLLATERAL DAMAGE

DECLASSIFIED

STORM FORCE

DAVID JACOBS

Based on the hit FOX series created by Joel Surnow & Robert Cochran

HarperEntertainment
An Imprint of HarperCollinsPublishers

This is a work of fiction. Names, characters, places, and incidents are products of the author's imagination or are used fictitiously and are not to be construed as real. Any resemblance to actual events, locales, organizations, or persons, living or dead, is entirely coincidental.

HARPERENTERTAINMENT
An Imprint of HarperCollins*Publishers*
10 East 53rd Street
New York, New York 10022-5299

ISBN: 978-0-06-137884-3

HarperCollins®, ▦®, and HarperEntertainment™ are registered trademarks of HarperCollins Publishers.

First HarperEntertainment paperback printing: January 2008

Printed in the United States of America

Visit HarperEntertainment on the World Wide Web at
www.harpercollins.com

10 9 8 7 6 5 4 3 2 1

After the 1993 World Trade Center attack, a division of the Central Intelligence Agency established a domestic unit tasked with protecting America from the threat of terrorism. Headquartered in Washington, D.C., the Counter Terrorist Unit established field offices in several American cities. From its inception, CTU faced hostility and skepticism from other Federal law enforcement agencies. Despite bureaucratic resistance, within a few years CTU had become a major force in the war against terror. After the events of 9/11, a number of early CTU missions were declassified. The following is one of them.

Due to the sensitive nature of the material, certain sites in New Orleans have had their names changed or been re-invented as composites. This has been done in the interests of national security, to avoid providing a blueprint for those who would destroy us.

• •

**THE FOLLOWING TAKES PLACE
BETWEEN THE HOURS OF
5 A.M. AND 6 A.M.
CENTRAL DAYLIGHT TIME**

• •

The Golden Pole, New Orleans

On the third Saturday morning in August, with dawn break-ing over New Orleans, CTU agents Jack Bauer and Pete Malo were staked out in an observation post across the street from a Bourbon Street strip club, waiting for a Venezuelan killer colonel to emerge from the love nest where he'd been spending the night with an exotic dancer.

Jack and Pete were top field agents for the Counter Ter-rorist Unit, a branch established in 1993 by the Central In-telligence Agency in response to the first bombing of the World Trade Center. Its mission was to deter and prevent acts of terrorism in the United States.

Jack Bauer was in his mid-thirties, athletic, blond, with a clean-shaven, agreeable face whose seeming openness was offset by a keen, restless, blue-eyed gaze. He was ex-Army, a former member of Delta Force.

Pete Malo was fortyish, of medium height, burly, with short-cropped black hair and a wide, thick-featured face and eyes so brown that they appeared black. He had a Navy background, having transferred out of the Office of Naval Intelligence some years ago to join CTU.

Ordinarily neat and clean in appearance, the two men now had a wan, wilted, hollow-eyed look, the result of having spent most of the night in the stifling hot box of the observation post, keeping watch on their quarry.

Colonel Martello Paz, a high-ranking hatchet man in the secret police apparatus of Venezuelan dictator Hugo Chavez, was a subject of intense and continuing interest to CTU, but he was not the subject of the two agents' ongoing surveillance. Their primary objective was to secure an interview with his paramour, dancer Vikki Valence.

Vikki kept an apartment on the second floor of the building housing the Golden Pole, the strip club where she headlined. The building fronted the north side of Bourbon Street. Vikki's apartment was on the long, east wall of the site, facing Fairview Street, a side street. She and Paz had been closeted there for some hours now.

The observation post was located on the opposite side of Fairview Street, facing the club. It was a tiny convenience store that had gone out of business several months ago and had remained empty ever since. A one-story, shotgun-shaped structure, it was one of a row of small, marginal shops and stores lining the west side of Fairview.

Bourbon Street lay at the heart of the French Quarter, a district whose high-ground location had spared it from the ravages of Hurricane Katrina several years ago. It was one of the first locales to make a comeback after the big storm.

Earlier, at a little past midnight on this Saturday morning, the area had been bustling with activity, its streets, squares, and sidewalks teeming with people looking for a good time.

At that time, Jack and Pete had been in a garbage-strewn alley, making a forced entry into the rear of the shuttered shop. Pete was a skilled lock picker, and with his pocket-sized case of specialized tools, it had taken him little more than a minute or two to unlock and open the back door.

The duo's arrival had gone unnoticed by all but the rats infesting the store, who had grudgingly given way to the intruders, squealing and chittering their resentment as they scurried into the corners, their red eyes glaring.

Inside, the shop had been picked clean down to the bare bones, long ago stripped of every item that could be pried off and carried away by repo men and thieving drug addicts. Electricity and water had both been shut off. The place was stark, dark, dirty, and stifling. But it made a good observation post.

Up front, a narrow street door stood beside a showcase window. The window was covered over on the inside with brown paper. The upper third of the door also featured a window, a square pane of reinforced glass that had been opaque with dirt. By tearing strategic holes in the window paper and rubbing some of the door pane clean, the agents had managed to provide themselves with solid sightlines on the street outside, allowing them to monitor it for relevant activity.

After that came the waiting, the long hours of the night watch.

At two A.M. a big black limousine with diplomatic plates had rolled up, parking in a yellow curb no-parking zone beside the club on the east side of Fairview Street. It had disgorged Colonel Paz and two bodyguards. Paz had gone inside the club just in time to catch Vikki's last set. Afterward he and the dancer had gone upstairs to her second-floor apartment, while his bodyguards waited outside, loitering around the limo while waiting for their chief to finish his dalliance.

Located on the Gulf Coast, New Orleans is generally hot and humid during the best of times. Whenever those times were, their opposite was now, in late August. The atmosphere on the street was not unlike that of a sauna, minus the health benefits.

Adding to the oppressive discomfort was the imminence of Hurricane Everette, a major storm several hundred miles out at sea whose present track was putting it on a collision course with the city.

It was worse in the observation post. The store's interior was greenhouse-hot, steamy, with moisture beading up on the windows. The agents' clothes hung on them like wet laundry, and every breath they drew caused them to break a fresh sweat.

Now, with night giving way to dawn, it could only get worse.

From time to time the two men spoke, soft-voiced. Now Pete Malo said, "The Colonel's making quite a night of it, the dirty so-and-so. He's up there in a cool, air-conditioned apartment with a hot blond, while we're stuck down here in this sweatbox."

"Let the good times roll," Jack said. "That's the city's official motto, isn't it?"

"I'd like to roll over him—with a tank. A real good-time Charlie, that's what he is. He's been making a big splash in every strip club and dive in the Quarter since his boss, Chavez, sent him up here," Pete said.

"That's another one who should have been rolled up a long time ago—Chavez, I mean," he added. "He could have been nipped in the bud, if somebody had a pair of balls."

Jack said, "How so?"

"A few years back, when Chavez first came into power in Venezuela, some Army officers down there attempted a coup against him. They held him prisoner for a day or two but finally threw in the towel and gave up."

"I remember," Jack said, nodding. "The old-line generals were against him, because they were happy with the old regime. But the rest of the Army, from the colonels on down, were for Chavez. Including Paz, who played a big role in keeping him from being put in front of a firing squad. That's how he got in solid with the new President."

"Well, it's a damned shame," Pete said. "The point is that the generals had the SOB and they let him go. The world would have been saved a whole lot of grief if they hadn't gotten cold feet. As it is, they wound up in front of a firing squad for their pains."

Jack said, "You know the old saying: 'If you strike against the king, strike hard!'"

"Ain't that the truth," Pete said. Scowling, he added, "Too bad they never heard that saying in Washington. Especially now, with Chavez cozying up to Cuba and Iran. Instead of biting the bullet and doing what has to be done in a timely manner, the politicians wait until it's crisis time before lifting a finger."

"That's the way it is," Jack said. He had reason to know, good reason, having been hung out to dry more than once, not only by self-serving politicos and bureaucrats, but also even by some of the higher-ups in CTU. Each time, when the showdown came, Jack had been smart enough, or lucky enough—or both—to have held an ace up his sleeve that managed to resolve the difficulties in his favor.

It was infuriating to have to fight a two-front war, one against the enemy, and one against the incompetents and worse on what was supposed to be the home team. But the good people in CTU far outweighed the bad, the unit's mission was vital to the national security, and so Jack Bauer soldiered on. He knew Pete Malo felt the same way.

"We're the shovel brigade," Jack said. "They call us out to clean up the mess after it's made, not before."

"Maybe this time we'll get a head start on the opposition," Pete said. Abruptly his mood changed, brightening up. "On the plus side, if not for Paz, we wouldn't be looking forward to meeting Vikki Valence."

"That should be quite an experience," Jack agreed, his tone dry, lightly mocking.

Pete said, "What makes a gal like Vikki, a stripper and a gold digger who probably never had a political thought in her head, contact CTU and request a meet?"

"Maybe she's patriotic."

"Maybe," Pete said, sounding doubtful.

Jack said, "You can ask her when Colonel Paz leaves."

"If he leaves. How much longer is he going to stay?"

Jack shrugged. "I'll say this, though. She sure knew the magic word: Beltran."

Beltran was a magic word as far as CTU was concerned, all right.

Venezuela's President Chavez was a great admirer of communist Cuba and had moved swiftly to forge an alliance with that island nation. A dangerous liaison, as Washington saw it. In the last twelve months, U.S. intelligence had noticed a heightened level of combined Venezuela/Cuba espionage operations, not only in Latin America, but also in the United States.

Recently Colonel Paz had been assigned to a special branch of the Venezuelan trade consulate here in New Orleans, a hotbed of spies and special action agents that had become an object of no small interest to a number of U.S. military and civilian spy agencies.

Less than twenty-four hours ago, Vikki Valence, stating that she had some important information to disclose, had contacted a special CTU phone hotline established for the purpose of receiving tips and information from the public. What the information was, she wouldn't say on the phone, but she offered up two nuggets that pushed her call to a priority level.

She said that she was Colonel Paz's girlfriend, and that Paz had linked up with a man named Beltran.

More than that she would not add, except to say that she was in some fear for her life and that she would tell all she knew in return for protection.

The vast majority of callers to the hotline were anonymous tipsters, so Vikki's having given her real name went a long way toward establishing her credibility. Colonel Paz was already on CTU's hot list, but it was the mention of Beltran's name that galvanized the agency's action arm.

General Hector Beltran was a high-ranking veteran officer for Fidel Castro's spy service. For decades he'd been a mainstay of communist Cuba's secret police and counter-espionage operations, ruthlessly suppressing dissidents at home while exporting subversion to other countries.

A brilliant and ruthless spymaster who'd scored notable successes during the Cold War era and afterward, Beltran had dropped off the radar in recent years, leading to the belief in U.S. intelligence circles, or rather the hope, that he was either retired, imprisoned in one of Castro's jails, or dead.

If he was alive and in the United States, as Vikki's call indicated, he could only be on active duty, engaged in some mission of vital importance to Cuba, one that associated him with the Venezuelan threat in the form of Colonel Paz. Vital indeed, for Beltran to risk his own neck by operating in person on U.S. soil, where he was subject to immediate arrest and imprisonment.

Catching him would rank as one of the intelligence coups of the new century.

So it was that Jack Bauer and Pete Malo found themselves in a stifling hole-in-the-wall just off Bourbon Street, surveilling a striptease club. The plan was to wait for Paz to conclude his nightlong assignation with Vikki Valence, then move in to contact her and remove her to safety after Paz had left the scene.

They had to move lightly, walk softly. Paz was no fool; Beltran was an old fox. A too-heavy CTU presence in the area risked tipping off either one or both that something was afoot. Beltran especially would go to ground at the least sign of trouble, thwarting any possibility of his capture. Jack and Pete were operating alone on the scene, to leave as light a CTU footprint as possible.

A tantalizing view of Vikki Valence could be seen in all her full-bodied glory on the opposite side of Fairview Street. Not in the flesh, but in the form of a life-sized photo image of the platinum-blond powerhouse mounted on reinforced cardboard and attached to a sandwich marquee standing outside the Golden Pole, as the club was named.

The Golden Pole was housed in a big, blocky, two-story rectangle of cream-colored stone that was trimmed with ornate, black iron grille work and topped with a mansard roof. The first floor housed the club proper, while the second floor was given over to private apartments—a useful arrangement for those who sought extracurricular, after-hours trysts with the dancers who occupied them. The upper floor had a roofed-over balcony that extended to three sides of the building, though not the front.

The club took its name from a set of shiny, gold-painted firehouse poles onstage that the dancers entwined themselves around during their sets. It was now closed, neon signs dark, windows curtained, doors locked. Even on Bourbon Street during the weekend, the joints have to close sometime, if only so their denizens could rest up for the next night's revels.

Jack stood at the shop's front door, peering through the smudgy glass pane set at eye level, looking across the street at the long east wall of the club building. There a side door, solid and now shut, stood at ground level. Mounted over the top of the door frame was a low-wattage night lamp, wan in the coming light of day.

To the right of the door, a black iron frame stairway angled up from sidewalk to balcony, accessing the row of apartments on the second floor. He knew that inside the building, several other stairwells also connected to the upper floor.

The apartment doors lining the second-floor balcony were closed and their curtained windows dark, including the third window from the right, Vikki Valence's apartment, into which she and the Colonel had retired several hours ago.

Below, at street level, the curb was painted yellow, and posted nearby in plain view was a NO PARKING sign. Parked alongside it was a long black limousine with diplomatic license plates, accessorized with two of Paz's bodyguards who stood waiting around on the sidewalk.

The vehicle seemed only slightly smaller than a cabin cruiser. Its front thrust forward aggressively and at length, terminating in a snarling chromium grille. The car body hung low and heavy on the chassis, leaving not much clearance between its underside and the street, a giveaway that it was an armor-plated job.

That meant that the tires would be solid clear through, reinforced to carry the extra weight of the plating. Bulletproof, too, just like the windows and windshields.

The machine had arrived at two A.M., and the bodyguards had been standing around outside since then, keeping watch over it and their surroundings. Both men were Paz associates whose identities were long known by CTU.

They were Aldo Baca and Ramon Espinosa, a pair of Venezuelan nationals officially assigned to the same trade consulate in New Orleans as Colonel Paz, and legally registered as members of the diplomatic corps. That little technicality gave them, like their boss, diplomatic immunity, shielding them from arrest and imprisonment by law enforcement agencies of the host country. If caught violating U.S. law, they could only be detained and deported.

Officially, that is. But CTU sometimes had ways of getting around red tape when it hampered national security.

Baca and Espinosa had similar backgrounds: both were mid-level operatives of the Venezuelan secret police, enforcers who could be relied on for strong-arm tactics, intimidation, violence, and murder. Both also shared a modest proficiency in English.

Baca was tall, rangy, and restless; Espinosa was a hulking bodybuilder type, oxlike and impassive. Despite the stifling heat and humidity, they both wore sport coats, the better to conceal the guns carried on their persons. Judging by the big bulges deforming the lightweight jackets, they were armed with mini-cannons.

Jack and Pete had guns, too. Everybody was packing.

It had been a long night for the Colonel's protectors. There wasn't much for them to do but chat, smoke, and eyeball their surroundings, watching for signs of threat or trouble.

They were completely oblivious and unsuspecting of the presence of Jack and Pete in the dark, shuttered shop across the street and remained so as the hours passed, night giving way to gray, misty predawn.

Now was the slack time, the ebb tide, the hour when Bourbon Street is as quiet and deserted as it ever gets. Not that quiet, though, thanks to the rumbling hum of countless air conditioners mounted in the windows of buildings throughout the neighborhood.

Still, the late night revelers had all gone home and the early morning lushes had not yet appeared, the bars and gin mills remaining as yet unopened for the day.

A figure appeared, emerging from the square, entering the south end of Fairview and walking north. A teenager, possibly Latino, small and slight, with thick, straight black hair hanging down to his jawline, covering much of his beardless face. He wore wire-rimmed glasses with oval lenses, a loose-fitting, short-sleeved shirt, baggy blue jeans, and sneakers. He walked with head down and hands jammed in the front pockets of his pants as he made his way, trudging along, minding his own business.

He couldn't have looked more inconsequential and inoffensive; bodyguards Baca and Espinosa barely gave him a second glance. He walked north to the next block, turning left at the corner and vanishing from sight.

The bodybuilder, Espinosa, lit up a little chocolate-brown cigarillo. Clamped between his massive jaws, it looked like a toothpick.

Aldo Baca spat, stretched, yawned. His jacket fell open, revealing a gun worn butt-out in a leather shoulder holster under his left arm. He crossed his arms over his chest and resumed leaning against the side of the limo.

Jack Bauer said, "Something's happening." He was looking at the second floor, at Vikki Valence's flat, where a light had just come on, showing behind a curtained window as a pale, yellow light.

"Looks like Paz is ready to call it a night," he said.

Baca and Espinosa saw it, too. They perked up—the long wait was over and soon they'd be on the move. The big man, Espinosa, glanced downward at the side door at street level, a tell indicating that that was where he expected his boss to emerge.

Aldo Baca straightened up from where he'd been leaning against the car's right rear fender. A smudged patch marred the finish of the machine's curved, gleaming black carapace. He took out a dirty handkerchief and rubbed the smudge, succeeding only in spreading it. He quickly pocketed the handkerchief and stepped away from the car, sticking his hands in his pockets and trying to look like he'd had nothing to do with soiling the finish of the car.

At the north end of Fairview Street, a utility truck rounded the corner and came into view, proceeding slowly southbound toward the Bourbon Street square.

Its cab fronted an oblong-shaped container box. Mounted on the roof of the box was a collapsible sectioned ladder. Blazoned on its sides was the logo of the local electric power company.

It rolled up alongside the limo, halted, and stood there in the street, idling. A heavy idle; the dirty gray exhaust clouds pouring from its tailpipe showed that it was long overdue for a much-needed tune-up. The cab windows were open on the driver's side and the passenger's side. Maybe the air conditioner was out of order.

It stood in place, not going anywhere. In the cab were two riders, a driver and a passenger. Both wore identical outfits of drab gray-green overalls.

The driver was in his mid-fifties, bareheaded, crew cut, with a pink, pear-shaped face and walrus mustache. Hands the size of oven mitts gripped the steering wheel. He was chomping on something, a piece of gum or a wad of chewing tobacco that made a walnut-sized lump in his cheek. He looked bored.

His partner, seated on the passenger side, wore a duck-billed baseball cap the same gray-green color as his overalls. He was slight, wiry, deeply tanned, his clean-shaven, wedge-shaped face a mass of fine lines and wrinkles set in a mask of perpetual irritation.

He rolled down his window, cupped a hand at the side of his mouth, and called to the men on the sidewalk, "Hey! Hey y'all!"

Baca and Espinosa turned to look at the speaker. The man in the baseball cap said, "That your car?"

Espinosa, shrugging his massive shoulders, said, "I don't know."

The newcomer was incredulous. "You don't know? You look like you belong to it. Y'all ain't standing around here waiting for no bus, that's for sure."

Baca spat, sneered, and said, "So what?"

"You got to move it, that's what," the man in the baseball cap said.

Baca's only reply was a widening of his sneer. Espinosa's gaze was mild, bovine, as he continued to puff away on his cigarillo. Neither moved to comply.

The truck driver turned to his companion. "Show them the work order, Dixie." He had a heavy Teutonic accent.

"Okay, Herm," Dixie said. He reached into the glove compartment, pulled out a sheaf of official-looking papers, and held them out the window toward the others.

"See this? I'm a power company repairman and I've got a work order to fix that lamppost," Dixie said, indicating the streetlight standing on the corner.

The lamp globe was still lit, pale and wan in the gray predawn gloom. Espinosa said, "It looks okay to me."

"We still got to inspect it. Orders," Dixie said, as if that were the definitive last word on the subject.

Espinosa said, "Who's stopping you?"

"You are. We got to use the ladder and we can't because your car's in the way," the repairman said. He stuck his head further out the window, cording his neck muscles. The veins standing out on the sides of his forehead were thick as pencils. He said, "You're parked in a no-parking area, or can't you read?"

Baca rose to the bait. "What do you care? You're no cop!"

The driver, Herm, remained facing front, staring straight ahead through the windshield at nothing, as though the conversation didn't concern him.

Dixie said, "You better haul ass and get that car out of here before I call a cop to come and have it towed away."

Baca, smug, played his trump card, gesturing toward the limo's license plates. "You blind? It says 'Diplomat.' That means we park where we like and to hell with your cops."

Dixie, stubborn, shook his head. "That don't cut no ice with me or the power company, neither. Get it in gear and haul ass out of here."

The building's side door swung open, outward, revealing a man standing framed in the doorway. Behind him, a long, steep flight of stairs slanted upward, quickly becoming lost in the gloomy dark of the stairwell.

Pete Malo nudged Jack, murmured, "Colonel Paz." Jack nodded, not taking his eyes off the scene playing out before him.

Paz stepped down to the sidewalk, a spring mechanism pulling the door shut behind him. A short, squat, bull-necked individual built like a fireplug, he had a head the shape of a pineapple, with a pockmarked complexion to match. His eyes were long, narrow slits. He sported a neatly trimmed little eyebrow mustache.

He wore a woven straw Borsalino-style hat; a dark blue blazer with gold buttons; a loud, floral print–patterned sport shirt; wide-cut khaki pants; and two-toned brown-and-white loafers with tasseled uppers. His right arm hung down at his side, holding an executive-style attaché case.

An unlit cigar jutted from the side of his mouth, clamped in place between steel-trap jaws. He glanced quizzically at the interplay between his bodyguards and the repairman.

Baca told the repairman, "Okay, we go now. Happy?"

"That's more like it," Dixie said. The hand holding the work orders retracted back into the cab, dropping out of sight below the top of the passenger side door. It flashed into view again, this time holding a gun, a semi-automatic pistol with what looked like a silver hot dog screwed onto the end of the barrel.

He squeezed the trigger, shooting Baca in the throat. The silver hot dog was a silencer, muffling the report to a sound like that of a piece of cloth tearing.

Baca lurched back a few steps, then folded at the knees, sitting down hard on the sidewalk. He clutched with both hands the hole in his neck that was jetting out blood. Streams of blood, so dark they looked black. Lots of it, geysering.

Baca choked, making sputtering noises. He went horizontal, writhing on the pavement, still holding his throat with both hands.

Dixie shot Espinosa in the eye, the bullet emerging out the back of his head. The big man toppled, smacking the concrete with a meaty thud.

Dixie's primary target was Paz, but the bodyguards had stood between him and the Colonel. He'd had to clear them away to get Paz in the firing line. Espinosa now lay stone dead, but Baca was still flopping around on the sidewalk. Dixie shot him in the chest, stilling him.

The instant it took him to finish off Baca was the margin of life or death for Paz, giving him time to counter with a secret weapon.

The attaché case had nagged at Jack Bauer from the instant he saw it, since it seemed out of character with the rest of Paz's leisure time outfit. But for all he knew, it could have held a couple bottles of booze and some sex toys to spice up the hours spent in Vikki's boudoir.

Now Jack realized that his first impression was right, and that the attaché case was more than it seemed.

Colonel Paz raised it at a tilted angle, pointing its narrow front side at Dixie. He made some quick, tricky little hand movement, fingers writhing, pulling at something on the handle.

Gunfire erupted from the side of the attaché case, sending a burst of rounds ripping up the side of the truck cab's passenger door and then ripping up Dixie, who jerked and flopped around in his seat as he was shot to pieces.

He looked outraged, as though indignant that Paz had committed some sort of unsportsmanlike conduct in not letting himself be slaughtered on the spot but instead terminating the assassin.

Herm the driver no longer looked bored. He flung open the door and jackknifed out of the cab, flopping heavily on the asphalt. The truck now screened him from Colonel Paz. He reached into the cab and hauled out a long-barreled .44.

Paz ducked down on the sidewalk, covering behind the bulk of his armored limousine. Hunkering down, he popped open the attaché case, flinging back the lid and revealing the gimmick that had let him shoot as if by magic.

Inside the shell of the gimmicked case was an Uzi-style machine pistol secured in a wooden frame. One end of a length of baling wire had been looped around the trigger, leaving a fraction of an inch or so of play in it. The wire was threaded through a set of eyelet screws mounted in the frame, emerging through a hole in the top of the case, where the opposite end was secured to the handle.

All he'd had to do was reach down around the underside of the handle, wrap his fingertips around the wire, and pull, tightening the wire noose around the trigger and firing the gun.

It was a neat little trick that had served him well in the past, back in the early years when he'd been a drug gang enforcer and executioner.

Paz now craved more direct action. The machine pistol's trigger guard had been removed, allowing him to slip the wire noose free and loose the weapon from its mounting in the case.

Herm had now regained his feet and stood crouching behind the truck cab, reaching around it to shoot at Paz, the big .44 reports booming like artillery fire.

It had all gone down like lightning: Dixie gunning down the bodyguards, Paz shredding Dixie with his attaché case gun, Herm the driver now taking potshots at Paz while the latter sheltered behind the armored limo, cradling a machine pistol.

Suddenly the situation was dealt another wild card, as the truck's back doors popped open and a new shooter popped out.

Jack recognized him as the long-haired youth in glasses who'd strolled down the street earlier, right before the advent of the utility truck. He must have been the spotter, casing the scene in advance of the other assassins. He now had a gun in each hand, shiny, chrome-plated .32 pistols, and he came out with both barrels blazing.

He hit the pavement running on sneakered feet, dashing behind the back of a car parked several lengths behind the limo and taking cover.

He blasted away in Paz's direction, not hitting him, but making plenty of noise.

Bullets spanged the limo's armor plating, turning into lead smears. Other rounds tagged the bulletproof windows, starring but not shattering them.

In his wake, the truck box yielded two more shooters, one a chunky guy and another wearing a red bandana knotted around the top of his head, pirate style.

The chunky guy featured an Elvis-style pompadour, sunglasses, and a goatee, and wielded a 9mm Beretta semiautomatic pistol. Hopping down to the asphalt, he dodged around the left rear corner of the truck, putting him on the same side as Herm the driver.

The third man, the bandana wearer, was reluctant to leave the cover of the truck box. Remaining inside, he peeped around the edge of the right rear of the door frame, reached around it with his gun, and snapped off shots at Paz.

He fired deliberately, methodically, mechanically. Bullets hit the club building, pecking out craters in the stone wall.

Jack Bauer and Pete Malo recovered quickly from the surprise, drawing their handguns and going into action like the professionals they were.

There was a stall for several heartbeats as the store's front door, sealed for months, balked at Jack's efforts to open it. Jack put a shoulder to it, popping it open and rushing outside, crouching low and dodging to the left. Pete followed, breaking right.

They knew what had to be done. The situation was unexpected, the solution simple.

Paz was necessary, a living link not only to the machinations of the Venezuelan spy apparatus he headed, but also possibly to the elusive and much-wanted General Beltran, himself the key to uncovering a subversive communist Cuban network that had been operating in the United States for decades.

Putting the would-be assassins in the expendable column.

The chunky guy caught a glimpse of the CTU agents coming, his eyebrows rising in surprise over the top of his sunglasses. He shot at Pete, missed.

Pete fired back, scoring. The chunky guy's knees buckled and he slid down the side of the truck, leaving a bloody smear to mark his descent. He sprawled on the street, motionless.

Herm the driver turned toward Jack, the two throwing down on each other at the same time. Jack fired first, pumping two slugs into the driver's middle, all but cutting him in two.

At that, Herm still had enough left to burn off a shot as he folded, firing wildly into the side of a parked car. The impact sounded like the vehicle had been broadsided by a wrecking ball.

Still sheltering inside the truck box, Bandana Top discovered that it wasn't bulletproof as he thought as Colonel Paz fired a burst through the walls and into him. He spun around in a half turn, falling from the truck into the street.

The two-gun kid with the glasses was in a tight spot, caught between the twin fires of Paz and the CTU agents. He alternated, firing one gun at Paz and the other at the agents, hitting neither. It was a technique that worked better in the movies than it did in real life.

Pete Malo threw a couple of shots his way and missed, shooting out a headlight and windshield of a car behind the one where the kid was sheltering.

The kid sent one Jack's way, coming so close that Jack could feel the passage of the round whizzing past his head. Jack fired back, Pete joining in.

A round tagged the kid on his left side, spinning him. His feet got tangled with each other and he tripped, falling sideways into the street, shooting away as he toppled.

He was still jerking the triggers when he caught the slug that finished him.

Absence of gunfire brought a sudden silence to the scene, leaving Jack's ears ringing. He became aware that Colonel Paz's machine pistol had stopped its chattering some seconds before the finale. He turned and looked just in time to see Paz round the front corner of the Golden Pole building and disappear, the soles of his shoes slapping the pavement as he ran away.

Jack stayed in place, focused on the immediate scene. It could be fatal to assume that all the downed were dead, rather than playing possum and waiting for the chance to take down one or both of their opponents.

As it happened, the downed were dead, all of them: Baca, Espinosa, Dixie, Herm, and the backup trio. Seven corpses.

Jack and Pete stood over the two-gun kid. There was no mistaking a telltale roundness and swelling at the breast and hips of the deceased. The agents exchanged glances.

"He's a she," Pete said. "A girl. And not so girlish, either. Up close, she looks a lot older than she did from a distance. She could be twenty-five, thirty, maybe."

Jack said, "That's a break. It narrows the search for her identity. There can't be too many like her on file."

"I hope not. One was too many," Pete said.

"Tell me about it. She damned near took the top of my head off with one of her shots."

Pete looked around at the carnage-littered street. His free hand, the one not holding a gun, rubbed the top of his head, while he frowned, puzzled. "What the hell happened here?"

"Offhand, I'd say somebody doesn't much like Colonel Paz," Jack said.

. . . .

THE FOLLOWING TAKES PLACE
BETWEEN THE HOURS OF
6 A.M. AND 7 A.M.
CENTRAL DAYLIGHT TIME

. . . .

The Golden Pole, New Orleans

Vikki Valence's apartment was like the dancer herself—
flamboyant and overstuffed.

Jack was in the living room, holding his gun in a two-
handed shooter's grip, his knees bent in a combat crouch.

Behind him, the door to the balcony gaped open, hanging
halfway off its hinges. It had been locked, compelling him
to make a forced entry. A couple of stomp-kicks had done
the trick.

Daylight shone through the open doorway, illuminating
the cavelike dimness of the interior. The windows fronting
the balcony were screened by both blinds and heavy drapes.
Even the wan light of an early, overcast morning was a help.

Jack stood to one side of the open doorway, to avoid out-
lining himself in it and making a better target for anybody

who might be lurking around inside. It seemed like the shooting was over, but . . . maybe not. Whoever was behind the attack on Paz might have decided to have Vikki taken care of at the same time.

Opposite the balcony door, on the far side of the living room, another door opened on a dark hallway inside the building. The door was partly ajar. As soon as he saw it, Jack figured that Vikki had fled that way, but he was taking nothing for granted. The apartment had to be cleared.

The premises showed all the signs of recent occupancy. The air conditioner was going full-blast. Coming in from the stifling heat and humidity outside, Jack could feel the sweat on his body turning cold.

The living room held a couch, several armchairs, and a coffee table. The plush couch was the size of a compact car; each plumply cushioned armchair looked big enough to swallow a medium-sized man. The furniture was festooned with lots of lacy black shawls and leopard-print coverlets.

The air was thick with the mingled scents of tobacco smoke, whiskey fumes, perfume, and sweat. The coffee table was crowded with bottles of booze, some empty, others half full; drinking glasses, an ice bowl, and a half-dozen or so bottles of club soda and tonic water for setups. Vikki and the Colonel must have had themselves quite a party.

The living room was empty of persons living or dead. To Jack's right, a short hallway opened onto several rooms. Doors opened on the right and left; at the far end of the corridor lay the bedroom. With his leveled gun leading the way, he padded soft-footed into the passageway.

On his left was a kitchenette. Jack looked in. There was a small, square table with a couple of straight-backed armless chairs, some cupboards, and a refrigerator sandwiched into an alcove. The sink and sideboard were covered with dirty dishes.

On the right was a bathroom. It was hot, steamy, cloyingly fragrant from the combined scents of dozens of bottles of creams, lotions, cosmetics, gels, hair sprays, and other beauty products. He looked behind the shower curtain to make sure nobody was hiding in the bathtub. Nobody was.

The inside of the shower curtain was dripping with moisture; the mirror over the sink was fogged with condensation, indicating that someone had taken a shower in it not long before. Vikki, the Colonel, or both.

A light showed in the bedroom, the glow of a bedside night-table lamp. The gun entered the room, Jack following it, moving light-footed, alert.

Dominating the space was a big brass bed slightly smaller than Cleopatra's barge, its pink satin sheets rumpled and sodden. Hanging on the wall above the ornate brass headboard was a painting of Vikki in the nude, all glossy pink and rendered on black velvet.

A flash of movement glimpsed in the corner of his eye jolted Jack, causing him to whip his gun around to cover it.

He realized that what he'd seen was merely his own reflection, imaged in a wall-length mirror. The looking glass was marbled with spidery gold veins. He grinned tightly, slowly letting out his breath.

He looked under the bed to make sure no one was hiding there. It was an old gag, one of the oldest in the book, but the reason it had lasted so long was that it worked. After the big gun-down outside, he wouldn't have been surprised to find a body, alive or dead, but it came up blank.

A walk-in closet held racks of garments, dresses, blouses, skirts, lingerie. The floor was covered with massed ranks of women's shoes. There was enough stuff inside there to stock a boutique, but no space for anybody to hide in.

Jack gave the room a quick scan, looking for anything that might prove useful in tracking Vikki down: an address book, diary, stack of letters, pocketbook, or anything along those lines. Later a CTU forensics team would go over the place with a fine-tooth comb. But he didn't want to take a chance on overlooking something that might turn out to be a vital clue. Nothing relevant showed up during his swift survey.

The main object of his search had been Vikki herself; his first impression was that she'd taken it on the run, but he had to be sure. He couldn't afford to linger overlong in her apartment, but he couldn't move on without clearing it.

Well, it had been cleared now. Jack retraced his steps, back into the living room. He crossed to the door opening onto the interior of the building, approaching it at an oblique angle that would keep him out of the firing line of any hostiles lurking on the landing.

Flattening his back against the wall, he used his foot to ease the door open all the way, then darted through the doorway.

He stepped into a long hallway, lined on both sides with closed doors. Sparsely placed ceiling lamps provided minimal illumination. The light was as murky as the waters of a fish tank that had gone too long without cleaning.

There was a chance, a slim one, that Vikki had found shelter in a neighboring apartment, but Jack lacked the time or resources now to make a room-to-room search. Instinct told him it was unlikely she was still in the building. If she was somewhere on the premises, that'd be a break, because she could be picked up later when CTU reinforcements had arrived. He wasn't counting on it, though.

Toward the front of the building was a landing and a stairwell. The stairs slanted down to a street-level door, the one used earlier by Paz when he'd stepped out onto the sidewalk and set off the fireworks.

In the opposite direction, toward the rear of the building, a second set of stairs led to a ground-floor back door. Outside, Pete Malo was covering that one, though it was probably a case of locking the barn door after the horse had vamoosed.

Jack made for the front stairs. Ahead, on the left, a door suddenly opened and a man stepped out onto the landing. Jack leveled the gun at him.

The other saw him at the same time. He was a fat man in a sleeveless undershirt and a pair of pants with suspenders. The suspenders were unfastened and hung in loops at his sides. His bare feet were stuffed into a pair of flip-flops.

He lurched, recoiling, the floorboards groaning under his weight. He threw up his arms in a hands-up position. His hands were empty of weapons. He cried, "Don't shoot!"

He goggled at the gun. Fear had drained the color from his face, leaving it white and pasty as baker's dough.

Jack moved closer, keeping him covered. He asked, "Who're you?"

"Shelburne! Drake Shelburne!" The fat man quivered, triple chins bobbing as he gasped for breath. "I'm the manager here!"

"Where's Vikki Valence?"

"I don't know!" Then, after a pause, he added, "I should have known she'd be mixed up in this!"

Jack said, "Why?"

"The company she keeps, playboys and artists and foreigners and I don't know what-all!"

Jack wagged the gun barrel, indicating the door through which Shelburne had just emerged. "That your place?"

"Yessir!"

"Go back inside and stay there."

Shelburne still had his hands up. "Jeez, you like to give me a heart attack, waving that gun around—I'm going now, I'm just letting you know so you won't shoot—"

"Move!"

"I'm moving, Oh Lordy, here I go—"

Shelburne edged back into his room, pausing at the threshold. He'd recovered enough nerve to ask, "Say, what's it all about, anyway?"

"Police business," Jack said, figuring that that was the kind of answer that the manager of a strip club like the Golden Pole would understand. "Go inside and stay there until you're told otherwise."

"I'm cooperating," Shelburne said over his shoulder as he waddled back inside his room, closing the door behind him. Not slamming it but easing it into place. A cautious man.

Jack descended the stairs and exited through the side door onto Fairview Street.

The scene was the same as when he'd left it. Littered with corpses. The two bodyguards, Baca and Espinosa, lay sprawled on the sidewalk; the five attackers, Herm, Dixie, and the three shooters from the back of the truck, were strewn about the street.

Seven dead. Quite a body count, even for New Orleans, the new-crowned murder capital of the United States.

So much for keeping a low profile to avoid scaring off Beltran.

The air was so still and dead that a pall of gun smoke still hazed the street, hovering motionlessly a few feet above the pavement, undisturbed by even the slightest breath of a breeze.

At the south end of Fairview, a pickup truck rolled west on Bourbon Street, the driver oblivious to the carnage. On the far side of the square, a handful of people stood together in a clump, peering and gawking at the gunfight site. Civilians, spectators. The curious.

Jack looked around, catching sight of Pete Malo standing north on Fairview, near the rear of the club. Earlier Jack had gone up the balcony stairs to check on Vikki's apartment, while Pete stayed at street level, covering the club's side and back doors.

Jack fitted his gun back into the shoulder holster and went to the other. Pete said, "Vikki?"

Jack shook his head no. "Gone."

"I figured as much. Our bird has flown the coop," Pete said. "She was already plenty jittery—on the tape of her call to the CTU hotline, she sounded spooked, scared. When the shooting started, she must've jumped like a scalded cat and hightailed it out of there."

He gestured toward the back of the building, where a brown-painted metal door was connected by three stone steps to an alley that met it at right angles. "Probably went out the back door," he said.

Jack said, "Let's hope so. At least that puts her in the opposite direction from Colonel Paz. It might not go so well for her if he should bump into her now—he might think she set him up for the slaughter. We know better—why contact CTU if the object was to lure Paz into a death trap?—but he doesn't know that."

Pete said, "The Colonel's a hard man to kill. The machine gun in the briefcase was a neat trick."

"One we missed."

Pete indicated the corpses in the street. "Better them than us."

Jack said, "Cal Randolph may have a different opinion on that score."

Randolph was Director of CTU's Gulf Coast Regional Center, the branch office located in the New Orleans area. Pete worked for him out of GCR Center. Jack worked out of CTU Los Angeles, but was on assignment here for the Beltran case.

Pete made a sour face. "Cal's been notified. I already talked to him and told him what happened."

Jack said, "How'd he take it?"

"About as well as you'd think. He's got a bloodbath before breakfast, and our lead to Beltran is gone, too."

"Maybe not. Vikki Valence isn't exactly inconspicuous. She'll have a tough time blending in with the woodwork," Jack said.

Pete said, "She doesn't drive, either—at least our preliminary background check revealed no driver's license or car registration in her name."

Jack said, "That's something, anyway."

Pete's expression was doubtful. "Trouble is, Vikki's been around. She knows her way around the Quarter. And a gal like her has plenty of friends she can lay up with—men friends—not to mention those who'd like to be her friend."

Jack made a quick decision. "If she's on foot, she may not have gotten very far. Maybe I can spot her hanging around in the vicinity. It's worth a try, anyway. Let me have the keys to the SUV."

Pete said, "I'll go. I know these streets a lot better than you do, Jack. This is my town."

"You also know the local lawmen better, too. It's best that they see a familiar face when they show up here. I'm a stranger to them, and a massacre is no place to strike up an acquaintanceship.

"Speaking of which, I'd have thought that the cops would be here by now," Jack added.

"You would—being an out-of-towner," Pete said. "Truth to tell, our New Orleans Police Department falls a long way off from being in the front ranks of law enforcement. With a storm coming—a big one, from the looks of it—there's already been a lot of absenteeism on the force. A number of the fellows don't want to be trapped here in the city if another one like Katrina hits."

He fished the car keys out of his pants pocket and tossed them to Jack, who snagged them out of the air. "Okay, Jack, you win."

"I'll cruise around and see if I can pick up her trail," Jack said. "Or Paz's."

"Good luck. I'll hold down the fort here," Pete said.

Standard security precautions dictated that their CTU-issued vehicle not be parked on the same street where Paz's bodyguards had kept their all-night vigil. They might have noticed it and become suspicious. Instead it stood on the next street running east of Fairview and parallel to it.

Jack cut through an alley to reach it, a passageway so narrow he could barely go through it without his shoulders brushing the walls.

The machine was there, right where they'd left it hours before on Friday night, parked at curbside on the west side of the street. A dark green SUV with a souped-up V–8 engine, bulletproof glass, armor-plated hull, reinforced chassis and suspension to carry the extra weight, and puncture-proof tires, solid all the way through. Plus an onboard wireless computer, satellite-phone communications capability, and an array of high-tech electronics hardware.

The vehicle was protected by an invisible, electromagnetic web woven by the sensors of a silent alarm system. So sophisticated were its threshold parameters that it could distinguish between random bumps and jostles such as any car might sustain when parked on a city street, as opposed to a deliberate attempt to tamper with the vehicle. In case of the latter, it would activate a receiver in the driver's handheld keying device, notifying him of the attempted breach.

No such alarm had been tripped during the night watch. Jack switched on the keying device, electronically unlocking the car.

He opened the door, stepping into a blast of heat. The SUV had been locked up tight all night, windows sealed shut. Inside it felt as hot as a pizza oven.

Jack, dehydrated and gasping, fired up the engine. It started right up, with a thrum of power. Smooth and potent. He lowered the windows to let out some of the heat and turned the air conditioner on full blast.

He angled the SUV out from between the two cars it was parked between and into the street. He turned right at the corner, going east along Bourbon, rolling past Fairview Street and the Golden Pole.

He cruised along, his search pattern an ever-expanding spiral whose center was the club building. Sticking his head out the open window on the driver's side, he peered into cross alleys, low-walled courts, recessed doorways, and similar places that offered cover to a fugitive.

He had two goals. Vikki was his primary objective, but he also kept an eye out for Paz. The Colonel had fled the scene on foot, too. He'd made his way south of the club, across Bourbon Street and beyond. Vikki had begun her flight by heading north.

He used his scrambled, comm-secure cell phone to contact CTU Gulf Coast Regional.

The Center was sited outside the city proper, New Orleans being a below-sea-level bowl bordered on the north by Lake Pontchartrain and the south by the Mississippi River. The facility was south of the river on the opposite shore, safely planted on high ground in Algiers, avoiding the danger of being trapped in the flooded bowl of the city, in the event of a reprise of an event like Katrina. A point that had now become more than academic, with Hurricane Everette churning its way across the Gulf on a course that was New Orleans–bound.

He drove with one hand on the wheel, the other holding the cell to the side of his head, his head craning out the open window, peering up and down various side streets, alleys, and footpaths in search of Vikki or Paz.

"Jack Bauer here."

A comm-sys operator at CTU GCR Center said, "Your call is being switched to Director Randolph."

Jack hadn't requested to speak to Randolph, he was just reporting in, but Randolph had some ideas of his own. The director was already up to speed on the Golden Pole massacre, having already been briefed by Pete Malo.

Randolph said, "We've got a forensics team and every available backup unit dispatched to the scene. They'll be there any minute now."

"They'll be needed. It's one unholy mess out there."

"What happened, Jack? How do you read it?"

"Somebody tried to liquidate Paz and botched the job. It was a professional job, a pretty slick setup. Unfortunately for them, Paz was slicker. And they had the bad luck to shoot their move when Pete and I were on the scene. They didn't know we were there, and got caught in a crossfire between us and Paz."

Randolph tsk-tsked. "Lord! This is the kind of thing you expect to find in Iraq or some banana republic, not in the United States of America. New Orleans is already on edge that Everette's going to swat it. An incident like this—well, it's the last thing we or the city needs right now."

Jack said, "I guess there's never a good time for a massacre."

"It's going to raise a big stink, Jack."

"Maybe the storm will wash it away."

• •

**THE FOLLOWING TAKES PLACE
BETWEEN THE HOURS OF
7 A.M. AND 8 A.M.
CENTRAL DAYLIGHT TIME**

• •

*Ministry of the Interior Substation,
Riyadh, Saudi Arabia
3:00 P.M., local time*

Because of the shape it takes, sandwiched between the lake and the river, New Orleans is known as the Crescent City.

On the other side of the world, the capital of the kingdom of Saudi Arabia, Riyadh, could fairly be called a "city of the crescent"—said crescent being the holy symbol of the faith of Islam.

Chance—or destiny—has seen fit to locate the world's richest sea of high-grade oil under the kingdom's desert sands. Petro-power has made it one of world's supreme wealth generators, whose power and influence has been a major geopolitical factor for the last half century and more. And whose economic and political clout can only increase, as world demand for oil inexorably rises as existing reserves steadily shrink.

Riyadh is a showcase for Arabian oil riches, a wonder city reared up in a desert wasteland, a vast, sprawling technopolis of skyscrapers and palaces, its modernistic urban complexes knit together by a network of superhighways.

There is luxury in Riyadh, opulence. Supreme master of the city and all the kingdom is the inner circle of the royal family of the House of Saud, a ruling cadre numbering several hundred individuals. They seek luxury and splendor the way flowering plants turn their faces to the sun.

But not the twelve men who now met in solemn conclave in the conference hall at an obscure substation of the Ministry of the Interior, located at the inland edge of the city, the borderland where the great desert begins.

Their rank and power entitled them to sit in the most august and respected precincts of power, but instead they preferred to assemble in the relative obscurity and anonymity of a minor office complex on the outskirts of the megalopolis.

It was safer that way. Their mission was a dangerous one, best shielded in secrecy.

The building was unprepossessing, one of the Ministry's more modest holdings. No lofty glass and steel needle tower, it was wide, squat, low-slung, and built close to the ground. It fronted south, its east wing facing the city, its west wing facing the dark immensity of the mainland, of vast stony plains marching inland to depths of desert solitudes.

The structure was integrated closely into the landscape, so that it seemed to be an outcropping of the hill on which it was set. There was something in its form suggestive of ancient stone forts and castles, updated to the modern era. A pile of tan and sandy vertical and horizontal slabs of stone and steel-reinforced concrete, with narrow, slitted windows. Arrays of satellite dishes mushroomed atop its flat roof.

On the third, top floor, in a conference room, the Special Council met. The meeting place had the aspect of a corporate boardroom. A rectangular wooden table, long and slender, occupied the central axis of the space. Grouped around it was an oval ring of high-backed swivel chairs. Occupying those chairs were the twelve members of the special committee.

Seated at the head of the table and master of the council was Prince Fedallah, chief of the Internal Security Section of the Ministry of the Interior—a secret police apparatus that worked directly for the King.

Fedallah was a royal, but only a minor princeling, one from a line far removed from the inner circle of the ruling class. His present prominence testified to his ability; he'd won his post as the King's trusted spy and hatchet man not through family connections but through a ruthless mastery of intrigue.

He was lean, wiry, balding, with leathery skin stretched taut across a long, bony face. His eyebrows rose in points in their middles. The hairs looked like individual copper wires. His nose was beaklike; his mouth was downturned.

He wore a red-and-white checked kaffiyeh headpiece and a khaki outfit that fell somewhere between a military uniform and a safari suit. It was custom-tailored, with crisp, sharp edges.

He provided his own security. Elite troopers from the enforcement arm of his Special Section guarded the building. A pair of them stood watch outside the closed conference room doors.

The others at the table were a mixed group of royals, clerics, and military intelligence officers. Most of them wore white ceremonial robes over business suits or Western-style clothes.

Conservative ceremonial attire for a tradition-bound land. Good protective cover for the council, whose task had already set them well on the way toward perdition according to the more ultraorthodox-minded of their coreligionists.

The majority were senior officials, graybeards, with a scattering of middle-aged members.

One of the youngest—and he was in his mid-forties— was Tariq bin Tassim. He was a prince, too. His family was much more closely connected to the ruling royals than Fedallah's.

He was one of the new breed, Western-educated, including a graduate degree from the Harvard Business School. He spoke English fluently; he had spent much time in America. He handled a number of major investments for leading royals, princes within the direct line of descent for the throne. He swam in a global monetary environment of the twenty-four-hour business cycle; of hedge funds, shell corporations, interlocking directorates and cartels, commodities and credits.

He piled up fortunes on Wall Street. He socialized with powerful U.S. politicians in Washington, D.C. He skied in Aspen, gambled at Monte Carlo, and yachted in the Aegean.

His friends included an ex-president of the United States, several current cabinet heads, a half-dozen or more senators, and a dozen senior congressional representatives.

A handsome man, he had dramatic features: thick, dark, wavy hair; dark brown eyes; a neatly trimmed ginger-colored beard.

He sat at the middle of the table, on Minister Fedallah's right-hand side. He was not the youngest council member. That role belonged to Prince Hassani.

Hassani had excellent royal connections but a somewhat checkered past. He was in his late thirties but looked younger. His watery-eyed gaze was blurred and unfocused behind the thick lenses of his black plastic-framed spectacles. His spade-shaped chin beard was thin and wispy.

Hassani's Western sojourns had been disappointing and unsuccessful. He'd had personal problems. He'd attended college in California and had lost direction, going off his moral compass. Repatriation to the kingdom, and extensive reimmersion in the ultraorthodox tenets of the kingdom's fundamentalist Wahabi sect, were the cure to his malaise, which was, at bottom, spiritual.

Farther up the table, seated in the penultimate place of power on Fedallah's right hand, was Imam Omar, better known throughout the kingdom and beyond as the Smiling Cleric.

He projected the image of a sweet, good-natured older uncle. He wore a white headpiece, glasses, and a bushy gray beard. His eyes were bright and merry. He smiled readily and often, and was ever ready with an old saw or pious saying.

The Imam represented a different source of power than royal connections or oil wealth. His was the power of faith and of the faithful. Traditionalist tenets are encoded in the Saudi Arabian operating system, at every level of the society. Even the highest are careful not to provoke the disapprobation of the powerful fundamentalist clerics, whose wrath has been known to unleash a whirlwind of mass fervor that can topple a throne.

Wahabism, the state religion of Saudi Arabia, is one of the strictest and most rigorously fundamentalist branches of Islam. The variety of Wahabism preached and practiced by Imam Omar was harsh and ascetic, rejecting much of the modern world, even the modern Muslim world.

Yet no matter how harsh his decrees, or uncompromising his rejectionism, his demeanor was unfailingly merry, with a twinkle in his eye. He was the spiritual leader of an influential mosque in Riyadh, one attended by some of the most devout and observant members of the royal dynasty.

The mosque was the beneficiary of royal patronage and largesse, receiving hundreds of millions of petro-dollars. Some of this money was used to fund a network of madrassas, religious schools, throughout not only the kingdom but also in Yemen, Jordan, Malaysia, and Indonesia.

A second branch of his organization was an equally far-flung chain of charities.

A third branch was the Imam's connections to the kingdom's religious police, the self-styled Committee for the Prevention of Vice and the Propagation of Virtue. Established in every city, town, and village, it consisted of thousands of zealots who volunteered to patrol and police their fellows to ensure orthodox obedience and suppress all deviations from the fundamentalism line. They had the authority to make arrests, close buildings, and administer whippings on the spot to violators of religious law.

Not a private army, perhaps, but a private police force, and one not necessarily under the sway of royal overlordship.

Which made Imam Omar a powerful man indeed. His influence reached both the urban masses of the Arab street and the desert dwellers of the inland settlements. He was a powerful force for tradition. His opposition to a government plan or decree was often enough to kill it.

A dangerous man, in a kingdom so precariously balanced on the edge of a sword.

The meeting having been called to order, Minister Fedallah addressed the other members of the council. "As you know, the King has charged me with carrying out a program vital to the security of the realm," he began.

The others knew it, all right. Fedallah never missed a chance to remind them of his position of preferment near the throne.

He went on, "His Majesty has charged me to carry out his plan, and I picked each and every one of you to serve as instruments of his will. Our task is not an easy one. It will continue to increase in difficulty. The purity of our intent is subject to misunderstanding by the very countrymen we seek to help. But there is no other alternative.

"To safeguard kingdom and throne, we must bestow a supreme gift to those very forces who would destroy us— the Americans. We must gift them with a surplus of the oil which they crave like a creature of Satan craves the blood of the innocent. This is our sacred task."

The planners and policymakers in Washington had labeled the mission Operation Petro Surge.

The Saudis of the secret council called it Cloak of Night.

Behind it lay the age-old enmity between the two leading branches of Islam, the division between Sunni and Shi'a. The Arab sect was the Sunnis; the Iranian sect was the Shiites.

In the latter half of the twentieth century, the leading Shiite power of Iran was offset by the Iraqi regime of dictator Saddam Hussein, a Sunni. Saddam and the Iranian ayatollahs fought a war in the 1980s that saw titanic clashes and bloodletting on a scale not seen since the battles of World War II. It ended in a draw.

The First Gulf War drastically checked Saddam's dreams of conquest, yet left the balance of power between Baghdad and Tehran fundamentally unchanged. The Second Gulf

War, the American liberation of Iraq, demonstrated the unpalatable truth that whatever else his faults were, Saddam knew how to rule his country. He ruled it with instant obliteration of foes and dissenters, mass executions, wholesale torture, and relentless terror. Thereby welding the fractious Iraqis into a nation.

Power, like nature, abhors a vacuum. The hole in the landscape left by the absence of Saddam was filled with the Iranians.

Iran's prospects for regional supremacy were bright. Few riper or more tempting targets for takeover existed in the region than the kingdom of Saudi Arabia. Its numbers were thin and threadbare compared to the far more populous Iran, with its teeming millions. Iran was well armed, with a huge conventional army as well as thousands of terrorists and guerrillas it could field to infiltrate, subvert, and destroy the foe.

Iran could take Saudi Arabia simply by marching an army into the kingdom. The mullahs in Tehran and the holy city of Qom would become the masters of the world's richest reserves of high-grade oil.

Standing between Iran's conquest of the kingdom was the bulwark of the United States. Washington and Riyadh have had a long and complicated relationship (like a hostile married couple, they stayed together for the sake of "the children")—that is, the oil fields.

Despite deep currents of hostility, suspicion, and mutual detestation, the two nations needed each other. The United States needs Saudi oil, and the Saudi royals need the United States to guarantee their throne and sovereignty.

Now a crisis was approaching. U.S. involvement in Iraqi nation building was reaching the beginning of the end. The misadventure had caused the United States to hemorrhage vast amounts of blood and treasure. Further gargantuan sums were required to keep the U.S. Navy and Air Force patrolling the vital sea-lanes of the Persian Gulf—Arabian Sea, by kingdom lights. The cruisers, destroyers, submarines, aircraft carriers, air bases, and all the other components of the U.S. military infrastructure burned vast reserves of oil every day to maintain the status quo.

Washington had recently made it clear to the royals in Riyadh that it needed some relief from the gnawing expense. Even the long-suffering American taxpayer was beginning to grumble with obvious signs of discontent. The Saudi royals' resistance to American pressure began to crumble.

The result was Cloak of Night.

Cloak of Night—that was the royals' term for a bold economic thrust on the world market.

The Americans, the oil executives, diplomats, and military attachés who'd helped broker the deal for Washington, called the forthcoming market glut Operation Petro Surge.

One result of the surge would be a sudden drop in gas prices at the pump and in home heating fuel costs. Extra money in the pockets of American consumers—a welcome event in what was shaping up as a tricky election year for the incumbent Administration.

The oil glut would be a onetime phenomenon. The Saudis had agreed to it this once because of the immediate threat presented by Iran's expansionist activities in the Gulf. It was a guarantor of American military protection.

Best of all, no real harm would be done to the kingdom's long-term interests. The oil glut would be soaked up and absorbed by the market, and prices would once more begin to rise, zooming upward. It would stifle any flickering impulses on the part of the Americans to develop some degree of energy independence, ultimately making them even more dependent on Saudi oil.

Most important of all, it would check the Iranians—hard.

The theory was simplicity itself: supply trumps demand. The kingdom maintained a vast sea of oil reserves, storage tank reservoirs containing millions of barrels of high-grade oil. They sat on it, carefully shepherding it to avoid putting too much on the market at once. A glut of oil would, at least temporarily, depress prices.

That cut into Saudi profits.

The boldness of Cloak of Night lay in its counterintuitive nature. It proposed to release those reserves, flooding them on the open market and dramatically driving down prices.

At first glance, it was seemingly contrary to Saudi interests. It also countered the dictates of OPEC, the global petroleum producers' price-fixing cartel, an organization of which Saudi Arabia was an integral part. As was Iran, the kingdom's dreaded rival and immediate threat.

Cloak of Night, the Saudi planners called it, a phrase with a self-consciously archaicizing feel. The newly freed reserves comprised a sea of night-black oil. But there was a deeper meaning. The oil ploy was an act of darkness, for it would directly benefit the unbelievers and crusaders of the Western adversary, particularly the Great Satan, U.S.A.

But not for long.

Minister Fedallah continued, "As expected, Cloak has produced no small amount of unrest at all levels of the populace, in cities and villages."

Khalid, of the religious police—a key ally of Imam Omar—was unreceptive, quarrelsome. "Who can blame them? Bad enough that we, the shepherds of the faithful, must oversee a process that rewards the Western foe who seeks to destroy us."

Fedallah countered, "Dissent is an act of disloyalty against His Majesty himself and therefore a crime, no matter how nicely motivated. To tolerate unrest is a betrayal."

Tariq noted, "No one will ever reproach your zeal in the service of the King, Fedallah."

Imam Omar said, "The King has spoken, his will must be done."

"I'm glad you feel that way, Imam," Fedallah said. "Some of the rioters and provocateurs are persons associated with your mosque."

"Then they are no followers of mine, for I counsel obedience to His Majesty's commands."

"Still, they listen to you and respect you. Words from you on cheerful obedience to the King's command would go a long way in quelling some of the more unruly and rebellious sentiment."

"I will speak on this matter on my very next program, Minister Fedallah."

Fedallah's gaze encompassed all eleven members seated at the table. He said, "Traitors and usurpers are everywhere, always seeking to exploit the thorny issues of the day to their own benefit. Yet in the end, their machinations and infamies shall yield them only . . . a mouthful of sand."

. . . .

THE FOLLOWING TAKES PLACE
BETWEEN THE HOURS OF
8 A.M. AND 9 A.M.
CENTRAL DAYLIGHT TIME

. . . .

An hour can make a world of difference.

Earlier, when Jack Bauer had jumped in the SUV and gone cruising in search of Vikki Valence or Colonel Paz, the scene he'd left behind at the Golden Pole had been one of bleak and forlorn stillness.

Except for the corpses cluttering Fairview Street and the presence of Pete Malo and a scattering of civilian early risers, the area had seemed deserted and abandoned. It had an eerie quality, like the bare stage of a theater after the performance has ended and the audience and players have all gone home.

Even Bourbon Street was bereft of all but a few lone vehicles rolling up and down the thoroughfare. Not only had the police not yet arrived, but the quietude of the dawn was unbroken by the sound of approaching sirens of patrol cars and emergency vehicles.

Now, little more than sixty minutes later, the scene had taken on an entirely different aspect. New Orleans had come awake and alive, to discover that the day had begun with a spectacular massacre.

The Golden Pole shootings had plenty of coverage now. The site was not only a crime scene; it was the center of a national security investigation with international implications.

The area was a hive of activity, swarming with police, press, and public officials.

A cordon had been thrown up around it, a blockade consisting of several concentric rings of barriers that grew tighter the closer one approached the center.

The outermost ring was made up of uniformed police who detoured unauthorized vehicles away from a cluster of several city blocks surrounding the club building.

The detour had created a traffic jam of impressive proportions, with noise to match.

A racketing clamor was compounded of honking car and truck horns, angry shouts of frustrated drivers, barked commands of traffic cops, the rumble of idling engines, the hiss of overheated car radiators, and the electronic wheep-beeping of police and emergency vehicles trying to make headway against the thicket of creeping masses of metal.

The heavy, humid air was now flavored with exhaust clouds from the vehicles stuck in the jam. No breath of wind stirred to disperse them; their blue-gray haze fogged the area, making eyes tear and throats burn.

Returning to the scene, Jack had wisely decided to avoid the jam, parking the SUV on a quiet side street well outside the area of congestion. It was strategically placed to make a quick getaway in the event he had to move fast to follow up a hot lead. He only hoped he would be so lucky.

He made his way inward on foot, wearing his CTU photo ID card on a lanyard around his neck, flashing it when needed to pass through the phalanx of cops cordoning off the area.

The square fronted by the Golden Pole was sealed off by a line of wooden sawhorse barricades stenciled with the letters NOPD: New Orleans Police Department. The barrier held back a crowd of gawkers, sensation seekers, and the morbidly curious.

The club building was the bull's-eye at the center of concentric rings of security barriers and checkpoints. Within the police lines, there was that combination of bustling energy and hurry-up-and-wait delay characteristic of the official response to a major disaster or other catastrophe.

Police and emergency vehicles flashed their rooftop light racks, the colorful sparking of blue and red lights adding an oddly festive note to the proceedings.

Two-way radios filled the air with garbled voice messages and crackling static.

Groups of plainclothes detectives and crime lab techs milled around with purposeful activity. Supervisors and senior investigators moved among the forensics teams, coordinating their efforts.

Forensics and criminality teams did their thing. Police photographers took still photos and video records of the carnage on Fairview Street, picturing the battle zone from all angles. Weapons were collected, identified with the investigator's personal mark, labeled, and sealed into evidence bags. Shell casings received similar treatment.

Diagrams were made of where shell casings had fallen; the brass shells were then collected, identified with the investigator's personal mark, labeled, and sealed into clear plastic envelopes. Chalk outlines were drawn around the bodies.

The paramedics alone were at loose ends. There were no wounded requiring medical attention.

The dead were bagged, tagged, and carted away.

Jack scanned the scene, looking for Pete Malo, spotting him standing on the sidewalk outside the Golden Pole's front entrance. Pete saw him at the same time and gave him the high sign, signaling him to come over. Jack slipped through the crowd, joining him.

Pete was not the demonstrative type, but there was about him an air of barely contained excitement. He motioned to Jack to step aside, out of the human traffic flow, into an alcove to one side of the club's front entrance.

He said, "Any sign of Vikki or Paz?"

Jack shook his head. "Not a trace. Not that I really expected to find anything. It was a long shot, but one I had to take. If I hadn't, I'd be kicking myself in the butt, wondering what would have happened if I had, if maybe I would have let the chance of catching them slip through my fingers."

"Trying to take back the initiative."

"You could say that, Pete. I take it that they're both still among the missing."

Pete nodded. "That's right. But all is not lost. There's been a few interesting developments since you left."

Jack felt the excitement rising in him. "You've got something?"

"A lead, a definite lead on one of the shooters."

"Ah. That's great, Pete. Which one?"

"The guy riding shotgun in the truck."

"Who is he?"

"I'll let you hear it from the horse's mouth. Come on."

"Where are we going?"

"Inside the club. There's someone I want you to meet. Two someones, actually."

"Who are they?"

"Cops." Seeing Jack's lackluster expression, Pete added quickly, "Not just any cops. These guys are something else. Two of the crookedest cops in New Orleans, if not the planet."

"Sounds promising."

"I have to warn you. They're a couple of characters who look like they just fell off the turnip truck, but don't let that fool you. They get results, and what they don't know about the local crime scene isn't worth telling."

"I'm all ears. Let's go."

"They're minding a couple of witnesses inside. The club manager and a couple of dancers who worked with Vikki."

"Lead on."

The CTU agents crossed to the front entrance of the Golden Pole. The door was guarded by a uniformed police officer, who nodded in recognition when he saw Pete. He lifted a hand in greeting. "Hey, Pete."

"Hey, Randy Joe," Pete replied.

The cop stepped aside to allow Pete to enter. Pete went in, Jack following. Jack held the ID card worn around his neck, tilting it so the cop could get a look at it. The patrolman barely glanced at it, waving Jack through.

Inside, the space was dim, cavelike, and coolly air-conditioned. The building was a rectangle whose short end fronted Bourbon Street and whose long sides met it at right angles. The long walls were made of rough, unpainted brick and were lined with tables and chairs. What few windows there were, were painted over with black paint.

The centerline of the space was dominated by a U-shaped wooden bar whose open end was at the rear of the structure. The open space inside the U was where the bartenders worked. The inner wall was lined with stainless steel sinks and coolers.

Opposite the twin ends at the top of the U was a stage platform level with the wooden bar top.

The stage featured a row of three gold-painted, vertical firemen's poles for dancers, the golden poles for which the place was named. The stage was at the same height as the bar top, so the dancers could step across on to the bar top and use it as a runway, allowing them to mingle with the drinking crowd lining the outer wall of the bar. They could work close with the clientele and pry loose better tip money from them with more personalized attentions.

Hinged half doors at the tops of the U allowed for entry and exit to the bartenders' area. Near the stage, a passageway led off into a couple of back rooms, where patrons could hire themselves some "private dances" (or whatever).

Bar stools lined the outer side of the U. The club was closed now and the stools were empty, or mostly empty. A handful of them down at the bottom of the U were occupied by two women and a fat man. They were bracketed by a man who looked like a retiree and was dressed in green, and a long, tall fellow with a mournful face.

A muscleman in a tight white T-shirt and white jeans stood behind the bar, chatting with the others.

Pete nudged Jack, saying out of the corner of his mouth, "The two characters bookending the group are Dooley and Buttrick, our cop friends. Try not to laugh."

Jack said, "No worry about that. I'm not in a very humorous mood this morning."

"This may pick up your spirits."

The elderly man sat facing the door. When he saw Jack and Pete enter, he slid off the bar stool and went to them. He approached them at a tangent, motioning for them to meet him off to one side of the club, away from the others seated at the bar.

Jack and Pete changed direction to meet him. Pete said, low-voiced, "That's Sergeant Dooley. Don't let that old codger act of his fool you. He's killed twenty-eight men in the line of duty. And who knows how many more, off the books."

Jack appraised Dooley with newfound interest. He was a prematurely elderly middle-aged man with a turtle's face: hairless, wrinkled, beaky. His head seemed too heavy for his neck and hung down between stooped shoulders. It was topped by a soft fabric, light-colored fisherman's hat.

He wore a yellow-green sport shirt, dark green golf pants, and green boat shoes.

His pants were high-waisted and came up a potbelly to a point just below his chest. A short-barreled .38 was worn in a holster clipped to the side of his right hip.

He said, "Hey, Pete."

"Hey, Floyd," Pete said.

Dooley said, "That was some mighty fancy shooting you did today."

Pete Malo smiled, a bland smile that committed him to nothing, neither confirming nor denying, but merely acknowledging that the other had made a remark.

He said, "Floyd, I'd like you meet an associate of mine, Jack Bauer. Jack, this is Sergeant Floyd Dooley, one of our outstanding peace officers. Not much goes down that he doesn't find out about."

Jack and Dooley shook hands. Dooley's hand was warm and dry, with a solid grip. Jack said, "Pleased to meet you."

"Likewise. You're the one helped Pete clean up on that killer crowd." It was not a question. Dooley held up a hand, palm out, as if to forestall any denials by the other.

"Now, you don't have to answer or crack to nothing. It's

none of my business. But that sure was some fine shooting. And I'm a man who appreciates some professional-type gun work."

Jack didn't know what to say to that. He smiled with his lips, uncertain, a bit tentative.

Dooley said, "You're another cloak-and-dagger fellow like Pete, eh?"

Jack glanced at Pete, who nodded yes.

"You could say that," Jack allowed.

"I could but I won't, at least not in public. I'm a man who knows how to keep a secret. Pete'll tell you about that. Well, now, Jack, I'm just a simple ol' New Orleans lawman, but I purely would appreciate it if you could give me some idea of what this killing and shooting in the streets is all about. 'Long as it ain't no top secret, official, and confidential material.

"Looks like Marty Paz's got hisself into a heap of hot water this time," he added.

Jack's face showed his surprise. Dooley chuckled. "Didn't think that an old backcountry cop like me has the lowdown on the Colonel from Caracas, huh? Let me clue you in on something, Jack. Marty Paz is quite well known here on Bourbon Street and in the Quarter, especially among what you might call the sporting crowd. Fancy gals, gamblers, whoremongers, that sort. Oh, he's a great favorite with that sort.

"He plays the babes like nobody's business. A real good-time Charlie, he is, livin' the high life. Playin' the babes, throwing money around hand over fist, living it up. Folks in New Orleans like the good life, and if that includes some fe-male companionship, ain't nobody gonna kick about it. Unless it comes up with a streetful of bodies, like it did here. That we take kind of personal.

"Not that there's any grief about him ventilating Dixie

Lee. That piece of trash's long overdue for a spot in the cemetery. It ain't right to speak ill of the dead, they say, so I'll just confine my remarks to saying, Good riddance to bad rubbish."

Jack, puzzled, said, "Who's Dixie Lee?"

Pete answered, "He was the passenger in the truck, the one who iced the bodyguards. I didn't know who he was myself, but Floyd identified him right off."

"Sure 'nuff," Dooley said. "Even with all those slugs in him, all I had to do was take one look at the body to know it was him. Dixie's a bad one; he's been long overdue for a date with the coroner for twenty years now.

"He's a graduate of Angola Prison; what with one thing and another, he's spent more'n half his life behind bars. Mean as a snake. Back shooter, robber, killer for hire. Gunrunner, mostly, but he dabbles in most anything, long as there's a dirty dollar in it. Looks like he run into the wrong gun this time, though."

Jack said, "I'm impressed, Sergeant Dooley."

"Floyd, son. Call me Floyd."

"Call me Jack, Floyd. Did you recognize any of the others with him?"

Dooley shook his head. "I took a look at each one, but I didn't know none of them from Adam. Neither did Buck. That's Buck Buttrick, my partner. I can tell you this, though: anybody that was siding with the likes of Dixie Lee needed killing, too."

He went on, "Soon as we heard that you wanted to have a talk with the club crowd, ol' Shelb and his people, we got 'em all together where we could keep an eye on 'em. And we didn't let 'em talk about nothing but the weather and such, so they couldn't put their heads together and cook up a story.

"What say we go over and jaw with 'em?"

* * *

Jack, Pete, and Dooley crossed to the group at the bar. Jack recognized the fat man as the fellow he'd held a gun on earlier, while searching the upper floor of the building looking for Vikki. Shelburne—Drake Shelburne—the club manager. "Ol' Shelb," as Dooley called him.

The women were undoubtedly dancers; they had the look. And the build. One was a redhead, the other, a brunette.

The fourth man must be Buck, Dooley's partner. He was a long, tall string bean of a man with a big sidearm holstered on his hip.

Shelburne sat with his back to the front entrance, leaning forward with his forearms on the bar, resting his weight on them. He now wore a sport shirt, slacks, and sneakers with no socks. He was drinking a cold drink in a clear plastic cup, sucking it up through a straw. Sweat made circles the size of medicine balls under his arms.

The muscular barkeep stood behind the bar, holding a white dishrag that he used every now and then to wipe a section of countertop. The females perked up, looking interested at the sight of the newcomers.

Shelburne glanced over his shoulder at them, uninterested; recognizing Jack, he did a double-take. Some of his drink must have gone down the wrong pipe, because he started choking, coughing, and sputtering. Dooley clapped a hand in the middle of Shelburne's back, between the shoulder blades. Shelburne got control of himself.

Wheezing, with tears running from his eyes, he said, "Sergeant Floyd, that's the man I was telling you about, the one who pulled a gun on me upstairs earlier this morning!"

"Relax, Shelb, you'll split a gut. And you got a lot of gut to split," Dooley said. He addressed his partner, the string bean with the big gun. "Buck, you know Pete here."

"Sure," Buttrick said, nodding at Pete Malo. "Hey, Pete."

"Hey, Buck."

Dooley went on, "This here's Jack. He's associated with Pete. He's okay."

Buck Buttrick was long-faced, with long, narrow, pale gray eyes; a turnip nose; and basset hound jowls. A farmer's straw hat with the sides pinned to the crown perched on his head. A faded, colorless, short-sleeved shirt hung in folds on his bony frame.

He wore a fancy leather belt with an oversized rodeo-themed plate metal buckle and blue jeans over cowboy boots with pointed toes. Hanging down at his right hip was a chrome-plated .357 magnum revolver in a fancy holster rig. He wore it gunfighter-style, low on his bony hip, so that when his arm was held at his side, his fingertips brushed the gun butt.

Jack and Buttrick shook hands. Buttrick's hand was sharp and bony.

The redhead looked up from her drink and said, "I thought you was a gentleman, Floyd. Ain't you going to introduce us to your friends?"

"I surely will," Dooley said.

The redhead's name was Francine and the brunette's was Dorinda. Dooley introduced the newcomers simply as Jack and Pete.

Francine's hair color was fire-engine red, straight out of a bottle. She was over thirty, sharp-eyed, with a button nose; wide, thin-lipped mouth; and a lot of (determined-looking) chin and jaw. She wore a thin, tight sleeveless shift with a thigh-high hem, and a pair of open-toed, high-heeled sandals.

Dorinda was in her early twenties, with a heart-shaped face framed by a mane of curly black hair that spilled over creamy shoulders, reaching down to mid-back. She wore a sleeveless T-shirt with a scooped neck, short-shorts, and flat shoes like ballet slippers. She was no ballerina, not with the abundant endowments given to her by nature and enhanced by cosmetic surgery.

The muscleman behind the bar was named Troy.

Shelburne said sarcastically, "Now that we've all gotten acquainted, you mind telling me what you want so I can get back to business? I've got a club to run here."

Buck Buttrick said, "Maybe not for long, Shelb."

The fat man looked up, his expression suddenly haunted and hunted. There was a lot of fear in him. "What—what do you mean?"

"The licensing board might take a dim view of all the goings-on here, all them murders and such."

"I had nothing to do with them!" Shelburne all but shrieked. "I'm a simple club owner!"

Dooley said, "He's just funnin' you, Shelb. Nobody figures you had any piece of this, 'cause you're a yellow belly. Now hush up for a minute."

Francine snickered, a dirty laugh. Shelburne turned to her, demanding, "What's so funny?"

"You," Francine said. "You should hear yourself. When you get excited, you start screeching like an old lady."

Shelburne turned on her. "Shut your mouth, you—"

"Yeah? Or what?" Francine was the type to rush into a confrontation, not back off from it. "What do you think you're going to do, fatso?"

Buttrick said, "Can the chatter."

Shelburne and Francine fell silent.

Dooley turned to Jack and Pete. "Which one do you want to question first?"

Jack indicated Shelburne. "Him."

While Jack was grilling Shelburne, Pete Malo and Floyd Dooley had a little private chat. Buttrick remained behind at the bar to keep an eye on Dorinda and Francine, to, as he put it, "make sure they don't put their heads together and cook up any stories."

Pete said, "That was nice work you did on identifying Dixie Lee so quickly."

"Shucks, that weren't nothing," Dooley said. "Lots of fellows on the force could have done that. Dixie's been around for a long time, with a long rap sheet."

"I appreciate that you passed the word to me first."

"What I do, I play the man. I know you, I know you got something on the ball, Pete, and I know that you know how to follow a hot lead when you got one.

"I also know you know how to keep a secret instead of blabbing it around to all creation," Dooley added.

He didn't have to come out and say what he and Pete both knew, namely that the streetwise CTU agent knew plenty about the deep-dyed corruption that lubricated the big-money machinery of the New Orleans infrastructure, including some shady doings that Dooley and his partner, Buck Buttrick, were involved with, and that Pete kept it strictly confidential.

And why not? CTU wasn't a law enforcement agency, it was a counterterrorism operation dedicated to protecting the people of the United States from catastrophic acts of mass destruction hatched by the nation's enemies. If that mission required looking the other way when it came to the sideline rackets of a couple of crooked cops who'd proved to be valuable informants in the past, why, then, so be it.

"'Sides, I figure you and your bunch will know what to do with it better than the rest of those clowns out there," Dooley said, gesturing toward the club's front windows, which looked out on the mass of investigators milling around the crime scene.

"Look at 'em. Everybody's trying to get into the act. The

District Attorney's got his special squad of investigators snooping around. The Mayor and the Governor have got their folks sticking their noses in. Then there's the parish Sheriff's Department; the State Police boys; the FBI; Homeland Security; the Alcohol, Tobacco, and Firearms revenuers; and who knows who else. They're all so busy stumbling over each other's feet that they wouldn't know what to do with a clue if it up and bit 'em on the ass," he said.

Pete said, "Was Dixie wired into the local mob?" The New Orleans Mafia had been established early in the twentieth century, and was one of the most powerful branches of the national crime syndicate.

"Hell, no," Dooley said, "though not for lack of trying. He was too political—that is, he was hip-deep in with the Klan and American Nazis and that sort. Supplying 'em with guns and bombs and whatnot. That brings down too much Federal heat, and that's one thing the Family don't need. Plus, them Ku Kluxers are down on the Catholics, and that don't sit right with them Mafia dons."

"You know how things work in this town, so I'd be grateful for any light you can throw on Dixie and where he fits in with the Paz hit try."

"Like I said, Pete, I made Dixie right off, but the rest of those jokers laid out on the street were strangers to me. They sure wasn't Mafia, I can tell you that. As to who they was, well, your guess is as good as mine. Probably better."

Dooley added, "Word is, Paz is big in the drug trade. Could be a rival gang tried to wipe out the competition—but I'm just guessing now."

"You've been a big help," Pete said. "What can I do for you?"

Dooley pushed his fishing hat back on his head. "This ain't no city matter, it's something much bigger. Just you being involved tells me that. That makes it Federal and puts it way over my head. Still, there's a local angle involved. Anything you can say to make me and Buck look good with the Police Department or the Mayor's office, put in a good word for us and say how we're cooperating, come up with some helpful clues, you know the routine, well, I'd surely appreciate it."

"Consider it done," Pete said. "And if you come up with anything else, you know where to reach me."

"Right now, you know what I know. Me and Buck'll keep our eyes and ears open. Anything comes up, we'll see that it gets to you in quick time."

Dooley frowned, shaking his head. "Thing like this, a mass killing on Bourbon Street, it's bad for business."

Where to take Shelburne for questioning? The manager had a private office in the back of the club, but Jack nixed that. Chances were that it might be bugged by the city's Vice Squad or some other law enforcement agency. The side rooms off the main floor, where patrons could go with the performers for private dances and whatnot, were also ruled out, for the reason that an operator like Shelburne was likely to have them outfitted with hidden video cameras to pick up some blackmail material.

Jack wound up taking Shelburne off to one side of the main floor, to an alcove where a pillar blocked the view of the stage. A table with bad sightlines was undesirable, a spot to be relegated to customers of no importance, and therefore least likely to be bugged or wired for sound. All the same, Jack looked under the table for evidence of eavesdropping devices, but found none.

Grouped around the table were four rickety, wooden armless chairs with woven cane bottom seats. Jack was doubtful that they could support the manager's massive weight, but Shelburne must have dealt with that problem before, because he came up with a ready-made solution. He pushed two chairs together and sat down on them with one meaty buttock perched on each chair.

Jack sat across the table from him. Shelburne said, "Why're you picking on me? I didn't do nothing. I'm a legitimate businessman. I've got no more to do with those killings than the man in the moon."

Jack said, "Vikki Valence works for you. She lives upstairs over the club. Her boyfriend was attacked outside your place in an ambush that left seven dead. Vikki's gone, disappeared. You're involved, all right."

Shelburne squirmed in his seat, the chairs creaking beneath him. "Sure, I rented the apartment to Vikki. Why not? It's standard business practice, see? It's a tradeoff. She gets a knockdown on the rent and the club gets a knockdown on her fee. She's a headliner and headliners are costly. It's the star system. It's a perk. If she don't get it from me, well, there's plenty of other clubs in the Quarter who'll give it to her."

He bobbed his melon-sized head in the direction of the two women seated at the bar. "Francine and Dorinda got a similar arrangement; they live upstairs, too. It's strictly business."

Jack said, "How long was Vikki going out with Paz?"

Shelburne shook his head, agitating his triple chins. "Hey, I'm not responsible for what the talent does during their off hours. These are healthy young women with normal physical appetites. What they do in their private lives is none of my business."

Jack, flat-eyed, looked at Shelburne until he was squirming again. He repeated his question. "How long was Vikki going out with Paz?"

"Coupla' months," Shelburne said.

"She have any other men friends?"

"She had her admirers, sure. All our dancers do. But she wasn't here long enough to pick up any steadies, because Paz moved in on her the first week she opened at the club. And there were no others after she took up with him. He liked to show her off, as arm candy. So everybody could see what a big shot he was, keeping company with a hottie like that. He liked to be seen with her, but he didn't want anyone else getting close to her. He's the jealous type.

"Besides, with the money and jewelry he was throwing at her, she didn't need no other sugar daddy. Why spoil a good thing?"

Shelburne was opening up. Jack soon learned the following:

Paz first started coming to the club in the spring. He'd gone out with several of the other dancers, including, most notably, Dorinda. In Shelburne's lexicon, "gone out" and "dating" were euphemisms for the same thing: having sex. Vikki started working at the club in late June. She was booked into the venue for the entire summer. When she hit the stage of the Golden Pole to do her star turn, Paz liked what he saw. He was smitten. He gave her the big rush, the full-court press, courting her with flowers and gifts of expensive jewelry, lingerie and the like. She and Paz hooked up in late June and had been an item ever since.

"It was a sweet deal for me," Shelburne said. "Paz spent a lot of money in the club, a bundle! He brought back the good times, money wise. He brought in a lot of other business, too, friends of his."

Jack said, "Who? We'll want their names."

Shelburne made a face. "Names? Who knows names? Every night we're packed to the rafters with customers, hundreds of 'em. Does a theater manager know the names of everybody who buys a ticket to a show?"

"Try."

Shelburne frowned heavily, as if to show that for him, remembering was hard work. "They were Latino dudes, that's all I know. Maybe they were from Venezuela, like him. I don't know, I don't speak the lingo. What I do know is that they were dough-heavy, too, and didn't mind spreading it around."

Jack said, "What about the other dancers? Any friends there that she might have contacted, gone to for help?"

"I don't mix in the dancers' personal lives, so I wouldn't know," Shelburne said. "But remember, Vikki was a headliner. A star. A real prima donna. She kept to herself, not buddying up much. Paz liked it that way."

Jack questioned Dorinda next, while in another corner of the club, Pete went to work on Shelburne, grilling him to see what else might be pried loose from the manager.

Dorinda was second-billed on the club roster, right below Vikki.

She was restless, fidgety, in constant motion. Not out of anxiety about the massacre, or at being questioned, but mostly because she was the type who couldn't sit still for a minute and always had to be doing something. That's how Jack read it. She might have had a drug habit of some kind, too, that was affecting her.

She kept running her fingers through her hair, pushing it away from her face, only to have the same strands keep falling back over her eyes whenever she moved her head.

She wore lots of gold bracelets that clinked and jingled as she moved. She chain-smoked filtered cigarettes and sipped from a plastic bottle of water throughout the interview.

Jack said, "What do you know about the shooting this morning?"

"Nothing. Not a thing," she said. "I was asleep when it

happened. The shots woke me up. I got out of bed and lay on the floor until the shooting stopped. I waited a couple of minutes before looking out the window and saw a bunch of dead guys in the street. I waited in my room for the cops to show up. That's all I know."

"So you didn't see Vikki Valence run away?"

"No, but I'm not surprised she's in the middle of this," Dorinda said, adding under her breath, "the little tramp."

"You don't like her much," Jack said, working the obvious.

Dorinda said, "I'm not in her fan club, if that's what you mean. Simply put, she's a conniving little bitch. I knew she was going to get Marty into a mess of trouble sooner or later."

"Marty? You mean Colonel Paz?"

"Who else? Martello, that's his real name, but I called him Marty. He seemed to like it."

"You and he were friends."

"You could say that. Good friends, very good friends, if you catch my drift."

Dorinda's long, narrow green eyes took on an inward look, remembering. "I had Marty first," she said. "Had him from the moment he first came into the club and saw me."

Jack said, "When was that?"

"Back in the spring, around April."

"You and Paz were together for how long?"

"Couple of months, until the end of June. I cut him loose."

Jack said, "You broke up with him."

"That's right," Dorinda said, eyes narrowing. "Men don't leave me, I leave them. Why? What'd you hear? Has that fat bastard Shelb been talking out of turn?"

Jack said, "Why'd you break up with Paz?"

Dorinda said, "It wasn't working. He was just too jealous.

It's that hot Latin blood, I guess. Once we were together, he didn't want me seeing any other men. Or even talking to them. Which isn't possible in this line of work, being a dancer, I mean. The job requires that we get along with the customers, be sociable, you know, to build goodwill and whatnot.

"When you're a star like me, you don't have to mingle much, not like the gals at the bottom of the bill, but even then, sometimes there's some guy who wants you to have a drink with him at his table, and it's easier to go along than to say no and make a big deal of it. A lot of heavy hitters come in here, powerful and important men, the real gentry, and you can't risk a shutdown because the invite you refused came from somebody high in City Hall or something. Marty didn't like that so well, even after I explained it to him a thousand times. He got used to it, but he didn't like it."

Jack said, "I understand he had a hot temper."

"Not with me," Dorinda said, "except once or twice when we had a few misunderstandings. As couples do. But he was a real gentleman. He never hit me. He could be scary when he got mad, though, his face would swell up and his eyes would turn all red. You've heard the expression, that somebody 'sees red'? I always thought it was just a saying. But when he gets mad, Marty's eyes, the whites of them, really do turn red. You knew he was nobody to mess with when he got in one of those moods.

"But they blew away fast, and most of the time he was—I wouldn't say a real nice guy. But he was decent enough," she said.

Jack changed the subject. "What about his bodyguards?"

Dorinda said, "What about them?"

"What were they like? Did you get along with them?"

She laughed, a harsh cawing sound. "Sure, I got along

with them. I'm the easygoing type. I get along with most everyone, especially men. Men like me, I wonder why?"

She made a show of stretching and yawning: lacing the fingers of both hands over her head, arching her back, and thrusting her breasts forward, so that they threatened to break loose from her low-cut blouse.

Jack asked, "Talk to them much?"

"Nah. A little, mostly hello-goodbye, how you doing. The two main ones I knew were Aldo and Espy—Espinosa, that is. He was killed, huh?"

"They both were."

"Too bad about Espy, he was a good-looking guy. What a waste of prime beef."

Jack said, "Did Paz have any enemies?"

Dorinda laughed again, that harsh cawing sound. "He must've, considering the trouble they went to try and kill him."

"Any that you know of, that he mentioned to you."

"Enemies? Yeah—you guys. That is, guys like you, cops. Cops and government guys. Marty was always going off about the government. Ours, that is, not his. The U.S. He kept sounding off about the FBI and the CIA, two of his pet peeves, and how they were always trying to bug him and follow him, and how they were the tools of the rich in this country and they only wanted to take back Venezuela from the revolution so they could go back to stealing the oil like they'd been doing before his crowd got in, and so on and so forth, and all that kind of crap. I didn't listen when he'd start spouting off; he could go on like that for hours."

Jack said, "Any other enemies. Apart from the government, that is. Any personal rivals, men he'd crossed in love or business?"

Dorinda shook her head. "Marty didn't talk about his business with me. He's one of those macho types who thinks a woman has no business being in business. But he had bodyguards with him all the time—well, not quite all the time, if you know what I mean. In bed," she added, just in case Jack didn't know what she meant.

"So he must have had enemies, or he wouldn't have had bodyguards with him all the time," she went on. "And I guess he was right, because somebody did try to kill him after all."

Jack asked, "What about friends? Did he have any of them?"

Dorinda's green cat eyes widened, then narrowed. In calculation. And malice.

"I know one!" she said. "Raoul—Raoul Garros."

Jack knew who Garros was, all right. CTU's GCR Center had a file on him, a big one. He said mildly, as if the matter was of little interest to him, "Raoul Garros? I believe I've heard that name. He's that big Venezuelan oilman, the one that's in the papers?"

"The very same," Dorinda said. "He and Marty were thick as thieves for a while. In fact, Raoul first brought Marty into the club."

Jack silently noted her familiar use of Garros's first name. "An odd couple. Paz is a roughneck and Garros seems like a smoothie. From what I read about him in the papers."

"Smooth? Slippery, that's the word you're looking for," Dorinda said, with no small bitterness of voice and expression. "Or oily, that's even better. Yeah, oily. That describes Raoul to a T."

"Sounds like you don't like him."

Dorinda's face was a porcelain mask, flawless, unlined, expressionless. Only the eyes were alive. Green eyes. Glittering, though, not sparkling. "Raoul? I don't like him or dislike him. I don't think about him. He's nothing to me. Less than nothing."

Jack couldn't help asking, "What was it about him you didn't like? His good looks, money, or celebrity?"

"All of the above," Dorinda said, her teeth clenched. "Raoul's greatest love is himself. He's vain, he's more stuck on his looks than any of the gals who work here. He's full of himself, a big bore.

"He didn't fool me with those phony manners," she went on. "He's a sneaky guy. I wouldn't trust him. He's always got a lot of big deals cooking, according to him."

"What kind of deals?" Jack asked.

Her shrug was dismissive. "How would I know? I'm not into that kind of crap. Men talking about business, to me it's boring."

"Were Raoul and Paz in business?"

Dorinda snickered. "Marty's not what you'd call a businessmen. He's a hard guy. A soldier. But he and Raoul were in pretty good together. Sometimes something would come up and they'd have to talk in private, so they'd tell us girls to go powder our noses or go shopping or get lost until they were done talking about whatever they were cooking up."

She fell silent, studying her nails. After a pause, she looked up. "Come to think of it, maybe Marty and Raoul are enemies at that."

"You said they were buddies," Jack said.

Dorinda said, "They were—but they had a big falling out."

"Why?"

"The oldest reason in the world."

"Money?"

"No," Dorinda said, irritated at his obtuseness, "a woman."

"Which woman?"

"Guess." Not waiting for his reply, she said quickly, "The one you're looking for. Vikki Valence."

"Why her?"

"Good question. I couldn't see the appeal, myself. But Raoul and Vikki used to play around. They were going at it pretty hot and heavy. Then she dropped him and took up with Marty."

Jack's tone was skeptical, disbelieving. "She dropped Garros for Paz?"

"Sure, why not?" Dorinda challenged. "It's the Bad Boy Thing. Raoul's a pretty boy. He's in love with his looks. If I didn't know better, I'd say that he and Vikki broke up after too many fights over who was hogging the mirror."

"But you know better."

"I know that Raoul stepped out of the picture when Marty made a play for Vikki."

Jack said, "Vikki was with Raoul, then Paz? Men you'd been intimate with? That didn't make you mad?"

Dorinda said, "Be serious. I had them first, then I got bored with them and moved on. All Vikki got out of it was sloppy seconds. My leavings. She could have them. They're her problem now. And it looks like it turned into a hell of a problem, too. A killing affair."

"Raoul tried to have Paz killed because he was jealous of him over Vikki?" Jack had a tough time maintaining a neutral tone and keeping the disbelief out of his voice.

Dorinda recovered some of her cool. "That's your spin on it. Don't put words in my mouth. I'm just saying that Marty took Raoul's girl away from him and Raoul was sore about it. After that, he stopped coming in the club. Raoul's rich and well-connected; I guess if he wanted to, he could find some guys to take his money for knocking off Marty. Especially in this town. Without looking too hard, either."

Jack, noncommittal, said, "Well, it's an interesting theory and we'll certainly follow it up."

"You do that," Dorinda said. "Just don't tell Raoul that it was me who put you on to him, okay?"

"Your confidentiality will be protected, just as we protect all our sources."

Jack stood up, indicating the interview was over. Dorinda's face lit up with a smile of genuine delight. "I just thought of something," she said.

"Oh? What's that?"

"With Vikki gone, that makes me the headliner!"

During her interview, redheaded Francine threw a different slant on things: "Dorinda had it bad for Raoul."

Jack said, "That's not what she says."

"She's kidding you, or herself," Francine scoffed. "She was real gone over the Caracas Romeo. Raoul's catnip to women, and he had Dorinda purring. But a guy like that is too good-looking to be good. Rich, too. He's a playboy; he's not going to settle for one woman. Besides, his family are big shots back in Venezuela; they'd never stand for their sonny boy marrying a Bourbon Street titty dancer."

Francine grinned, relishing her own malice. "Not that he was ever going to marry her anyway. He's not that dumb. That was Dorinda's fantasy—she is that dumb. To him, she was strictly for laughs. That goes for Vikki, too."

Jack said, "Did Raoul and Paz get along?"

"They palled around."

"I heard they had a falling out after Paz took Vikki away from Raoul."

"You must've heard that from Dorinda. What else is she going to say? She's just trying to save her face," Francine said. "Listen, friend, nobody could take any girl away from Raoul until he was good and done with her. Take it from one who knows."

"You were with Garros, too?"

"A lady never kisses and tells," Francine said, smirking. "Vikki had nothing to do with Raoul throwing over Dorinda. He was tired of her long before he ever laid eyes on Vikki. He dumped her at least a month before Vikki began her engagement here."

Francine went on, eyes bright with anticipation of her next revelation. "Raoul and Paz were pals. Bosom chums. When Raoul got tired of Dorinda, he passed her along to Marty. Then Vikki came along, and Raoul gave her a big play, until he got tired of her. Then he passed her along to Paz."

Jack said, "But Raoul stopped coming in the club around then?"

"But definitely. He had bigger fish to fry. Don't you read the society pages, chum?" She gave Jack the once-over and said, "No, I guess not. You're not the type. But you'd have to live in a tree somewhere not to know that Raoul's giving a big play to that stuck-up Keehan bitch."

"I may have heard something about it," Jack allowed. "That's Susan Keehan, the heiress?"

"The very same. Talk about being full of yourself! She makes Raoul look publicity shy. She may not be built like Vikki or a master of sexpertise like Dorinda, but she's got her share of the Keehan family fortune to bring to the table. With a prize catch like that on the hook, why would he bother fishing around these waters? Especially since he'd already netted his limit here."

Jack nailed it down. "So as far as you know, there was no enmity between Raoul and Paz?"

"The reverse," Francine said. "If you ask me, Raoul was kind of a high-class pimp for Marty. Not that Marty can't get his own girls if he wants them; Lord knows he's not shy. But Raoul's a talent scout for him. He'd try out the merchandise, give it a test drive, and when the ashtrays were full, turn it over to Paz. Something a little sick about the way they trade girlfriends, but it takes all kinds."

A happy thought struck her. "Hey, who knows? Maybe after Raoul gets tired of the Keehan girl, he'll pass her along to Marty, too," Francine said.

A uniformed cop entered the club, spotted Dooley, and hurried over to him. He passed along some information to Dooley and went back outside.

Dooley crossed to Jack and Pete, said, "Got some news that might interest you. Looks like we've got a lead on Paz."

. . . .

THE FOLLOWING TAKES PLACE
BETWEEN THE HOURS OF
9 A.M. AND 10 A.M.
CENTRAL DAYLIGHT TIME

. . . .

Top field agents such as Jack Bauer and Pete Malo were the
tip of the antennae of the military-intelligence entity that
was CTU.

Just as the human organism produces antibodies designed to seek out and destroy opportunistic infections and
diseases, the American nation had created in CTU a specialized defense mechanism to deter, seek out, and destroy
the global pandemic of hostile terrorist cells inflamed by
murderous fanaticism and empowered with the awesome
overkill potential of weapons of mass destruction. CTU was
a national resource with worldwide reach.

From the moment that Vikki Valence had first contacted
the CTU public tips hotline and uttered the key word Beltran, the agency had begun focusing its formidable array of
institutional instruments and abilities on the case. Unfortunately, the ceaseless and pervasive threat level directed from

all corners of the globe against the United States prevented the agency from channeling more than a part of its energies to the developing incident.

As with all other U.S. civilian and military outfits in the new age of the War on Terror, CTU's mandate and responsibilities exceeded the human power and budget allocated it by a government whose treasury was already stretched dangerously thin from the demands of meeting its overwhelming superpower commitments.

The early morning massacre on Bourbon Street had further prioritized the Beltran affair in CTU's caseload, allowing a greater allocation of time, technology, and personnel to the matter. The ultraviolence of the would-be assassins, and the involvement of hostile Venezuelan and communist Cuban elements, threw what was already a red-flagged incident into overdrive.

In the immediate aftermath of the shootout, Pete Malo had used his cell phone camera to photograph the dead men and woman, capturing each in full-frontal and profile views. CTU already had photos of Baca and Espinosa on file, but he'd photographed them in death, too, in the interests of completeness.

The information was instantly sent to CTU's Gulf Coast Regional Center for processing by the technicians and operators of the facility's Analytical Division.

The images were examined using the latest facial recognition and identity imaging software for purposes of identification.

From here, the images were also uploaded to CTU Headquarters in Washington, D.C., for further analysis by the agency's linked national network of supercomputers—themselves cross-linked to the databanks of the FBI, CIA,

NSA, the Pentagon, and all other associated intelligence services who might be able to throw some light on the case.

As House Committee on Un-American Activities ace investigator James McClain had once observed, "These are the mills that grind so very fine and not so very slow." And that was in the precomputer age of filing cabinets and index cards.

The bulk of hands-on investigative chores in the Beltran affair fell to CTU's Gulf Coast Regional Center under the leadership of Director Cal Randolph. Within minutes of being notified of the Golden Pole massacre, Center dispatched teams to secure the site and subject it to forensic analysis.

Long before police investigators had arrived, CTU agents had photographed and videotaped the crime scene from all relevant angles.

The ambushers' utility truck and Paz's armored limo were impounded and towed away to the Center, to be exhaustively examined by mechanics and technicians.

It was important that the limo be whisked away before any members of the New Orleans branch of the Venezuelan Consulate could arrive at the scene to claim possession of the vehicle. The consulate as yet had received no official notification from U.S. government agencies of the attack, CTU having judged that any "premature" notification would be counterproductive. For the same reason, the U.S. State Department had also been kept out of the loop, to prevent their meddling from hampering the investigation.

Both decisions had been enthusiastically endorsed by high-level White House national security advisors.

All weapons found at the scene were collected and inventoried. One fact immediately stood out: all the attackers' weapons had their serial numbers intact and unaltered; no attempt had been made to obliterate them. This indicated that the weapons were "sterile," that is, probably stolen and without any paperwork or history to directly link them to the users.

All the same, the serial numbers were input into the CTU computer net for identification and determination of point of origin. Even stolen weapons could furnish potentially valuable clues for triangulation with other bits of evidence to build a profile of the assassin team and, more important, its sponsors.

CTU moved early on to secure the club building and prevent its occupants from leaving. The site was searched from top to bottom to ensure that Vikki Valence was not secreted somewhere on the premises, alive or dead. Results were negative. Wherever she was, she was gone from the Golden Pole.

A forensics team focused on her apartment, inspecting and inventorying its contents, and taking away any material that might prove germane to the investigation. This included several boxes of personal material, most of which was publicity-related photos and press releases, but also including several stacks of private correspondence and fan letters.

During Vikki's initial contact with the CTU hotline, she'd identified herself and where she could be found. Intentionally or not, she'd neglected to supply a cell phone number. The source of the call had been tracked to a pay telephone located several blocks away from the Golden Pole.

A computerized search of the customer lists of various telecom company records identified her cell phone provider and through it, her telephone number. This gold mine of information provided the ability to contact her directly, as well as to track her movements by way of the cell phone towers and substations she used to make her cell phone calls.

But this major lead was neutralized by the simple fact that, from the moment the number was identified until the present time, her phone was switched off. She might have turned if off deliberately for reasons of her own, she might have misplaced the cell and fled without it, or she might have met with foul play and, like the phone itself, been switched off—perhaps permanently.

Until it was turned on, the cell was no more than a blind alley.

A copy of her phone records had been acquired by CTU; her incoming and outgoing calls were being analyzed to build up a profile of her contacts and associates, all of whom would be investigated as part of the ongoing search.

The Golden Pole and wider Bourbon Street area were monitored by a variety of private and official surveillance devices, including police traffic cameras mounted at key intersections, monitors posted at high-crime areas to discourage street prostitution and drug dealing, and security cameras serving as anti-theft devices at stores, shops, and parking lots.

Center was in the process of accessing the videotaped records of such cameras that were in operation at prime locations during the relevant time periods.

After being interviewed by Jack and Pete at the Golden Pole, Drake Shelburne, Dorinda, Francine, and Troy the bartender were escorted by CTU agents to the Center facility across the river in Algiers, for further and more extensive debriefing.

This was an application of the well-known fact that detaining in custody reluctant or hostile witnesses and persons of interest tended to wonderfully improve their memories and powers of recall.

The mill wheels were turning.

Sisters of Mercy Hospital
New Orleans

Thurlow J. Meade, forty-five, stood a few inches short of six feet and a few pounds short of the two hundred mark. He had a big gut but was still hard and strong. Even the gut, a kettle belly, was taut and solid.

He was a native of New Orleans, a lifelong denizen. He could take care of himself; he'd worked on the docks for all his adult life, and you didn't last on the waterfront if you couldn't stand the gaff. By some (including himself), he was regarded as a pretty tough character.

He was currently employed as a forklift operator in a riverside warehouse.

Normally the warehouse was open on Saturday, for a half day, from six A.M. till noon. Not today. Today it was closed, because of the threat from Hurricane Everette.

Meade was of two minds as to how to respond to the oncoming storm.

Several years back, at the last possible moment, he'd heeded his wife's urgings that they get out of New Orleans before Katrina hit. They'd been safely north on high ground, staying with relatives, when eighty percent of New Orleans had been submerged.

That was one narrowly escaped nightmare not to be soon forgotten, and went into the plus side of the scale weighing the benefits this time of staying or going.

On the staying side was the fact that since then, there had been no catastrophic storm. This season, the city had already escaped being struck by two imminent hurricanes that at the last minute veered off to make landfall somewhere else.

Both times Meade, his wife, and the family dog had piled

into his pickup truck (the bed of which was laden with their belongings, wrapped in waterproof tarps) and taken it north, along with thousands of other evacuees fleeing the city. It had been no picnic, enduring endless traffic jams that took hours to travel miles, not to mention the hardship and discomfort of having to take refuge with their kinfolk. Who no matter how they tried to extend the welcome wagon, couldn't help but make Meade and family feel like poor relations.

Two false alarms in a row had Meade deciding this time on staying put and sticking it out. As Everette neared, his resolve began wavering.

The window of opportunity was closing; today, Saturday, was the last day on which to make good an escape from New Orleans. The last two trips, the worst he'd had to suffer was another "damned, time-wasting, backbreaking inconvenience" of the type he'd swear was sending him to an early grave. But if he stuck, and Everette proved to be the real deal, well, then he'd be taking his and his family's lives into his hands.

Because New Orleans was in worse shape now than it had been before Katrina. The resources were less, and so were the reinforcements. The gangs were bigger, bolder, and more arrogant; violent crime and killings were way up; and one could only imagine the orgy of lawlessness and sadistic brutality that another major storm would evoke.

Early this Saturday morning, then, Meade had gotten into his car, a late model gray sedan, his pickup truck being in the process of being loaded yet again with the family possessions, such as they were.

His goal was a greasy spoon diner where he'd pick up some fried egg sandwiches and a couple of thermoses of coffee to fortify himself for the exodus. The diner was located on a little-traveled byway riverward of Bourbon

Street. Meade left his wife still stowing some gear in the pickup while he headed downtown.

It was a little past six A.M. Meade had the air conditioner in his car on and the windows down. The air conditioner lacked the muscle to make a dent in this oily, seething, suffocating air. Sweat started from his every pore.

Driving along an approach to Bourbon, he halted for a red light. His car was second in line, sandwiched between a tan minivan ahead and a compact car behind.

He was muttering to himself about the heat and humidity and not paying attention when suddenly a figure loomed alongside him in the driver's side.

A glimmer of movement on his left came simultaneously with the driver's side door being yanked open. A hand reached in, grabbed Meade by the back of the neck, and hauled him bodily out of the car.

His car was idling in drive. With his foot now off the brake pedal, the machine rolled forward several feet before bumping hard into the bumper of the minivan in front of it, which was also halted for the red light. Metal and plastic crunched, glass broke, and Meade's car bumped to a stop.

Meade lay on the asphalt, dazed, winded, his elbows and knees scraped and his side and hip bruised. Shaking his head to clear it, he started to raise himself up on his elbows.

Before he could do more, a gun loomed in front of his face. And not just any gun. A monster gun, a mini–machine gun whose big-bore muzzle was staring him straight in the face.

The gun was in the hand of a medium-sized, stocky man whose head looked like a pineapple. A pineapple with red eyes. They were the only live, moving things in his rough-textured visage.

Most likely, he'd decided on the sedan because it looked faster than the minivan.

The minivan's driver started to get out to inspect the damage to his vehicle from the fender-bender, until he saw the man with the gun. He froze.

The gunman hopped into the driver's seat of the gray sedan. He threw the car into reverse, backing up hard into the car behind him, smashing the headlights and front grille of the latter and crumpling the rear of the sedan.

He was making room for his exit, pushing the car behind him backward. He executed a rubber-burning U-turn, wheeling across the yellow line into the opposite lane.

Meade got his feet under him, scrambling to get out of the way of his own stolen car coming at him.

The carjacker whipped the machine around 180 degrees. Tires yelped like a dog with a stepped-on tail as the gray sedan whipped around and headed away down the opposite side of the street.

It turned right at the next intersection, scooting around the corner and out of sight.

Such was the tale told by Meade himself, while he was being treated in the emergency room of a nearby hospital.

He'd been there for several hours already, in crowded corridors filled with screaming kids, groaning pain sufferers, and scared-looking loved ones, relatives, and friends. Doctors, nurses, and orderlies moved with purpose along the halls, flanking wheeled patient-laden stretchers along linoleum-floored corridors.

Hospital security guards (unarmed) grouped in clusters at strategic points along the halls; there were also uniformed NOPD cops stationed there to help enforce the peace in this time of prestorm jitters.

Several hundred miles from landfall, Everette was already racking up a casualty count. There were those who'd been injured during hurried preparations to escape, falling victim to stress or strain: cardiacs, panic attacks, even hernias induced by trying to tote too much away. Crimes of violence had spiked dramatically: shootings, stabbings, beatings. Abandonments, too: a number of elderly relatives, wheelchair or bedridden invalids, had been left by their families on the outskirts of the hospital grounds.

Not least of those present was Thurlow J. Meade, who'd just finished telling his story to Jack Bauer and Pete Malo, following up the tip furnished to them by Floyd Dooley.

A police officer on duty in the ER had originally taken Meade's statement and passed it along to headquarters; now, as the incident assumed vital importance in light of the Golden Pole massacre and manhunt, a detective stood alongside the victim, minding him until the CTU agents arrived.

The detective, Stankey, balding and sharp-featured, wore a rumpled summer-weight suit, pale yellow shirt, and charcoal-gray tie. He said, "What with all the extra calls coming in because of the storm, this one got lost in the shuffle for a while."

Meade was sitting on top of an examining table. He wore a hospital gown. Bandages patched his face and skinned elbows. His right ankle was taped up.

"Do you recognize any of these men?" Jack said, using his cell phone monitor to show Meade a series of six photographs, head shots of different men. Five of the shots were ringers, the sixth was Colonel Paz. The purpose was to avoid leading the witness while certifying the validity of the identification, should any be made.

At the last photo, the one of Paz, Meade sat up straight—an action that caused him to groan with pain—

and said, "That's him! That's the guy! I'll never forget that face!"

"Thanks, Mr. Meade, you've been very helpful," Jack said. He and Pete were already in motion, heading toward the exit.

Meade called after them, "If you catch up to that guy, watch out for his gun. It's a big mother!"

CTU Center contacted the NOPD to put out an all-points bulletin on the stolen car, yielding swift results. A police patrol car found it several miles away from where it had been taken.

Jack and Pete arrived at the locale, which was several miles north and inland from the French Quarter. It was a working-class neighborhood of small, modest houses laid out on a grid of cracked-pavement streets. The area had suffered some Katrina damage but had remained largely intact.

A fair-sized crowd of neighborhood folk, men, women, and children, stood grouped around the gray sedan. Not many residents would evacuate this area. Few cared to leave behind their meager, hard-earned worldly goods to the tender mercies of thieves and looters. Most were staying. The area was on a gentle rise, most of it above sea level, but potentially exposed to gale force winds that could sweep the knoll clear if the storm came roaring in at full strength.

There were lots of kids around, running in circles, dodging in and around the clusters of adults, narrowly avoiding collisions, the adults snarling at them but the kids already gone, out of reach.

The gray sedan had been found quickly because it had been involved in another carjacking, this time of a boxy Korean-made tan-colored coupe. The sedan had cut off the coupe, blocking it and forcing it to a halt. Its gun-toting driver, who was undoubtedly Colonel Paz, had abandoned the sedan, charging the coupe on the driver's side and forcing out the two occupants, an elderly couple.

They'd been slow on the uptake, stunned by events, and for a moment remained frozen in place in their machine.

Paz had goosed them into action with a burst of machine-gun fire, emptying it into the side of the sedan he'd just quitted. Glass windows blew, doors cratering and crumpling under the burst. Then he waved it at the duo in the coupe. This time they got the message, piling out of their car and scuttling away.

Paz jumped in the coupe and took off. He was long gone when the first patrol car arrived on the scene.

Pete Malo shook his head, grinning wryly. "The Colonel is sure cutting a wide swath across town."

Jack said, "But where's he headed? And to what purpose?"

New Orleans is a big city that covers a lot of ground, a crazy-quilt patchwork of neighborhoods and districts that includes such disparate walks of life as the urban cityscapes of the business and commercial precincts, the French Quarter with its Old World charm spiced with sleaze, the suburban sprawl of the Lakeview District, and such blighted zones as the lower Ninth Ward and East New Orleans.

Sandwiched inland where the business district ends and the residential neighborhoods begin is a decaying factory-warehouse area that began running to seed a long time ago.

A rough, scrappy patch of reclaimed marshland knit together by a spidery skein of canals, truck routes, and access roads, it features mostly warehouse buildings, transport company depots, and junkyards, aging sites mostly bordered by tall chain metal fences topped with spiraling loops of razor-sharp concertina wire.

An eyesore for decades, it's now a full-blown industrial wasteland. Katrina had seen to that. The storm surge had swamped the area, flooding the flats. Floodwater alone is bad enough, brackish and diseased, but the Katrina-borne deluge had served as a kind of universal solvent, leaching out tons of chemical, oil, and sewage pollutants that had been buried underground and surfacing them.

The citizenry called the sludge "toxic gumbo." When the waters finally receded, they left behind the residue, a noxious ooze several inches deep that contaminated all it touched.

This area had been hard hit. The polluted residue was plain to see, a silver-gray coating resembling metallic frost that blanketed fields, lots, and canebrakes. From a distance it was oddly beautiful, like a November frost, but every piece of plant life it touched, it killed, while leaving them perfectly preserved, like museum pieces.

Running through the middle of the badlands was a truck route, a two-lane blacktop ribbon. During the weekdays the road was lively with truck traffic, big rigs, flatbeds, deuce-and-a-half carriers, and pickups, all ferrying material to and fro.

Saturdays, with many of the trucking companies closed for business, traffic was much less.

Today, this Saturday, with a storm imminent, traffic was close to nonexistent.

In the middle of this emptiness, on the west side of the north-south road, stood an abandoned gas station. A rusting marquee sign's faded letters were just barely legible to make out the name of its long-defunct off-brand: JIFFY PUMP.

The pavement was cracked and weed-grown. The gas pumps were long gone, removed, though the underground fuel tanks remained, rusting, corroding, leaking oily residue into the subsoil. A flat-roofed cube that had once housed a combination garage and convenience store now stood with its doors and windows boarded up.

The dreary solitude of the setting was broken by a tan coupe that scooted southbound and riverward along the roadway. It slowed as it neared the abandoned station on the west, turning into the driveway and rolling around to the back of the building.

It was now screened from view of any other vehicles that might pass along the route.

The car stopped, its engine chugging and gurgling for another half minute or so after the ignition had been switched off before thudding to a halt.

Clambering out of the vehicle was Colonel Paz.

Take a piece of lead pipe and slam it against a hornet's nest a few times; the results are explosive. Such was the mindset of Martello Paz. The assassination attempt was the lead pipe, and the inside of his head was the hornet's nest.

He was buzzing, electric with fury. Red eyes rolled in the dark, lumpish mask of his face. His machine pistol was clutched in one hand. He was dangerously low on ammo, with barely a few rounds left in the sole remaining clip.

Somewhat the worse for wear, he'd lost his hat, his clothes were filthy and torn from rolling around on sidewalk and street scrambling for cover during the shootout, and his body was bruised, sore, and aching. Otherwise, though, he'd come out of the kill zone pretty much unscathed.

He talked to himself, maintaining a running monologue under his breath. "All those bullets flying and not a mark on me! That's because my guardian saint is looking after me. Saint Barbara! She protects her favorite son!"

In his way, Paz was a religious man: a diabolist. Like many narco traffickers and killers, he looked to the spirits of the invisible world for protection in this one. His was not so uncommon a belief in the violent underworld, the vida loca of South American drug cartels, where a trafficker must fear his rivals, his allies, and the police, while the ever-present fear of betrayal, torture, and violent death hangs miasma-like over the milieu.

A trafficker seeks to up his odds of survival any way he can. That includes help from the beyond, the domain of spirits, ghosts and phantasms; the dark world of devils, demons and dark gods. Many pistoleros take to the practice of magic, witchcraft, the invoking of presences and spirits for supernatural protection against earthly foes.

Paz's guardian spirit was Saint Barbara, traditionally the patron saint of gunpowder, a Christian icon who in the realms of voodoo and Santeria stood for Ogun, the god of war.

Around his neck, strung on a thin chain, Paz wore a medallion stamped with the image of the saint, a vital protective talisman that had been blessed by a powerful bruja, or witch.

Paz reached into the top of his shirt, wrapping a hand around the medallion of Saint Barbara and squeezing it as he made a sacred vow to the deity.

"I, Martello Paz, give thanks for deliverance from my enemies. I will send many souls to serve You in the afterlife, I promise You that, and You know that is one promise that Paz never fails to keep. There will be blood—"

Paz set about turning sacred vows into secular reality. He had already been surprised once today; it would not happen again. Gun in hand, he prowled around the site, making sure it was as lonely and abandoned as it looked. Doors remained locked; the plywood boards covering plate-glass windows were intact and untouched.

He'd just completed his survey when he glimpsed a blur of motion to the north.

He ducked behind the rear of the building, out of sight, peeking around the corner.

Instinct had proved right, as he now observed a police car driving south along the road.

Paz at this moment was in no mood to be trifled with by anybody. If the lawmen were on his trail, it would be just too bad for them. However few rounds he had left in his machine pistol's clip, he'd put them to good use. When the bullets ran out, he still had his bare hands. He was Paz, Martello Paz.

The stolen car was parked behind the back of the station, which should hide it from casual observers passing by along the road.

The oncoming police car was in no hot pursuit; its emergency lights and flashers were dark. It rolled past the Jiffy Pump ghost station and kept on going, not slowing down, rolling southbound and away until it was out of sight.

"Lucky for you, bastardos," Paz said to the rear of the police car as it dwindled in the distance, becoming a blur, then a dot, then winking out into nothingness. He spat in their direction.

He lingered long enough to note that there was a light but steady flow of traffic on the road. Generally, at any one time, it was never empty; there were always a few vehicles following it north and south. He saw no immediate threat implicit in that fact.

Restless, he prowled around the back of the lot, making sure there were no homeless derelicts, winos, or bums encamped in the brush, and no youngsters exploring the nearby polluted creeks and fields. If any witnesses saw him making use of the station hideout, he'd kill them. Which bothered him not at all, but hiding the bodies afterward would be real work, especially in the suffocating heat, already oppressive at this hour of the morning.

The station building was a flat-roofed blockhouse consisting of two parts, an office/convenience store area and the larger section, a two-bay garage. The outer shell of the station was faced with white ceramic tiles, now faded to a dingy gray, set in a grid pattern. The plate-glass window display area was encased behind sheets of nailed-up plywood. All other windows, large and small, were also boarded up

Paz went around to the rear door. It was made of solid metal, with a door handle but no keyhole.

He reached around to the left door frame, at about chest height, probing and feeling around the tiles and the grouting until he felt one tile move under his touch. He pushed in on it, hard. A metallic clicking sound came from within; he'd tripped some kind of concealed internal locking mechanism.

The tile under his fingertips was mounted on a hinged metal square plate. With the release tripped, the hinge-mounted tile flipped up, jutting at right angles to the wall. Beneath it lay a hidden recess containing a numerical keypad.

Paz's stubby, strangler's fingers punched out a six-digit numerical code number and pressed enter. Triggering an electronic impulse that released a concealed locking mechanism in the door. The bolt retracted, unsealing the door.

Paz opened it, stepping aside as a blast of hot, stale air wafted out. It reminded him of the "hot box" cells he'd used back in the Venezuelan jungles, penning prisoners in them for days and weeks at a time to break them; or, having broken them, to let them rot in their own filth.

Light shone through the doorway, illuminating the office side of the building. A long wooden counter ran down the long axis of the space, dividing it in half. The countertop bore a faded imprint of where a cash register had once sat, back when the station was actually a going concern.

The front of the building had featured a large plate-glass window front and glass door. They'd been painted black and encased from within with metal grilles. Thieves would need heavy-duty equipment to break in, deterring kids, crackheads, and all but the most determined burglars.

A pall of dust covering the floor was undisturbed. No one had entered the hideout since he'd last been here over a month ago.

He set his gun down on the counter. Stacked under it were supplies, boxes of dried foods that would keep forever, stacks of half-gallon containers of bottled water. Not to mention other, vital creature comforts, such as a humidor of top-quality Cuban cigars. And adult beverages.

He hauled out a cardboard carton containing four bottles of rum. Dark Jamaican rum. He pulled one out, broke the seal on it, unscrewed the cap, and took a long pull from it. It poured liquid fire down his gullet into his belly, then all through the rest of him. It felt good, nerving him with energy.

He followed up with several more solid belts, leaving the bottle half empty when he set it down. He let out his breath in a long sigh: "Ahhhh . . ."

For the first time since the gunfire at dawn, he finally felt like he had time to catch his breath.

Martello Paz had come up in a hard league and had never forgotten it. He'd come far and risen high, but it could all vanish in the blink of an eye. The wheel of fortune throws down as capriciously as it lifts up. The regime that prized his services today might seek to liquidate him tomorrow.

Paz was careful. He always left himself a way out. The gas station was a safe house known only to him. A bolthole, a safe house to hide in if things went sour.

Nemesis, he knew, could come knocking for him in the

form of any of his colleagues at the New Orleans consulate, virtually all of whom were involved in Venezuela's spy services. Military spies, secret police spies, even political spies. When they weren't spying on the Americans, they were spying on one another. Sometimes they spent more time spying on one another than the opposition, monitoring their fellows for loyalty to President Chavez and his "twenty-first-century socialist" regime.

Opposition there was aplenty. Emissaries of Chavez's socialist state were radioactive as far as the American intelligence agencies were concerned. All consulate staffers were on the Yankees' watch lists. So were their contacts, colleagues, chance acquaintances, friends, family members, and mistresses, their cooks and servants and gardeners.

Handicapping the U.S.'s military intelligence apparatus was the fact that it was stretched and stressed to the breaking point. So many persons of interest were wandering loose and abroad in the nation that it was impossible for the home team to keep track of them all at any one time. America's open society provided an incredible advantage for the aggressor.

Paz swam in a sea of treachery. Betrayal was endemic to his profession. It could come from any direction. Therefore, real security could come only from relying on oneself. He had established this little bolt-hole early in his tenure at the consulate. It presented no great difficulty to a man in his position of power and trust.

Oil was the motive force of Venezuela's move to center stage of world power plays. The state oil company's overseas division, LAGO, was politicized from top to bottom. More than merely politicized, it had become a vehicle to insert an entire espionage infrastructure within the United States and every other nation where it was in business.

Here in New Orleans, LAGO had established a major

presence in areas both overt and covert. Raoul Garros, the real power in LAGO's New Orleans branch, was Paz's man.

Paz was a past master at feathering his own nest. He'd carried out the establishment of the safe house strictly by himself, going outside channels to avoid leaving any trail, paper or other. The official spy organization being run out of the consulate had a number of safe houses in the city at its disposal. That was no good to Paz. He needed his own private safe house (or bolt-hole), known only to him.

He had several million dollars salted away in various offshore banking concerns.

He'd set up a dummy corporation, using it to buy the site of the abandoned Jiffy Pump gas station. His ownership and identity were hidden behind an intricate assemblage of false-front companies and cutouts.

He hired a construction firm from neighboring Mobile, Alabama, to refurbish it to his liking. They'd installed the security hardware, the keypad-activated electronic locks, the reinforced doors, roll-down bay doors, metal mesh grilles protecting the windows.

Paz's shell company had the electric power switched on, paying the monthly bills.

He'd also fitted the site with some extras.

He swilled another long pull of rum, crossed to the left wall of the office, the one adjacent to the garage. Bottle in one hand and machine pistol in the other, he crossed to the left wall of the office, where a door stood, and opened it. No tricky mechanism involved here; he turned the knob and the door opened. The smell of oil and stale grease hung heavy in the air.

He switched on the overhead fluorescent lights. The garage was rigged like the office, windows blacked out to prevent the escape of a single beam of light. A precaution that mattered little during the day but would be important after dark.

The bay nearest the office featured a late-model Explorer SUV. "The SUV of Death," as he liked to call it. It was parked facing the closed bay door. Its plates were legal, as was its registration.

Standing in a rear corner of the garage was an old air compressor, a bulky and ancient hulk of disused machinery set in a housing whose base was bolted to the floor. Paz went to one knee beside it, turning two of the heads of the bolts. The bolts turned easily, unlocking a concealed mechanism.

He gripped the edges of the housing, putting his shoulder to it. The base with its flaring metal flanges was mounted on a hidden axle, pivoting easily enough under his efforts. He pushed it to one side, out of the way, revealing an oblong space cut into the floor. It contained several suitcases. Paz hauled them out and opened them up.

They contained weapons: a Kalashnikov assault rifle complete with grenade launcher, a half-dozen grenades, an Uzi-style machine gun, a number of big-bore handguns (revolvers and semi-automatics), plus plenty of boxes of ammunition and spare clips for each.

Paz selected a pair of 9mm pistols, Berettas, loading each with full magazines. He stuck the pistols in his waistband at his hips, Wild West style. He stuffed some more magazines into the side pockets of his tattered sports coat.

Now that he had some more firepower to fall back on, he felt physically relieved, able to cope. It was like a shot of dope.

Other pressing needs demanded his immediate attention. The stolen car, for one. He couldn't leave it out in the open, for fear that a cruising police helicopter might spot it

He unlocked and opened the front door of the empty garage bay and raised it, the segmented sliding door rising and retracting along the curved tracks overhead. Light filled the cavelike garage space; heat poured out of it.

Paz stepped through the open bay door and went around to the back of the building. He started up the tan coupe, circling around to the front, and backing the machine into the bay.

He stood in the open bay doorway, scanning the scene. Vehicles continued to roll past in both directions, none showing any sign of interest or even notice of the activity at the station. He pulled down the sliding door, closed and locked it. So much for the stolen car, putting it out of sight.

He turned his attention to the assault rifle, quickly assembling and loading it. His touch was sure, betraying no slightest trace of hesitation of clumsiness. Guns, he knew. They'd been an integral part of his life since early boyhood days.

Addressing an invisible foe, he said, "You want a fight, you can have one!"

Martello Paz first saw the light of day in a Caracas slum, one of ten children by as many different fathers. An unattractive youth, lumpish-featured and thick-bodied, he early on demonstrated a penchant for lawlessness and a flair for violence. Law-abiding citizens, such few as there were in his crime-ridden barrio, marked him out as "a bad one."

He possessed the virtues of strength, cunning, and endurance. He was a fierce brawler and street fighter, traits that served him well in the street gangs which he'd joined as soon as he was able.

At thirteen he was as self-possessed and independent as a grown man—a hard, dour one. He smoked, drank, took drugs, and had sex with women and girls whenever he could get it. Two kills were already under his belt: a fifteen-year-old bully he'd stabbed to death; and an adult, a middle-aged shopkeeper who'd threatened to inform on Paz for stealing and had had his brains bashed out by a lead pipe wielded by the youngster.

At this point, he experienced a life-changing event.

The street gang he ran with was so full of itself that it valued hell-raising more than moneymaking, a sure sign of madness. They were rabid, and there's only one thing to be done with rabid dogs, and that's to put them down.

Sheer chance saved Martello from the kill-off. The night it came, by sheer chance he'd gotten drunk by himself and passed out in a clearing on a hillside.

He was awakened from a sodden stupor by the sound of shots and screams. The clamor came from the village below. Gunfire popped and rattled, punctuated by the explosive boom of shotguns.

Smoke clouds rose, underlit by red firelight. The blaze was coming from an old shack that the gang used as a clubhouse. Inside, the one-story structure was a mass of flames. The light spilling from it revealed several dark forms—bodies, dead bodies—sprawled on the ground in front of the structure.

A couple of jeeps were parked along one end of the plaza, headlights on, illuminating the town's central square. Figures were chasing down other figures and shooting them dead. The shooters were strangers; the ones they were shooting down were Martello's fellow gang members. The strangers were grown men, wielding handguns and shotguns.

A death squad.

The victims were teen gang members. Most of the killing had been done by the time Martello awoke. The square was littered with bodies. A heap of corpses lay at the foot of an adobe wall that had served as the backdrop for a firing squad. The executioners manhandled the ever-mounting pile of bodies, delivering the coup de grâce of a bullet in the brain to the wounded.

Hot night. Hot work! When the job was done, one of the shooters, a leader from the way the others deferred to him, took off his cap and used a bandana to mop the sweat from his face. His visage was revealed in the firelight, a face Martello would never forget. The killers climbed into their jeeps and drove away.

At dawn, the villagers emerged from their huts to examine the carnage. In the main, they were able to control their grief. One or two heartrending cries sounded from mothers and sisters when they recognized their own flesh and blood among the bodies, but such unseemly displays were quickly shushed and silenced by their stoical menfolk.

Martello Paz took advantage of the opportunity to sneak into one or two houses, stealing food and water and anything else of value he could find. He sneaked back into the hills, deeming it best to maintain a low profile for the moment.

Later that day, the police arrived to deal with the mess. The "investigation" was a desultory effort at best, police and villagers being equally unenthusiastic about solving the slaughter.

Martello Paz watched the cleanup effort from a hiding place in the brush bordering the outskirts of the town square. He particularly took note of the police official heading the operation.

It was the man who'd been leading the executioners the night before, whose face Martello had seen in the firelight.

The solution to the case was simple. The local shopkeepers and vendors had scraped up what little money they had, until they had enough to commission the services of a death squad. A police death squad.

Such arrangements were common, a way for ill-paid lawmen to combine extracurricular profit and justice. They'd taken the contract and come by night to eliminate the gang. Summary executions. No gang, no problem.

Investigation? No such animal—what were the police going to do, investigate themselves?

Martello Paz knelt in the bush, fascinated, watching the entire show. The last body was loaded in the back of a dump truck; the cleanup crew and the cops went away.

The entire experience had been a revelation to young Paz. He felt no resentment toward the executioners who'd wiped out the gang and would have done the same to him if fate hadn't spared him.

He was instead inspired with a profound sense of admiration and envy. Gangs made the world go round. His world, anyway, and that of his fellow slum dwellers, dwellers in one of scores, if not hundreds, of similar districts scattered in and around Caracas and its outlying districts.

The police were just another gang, better armed and more efficient than most.

Young Paz now had a role model: the police officer who'd bossed the death squad. The police, that was where the real power lay.

From that moment on, Paz resolved to become like them. One of them. A policeman.

Fortunately, this ambition did not require in him any notions or moves toward reform. Quite the contrary. An honest policeman in his society was doomed to, if not an early grave, then a miserable existence of poverty and ridicule.

So it began.

Paz surfaced in another part of Caracas, one far enough away from his old haunts to insulate him against comebacks for his former misdeeds. Crime remained his means of livelihood. He certainly wasn't going to go to work for a living, he'd starve to death!

He quickly attached himself to a drug gang. He was a prize acquisition, a youngster who was already a stone killer. Not for him the menial tasks of gofer and runner; he held the prestige of the life taker, mixed with the novelty of his youth. That tender age proved invaluable when it came to assassinating rival gang members, none of whom imagined that the short, squat, unattractive kid—often in the guise of shoeshine boy, newspaper vendor, or errand boy—would empty a revolver into their faces to achieve their deaths.

At the same time, he was learning all he could about the interface between the gangs and the law, and began playing a dangerous double game. He became a police informant, fingering and setting up those gangs and independent operators who'd failed to pay off the police for the privilege of operating. Building solid contacts.

The gang bosses pushed the idea of Paz joining the cops as their inside man, not knowing that he'd manipulated them toward this very end. The same attributes of fearlessness, amorality, and ultraviolence served him as well in the ranks of the police force as they had in the criminal gangs.

Inevitably, inexorably, he followed an irresistible rise to the top of the city police establishment, then the regional, and finally the national police establishment.

After three decades, Martello Paz was simultaneously at the top of the secret police corps and the Venezuelan drug cartels.

It was at this point that Colonel Hugo Chavez began his own rise to supreme power. Chavez came out of the Army ranks, a fiery speechmaker and demagogic radical.

At first he'd masked his true beliefs behind a facade of populism, appealing to the masses by promising them that they'd get their rightful share and more of the riches that had been stolen from them by the oligarchy and its American capitalist masters.

Paz sensed in Chavez a kindred spirit. Paz was a bandit in a police uniform; Chavez was a bandit in Army fatigues. Paz operated behind the scenes to consolidate his power; Chavez operated at center stage, brandishing a bold, fiery rhetoric of "economic justice for the masses" and "due process of law." Chavez was using a front of socialist ideology to steal a country. He and Paz were a natural fit.

Chavez was a strongman; the Venezuelan oligarchy was weak. The ruling class had long ago lost the taste for blood so necessary to secure and maintain absolute power.

They were shortsighted, too. They'd bought the generals but not the rest of the Army. The generals were too stupid and greedy to share the wealth, alienating the colonels and all other ranks down. Chavez had the Army and the masses.

Paz threw in with Chavez early, putting his formidable police apparatus to work for the promising presidential candidate. Anything from providing police presence for crowd control and security at Chavez political rallies; supplying intelligence on all the dirty secrets of the opposition—vital blackmail material to make the most recalcitrant foes fall in line; guarding the person of the candidate; harassing dissidents and political foes; breaking up opposition efforts, smashing their printing presses—and their heads, if they failed to get the message.

Paz's position at the top of the national police hierarchy proved invaluable in collecting massive campaign fund "donations" from gang bosses and drug lords. As did his clout with the caudillos, the powerful political bosses in every city, town and village, with their ability to get out the vote (not once, but often), facilitated by their election day workers, poll watchers, vote thieves, and ballot box stuffers.

No less important was the use of the caudillos' goon squads, comprising thugs, enforcers, and gunmen. The really important political murders were the province of Colonel Paz himself. He oversaw the murder of intractable political foes, including clerics, labor bosses, newspaper owners, editors and reporters, political dissidents, and others whose timely removal was judged necessary for the success of Chavez's political campaign.

The other side did it, too; unlike previous elections, though, this time out they lacked the inestimable services of Martello Paz, who did it better.

Chavez was elected president, and duly appointed Paz as the head of his secret police apparatus. Soon after election, Chavez was seized by a rebel cadre of high-ranking Army officers in a coup attempt. Paz was unable to forestall the seizure, but his behind-the-scenes efforts, including the taking of key hostages from among the plot's oligarchic sponsors, was instrumental in Chavez's quick release and triumphant return to office.

Most recently, Paz's services had won for him the coveted post of top military attaché to the Venezuelan Consulate in New Orleans. A post that also placed him at the head of Caracas's espionage efforts in the U.S. Gulf Coast.

Now, sitting in the safe house of the Jiffy Pump gas station, cradling an assembled and fully loaded Kalash across his knees, Paz lit up a cigar. He puffed away, aromatic smoke clouds wreathing his head, the orange-colored tip of the cigar flashing like an emergency beacon.

President Chavez was really high on his alliance with communist Cuba. He idolized Castro for having kept his Marxist-Leninist regime a going concern for a half century, despite the intractable hostility and diabolical machinations of the Norte Americano arch-capitalists. He saw himself as the new Fidel; no, beyond that, the new Bolívar, near-future liberator of all Latin America.

The result of their newfound entente was that Cuba got much-needed oil from Venezuela; Venezuela got much-needed intelligence from Cuba. Colonel Paz's key Cuban contact and ally in the United States was the formidable, elusive General Beltran himself.

The cigar that Paz now smoked was one from a humidor with which Beltran had gifted him, claiming that their quality was beyond that even of Cuba's superb Monte Cristo variety: "These are from a blend specially made for Fidel himself!"

Yet there was trouble in the workers' paradise, the new Latin American Socialist Internationale. For Beltran was the one who'd tried to have Paz hit.

Beltran had inadvertently betrayed his authorship of the attempt by using the female shooter, an exotic, deep-cover operative whom Paz knew without doubt was one of Beltran's creatures. Beltran thought his association with her was a closely held secret, but Paz was not without confidential sources himself and had undoubted proof of the connection. The Cuban wasn't the only spymaster in the game; Paz had been playing, too.

Whether or not Beltran had been acting on his own or following orders from Havana was a question purely academic. In either case, the answer was the same: Beltran must die.

Still, in all honesty, Paz had to admit that it really was a superior brand of cigar. He promised himself he'd smoke one over Beltran's dead body. Soon.

"There will be blood."

. . . .

**THE FOLLOWING TAKES PLACE
BETWEEN THE HOURS OF
10 A.M. AND 11 A.M.
CENTRAL DAYLIGHT TIME**

. . . .

Jack Bauer and Pete Malo prowled around in their SUV, trying to pick up Colonel Paz's trail. Pete drove, Jack riding shotgun in the passenger seat.

Valuable time was eaten up pursuing false leads. A complicating factor was that, as in any other major U.S. city, carjackings and auto thefts in New Orleans were a routine, round-the-clock daily occurrence. The number of incidents was spiking dramatically higher due to the approach of Hurricane Everette, which caused an already understaffed police force to be spread ever thinner, creating a climate of rising anarchy that encouraged the criminal element to take advantage of the opportunities it offered.

Jack and Pete crisscrossed the New Orleans area, receiving a steady stream of information and updates via their secure comm link with CTU Center across the river in Algiers.

No sooner had one new lead developed than it was quickly shot down. There were plenty of carjackings taking place, but they all turned out to be common, garden-variety auto thefts, none of which could be laid to Colonel Paz.

NOPD traffic cameras monitoring key intersections, squares, and thoroughfares for moving violations registered a blank when it came to sightings of the tan coupe stolen by Paz. The same went for cameras covering bridge approaches and entrance ramps to the major highways out of town.

Results: negative.

Jack said, "I see a pattern here. Paz grabbed his first car within a few blocks of the Golden Pole in the heart of the city. His second car was stolen out in the boondocks. He knows what he's doing. He's moving away from the urban hub where surveillance is heaviest and out into the outlying districts where coverage is lightest."

Pete nodded, his face glum. "He may have switched cars again and the reports haven't reached us. Or he's in the same car but cruising along the outskirts where the cameras and the cops are few and far between. Or he's gone to ground and is laying low."

Jack said, "Looks like the trail's gone cold for now."

The Garden District is one of the oldest and wealthiest neighborhoods in New Orleans, an opulent domain of palatial mansions and parklike estates. Located on high ground, it had escaped most of the ravages of Hurricane Katrina, and what damage could not be avoided had been quickly repaired and made right.

One of the most imposing and storied old homes in this historic area was Venable House, a majestic Neo-Georgian structure with a white-columned front and extensive, exquisitely landscaped gardens. Its grounds were bordered by an eight-foot-high, black iron spear fence.

Venable House now served as the site of the Venezuelan Consulate.

Because of its current owners' antagonistic stance in regard to the host country, the locale remained under constant surveillance by U.S. intelligence, most prominently by CTU and the FBI, who maintained a joint operation that used both human agents and electronic eavesdropping devices to keep a close watch on the consulate.

Observers now reported that the consulate had gone into maximum security lockdown. Word must have finally reached its occupants of the attack on Colonel Paz and the massacre at the Golden Pole. With Paz missing in action, command of the security sector devolved to his second-in-command, Major Delaparra.

Now the massive, motorized front gates accessing the long, curving driveway through a broad expanse of front lawn were closed and locked. A heavy-duty SUV was parked broadside just behind the gates, to serve as a further obstacle to deter and resist the onslaught of any car or truck bombs. The machine had to be moved to allow the passage of vehicles containing security teams, the only vehicles that were allowed to enter or exit the compound.

Normally there were two guards armed with sidearms on duty at the entrance.

That had been upped to a squad of six men, helmeted and flak-jacketed, armed with assault rifles.

Similarly equipped teams of guards had been posted at strategic points around the grounds, stationed so they commanded a 360-degree field of fire to engage intruders from any direction in which they might try to launch an assault.

The main building's ground-floor windows—already made of bulletproof glass—were sealed behind bombproof shutters. Except for security forces, all other consular personnel remained inside the building and out of sight.

That included the consul himself, Professor Gabriel Vargas Obregon, his wife, and daughters, all of them occupants of the mansion's luxurious living quarters, and all of whom had been at home at the time of the lockdown.

A plan was already in place to meet the threat of Hurricane Everette by concentrating diplomatic personnel and their families at the consulate and riding out the storm there, rather than evacuating them from the city. The building had its own generator and stocks of food and water. Since the consulate had weathered Katrina with minimal damage and disruption, it was felt that the precautions were adequate to survive whatever onslaught Everette could muster.

A more militarized, action-oriented version of that plan was now set in motion, as members of the consular staff who resided off-site in houses and apartments around the city were notified to lock themselves in and remain at home, where they would be picked up by security squads and delivered to the Garden District mansion.

A half-dozen armored limos similar to the one driven by Colonel Paz now conducted a ferry system, going abroad into the city to pick up staffers and their families and bring them back to the hardened strongpoint of the consulate.

Despite the home regime's official line of a socialist system without the preferments of caste and class, it was noticeable that off-premises staffers were secured and delivered to the mansion according to their rank in the diplomatic hierarchy. Those highest in the chain of command, assistants and deputies to the consul and such, were picked up first, then middle-level bureaucrats, and lastly clerks and secretaries.

Not only the consulate's physical but also its electronic security had been hardened. No phone messages, e-mails, cables, or faxes were allowed to go out or come in without being screened to protect against further, updated instructions being passed in either direction to potential traitors or double agents in on the conspiracy.

U.S. electronic intelligence—ELINT—devices detected a major increase in signal traffic going into and out of the consulate's core, shielded, top secret communications center. The communiqués were scrambled and encoded. They were intercepted by National Security Agency "big ear" devices and downloaded to NSA supercomputers for decrypting. Results would be transmitted to CTU as soon as available.

U.S. government agents posted throughout the surrounding neighborhood at all critical avenues of approach continued to file updated reports stating that no potential physical threat elements to the consulate had yet been detected.

The twin-chambered heart of the Venezuelan government's presence in New Orleans consisted of the consulate and the LAGO offices. LAGO was an overseas subsidiary of Petroleos de Venezuela, the state oil company. Its offices were located in a skyscraper in the urban cluster of the downtown business district.

Like the consulate, the office building was itself a strongpoint, protected by LAGO's on-site security force, all of whose members had been personally selected and trained, and were under the command of Colonel Paz. Their leader's unexplained absence failed to affect the efficiency of the unit, which moved swiftly to defend the locale with a phalanx of cold-eyed, combat-ready troopers.

LAGO maintained a sizable staff of high-ranking executives, mid-level managers, and rank-and-file administrators. An operation similar to that which concentrated the diplomatic staff at the consulate site was conducted by the LAGO contingent.

It would have been impossible to succor the oil company personnel at the consulate; their numbers would have swamped the site's resources. Instead, LAGO staffers and their families were secured and delivered to the company building, which also boasted its own private generator and reserves of fresh water and food.

They were prepared to ride out the storm; now they would also ride out any armed assault.

The dark green SUV manned by Jack Bauer and Pete Malo pulled over to the side of the road and stood there, idling. They had been notified of an important incoming transmission from Director Cal Randolph at CTU Center, one that would be beamed to the transceivers that were part of the vehicle's array of onboard electronic communications hardware.

This included a monitor screen that was part of a console built into the dashboard housing. The screen was treated with a polarizing glaze process that rendered it opaque to any person or surveillance device that attempted to view it from outside the windows of the SUV. Audio was supplied by a speakerphone grid. Condenser microphones with fine-tuned pickup allowed Jack and Pete to respond directly to Cal in real-time, two-way conversation.

Cal said, "We have a positive identification of the female shooter."

The monitor screen imaged full-face and profile shots of the distaff member of the hit team, dead.

These were followed by a different photo of the assassin, one taken elsewhere and earlier, when she was alive. From the look of it, it was the product of a surveillance camera whose subject was unaware that she was being photographed.

It was an exterior shot, a street scene in an anonymous, unrecognizable urban locale. It pictured the woman standing on a street corner. She wore civilian clothes, a short-sleeved blouse and slacks, toting a handbag with a long shoulder strap. Her dark hair was much shorter than at the time of her death, a boyish pixie cut whose ends reached down to her firm jawline. She wore the same characteristic wire-rimmed spectacles with the oval lenses. Her forehead was high and smooth, almost bulbous; her mouth was a tightly compressed straight line.

Cal Randolph's disembodied voice came loud and clear through the speaker grid.

"This picture was taken by one of our sources eighteen months ago in Lima, Peru. The subject is Beatriz Ortiz, a Maoist, radical terrorist, and self-styled urban guerrilla."

The name rang no bells with Jack. He'd worked some Latin American assignments, but his real area of expertise was the Middle East, South Asia, and the Balkans. He glanced at Pete Malo, whose face showed no sign of recognizing the woman.

Cal said, "She's of Argentinean origin. Thirty years old, according to the record."

The director continued, "Her father was a college professor, her mother a dental technician. The father got on the wrong side of the Argentine military junta during the era of its 'Dirty War' against the left. He only signed a few human rights petitions, but that was enough to get him denounced, arrested, and sent to jail. He was never seen again and became one of the thousands of Desparacus, the Disappeared Ones. Presumably, like the others, he was tortured, executed, and buried in an anonymous mass grave.

"This radicalized the daughter. By the time she came of age and went to university in Buenos Aires, the junta was long gone and she was able to pursue her ideological passions with a minimum of scrutiny by the authorities. She began her student days as a committed Marxist-Leninist. She was spotted by a radical professor who steered her to a

Cuban communist recruiter. She dropped out of sight sometime before graduation, her whereabouts a mystery to her family and few friends.

"We believe she was smuggled out of the country to Cuba, where she was extensively trained at a school for spies. Her training period took several years, during which she demonstrated real expertise in the clandestine arts, including demolitions and assassination.

"She surfaced in Colombia, where she was associated with FARC, the rural-based revolutionary militia that's fought a civil war against the government for over twenty years now. The record shows that she operated with equal facility in the cities or the jungle. In the cities, she helped blow up buildings and assassinate government officials, journalists, judges, and prominent capitalists. In the jungle, her targets were landowners large and small, priests, teachers, ranchers, farmers, villagers who wanted to stay neutral, and all others she deemed 'enemies of the revolution.'

"This experience further radicalized her, causing her to cast aside Marxism-Leninism as 'too gradualist' and embrace Maoism, specifically the most violent revolutionary excesses of the Red Guard era during the sixties, a program that was defunct years before she was born. She expressed admiration for the genocidal regime of Pol Pot's Cambodia, and was *muy simpatico* with the Maoist Shining Path guerrillas during their reign of terror in Peru.

"If Havana had ever fully controlled her—and there's some doubt on that score, the late Ms. Ortiz apparently having been something of a wildcard when it came to following party directives, due to her frequent denunciation of the Fidelista ruling clique as self-serving moderates afraid to get their hands dirty—she became a fully independent free agent following her years in Colombia with FARC.

"Since then, she's been a freelance radical terrorist and

killer, working with the most extreme ultraleft elements in South and Central America and the Caribbean. She was sentenced to death in absentia in Brazil. Most recently, she's been spotted in Puerto Rico and the Dominican Republic.

"And get this: in the last year, she's reported as having been in the Orinoco in Venezuela, allied with a radical militia group terrorizing and killing owners of big estates and plantations opposed to Chavez's socialist takeover.

"A lot of governments will be happy to write 'Closed' on her files. Including ours. By the way, there's no record of her having entered this country legally—or any other way. It'll be tough to get a line on her. She was a pro. She went on the Paz hit job with no identifying documents, real or fake. No laundry marks in her clothes. Garments and sneakers that're mass-produced items available in hundreds of stores around the city. No leads there."

Jack said, "How about the glasses, Cal? Maybe she had them made in New Orleans. Or the States. Maybe we could get a fix on her from the prescription of the glasses, the grinding of the lens and the house style."

"We're checking it out," Cal said, matter-of-factly. "So there you have her, the late, unlamented—unlamented by our side, that is—Beatriz Ortiz. Make of her what you will."

Jack asked, "Anything on the other three shooters?"

"That's all we've got for now. We'll keep you posted on anything else that comes in."

Cal signed off, ending the transmission. Jack and Pete sat in silence for a moment, thinking, oblivious of the throbbing rumble of the SUV's idling engine.

Pete spoke first: "That Chavez connection makes her a natural to link up with Paz."

Jack said, "Except that she tried to link him up with a bullet."

"Thieves fall out. Maybe she was part of Paz's apparatus

here in New Orleans until she had a change of heart and thought he was going soft and decided to purge him for 'deviationist tendencies.'"

"It could happen," Jack conceded. "But that communist Cuba background could also tie her straight to Beltran—the joker in this deck."

Pete pointed out, "Havana's too moderate for her liking, according to Cal."

"She might have been able to overcome her distaste if Beltran's got something really hot cooking, something big enough and explosive enough to whet her appetite."

Pete said, frowning, "When you put it that way, it sounds worrisome."

Jack stroked his chin between thumb and forefinger. "Here's a puzzler: how does a hard-core Maoist urban guerrilla like Beatriz Ortiz wind up siding with a piece of neo-Nazi trash like Dixie Lee? Talk about your odd couples!"

Pete shrugged. "Politics makes strange bedfellows, they say. Still, according to Floyd Dooley, who knows his stuff, Dixie was a money-hungry cuss who wouldn't lift a finger unless there was a dirty buck in it."

Jack said, "While Beatriz Ortiz reads as a stone-cold ideologue and revolutionist who couldn't care less about personal gain. You couldn't buy her for anything she might consider counterrevolutionary, no matter how high the price.

"And another thing: why would Beatriz try to hit Paz? Whatever else he is, he's a bulwark of Venezuela's 'twenty-first-century socialist' regime. By her standards, a Chavez stalwart like Paz should be the last of her targets. We know she's a committed ideologue through and through; where does the Paz hit fit in with her ideology?"

Pete said, "Paz is dirty as hell. A big-time drug dealer. Maybe that makes him counterrevolutionary."

"FARC's a major cocaine supplier; they move product in volume to help fund the struggle. It's revolutionary drug dealing. She stuck with them in Colombia for years. So why get squeamish about narcotics trafficking now?"

"You're asking the questions, Jack. What's your take on it?"

"What could bring two polar opposites like Ortiz and Dixie together in a hit on Paz?" Jack said, responding with another question and then answering it: "Maybe—Beltran."

Pete made a face. "Sounds iffy."

"Who made the try on Paz? Let's reason by process of elimination," Jack said. "Who didn't make it? Venezuela. If Caracas wanted to give Paz the chop, there was a lot easier and more discreet way of handling it. All they had to do is recall him home and execute him there. Or they could have farmed it out to someone close to him who could have carried it out with a minimum of fuss, like one of his bodyguards.

"They sure wouldn't go gunning for him with a hit team when he's coming out of his stripper girlfriend's apartment. That's not the kind of headlines that the regime— any regime—likes. It creates a scandal. Headlines. Bad publicity. It would have made Paz look ridiculous—him, and by extension his boss, Chavez."

Pete challenged, "Okay, Caracas didn't do it. Who pushed the button, then?"

Jack said, "That brings us back to Beltran. We know Paz is a thief, trafficker, and killer. Beltran's more of the same, only older and more experienced. One or both of them might have gone off the reservation and gone into business for themselves. Maybe they worked up some private deal, unknown to their masters in Caracas and Havana.

"Then, like you said, thieves fall out. Maybe Beltran discovered that Vikki contacted CTU and decided that anybody who had an indiscreet girlfriend who knew too much was too unreliable to do business with. So he decided to dissolve their partnership by dissolving Paz."

Pete's head tilted, as if he were looking at the problem from a different angle. "I'm not saying I buy it, but just for the sake of argument, where does Dixie Lee fit in? I can see where the Ortiz gal fits in with Beltran, but Dixie Lee?"

Jack said, "I admit it's a loose end. But Beltran's been operating in the area for a lot longer than Paz has. He might have crossed paths with Dixie sometime in the past and decided to use him as a cutout or red herring to obscure the true sponsor of the hit."

Pete looked as uncertain as a customer in a used-car lot. "Seems like a cowboy job for a shadowy character like Beltran who shuns the limelight."

Jack said, "Maybe he had to act fast. Vikki's contacting us might have set a time clock ticking. A corollary to that is that some Beltran-Paz operation in the works threw a scare into her and sent her scurrying to CTU."

Pete chewed over the idea for a minute before replying. "You know, if Beltran did try to chop Paz, that would be a hell of a situation."

"Wouldn't it? Lots of possibilities there," Jack said.

Saturday was a work day at the Supremo Hat Company, a full day's work, from six in the morning until eight at night. Despite the storm threat, today it was business as usual. All employees were expected to clock in at their usual time, work their full hours, and clock out at closing time. No exceptions.

An independent small business lacks the leeway of the bigger corporate chains. It has to hustle to outpace the bigger, better-funded competition.

Supremo Hat was located in a single block building on

the edge of a run-down area where the city's commercial business district petered out, blending into an equally run-down residential neighborhood. Most of the buildings here had gone up during the 1920s, and there had been little new construction since.

No developers were rushing to gentrify this area. The skyline was unimposing, with few structures standing more than a few stories tall. The heart of the small business zone area was an intersection where two main thoroughfares crossed. Streets were cracked and potholed; sidewalks were uneven, with slabs of different heights. One square farther east, a block of down-at-the-heels tenements began.

Modest and unassuming at best, most of the businesses lining the square were going concerns: that is, they were concerned about going out of business. There was a furniture store specializing in selling factory seconds, off-brands, and more than slightly damaged goods. An E-Z Loan finance company. A combination cut-rate drugstore and gift shop. A Salvation Army thrift shop. A shoe repair store. A coin-operated Laundromat. A storefront church. A corner convenience store and smoke shop.

The Supremo Hat Company seemed a happy exception to the general air of shabbiness and neglect. It occupied a single-story building, a shedlike rectangle whose short end fronted the square.

The brown brick structure featured a tan cornice, window and door moldings. It was divided into two sections, a display and office space occupying the front third of the space, with the other two-thirds taken up by a work and storage area. At the rear of the building was a loading platform, and beyond that, a company parking lot. The gravel lot was bordered by a ten-foot-high chain-link fence topped with three strands of barbed wire. A company panel van and a half-dozen or so vehicles belonging to employees were parked in the back lot.

At the front of the building, a display window showcased the various styles of hats made by the company. In the bottom corners of the window, a pair of signs proclaimed the same message in two languages: POR LA MEJOR and FOR THE TRADE.

No casual customer could just walk in off the street and buy a hat. It wasn't that kind of a setup. The showroom was closed to the general public and reserved for garment industry professionals; even for the latter, it was preferred that they make an appointment in advance to see the line. The showroom was almost a formality, since company policy was to send its salesmen directly to the stores to display their wares for the buyers.

New Orleans takes its fashion seriously. Part of living well is dressing well. Hats are a necessary accessory.

Supremo made and sold men's hats only. Its specialty was handmade and woven straw hats. These were not crude things but works of art, with fine-mesh weaves. Panamas, Borsalinos, stingy brims, porkpies, planters, and other classic styles. Not cheap, either. Supremo made a quality product, with prices to match.

A couple of administrative staffers worked up front in the showroom and office area. At any given time, anywhere from eight to a dozen employees were at work in the back rooms.

The showroom featured a central display stand, stepped and velvet draped, covered at all levels with hats. Each hat bore a white, plastic-encased card with the style name and number. There was a quaint, old-timey feel to the decor, with its wicker-bladed overhead fan and array of globe lights.

To one side, a reception desk guarded the closed-door entrance to a private office.

Within, seated behind a dark wooden desk the size of a compact car, was the company's owner/manager, Felix Monatero.

He was in his fifties, well-groomed, with an athletic build. His face was long, rectangular, with a hawklike nose, arched eyebrows that came to a point in the centers, and a mustache that looked like it had been penciled in, but wasn't. Hair, brows, and mustache were all dyed jet-black, so black they had blue highlights.

Monatero sat behind his desk, examining an open ledger, going over some accounts. He peered at the entries through a pair of reading glasses.

A knock sounded on the door, one whose cadence and rhythm was familiar to him. He took off his glasses, slipped them into the breast pocket of his shirt, and said, "Come in."

The door opened and in stepped Mrs. Ybarra, his receptionist and confidential assistant. She was fortyish, matronly, short, chubby, with a large bust and wide rear. A heart-shaped face showed wide dark eyes and a red-painted Kewpie-doll mouth with a beauty mark to one side of it. She wore a cocoa-colored dress and dark brown leather shoes. Earrings, necklace, bracelets, and watchband were all made of heavy gold.

Closing the door behind her, she crossed to his desk, a sheet of paper held in one hand. She said, "This just came in over the fax."

She handed it to him. It was a printed circular, an ad whose heading said, "Red Sail Travel Tours" in such bold letters and oversized print that he could make it out without his glasses. He frowned at it. "Just came in, you say?"

"This very minute," she said. "I knew you'd want to see it right away."

"Indeed I do. Thank you, Mrs. Ybarra."

"You're welcome, Mr. Monatero."

He nodded, indicating that the encounter was at an end and she should go. She took her cue with no seeming reaction, her painted face expressionless, masklike. She went out, closing the door behind her.

Monatero put on his glasses and studied the missive. At first glance, it seemed no more than just another piece of spam, one of the many pieces of unsolicited advertising that comes in during the routine course of operation of a business fax machine.

He squinted at it. The tour agency ad hawked their "island getaway" special, a series of price-cut packages for budget-minded vacationers seeking fun-fested Caribbean holidays. One might have thought that the timing was a little off, considering that Hurricane Everette was now churning across the waters of the Gulf on a collision course with New Orleans, and the only getaway the locals were contemplating was a run to high and dry ground.

But this was no mere advertising circular, it was a notice of intent, a heads-up message for those such as Monatero who could read the signs.

He rose, crossing to a corner filing cabinet, a chest-high, gray metal job topped by a decorative potted plant with big waxy green fronds that looked fake but wasn't. The cabinet's vertically stacked row of drawers was secured by a combination lock. Montero knew the combination by heart, dialing it without hesitation and unsealing the lock.

Opening the top drawer, he reached in and took out its sole contents, a laptop computer. He quivered with alertness, experiencing an adrenaline rush that made his hands tremble.

That's what he told himself, that it was adrenaline which made his hands shake, and not . . . fear.

Carrying the machine in both hands, he set it down on

his desktop, sat down facing it, lifted the lid, and booted it up. He input his password, a twelve-digit combination of letters and numbers. When it was functioning properly, he activated its wireless transceiver.

The faxed message had been his cue to make ready for an incoming message. A prime communiqué.

Red Sail—that was the code name of a contact with extraordinary authority and clout, whose word was law to Monatero and the organization of which he was the head.

Monatero was a deep-cover agent for communist Cuba. The Supremo Hat Company was a cover, a false front for a clandestine espionage network which had taken a decade to establish.

Monatero, Mrs. Ybarra, and all the company employees, including the hatmakers and the delivery truck driver, were all members of the spy cell.

That they had transformed their cover operation into a profitable business with a reputation for making a quality product was merely one measure of just how effective that camouflage was. It was a manifestation of the classic espionage resident/illegal two-step.

Cuba and the United States maintain diplomatic relations of sorts, however strained those relations may be. There's an American Embassy in Havana and similar Cuban facilities in the United States. Each side assumes as a matter of course that all the diplomatic cadre of the other side is made up of spies. Being protected by their respective diplomatic credentials, they are immune to arrest and prosecution by the host countries.

That's what is called the resident system. Residents possess the equivalent of a get-out-of-jail-free card. If caught spying, the worst they can expect is to be deported back home. Of course, such residents come under relentless scrutiny by their opposite numbers in the rival intelligence services, who put them under the microscope night and day, around the clock.

Such total surveillance is a major obstacle to carrying out acts of covert and clandestine subterfuge so vital for effective espionage, counterintelligence, and action operations. The real meat and potatoes of the spy game.

To accomplish those ends, a second parallel system or network is required. One made up of persons not diplomatically accredited and therefore not necessarily subject to total surveillance by the host country's counterespionage and counterintelligence agencies.

These spies, who may pose as journalists, businesspersons, tourists, students, and the like, are known as illegals. If caught, they are potentially subject to arrest, interrogation, imprisonment, torture, and, in extreme cases, execution.

Monatero and the spy cell he ran behind the facade of Supremo Hat were all illegals. They were all very good at what they did, having escaped penetration or even detection by U.S. intelligence for many years now. They carried out the real nuts-and-bolts espionage operations that the Cuban diplomatic residents, the legals, were unable to perform due to the constant surveillance maintained on them by the United States.

An elaborate system of third-party cutouts, brush contacts, dead drops, and similar tradecraft tactics was in place to allow for two-way communication between the residents and the illegals.

Monatero was part of a chain of command linking him to his masters in Havana.

But there was a second line of authority, one whose existence was beyond top secret, linking Monatero to Havana's supreme deep cover agent operating in the U.S. Gulf Coast.

That shadowy spymaster was General Hector Beltran,

"the Generalissimo." Beltran's extraordinary status gave him top priority when it came to calling on the services of Monatero and the Supremo cell, allowing him to mobilize their full resources in support of whatever mission he desired to carry out.

It was a measure of Monatero's effectiveness and the confidence and trust reposed in him by Havana that he had been allowed to know the nature of the Beltran connection.

He was the only member of the Supremo cell to possess that knowledge.

Red Sail was a Beltran cryptonym. The Generalissimo had many different ways to contact Monatero and make his wishes known to him. The fax machine cue was just one of them.

When Beltran wanted something, it got done. Period. Monatero and his whole Supremo cell had to drop whatever ongoing operation they were engaged in, no matter how urgent it might be, even if the current op might be burned or blown by reason of neglect while they were carrying out Beltran's orders. That was how Havana wanted it; that was the way it had to be.

Months might pass, sometimes even a year or more, between Beltran's contacts with Supremo. Months had passed since Monatero had last been required to serve the Generalissimo.

Now Beltran had opened up communication with the cell. His encrypted message was downloaded into the laptop Monatero reserved for such communiqués. Monatero went to work on the message, keying in a series of passwords that were operative for today's twenty-four-hour window of opportunity.

Text flashed across his monitor screen, an alphabet soup of letters, numbers, and symbols that abruptly reconfigured into lines of text message:

```
(begin)
GRAND SLAM
LITTLE BROTHER LOCAL IN VIOLATION OF
    CONTRACT.
DEAL NULL & VOID.
PROJECT CANCELED.
SOONEST:
FIRE CARPENTER
TRIPLE PLAY FOR RUBI SUSPENSION
(end)
```

Decrypted, it was still opaque to those unaware of a lexicon previously worked out between Beltran and Monatero, a system of code words, private allusions, and euphemisms designed to add yet another layer of complexity to the text.

Monatero translated the message in his head. Spying was never less than intense, but Beltran always worked at the cutting edge, demanding the near-impossible and insisting that it be done in record time.

Monatero's nerves, already taut, underwent several more turns of the screw, keying him up to near-breathless levels of anxiety as the full import of the text took hold.

"Grand slam": that was a priority notification putting Monatero and by extension the entire Supremo cell on a maximum security alert—basically a wartime, combat-ready status.

What was afoot? Had the U.S. declared war on Cuba? "Grand slam" implied a crisis level of similar magnitude.

Monatero mentally clamped down on his physical reaction, his heart rate mercifully slowing down some as he read on. "Little brother" was Venezuela's new socialist regime. To Havana's dedicated Fidelistas, late-blooming Caracas could never be regarded as anything but a junior partner in the business of world revolution.

"Local" meant Venezuela's New Orleans consulate, specifically the spy apparatus being run out of the site.

"Violation of contract, deal null & void" and "project canceled" were all straightforward enough: there had been a falling-out due to some perfidy on the part of the Venezuelans; the working relationship between Cuban and Venezuelan spy nets, at least in New Orleans, was over, finished. Kaput.

"Soonest" was equivalent to "take immediate action." "Carpenter," Colonel Paz, was to be "fired"—that is, killed on sight or as soon as possible.

"Triple play for Rubi suspension": "triple play" was a three-man action team. Enforcers. Wet work specialists. "Suspension" was kidnapping.

"Rubi" contained a little private joke of Beltran's. It was short for Rubirosa. Porfirio Rubirosa had been the confidential agent of the fearsome Dominican dictator Trujillo, during the 1940s and 1950s. He'd also been an international playboy, a real-life Don Juan whose conquests included a string of movie starlets and heiresses.

Rubi was Beltran's sardonic code name for Raoul Garros, Venezuelan scion and womanizer, LAGO's smooth front man in New Orleans and a vital component of Paz's organization.

The message was dismaying, a red alert that conditions between Havana and Caracas had undergone a 180-degree reversal, from comity and close cooperation, to enmity and virtual all-out war. It specifically concerned operations in the New Orleans area, where Paz and Beltran had been conducting joint ventures, the nature of which was unknown to Monatero, who lacked the "need to know."

Monatero and his Supremo cell could expect an attack from Paz at any time. He was instructed to put Paz at the top of his A-list of targets marked for immediate execution.

Raoul Garros, a vital Paz associate, had escaped being marked for death, but was instead reserved for abduction, to be taken alive—for interrogation, exchange purposes, or whatever; that was a mystery to Monatero. Beltran would be handling the Garros kidnapping himself, and required a team of three top agents to immediately be put at his disposal.

Monatero reread the message, committing it to memory. He hit enter, and the text disappeared, winking into nothingness. Had he not hit the key, the message would have automatically deleted itself at the end of five minutes.

Monatero decided to have a smoke. That would give him something to do physically while his brain and nervous system were integrating the import of the instructions. He took out a custom-blend, brown paper cigarette and set fire to one end of it. After a few puffs, he became restless, eager to be in motion.

He set the still-burning cigarette in the ashtray and switched off the laptop. The screen's going black-dark gave him a start, making him flinch.

He unlocked the bottom right-hand drawer of his desk. In it were a gun and some boxes of ammo. The weapon was a short, snouty .380-caliber semi-automatic pistol, graphite-colored steel with dark inset walnut grips. It held a full clip, but the chamber was empty.

It was legal; he had a permit for it. Also a permit to carry a concealed weapon, obtained on the basis of his being the manager of a company that frequently required him to carry large sums of money. Ordinarily he rarely went about armed.

"Ah, well, there's no end for it but to follow orders," he told himself. Sighing, he slipped the weapon into the right side pocket of his sport jacket, then winced; the weighty pistol tended to ruin the linings of his pockets.

He closed the laptop, toted it back to the filing cabinet, and placed it in the top drawer. He closed the drawer, the lock clicking into place, and gave the combination dial a spin for further security.

Now to notify the rest of the cell of the change in status . . .

Something nagged at him, irritating him for no discernible reason and setting his teeth on edge, even more than they already were from the devastating new developments.

Whatever was bothering him was somewhere below the threshold of consciousness, and he couldn't put a finger on what it was, irking him all the more.

Suddenly awareness came and he realized what it was. The source of his annoyance was external, it was in the air all around him, and must have been so for several moments.

It was a tune, a mindlessly simple, catchy little tune that was being played repeatedly on some kind of electronically amplified, computerized music maker.

It came from outside, from the front of the building. His window was closed, the air conditioner was on, but the music still came through, loud and clear, maddening in its infantile simplicity and mind-numbing repetition.

It was that old folk song "La Cucaracha," rendered in the idiotically simplest, piping electronic tones.

Crossing to the window, he fingered open two slats of the Venetian blinds and peered between them, looking out through the glass.

The music came from a loudspeaker mounted on a lunch wagon parked at the curb in front of the building. An old, beat-up vehicle with a cab up front and quilted metal box behind. The box's side panels were hinged to open up and outward, revealing shelves stocked with plastic-wrapped sandwiches, coffee, soft drinks, buttered rolls, bags of potato chips and pretzels, and other quick snack foods.

It was what some of the men working in the back of the building jokingly called a "roach coach," although they patronized it religiously as it made its daily stops at the hat company.

A familiar sight, an icon, operated by Tio Rico, an oldster and well-known neighborhood character. He'd been doing business in the neighborhood for years, as far back as Monatero could remember. Supremo Hat was one of his regular stops, twice a day, six days a week. Regular as clockwork—had he ever missed a day?

The music was his way of announcing his arrival, just as ice cream vendors play similar ditties to advertise their presence and attract the kiddies to their truck.

Monatero had never before realized how annoying such music could be. It worked on his nerves like a dentist's drill. The mechanical, moronic repetition of the tune, reduced to its simplest elements, was maddening.

Or maybe it was the same as always, and it was he, Monatero, who was different, twitchy with a skinful of adrenaline and a skein of tautly strung nerves.

Letting the blinds fall shut, he turned and crossed to the outer office of his door. Beyond it, he heard the sound of voices, laughter.

He opened the door, stepping into the showroom. His nostrils tasted the mixed scents of hot coffee and fresh-baked goods. They arose from a thin cardboard box on Mrs. Ybarra's desktop, her workstation and reception area being placed just outside Monatero's inner office. She sat behind her desk, chatting with Tio Rico, the aged deliveryman and vendor who'd brought the snacks.

Tio Rico—"Uncle Rico"—was a little old man, balding, clean-shaven, deeply tanned, with white eyebrows and bright brown eyes. He wore a stingy-brim straw hat, button-down short-sleeved shirt over baggy khaki trousers, and a pair of blue-canvas, rubber-soled deck shoes.

Joaquin stood nearby. A veteran protector, competent, dangerous, he was the showroom's doorkeeper and security guard. A big man with a big gun worn beneath his white-on-white guayabera short-sleeved shirt, worn loose outside his pants and not tucked in. A professional, good at what he did, but as yet unaware that the cell had moved into the danger zone. He was focused on the good eats that Tio Rico had brought into the showroom.

Tio's face lit up when he laid eyes on Monatero. His head bobbed, nodding respectfully. "Good morning, senor."

"Good morning to you, Uncle," Monatero said. No kinship existed between the two. Everybody called old Rico uncle. Monatero said, "Is it snack time already? I must have lost track of the hour."

Tio executed more head bobbing and smiling. "That is because you work so hard, senor."

The coffee and baked goods did smell good, Monatero realized. He was aware of a hollowness in his belly as appetite began supplanting angst.

Joaquin unconsciously smacked his lips. He held back, as did Mrs. Ybarra; protocol dictated that Monatero make his selection first, then the others could follow.

Tio indicated the box of goodies. "Fresh-baked crullers for you, as always, senor." Monatero thanked the old man.

Inhaling deeply, Mrs. Ybarra said, "That coffee smells heavenly, Tio."

"Just the way you like it, senora. *Con leche* and sweet, sweet like you."

Monatero had other things on his mind than passing the time of day with the oldster. Tio Rico was the type to stand around and gab for five or ten minutes, if given the least sign of encouragement.

Monatero suppressed the urge to be curt and peremptory, maintaining his smooth front. "You'll have to forgive me, Uncle; I'm in a bit of a hurry today. A special order that must be filled immediately . . ."

Mrs. Ybarra glanced at Monatero, her facial expression blandly composed but her dark-eyed gaze alert, intent.

One thing about Tio, he could take a hint. "Yes, of course, senor, you are a very busy man; I won't take up an instant more of your valuable time."

Monatero pulled out his billfold and paid the man. Tio made a show of reaching into his pocket to make change, only to have the other wave off the effort. "For you, Uncle."

Tio protested, "No, I can't, senor, it's too much—"

"Please." Monatero held up a hand, indicating the matter was at an end.

"You're too generous, senor! And very kind. I thank you," Tio said. He thanked Mrs. Ybarra and Joaquin, too. He all but bowed his way out of the showroom backward, like a courtier making his withdrawal from the royal presence.

He exited, crossing the pavement to his truck, scuttling along bent forward, but surprisingly nimble for a man of his years. Scooting around the front, he got behind the wheel and started up the engine, rounding the corner and making for the parking lot behind the building, to vend his wares to the workroom crew.

Joaquin was gobbling a donut, while his other hand held in reserve a fistful of sandwiches. He could finish one off in a couple of bites, and needed several to satisfy his snack time appetite.

Monatero's face was frozen in the blandly beneficent smile he'd plastered on it for his dealings with the old man, but behind it, he was now all business. He told Joaquin, "When you finish stuffing your face, you can start doing your job. We're on a red alert—maximum security."

Joaquin went on chewing, but without savor. Mechanically. His mouth full, he said, "Who is it? The gringos? Is it the gringos? I always knew it would be them, in the end—"

Monatero said, "It's not the gringos, it's the Cousins." The Cousins was Havana-speak for the Venezuelans.

"The Cousins!" Joaquin echoed. "Well, I can't say I'm surprised. I always knew it would come to a falling-out. That Paz is a thug, a crook. He serves the revolution only as it serves himself. When the two conflict, the revolution goes out the window."

He gestured toward the rear of the building. "What of the others? Have they been told?"

"Not yet. Let them get their bellies full of Tio's snacks. It may be the last regular meal they get for some time," Monatero said. "Besides, we don't want to tip our hand. The Cousins may or may not know we're aware of their intentions. In either case, we must act as if we're not. That means carrying on as we ordinarily do, business as usual. No break from the pattern. To get the wind up now, when Tio is here to see them, would be a mistake. When the men are back inside, where no outsiders can see them, we'll tell them. Not before."

Joaquin frowned, his low forehead corrugating. "What if the Cousins strike now, before we're ready?"

"We'll just have to count on you holding them off," Monatero said, clapping the other on his broad back. He felt better now, in command. Almost merry. Joaquin's worry had helped restore some of his own confidence.

"I'll feel secure, knowing that you're here to take a bullet for us, Joaquin, to make the supreme sacrifice. I should say, the Supremo sacrifice, eh? Ha-ha."

Monatero smiled, the grin failing to reach his eyes.

• •

THE FOLLOWING TAKES PLACE
BETWEEN THE HOURS OF
11 A.M. AND 12 P.M.
CENTRAL DAYLIGHT TIME

• •

De Lesseps Plaza, New Orleans

There was movement above, high over New Orleans. Earlier, the sky bowl had been roofed by a smooth, unbroken cloud covering, a solid gray dome stretching from horizon to horizon.

Now the dead calm of that milky cataract was giving way, replaced by streaming masses of low, dark, ominous storm clouds. Heavy, moisture-laden, they rushed north in advance of Hurricane Everette, churning its way across the Gulf, landward bound. With them came rising winds, intermittently at first, beginning to sweep across the river and through the cityscape.

The sky ceiling lowered, the bottoms of charcoal-gray clouds grazing the tips of spires of skyscrapers in the central business district where Jack Bauer and Pete Malo kept vigil of the LAGO stronghold.

The agents were in their SUV, which stood parked facing the southeast corner of De Lesseps Plaza, where the Venezuelan oil company had its headquarters.

When New Orleans boosters issued promotional material designed to attract out-of-state investors, they focused on the midtown business district to convey the impression that the city was a state-of-the-art hub of industry and commerce, a world-class economic powerhouse.

Here was a citadel reared by the region's fiscal titans, a concentration of banking, shipping, and energy interests, embodied in a breathtaking cluster of sparkling, modernistic steel and glass towers. A showcase of the complex was De Lesseps Plaza, a sprawling site taking up several city blocks, a lofty mass of office buildings housing rich and powerful corporations, cartels, and global conglomerates.

Among the mighty was LAGO Corporation, an offshoot of Venezuela's state-owned oil company. Awash in petro-wealth, it had bought outright the office tower that housed its corporate facilities.

It was in the vicinity of that building where Jack Bauer and Pete Malo now kept vigil, waiting for some inside word regarding the whereabouts of one of LAGO's key players, Raoul Garros.

Garros was a person of interest for many reasons, such as his key role as company emissary to the New Orleans business community in particular and U.S. financial interests in general; his close personal and professional association with Colonel Paz; his engagement to Susan Keehan of the powerful and potent Keehan political dynasty; and, most pointedly, his recent liaison with exotic dancer and Paz paramour Vikki Valence.

LAGO Tower was a prime target of U.S. intelligence,

which ran heavy surveillance on it inside and out, but it was a tough nut to crack. Its security system had been overseen by Colonel Paz, whose paranoid suspiciousness and instinct for treachery had caused the installation of a variety of internal security mechanisms, human and electronic, designed to thwart U.S. spy probes.

Now, in the aftermath of the botched hit on Paz and his having dropped off the radar, the defensive system he had masterminded had gone into hyper drive, causing the Venezuelan Consulate and LAGO Tower to go into their maximum security mode.

CTU had a special source, an insider planted deep in the heart of LAGO's labyrinthine corporate maze. Jack and Pete were waiting for an update from that source before making their next move. They weren't just posted there in the SUV killing time, hoping that something would come in. It wasn't a case of sitting by the fishing hole, hoping that maybe they'd get a bite. This wasn't fishing; it was hunting.

Just as LAGO Tower had its ultrahardened, maximum security mode to fall back on in a crisis like this, CTU had a plan in place to defeat that system. Jack and Pete were waiting for it to kick in.

As top field man of the local CTU Center, Pete had the inside information on the LAGO leak and was explaining it to Jack. He said, "We've got a confidential informant placed high in the corporate hierarchy, basically right up there in the executive suite with Garros.

"It's a CTU asset, nobody else knows about it, not the FBI or NSA or any of the other agencies keeping an eye on that spies' den. No need to go into the identity of that source here. Let's just say that it's a good one, ideally placed to know Garros's comings and goings."

Jack nodded, taking for granted Pete's lack of disclosure of the source's identity. Compartmentalization was the ultimate safeguard of any intelligence service. You can't betray a secret you don't know. At this point in the investigation, Jack had no need to know the name of the LAGO source. Later on, if for some reason Jack thought it necessary for him to have that information to facilitate the hunt, CTU Center Director Cal Randolph would rule on whether to put him in the loop. It was Cal's asset and his call. Cal might decide to continue withholding the information. If Jack really wanted to push it, there was an appeals mechanism in place, but it would be an extraordinary step for him to take, and he would really have to make a case to justify the request, the final ruling on which would be made by the Director at CTU Headquarters in Washington, D.C.

Who knew? It was quite possible that Pete Malo was unaware of the source's identity, too, and that his knowledge extended only to the fact that such a source did exist.

Pete went on, "The current lockdown compounds the difficulty of our source getting the intelligence to us. Because of the attack on Paz, the Venezuelans are bringing their people in. The consular staff is being collected at the Garden District site, while the LAGO crowd is being brought into the Tower.

"Those folks already inside are prohibited from leaving, so that quashes any chance of our source making physical contact with a CTU agent to deliver an oral or written message. As for electronic messaging, forget it. All telephones, fax machines, and computers, all landline communications devices in the LAGO offices are centralized, channeled to go through one tightly controlled exit port which is constantly monitored by Paz's security staff."

Jack said, "What about wireless—cell phones and text messages?"

Pete's expression was half grin, half grimace. "That's

covered, too. Installed in the office areas are jamming machines, hardware designed to make such wireless devices
inoperable. The technology's similar to the kind used in
some live theaters and concert halls, to prevent audience
members' cell phones from going off in the middle of a
performance.

"As a final stopgap, the Tower's windows are sealed shut
and can't be opened by anything short of a crowbar, preventing our source from writing a note on a paper plane and
sailing it out the window down to the ground level where
one of our people could pick it up."

Jack said, "So what's the gimmick? There must be one,
or we wouldn't be sitting here right now, waiting for the go-
ahead. Or is that a state secret, too?"

"Sure, there's an angle," Pete said, "an old gag, and one
about as low-tech as you can get. We've got an observation
post in a building on the opposite side of the plaza, in an
upper floor facing LAGO Tower. The room's about the same
height as LAGO's executive offices, give or take a floor. Inside, there's a spotter with a camera with a telescopic lens
focused on the Tower.

"When the information comes through, our source inside
LAGO goes to the window and looks out, facing the building where our OP is. Nothing suspicious there, what could
be more natural than looking out the window, especially
now, with a storm coming?

"Our source silently mouths the information, saying it
without speaking aloud. It's picked up and filmed by our spotter's long-lens camera. The footage is transmitted to Center,
where it's examined by an expert lip-reader. The lip-reader
interprets the message and Center passes it along to us."

Jack was suitably impressed. "A lip-reader! That's quite
an angle, all right."

"Sneaky as hell, that's us," Pete said, trying not to sound smug and failing.

Jack said, "Now all we need is the info."

"Well, yes, there's that," Pete conceded.

Several minutes passed, then the comm system came alive with a message from Center. Not the go-ahead that the two agents were waiting for, but rather an update on the utility truck that had been used in the try on Paz.

An operator at Center reported, "The truck was stolen sometime last night from a power company motor pool. It wasn't missed until this morning—in fact, they didn't know it was gone until we called to check on it."

Jack said, "Any leads there? Any surveillance cameras that might have caught something?"

"Negative," came the reply. "It's not that kind of setup. It's a big lot with a hundred or more trucks parked there at any one time, with vehicles driving in and out at all hours of the night and day. Whoever took it must have had the paperwork to drive it off the lot without attracting suspicion, but security's none too tight there to begin with. The only records are logs kept of the vehicles coming in and going out. We've got somebody down there examining the files. Maybe something will turn up."

"Or maybe not," Pete said, after Center had signed off.

Jack used the SUV's dashboard monitor screen to call up images of the utility truck's driver, the man called Herm. No identification of him had been made yet.

The screen pictured the only photos available of him, ones taken at death. He was a potato-headed individual with a lumpish face, meatball nose, and protuberant eyes that stared fixedly at some point on the other side of here.

Jack's eyes narrowed as he studied the dead man long and hard. When he finally looked up, his gaze was inward and faraway, his mouth a tight line with the corners turned down.

Pete said, "Got something?"

"I thought I might—but no," Jack said, shaking his head. Still, he couldn't let it go. "I know I've seen that face before. Not a photo, either, but the man. I can't remember where or when, but I think it was several years back. But it just won't come together for me.

"I'll tell you this, though," he went on, "it wasn't in the States. I'm pretty sure about that. I'm thinking Europe . . ."

Not much to go on, but it was something, maybe a starting point. The more he thought about it, the more he thought there was something to it, that he had seen the other man in Europe sometime, somewhere, though the rest of it eluded him.

He contacted Center and passed along his thoughts on Herm. "Sorry I can't come up with more than that, but maybe it'll come back to me."

The Center operator replied, "The photo's been distributed to Interpol and our West European allies."

Jack said, "Okay," and signed off.

Center came back five minutes later. Jack and Pete were keyed up, waiting for the go-ahead, and the start of the incoming message caused them to involuntarily lunge forward in their seats, like a pair of racehorses eager to be off at the starting gate.

But the communiqué was related to a different matter. The operator said, "Cal thought you'd want to see this."

Streaming video filled the monitor screen with light and movement.

Center said, "This was taken at a few minutes after seven this morning by a surveillance camera at the Shelton Street arcade, about an eighth of a mile from the Golden Pole club."

Pete nodded, said, "Sure, I know where that is."

The footage was taken by a black-and-white camera, which meant that it was in shades of gray. The camera must have been wall-mounted about ten feet off the ground and was aimed downward at a forty-five-degree angle, depicting what appeared to be a tunnel enclosing a walkway. The tunnel was lit with a row of overhead electric lights, wan bulbs enclosed in wire-mesh screens whose light cast a web of spidery shadows along the arcade.

The tunnel's long sides were lined with storefront-type shops: a botanical selling herbal potions and remedies; a souvenir stand; a lingerie shop whose armless, limbless female mannequin torsos were adorned with sleazy lingerie; a surgical supply shop; and a palm-reading and fortune-telling parlor. The storefronts were closed, dark; some had metal security grilles in place.

At the far end, an archway opened on the bleak emptiness of early morning light.

The archway was filled by a figure stepping into view. The figure advanced, moving along the arcade toward the camera.

The scene was imaged not in real time but compressed, with one frame every few seconds, giving it a flickering, herky-jerky quality, like a sequence from an old-time silent movie.

The figure neared, resolving into a female figure. Outrageously female. Pete cracked, "I can't place the face, but the body is familiar."

The woman wore sunglasses and a light-colored scarf wrapped around her head, covering her hair. Her sharp-pointed face was worried, intent. She wore a sleeveless, one-piece dark dress whose hem reached to mid-thigh; her feet were shod in low-heeled sandals. She carried a handbag whose strap was slung across one shoulder.

She passed beyond the camera and out of range. End of sequence.

That was all.

Jack said, "Run it again, only this time freeze it on the face."

This was done. Jack said, "Vikki Valence."

Pete said, "In the flesh."

"We know one thing, at least: she was alive at seven o'clock."

"I know that arcade, too," Pete said. "That Shelton Street neighborhood's like a maze, filled with back alleys and passageways. You couldn't ask for a better place to get lost in—or to lose anybody that's looking for you. She knew what she was doing when she ducked in there.

"But it cuts both ways. Because of the layout, it's a natural for criminal activities, namely drug dealing, prostitution, muggings, public urination. So it's covered by a lot of cameras. Too bad most of them don't work. Not since Katrina."

Jack said, "It's something, anyway."

Center said, "We're checking on other cameras in the area and beyond to see if we can pick her up. But we're hampered by the technology gap. The NOPD surveillance system is spotty, glitchy. Whatever they've got, it takes time for them to call it up and send it to us. They're understaffed, too, more than usual, since a lot of personnel took off from work in order to evacuate ahead of Everette. We'll get what they've got—eventually."

Jack said, "Any police patrol cars operating in that or adjacent areas that might have spotted her before the alert was given?"

"If they did, they haven't reported it to us yet," Center said.

Pete said, "Try the streetcar conductors in that zone at around that time; maybe Vikki boarded one."

Center said, "We're checking on that that, and on the taxicab companies too. No luck so far."

Center signed off. Jack said, "Vikki's not the type who can fade back into the woodwork so easily. So how does she slip the dragnet and drop out of sight?"

Pete said, "She knows the turf and how to work it. She could've gotten clear of the area before it was cordoned off. Or she could still be hiding in it, somewhere. At that hour, there weren't a lot of public places open for her to duck into, like cafés and whatnot. But there's plenty of private places she might know about, illegal gambling dens, brothels, bottle clubs, after-hours clubs—hell, crack houses and heroin shooting galleries, if it comes to that. She knows the spots; she's a player and a party girl."

Center came back on the line. Pete was so pent with frustration that he answered by saying, "What?"

But this time Center came back with something solid. "Our LAGO source reported in. Raoul Garros is at the Mega Mart building."

Pete said, "Susan Keehan's place."

Jack said, "Let's go."

They went.

Where the Mississippi River empties into the Gulf of Mexico, it was inevitable that a mighty port would come into being. The locale was strategically and commercially valuable, the advantages irresistible. Such was the seed of New Orleans, now one of the great port cities of the world, ranking with such other maritime giants as London, San Francisco, Macao, and Hong Kong.

Its waterfront is extensive, encompassing mile after mile of docks, piers, quays, wharves, shipyards, and warehouses. A city within a city, it's part of New Orleans but apart from it, a kind of private floating world.

Dockside facilities are generally self-contained. Like other places of business, such as factories and truck terminals, they're off-limits to the casual visitor. An industrial zone, not a public playground.

Crime is rampant on the docks. Smuggling, of such contraband as drugs, weapons, exotic animals, and people. Labor racketeering. Cargo theft.

Law enforcement is no less involved, with officialdom represented by the Coast Guard, Harbor Patrol, tax collectors, safety inspectors, maritime regulating agencies, and occupational and environmental groups.

The sheer size and sprawl of the waterfront is a great guarantor of anonymity, offering innumerable cracks and crannies to hide in, lending itself to covert activities. The riverside booms with places that are alive with activity; colorful, dynamic wealth generators.

Pelican Pier was not one of them.

It sat on the right bank of the river, the New Orleans side, in a relatively isolated and run-down area several miles upstream from the Mississippi River Bridge that connects the city with the left bank.

A two-lane roadway ran parallel to the shoreline. The road carried plenty of truck traffic day and night, making deliveries to and from the docks. Between the road and the water stood Pelican Pier, a long wharf jutting out from the shoreline at right angles. There was seemingly nothing about it to make it stand out from its similarly drab neighboring facilities.

The shoreward side of the pier was walled in and fenced off, restricting access and screening the site from public view. Above the top of the wall could be seen the roof of a warehouse and, at the far end of the wharf, an old, rusted derrick crane for loading and unloading cargo.

* * *

The absence of a thing can be as significant as its presence. Sherlock Holmes once famously solved a case based on the clue of what a dog didn't do at night.

In an ecosystem, the sudden disappearance of a species is a red flag pointing to a serious imbalance in the environment.

A similar warning was to be found in the lack of something in the vicinity of Pelican Pier. What was missing were the human derelicts with which the rest of the waterfront abounded.

These were the folks who'd fallen into society's abyss, homeless outcasts who haunted the docks and made them their homes. Among them were hopeless alcoholics, drug addicts, the mentally ill, those broken in spirit or body or both.

On dry land, they would have gravitated to the local equivalent of skid row, that sinkhole where the defeated follow their downward path to the null point where they come to rest.

In a port city such as New Orleans, though, legions of the lost wind up on the waterfront, to grub for such minimal necessities as a crust of bread, a bottle of cheap wine, a rock of crack cocaine, and a hole to hide in.

Previously Pelican Pier had been such a resting place, a closed site turned den for these living ghosts of the waterfront.

Then, no more than a month ago, the pier had been reopened and reclaimed, occupied by a new crew of tough, hard-eyed strangers. They were on a mission, and the pier site clanged with their cryptic activities.

And a not so funny thing began happening: the living ghosts that were the derelicts haunting Pelican Pier began disappearing. Vanishing without a trace, except for an occasional shriek in the night or a pattern of blood spatters left drying on a wall.

Word went out along the grapevine that these living ghosts weren't living anymore, that they'd been done in and dumped in the river, which carried their bodies away.

Those who'd managed to avoid the initial purge spread the news that Pelican Pier was a place to be avoided like, well, death.

So the creatures of the night, the winos, crackheads, bums, and crazies, all absented themselves from the area, finding new places to dwell.

The cops were ignorant of the incident. They had better things to do than go in search of a bunch of missing bums, even if they'd known they were missing. They'd just as soon have said good riddance to them, had they been aware of the great disappearance.

Whatever purpose Pelican Pier was being used for continued to advance without interference or even outside observation toward fruition.

Now, today, that purpose was about to be made manifest. Saturday, an hour or so away from noon, when seen from the outside, Pelican Pier resembled nothing more than another dockside facility, indistinguishable from its neighbors.

The shoreward side of the pier was fenced and gated, with masses of green tarps strung behind the fence to screen what lay beyond from the prying eyes of outsiders.

The front gate, wide enough when open to permit the passage of a delivery truck, was now closed, barred from the inside.

Inside the fence, to one side of the gate, stood a guardhouse, a simple one-room structure. Fence and guardhouse were relatively new, as were the floodlights mounted atop the gateposts.

The guardhouse was manned by a lone sentry, who wore a gray uniform and commander's cap, an outfit standard for private security guards. With this exception: there were no badges, emblems, or insignia to indicate to which firm the guard belonged.

No nameplate to identify him, either.

He was about forty, big, and tough-looking. He wore a big-bore belt gun, a heavy-caliber man stopper. Inside the guard shack, standing against the wall within easy access, was a machine gun.

Sharp, hard-edged, he seemed a breed apart from the usual run of rent-a-cops. There was something martial, soldierly, in his bearing, his watchful gaze, and the way he carried himself. His attitude was that of a sentry on guard duty.

Other guards were posted around the site. They, too, projected that same aura of deadly competence.

A warehouse sat atop the pier, its long axis parallel to it. The structure was a shoe box–shaped, high-walled shed with a peaked roof. Narrow horizontal bands of windows were set high atop the long walls. It was a dilapidated, barnlike shed, its walls faced with sheets of corrugated tin. The tin was corroded, rusted through, giving it a ruddy color, like the planet Mars.

At the far end of the pier, out over the water, stood a heavy-duty lifting crane.

Its boxy cab sat atop a steel framework derrick tower several stories tall. The rig was old, rusted, and hadn't worked for many years. But the control cabin served as an excellent watchtower, affording views of the river and the shore.

It was manned by a couple of sentries equipped with binoculars, cell phones, and assault rifles. One kept watch over the land, and the other over the river.

It had been years, almost a decade, since the pier had last housed a going concern. The warehouse was decrepit, a potential safety hazard. The crane had broken long ago, and now the machinery was beyond repair.

That was before the arrival of the New People.

In the last month or so since then, the site had enjoyed a kind of rebirth. It was back in business. The recent spurt of activity was for a limited time only, and was about to reach its end.

The pier was raised up on a framework of massive wooden pilings reinforced with X-shaped cross braces, raising it twenty feet above the river. On the downriver side of the pier, a ramp zigzagged downward to a massive floating dock, a raftlike platform now bobbing on the surface of the water.

Moored alongside it was a barge. A gangway with side rails slanted upward from the floating dock to the bridge.

The vessel was an old hulk of a freight-hauling scow, crude and massive.

Rectangular-shaped, its upper works wider than its base, with slanted sides, bow, and stern. It was equipped with a bridge amidships and portside deckhouse. A distinctive touch: its starboard side sported davits designed for offloading a whaler-style motorboat that was secured to them.

The barge was marked with a series of identifying numbers matching those inscribed on the ship's papers in a cabinet in the wheelhouse. The numbers and the documents were fakes, although they were good enough to pass a superficial inspection by the authorities.

No Coast Guard or Harbor Patrol boat or any other minions of maritime officialdom had yet arrived to inquire about the barge or the site, and it was unlikely that any would, in the relatively brief time remaining before it began its final, fatal voyage downriver.

Why should they? The New Orleans waterfront was huge, sprawling, teeming with hundreds of ships of all sizes and thousands of men. There was nothing in this near-derelict hulk and faceless facility to attract the interest of officialdom.

The barge displayed numbers but no name. Whatever original name it had once borne had been painted over and blacked out.

Arm-thick hawser lines secured it to sturdy wooden bollards on the floating dock.

The vessel rode bobbing on turbid waters. The river was long, wide, snakelike, coiling with heavy, powerful currents and churns. Thick and murky as black coffee, complete with the grounds.

Above the water, the sky seethed with masses of gray clouds streaming northward. Gusts of wind began picking up little, spiky whitecaps on the river's surface.

The nameless scow was as seaworthy as it could be made in the limited time allowed before its mission. Besides, it wasn't supposed to look too good. That would break cover and make it stand out from the ordinary run of similar bargelike vessels, scores of which were seen ceaselessly plying their courses up and down the river.

Major Marc Vollard didn't have to be there while the final rigging and arming was done. His role now was strictly as an observer. Huygens was an expert and didn't need a commanding officer looking over his shoulder to ensure that he performed up to his usual standard of excellence.

By all rights, Vollard shouldn't have been there at all. It was a contravention of sound military doctrine for the team leader to risk his own neck on the threshhold of a mission, because if something did go wrong and catastrophe resulted, the mission would be without its commanding officer.

The mission was two-pronged; the explosives-laden barge was only one-half of it; and even without it, the other half promised to supply the necessary quota of destruction contracted for by his clients.

Vollard had no doubt that his second-in-command, Rex de Groot, would carry on and complete that portion of the mission in the unlikely event that Huygens got his wires crossed and blew the boat, its occupants, and the pier sky-high. De Groot and the main body of the mercenary storm force were off-site now, at a secluded compound outside city limits, waiting for nightfall to make their rendezvous at Pelican Pier, the staging area from which the raid would be launched. No pier, no problem; de Groot would merely lead the force from the compound to the target area.

No, Vollard didn't have to be there. That's why he was present. In the business of soldiering, one led from the front and by example. Mystique was part of leadership. Vollard delighted in sharing the risks taken by the least of his troops. Private troops, mercenary force.

He liked the action, the thrill of being poised on the swordblade's razor edge.

The wheelhouse was a square-shaped cabin that stood amidships on the port side, containing the controls for the barge. Vollard stood in the doorway, looking in.

Inside the cabin were three men: Piet Huygens, the demolitionist who was completing the rigging of the arming device; and Ahmed and Rashid, a pair of Yemeni sea captains and would-be martyrs who would pilot the boat on its final run.

Vollard was Belgian, Huygens was Dutch, but both essentially were men without a country. Hardcore professsional mercs, the only banners they fought under were the black flag and the certified check. Freelances in a rogue's regiment of Dogs of War.

Ahmed and Rashid, something different, had been furnished by the mission's Saudi backers. Their part in the operation was a suicide run, a one-way ticket to Paradise. That was a job not for mercs but for True Believers.

Huygens was an innovator and skilled mechanic in the field of destructive delivery systems. He had a thatch of strawcolored hair, a same-colored mustache, and a red face. Arm muscles bulged in his short-sleeved shirt as he connected the end of the wiring's trunk cable to the arming device.

The crates of explosives in the hold were rigged with a network of wires and detonators. The detonators were arranged in spaced clusters to maximize the force and impact of the cumulative explosions. Individual wires stretched back into bundled branches of wires, themselves combining further on into a single, trunk cable which emerged from the hold and into the wheelhouse, where Huygens was finishing the work of connecting it to an arming device which combined a timer and a triggering device.

The arming device was housed in a horn-shaped piece of plastic similar in size and shape to the joystick of a video game console board. It contained a digital electronic clock, a keying switch, and several built-in fail-safe devices, all of which had to be tripped before the master switch could be thrown.

The arming device was connected by a bolted-on housing to the control board of the barge. The arrangement would allow the barge pilot to arm the floating bomb as it made its final run.

Huygens stood on one knee on the floor, screwdriver in hand, tightening the connections from the pluglike end of the firing cable trunk to a socket set in the base of the arming device.

Ahmed and Rashid stood nearby, watching with interest.

Ahmed, forty, was medium-sized, with close-cropped dark hair and a short black beard. Rashid, in his mid-twenties, was long and rangy, with warm, sympathetic brown eyes and a wispy mustache and beard. Ahmed spoke English and was the leader of the duo; Rashid, his backup and assistant, knew only a few words of the language and relied on him for translation.

Huygens continued to labor over the assembly, fresh sweat pouring from him with every breath. From time to time, he wiped his brow on the sleeve of his shortsleeved shirt, to keep the sweat from trickling into and stinging his eyes. He sweated not from fear but from the heat, even though the slightest fumbling of crossed wires at this point risked blowing them all sky-high. Bombs were his business and he didn't make those kind of mistakes.

He finished making a final adjustment and lowered the screwdriver. "Done," he said. Easing away from the mechanism, he straightened, standing up, groaning softly from the pain of moving after having knelt in one position for so long. He shook his leg to work out some of the kinks.

Vollard said, "Bravo."

Huygens lifted his shirt front, using it as a towel to wipe the sweat from his face. Fresh sweat instantly replaced it. Vollard padded into the cabin, eyeing the arming device.

Huygens said, "It is a simple rig. Primitive, really. It has to be, to make it effective."

Vollard said, "It looks all right to me."

"A tricky problem," Huygens said, "complicated by the storm. Everette could throw off the electronics. Too much electricity in the air. We cannot rely on a remote, wireless detonator to set it off from a distance. The storm force could glitch the signal, suppress it, canceling it out. It could happen. Wireless devices are too fragile for a big blow.

"So, we use a timing device which can be set from here

in the wheelhouse. It all shall be done with wires, not wireless. The operator sets the timing device for say, five or ten minutes before final impact. At zero hour, an electrical impulse goes from here down the nerve net trunk, through the wires fanning out from here into the individual detonators of the bomb sub-clusters. Simplicity itself."

Simple to Huygens, perhaps, but then he was the expert. Vollard turned to the senior boat pilot. "What do you think, Ahmed? You're the one who has to ride the tiger."

Ahmed stood with arms folded over his chest. He nodded, said, "It is well."

Vollard said, "You'll run into some rough waters when the storm is rising."

Ahmed bared teeth the color of old ivory in a half-sneer, half-grimace that might have been a smile. "I have sailed wooden fishing boats in the Arabian Sea during monsoon season. A little wind and rain on this river is nothing."

Huygens smirked, said, "Make no mistake, my friend. An incoming hurricane is no joke."

Ahmed said, "Allah willing, Rashid and I will be in Paradise long before the storm reaches its height."

Vollard said, "May it be so." Here was the variable in Vollard's plan, the unanticipated X-factor. The approach of Hurricane Everette presented threat and opportunity. According to his calculations, even if the storm did make landfall in New Orleans, it would not do so until some hours after the job was done. The mission would be accomplished well before the storm peaked. That said, it was still a risk, but he was used to taking risks and so were his men. That was one of the things they were paid for.

The storm cut two ways. The chaos it would produce was his ally; he and his men were trained professionals used to operating at peak efficiency while havoc reigned. It would confound and confuse the authorities and reduce their already modest level of competency to new lows. Once the mission was done, the storm would help thwart all pursuit and give the mercenary force a long lead time to make their getaway.

As for Ahmed and Rashid, they would make their getaway upon completion of their part of the mission. Final, earthly getaway.

1 2 3 4 5 6 7 **8** 9
10 11 12 13 14 15 16 17
18 19 20 21 22 23 24

· ·

· ·

House of the Green Fountain,
Riyadh, Saudi Arabia
8:05 P.M., local time

It was a scene that could have taken place a thousand years,
back in the era of the Caliphate of Haroun al-Raschid, when
the *Tales of a Thousand Nights and a Night*, now known as
the *Arabian Nights*, was first penned.

The setting was a pleasure garden, a place designed to
please the senses of desert-dwelling folk. At the middle of it
stood an octagonal basin, whose centerpiece was a stepped
pillar, rising to the height of a man.

The pillar contained a fountain, which continually
sprayed jets of water from its top. The water cascaded
down into a series of shell-shaped catch basins, each pro-
gressively wider than the one above it, finally spilling into

the octagonal pool, where hidden pumps recirculated it, sucking it up a pipe in the center of the pillar, and resuming the process.

The waterfall effect was a thing of great beauty; fluid, ever-changing curtains of clear liquid tumbling from basin to basin into the eight-sided pool.

The fountain was faced with tiles, green tiles, in a range of color varying from pale green to dark green and all shades in between. They formed a mosaic, a pattern of intricate arabesques that spiraled and entwined around the fountain from top to bottom.

The garden floor was made of larger, hexagonal tiles of black and green, themselves forming dynamic geometric patterns. Grouped around the fountain were marble benches and rows of enormous reddish-brown ceramic planters holding orange, lemon, and apricot trees. Interspersed among them were rows of thick, dark hedges, seven feet tall, set in long, troughlike planters. Benches, fruit trees, and hedgerows broke up the garden space, creating a variety of nooks, alcoves, and arcades. The air was cool, moist, fragrant with the scents of flower beds and fruit trees.

The garden would have looked right at home in a fabulous storybook illustration, yet it was a reality that existed right in the heart of the futuropolis that is today's Riyadh.

It was indoors, located in an atrium of a house occupied by Imam Omar, the Smiling Cleric—who, with a piece of property like this, had much to smile about. The atrium was a central shaft, several stories tall, whose top was roofed over with a clear, Plexiglas bubble dome.

The palatial residence had been donated to the Imam by one of his followers who was a well-placed member of the House of Saud. It was one of several such houses, all equally magnificent, located in and about Riyadh, that belonged to the Imam.

Counterpointing the sounds of running water from the fountain came the rhythmic rise and fall of voices chanting prayers.

The praying took place in a room that served as a place of worship, located off the atrium. Entrance was obtained through a pointed archway. Posted outside it were two guards, trusted members of the mutawayin, the religious police.

The mutawayin was the militia of Imam Omar and his militant sect of ultrafundamentalist Wahabists.

Minister Fedallah had his own private army in the form of his Internal Special Squad. But Fedallah was only the steward of the corps, not its master. The section was the property of His Majesty the King, to whom all its members had pledged fealty.

Whereas the mutawayin's ultimate loyalty lay not with the King, but to God, who was represented on earth in the form of his servant and messenger, Imam Omar.

Fedallah—and for that matter, the King himself—would have given much to know what now transpired in the inner sanctum of the prayer room of the House of the Green Fountain.

The entire site was guarded by a phalanx of religious police, stationed throughout the house and in the grounds beyond. Fanatical bodyguards whose lives were pledged to protect the sanctity of this place.

The prayer room was large, spacious, high-ceilinged. Its walls were paneled in rare, costly woods polished to a mirrorlike finish, its marble floor covered with ornate rugs. There were low divans and mounds of overstuffed cushions and pillows.

Within, a joyful celebration was taking place. Twelve men in all were assembled, a mirror image of His Majesty's Special Council, the overseers of the petroleum market glut operation veiled under the cryptic tag of Cloak of Night.

Some of those now present in the prayer room had also been present earlier in the afternoon, in the conference room of the Special Council.

Chief among them was Imam Omar himself, who now conducted this special service of prayer and thanksgiving. The Smiling Cleric was their undisputed arbiter of matters devotional and religious.

All the celebrants stood, open prayer books in hand, rocking slightly back and forth as they chanted their holy verses, God-intoxicated. It was a call-and-response ceremony, Omar passionately intoning the stanzas, his rapturous followers venting their corresponding choruses in unison.

The devotions had been going on for some time now, more than an hour, but the energy and enthusiasm of the participants never flagged, instead seemed to steadily increase.

The uninitiated might have been most surprised by the presence and fervent, wholehearted participation of Prince Tariq. Those who knew him only as a worldly, Westernized man of affairs, the smoothly polished diplomat and dealmaker of the corporate boardrooms and ministerial conclaves, would have been surprised to see him here, seemingly giving himself up heart and soul to the ritualized worship.

Still more God-maddened and inspired was Prince Hassani, caught up in the throes of an ecstatic trance. His expression was otherworldly. His gaze was fixed, the object of his glazed-eyed stare placed somewhere beyond worldly ken—perhaps on the promise of Paradise.

Such worship—one-point consciousness, channeled, underlined by repetition—can induce mystical intimations. A hypnotic quality underlay the ritual, evoked by the rhythmical chanting, the call-and-response, the rise and fall of words that lost their individual meaning and became a sonic pattern as abstract and primal as crashing surf or winds wailing across a wasteland.

The worshippers were transported beyond earthly cares into the realm of the blessed. For what could be more blessed, more joyful, than to know that one of their own, one present here tonight, would be in Paradise tomorrow?

This would-be homicidal suicide had elected to make the supreme sacrifice by taking unto himself the honor of holy martyrdom.

Tomorrow, he would kill. A sanctified killing, righteous and just, yet one that could not be accomplished without bringing death to the slayer.

The Cloak of Night had a dagger hidden up its sleeve, the dagger of an assassin.

De Lesseps Plaza, New Orleans

Another showpiece of the midtown business district was the Mega Mart building.

It was visible from De Lesseps Plaza, where Jack Bauer and Pete Malo were. Pete pointed to a needlelike spire rising to the northeast behind a row of buildings lining the plaza's east side.

"There it is," he said. "Not far from here, as the crow flies. Too bad we're driving. We've got to go the long way around. Like the man said, 'You can't get there from here.'"

The midtown area was suggestive of a medieval fortress town, its central keep surrounded by a maze of pathways. The SUV rolled along one-way streets, making frequent detours to access the route it wanted, only to find progress blocked by a high wall, construction site, or cul-de-sac, requiring it to make another circuitous go-round.

It stopped for a red light, Jack taking advantage of the

pause to reach into the inside breast pocket of his jacket and remove a nondescript metal container that was about the size and shape of a pack of cigarettes. He lifted the lid, opening it.

Inside, each nestled in its own hollow in a lining in the bottom of the box, were a half-dozen objects that looked like fuzzy black aspirin tablets.

Pete glanced away from the road ahead and at the container nestled in Jack's palm. "What're you going to do with those?"

Jack said, "Hang one on Garros."

"A nice trick, if you can get away with it."

Jack smiled with his lips. "What's one more flea to a horndog like him?"

"It's not him I'm worried about, it's Susan Keehan. And her palace guard," Pete said.

"Flea"—that's what the technical division called it. Unofficially. A new refinement on traditional bugging devices, it operated along lines similar to those of the microchips that pet owners have implanted in their dogs and cats to find them if they got lost. Except that it didn't have to be injected under the skin, but could be attached by a casual "brush" contact.

Each one contained an ultraminiaturized transponder, audio pickup unit, and transmitter, all enabled by a fleck-sized power cell. The entire surface was a compound poly-fabric condenser microphone. Powerful and sophisticated, it could hear what was going on around the general vicinity of its wearer and stream the audio to a receiver.

Its sticky matte-black exterior shell was modeled after a thistle burr, and once attached to the target, unlikely to work loose and come off. The transponder also served as a locator, enabling the operator to maintain a continuous fix on the subject's location.

The light turned green and Pete drove on, wending his way Mega Mart–ward.

He said, "You don't think Garros is going to stand still while you slap one of those on him, do you?"

Jack said, "It'll be over before he knows what happened. It'll only take a second to stick it to him."

Pete scoffed. "A second, huh? What makes you think you'll get it? We're not just bucking Paz's crew this time, we're going up against the Keehan machine."

"I'll keep that in mind."

"Center'll make sure you do. So will headquarters in Washington."

Jack quirked a smile, with one corner of his mouth turned down, the other turned up. "Deep politics, eh?"

"With a vengeance," Pete said. "Susan's uncle, Senator Keehan, holds a top post on the Senate Intelligence Committee."

Jack said, "I know; I've met him a few times when I was testifying before the committee in closed-door session."

Pete shot him a quick side glance. "Is he as big a horse's ass in person as he is on TV?"

"Depends," Jack said. "He's Mr. Senatorial Courtesy and Decorum until the testimony contradicts some policy line that he's taken. Then he repeats his question in the form of a statement, telling you what he wants to hear from you."

"What did you tell him?"

"Just the facts, Pete, just the facts. That's why I'm sitting here right now, instead of holding down a top administrative job at CTU Washington."

Pete laughed, said, "Aw, you wouldn't like it at HQ anyhow. All that politics and paperwork."

"Not to mention that big pay raise and all those perks. That'd be tough to take," Jack said.

Pete's tone was upbeat. "Maybe this time the Senator's

bitten off more than he can chew, getting into bed with Chavez on that oil deal."

Jack said, "It hasn't hurt him so far. But who knows, now that the shooting's started. Maybe we can monkey wrench that gruesome twosome."

A parked car lurched away from curbside into the street, causing Pete to have to swerve the wheel hard to avoid getting hit. He hammered the heel of his hand against the horn, cursing.

The other driver flinched, looking sheepish. This was no sinister aggressor shooting a move, it was just another careless, heedless driver. He hung back a few car lengths, keeping his distance.

A few blocks later, the veins standing out on Pete's forehead started to reduce in size. He said, "We're almost there now. That's Mega Mart up ahead. The building's got its own EXECPROTEK unit."

EXECPROTEK was a civilian security and confidential investigations agency with plenty of clout, originally founded by Brinsley S. Wolters, former ace sleuth and opposition researcher on the Senator's staff. Senator Keehan's own private eye.

Pete said, "Goofy name, EXECPROTEK. Sounds like some sort of fancy condom."

Jack remained straight-faced. "Nice to have your own private police force, though. Every dynasty should have one."

Pete nodded. "They've got Mylon Sears over there, honchoing the operation. He's nobody's fool."

Jack, thoughtful, said, "Sears is Wolters's top lieutenant. Shows you how much store the Senator sets on this Chavez thing."

Pete grinned, said, "Maybe it won't look so sweet to him now that the bodies are piling up."

"Might make Sears more cooperative."

"Uh-uh. Susan wouldn't like it."

"What's her problem, anyway, Pete?"

"She thinks we're picking on her because of her tie-up with LAGO. She's right, of course."

"Garros might be inclined to meet us halfway," Jack said, "considering that we know about his hookups with the Golden Pole dancers, Vikki and Dorinda. He doesn't need that kind of heat while he's romancing Susan Keehan. That gives us some leverage."

Pete shook his head. "She's so stuck on that guy, she'll just figure we're making things up to smear him. On the other hand, Caracas might not like it that he's risking a mul-timillion-dollar romance by two-timing the heiress. Or is that three-timing? In any case, he's got the boys back home to worry about."

Jack said, "Plus whoever it is that tried to whack Paz."

"Yeah, there's that, too."

The Mega Mart building looked like a starship poised for takeoff on the launching pad. It had been built and was owned by the powerful Keehan clan. A decade earlier, they'd gambled big on the future of New Orleans, and it had paid off.

Even now, in the post-Katrina climate, it continued to thrive and its prospects remained bright. Much of the sky-scraper's space was occupied by Keehan business interests, not only the family's primary and openly acknowledged financial vehicles, but also a number of subsidiaries, satellite and shell corporations linked to it by a complex and tenuous web of cutouts and holding companies.

Office space in the Mart was eagerly sought after by companies independent of any association with Keehan in-terests, attracted by the site's first-rate accommodations and the charismatic allure of the dynasty's name.

The Keehans were one of the richest families in the United States. Back in the nineteenth century, the fledgling dynasts had been a clan of Philadelphia lawyers and bankers who'd gotten into the oil business on the heels of the state's rich Spindletop strike. Pennsylvania's oil deposits were soon exhausted, but not before the family had diversified its holdings into coal, steel, railroads, and real estate, taking their place among the great robber barons of the Gilded Age.

In this, they were no different from many other hardheaded, hardfisted plutocrats of the era. The Keehan genius lay in an early and intensive concentration in the field of politics.

Most of their fellow titans of industry shunned direct involvement in partisan politics, disdaining the whole grubby business of electioneering, preferring to take the easier course of buying politicians rather than filling the offices themselves.

The Keehans knew better, realizing early on that elective office was where the real money and power lay.

Politicos controlled the building of schools, hospitals, government buildings, roads, canals, and all the vast, ever-growing infrastructure of the public sector.

They decided where the projects were sited, who would get the contracts to build them, and which banks and brokerage houses would oversee the issuing of bonds and stock offerings necessary to finance them.

Here was where the real money was made for oneself and one's friends; here lay the power and influence to make sure that nobody else could take away those gains.

Paid publicists ballyhooed the notion of a Keehan tradition of public service, playing it up big. After a while, even the Keehans had come to believe it themselves.

Pennsylvania was the fountainhead of the family's financial and political power and continued to remain its stronghold and home base. The state had elected one Keehan governor and sent several more to Congress.

The family had long since branched out, going nationwide, establishing tentacles north, south, east, and west. Its business and politics went hand in hand. Getting Keehans and their allies elected built an ever-expanding continuum of power.

Behind it all lay the motive force of the family fortune, source of all good things.

In the time-honored mode of the super-rich, they'd established a number of philanthropic endowments, funds, and foundations. It was another way to augment the family's access and influence throughout the national economy—and it was all tax-free, too.

The foundations fed into the political zone, which fed into the financial zone, which fed back into the philanthropic and political zones. A colossal daisy chain to promote all things Keehan.

In recent political history, Keehans had filled such cabinet posts as secretary of state and attorney general, as well as being appointed ambassadors and Federal court judges. By the first decade of the twenty-first century, the current generation of Keehans held office throughout the land on the city, county, state, and national levels.

No Keehan had yet been elected president, though several had tried and failed—an ever-rankling sore spot to the family pride. They were still in there pitching.

Patriarch of the clan was Burl Keehan of the Pennsylvania Keehans, the original root and branch of the dynasty. He was the family's preeminent politician, the born backslapper and dealmaker, Mr. Personality. As Senator Keehan, he was a long-serving senior legislator with a safe seat in Congress and a high-ranking member of several all-important committees, including Intelligence and Appropriations.

His brother, Wilmont, was the family's top financial man and wealth generator, Mr. Money Bags. Wilmont was the father of Susan Keehan.

Life is good, Raoul Garros said to himself. He was on top of the world, in more ways than one.

He was in a room on a floor near the top of the Mega Mart building, up so high that he could look down on the tops of the other skyscrapers in the midtown business district. The room was the inner sanctum of a suite of rooms belonging to Susan Keehan, director of the New Orleans branch of the Keehan Humanistics Fund and mistress of the building and all it contained.

She belonged to him. She was his lover, his fiancée, and she stood naked in his embrace, pressing against him. The room they now shared, this eagle's nest, was also their love nest.

The combination of the time, the place, and the woman was intoxicating. Cooler heads than Raoul's might well have overheated amid such surroundings. They reeked of wealth and power, blazoning the pride and prestige of their possessor.

This upper floor of the building was the headquarters for the Keehan Humanistics Fund, the controlling corporate entity of the entire structure and much more besides. A suite of rooms had been set aside for Susan's personal use, luxury, and comfort. The suite contained her office, as well as an adjacent room that served as her living quarters and inner sanctum. It was strictly for her personal convenience and comfort while she was at her place of business. Her main residence in the city was a mansion in the Faubourg Marigny, a neighborhood as old, storied, and rich as the Garden District.

Here, in the Mega Mart monolith, these rich and secluded

surroundings were her private world, her retreat. Inner sanctum. In here, Susan Keehan was as naked as she was ever
going to be. And not just physically. Though there was that,
too. Right now.

Raoul Garros was thirty-five, handsome, athletic, of good
family, a playboy and a power player in the hierarchy of
LAGO, Venezuela's state-owned oil outlet in New Orleans.

He was clean-shaven, with clean-lined, chiseled features,
his dark, thick hair worn brushed straight back from the
forehead. He was a handsome man and he knew it, worked
it, traded on it.

Susan was in his arms right now. They'd spent much of
the morning closeted away in her private retreat making
love. After, they'd showered. Raoul had dressed and was
in his shirt and slacks; Susan was still naked. She pressed
against him.

She was tall, almost as tall as he, and he was over six
feet. Her face was turned up and he kissed her on the mouth.
Openmouthed. Her mouth was wet and warm; her breath
was sweet.

She was tanned, her long, straight, dark blond hair glinting
with metallic gold highlights. Long-limbed, high-breasted,
with a pertly rounded rump and long legs. Her eyes were
gray, her brows were thick and arched, her nose straight and
thin, her mouth sensitive, if inclined to pouting.

She smelled good and tasted sweet when he kissed her.
She was in her mid-thirties, a few years older than Raoul, a
fact she preferred to ignore. She was twice-married, twice-
divorced, and childless.

"Third time's the charm"—she'd accepted Raoul's pro-
posal of marriage; if he hadn't asked her, she'd have asked
him, of that he was sure. Their relationship was strongly
physical; the sex was good. Better for her than for him, but
then for Raoul there was an element of work involved.

She was in love with Raoul, of that he had no doubts. She showed all the signs. And he knew them. He had been with many women, no small number of whom had been international celebrities in their own right, stellar on a level equal to that of Wilmont Keehan's daughter, and some more beautiful and passionate, too.

And yet—more than an heiress, she was the living link to a powerhouse political dynasty, the Keehan clan, with all their global reach, their clout, their money.

Susan kissed with her eyes closed. Raoul's were open, and he glanced around, enjoying the view and the luxuriousness of his surroundings.

The room and everything about it was first-class. A high-priced professional designer had put it together, according to Susan's instructions. She was not without taste; her eye, instincts, and aesthetics were good, though inclined toward the safe choice, the conventional choice.

One wall was solid plate glass, opening on the heights, offering a spectacular view of the sky-high vista. Even here in the midtown business district, known for its tall buildings, none of the other structures came up to the heights of the Mega Mart; Raoul was able to look down even on the tallest.

A pleasing prospect: up here, his companions were eagles and airplanes. Neither of which was in evidence today, not with the storm coming.

Today's view was constrained, claustrophobic in comparison to the vaunting sky-high vistas of a clear day. The sky was blanketed by low-hanging cloud cover. If it got any lower, it would engulf the office floor and cut off the view below.

Solid cloud cover in shades of gray: charcoal for the interior masses of the cloud cover, slate for the outlines of stacked masses, silvery ash-gray showing at the few, infrequent rents in the cloud ceiling.

The clouds were in motion, the vanguard of Hurricane Everette.

It was a dark day; even with the window blinds and curtains drawn, the room was thick with shadow. The gloom was broken by artfully spaced overhead lighting; dimmers that kept the lights down low, warm, intimate.

Dark, rich, wood-paneled walls were hung with framed paintings. A key element of the decor was a long, well-padded couch, upholstered in black leather. It could fold out into a bed, but it was large enough even when unfolded to accommodate a carnal coupling and had; several, in fact, and recently, for that's where he had been with Susan for the past few hours.

The room featured a private bar, complete with a mini-refrigerator and a stainless steel sink. Mounted on one wall was an oversized plasma TV screen, now dark. An oversized alcove held an intimate dining nook for two, complete with table and two chairs.

Off to one side, an open door accessed a bathroom that would not have been out of place in the suite of a luxury hotel. Inside it, the light was on, bright light that slanted out the doorway and into the office. It had recently been quitted by Raoul and Susan, who'd showered after a strenuous bout of mid-morning lovemaking.

He was now mostly dressed; she was naked, save for a towel. They made a handsome couple, a power couple; they exuded wealth, attractiveness, glamour.

Taking it all in, the whole luxurious milieu, Raoul could not help but congratulate himself, thinking, Truly, someday this will all be mine.

And soon.

The family Garros was a pillar of Venezuela's old-line,

traditional oligarchy, that narrow apex of the social pyramid that controlled the vast majority of the country's wealth.

Raoul's breeding and background were impeccable. His mother was half French, and his Christian name had been rendered according to the French spelling Raoul, rather than the more Hispanicized Raul. The family had considerable holdings in shipbuilding, telecommunications, and real estate.

He was handsome, educated, athletic, and wealthy. The world should have been his oyster. All would have been well, but for the advent—or rather, onslaught—of Hugo Chavez.

This was a bad time in Venezuela for the clique of ruling families, for the oligarchy was all-powerful no more. Chavez had the power. He had the Army on his side and the impoverished masses. Once having been elected president, he would retain the office for life. He would no more be voted out than he would willingly relinquish power. His was the power supreme.

To be rich was no longer enough in Venezuela. Now, to be rich was to be vulnerable. Vulnerable to the prosecutions and nationalizations of the state, decreed by the President in his role as supreme representative of the people.

Many if not most of the oligarchs were too hidebound and fossilized to adapt to the new order of "twenty-first-century socialism," the regime's supreme buzzword and sacred cow. Not so the family Garros. They saw things clearly enough, without illusion.

Chavez was going nowhere, except to stay in place at the top of the heap for the foreseeable future. There was no telling what idea he might cook up next, he and his cadre of like-minded sycophants, ideologues, and newly empowered bandits.

Key sectors of the Venezuelan economy had been nationalized early. Companies foreign and domestic had been bulldozed by the strongman, including big global megaconglomerates that were forced to bow down and submit.

The family Garros had unreservedly put all its resources at the President's disposal. It was the only way to deal with such a man: total surrender. Let him have what he wants. It was less trouble for him to replace the existing infrastructure with his own people than it was for him to leave the system in place under the nominal control of the Garroses to serve him.

"We have lost much, my son. We will lose more. But, with the help of Providence, perhaps we will not lose all."

Such were the words of Raoul's father, during a final meeting before the younger Garros was due to depart for New Orleans to serve as a high-ranking executive in the overseas branch of LAGO.

Raoul had said, "I'll do my part, Father. I won't let the family down." And so he had done his part, in his fashion.

Some men are fighters; he was a lover. It was his vocation and his avocation.

Hence, Susan Keehan. Because Raoul was on a mission for Caracas. A mission to marry into one of America's richest and most powerful families. A mission now on the verge of accomplishment.

Soon he would be wed to the daughter of doting father Wilmont Keehan, multimillionaire dynast and brother of Senator Burl Keehan.

Topping it all off, the woman was good-looking, too. That didn't hurt, although he would have gone ahead and romanced her no matter what her looks. That was the plan, cooked up by the master plotters back in Caracas. It was a plan with which Raoul thoroughly agreed.

* * *

The springboard for the scheme was the alliance between Senator Keehan and President Chavez.

With great fanfare, Chavez had announced he was making available a free supply of oil, earmarked to serve as heating fuel in the winter months for poor people in impoverished urban neighborhoods in the United States.

The Venezuelan end of the project would be handled by LAGO; expediting and assisting the operation at the U.S. end of the pipeline was the Keehan clan.

Chavez was the strongman of a socialist regime, belligerent and anti-American.

The current Administration in Washington was a frequent target of the dictator's strident, abusive tirades. Senator Keehan was a leader of the opposition party. Free heating fuel would be a powerful vote getter, for himself and his party.

But the matter had to be handled carefully. Chavez—splendid fellow that he was, a "diamond in the rough" according to the thinking of the Keehan policy advisors and their media echo chamber—was still a volatile and unpredictable character who might yet go off the reservation. Way off.

The Senator needed deniability, a middleman to handle the organizational chores while insulating him from too-direct involvement in case the deal soured. A perfect solution existed, in the form of one of the numerous funds, endowments, and foundations established by Keehan capital.

The vehicle in this case was the Keehan Humanistics Fund, KHF, whose charter was sufficiently airy and elastic to serve as the operating entity. KHF was a do-good operation, perfectly suited to handle the chores of getting all that free Venezuelan crude refined into home heating oil and distributed to the target neighborhoods/communities up north.

The Fund was designated as the entity to partner with LAGO in the free fuel oil operation that a public relations firm had tagged with the innocuous-sounding label, the Hearthstone Initiative. Its slogan, "Warm Homes, Warm Hearts."

New Orleans was where the project was centered. The city, a prime receiving point for maritime oil imports, was where Venezuelan tankers would offload their oil. This complemented Keehan family business interests. The family-owned Mega Mart would be used to support the Initiative.

Susan Keehan would head the KHF part of the venture. Her business skills were good, she had a head for figures and details, and she possessed in full the characteristic Keehan drive and ambition.

On the other hand, nobody could know it all and do it all, not even a Keehan. For that, the family relied on its executive leadership cadre, a pool of expert lawyers, brokers, analysts, engineers, and the like—specialists to safeguard the family role and make sure that the oil Initiative did no harm to short-, medium-, or long-term dynastic interests.

In New Orleans, a number of such advisors were assigned to Susan's staff, the two most prominent (and capable) being operating manager Hal Dendron and executive assistant Alma Butterworth. Also on tap was Mylon Sears, number two in the EXECPROTEK private security firm, now officially in charge of Mega Mart security and unofficially protecting family interests while reporting directly to Senator Keehan.

The White House was steamed to the max about the entire venture, seeing it (rightly) as a Chavez propaganda ploy designed to embarrass the Administration—a goal that Caracas shared with Senator Keehan.

But there wasn't much they could do about it. It was all

perfectly legal. After all, LAGO service stations sold gas in a majority of states in the United States. Irksome as Chavez was, Uncle Sam needed that Venezuelan oil, which made up ten percent of all U.S. oil imports. Any curtailment of which would wreak havoc at the pumps, and in the public opinion polls.

What Washington could do, however, was to keep a very close eye on all LAGO and Initiative doings in New Orleans.

The Administration had to move carefully here, to avoid doing anything that would allow Senator Keehan and his party to claim politically motivated persecution and kick up a corresponding media fuss about it.

Which meant that CTU had to walk softly in the matter, too.

Now, Susan Keehan said, "That's the good thing about being the head of the company. I can always put everything on hold to take a very important private meeting."

She and Raoul had moved to the bathroom, a bathroom bigger than many top-level executives' offices. He'd gone in to fix his hair, and she'd followed.

Raoul stood facing the mirror over the sink; Susan stood behind him, embracing him. He was mostly dressed, she was still naked save for a bath towel that stood pressed between her front and his back. He'd finished knotting his tie and was now brushing his hair, a more exacting operation than it might sound. The part had to be just-so. It wouldn't do to have a few strands out of place, making him look ridiculous.

She'd just showered, and even though she'd dried herself, she was still damp. Raoul didn't like her rubbing against him at such times; it mussed his shirt and slacks. Which was why she held the towel pressed between the two of them.

He reached behind himself to squeeze her naked flank.

"I celebrate our being together, I want to shout it from the rooftops."

Susan said, "Better let me work on Daddy some more first."

Raoul frowned. "He doesn't like me."

She said, "It's nothing personal, Raoul, that's just his way."

"He hates me."

"He doesn't hate you, Raoul," Susan said, sighing. "We've been over this time and again—"

"He thinks I'm not good enough to marry his daughter."

She didn't deny it. "He doesn't think anybody is good enough to marry me. He felt that way about Dale and Drew, too." Dale and Drew were her two ex-husbands.

Raoul finished brushing his hair to his exacting specifications. "My family were aristocrats in Venezuela for two hundred years before your ancestors stole their first million."

Susan nodded. "We Keehans were great thieves, reprobates, and pirates."

"'Were'?"

"Not anymore. That was in the bad old days."

"You think so, eh."

"I know it. We're revoltingly legal these days," she said.

Raoul set down the hairbrush and stepped away from the mirror and sink. Susan said, "When Daddy gets to know you better, he'll love you like I do."

"Not quite exactly like you do, I hope."

"Stop talking dirty, Raoul. You're getting me excited again."

"Me, also. Alas, much as I would like to remain in your delightful company, Susan, I have things I must do. I fear that I have already neglected my duties too much—but then, how could I resist so tender an interlude?"

The smile he gave her was dazzling. His teeth were first-rate, all white and gleaming and perfectly capped. That smile made her tingle deep down.

Outside, in the main room, near the connecting door to her outer office, was an old-fashioned writing desk. Susan sometimes used it for minor chores, such as writing thank-you notes and similar minor but not unimportant communiqués. On it was a laptop and a combination phone/intercom setup.

The communicator now buzzed, sharp, insistent, annoying. Imperative.

Susan, cross, said, "Damn! They know my standing instructions are that I'm not to be disturbed when I'm in conference here with you."

Raoul said, "In conference—that's what you call it?"

She said, "That's one way of putting it."

Raoul's leer was amiable. He'd been satisfied. He'd be leaving soon, and that inclined him to be indulgent. But he was grateful for the interruption; it would help cut short his departure time. Unlike Susan, he hated long goodbyes. It was perfectly understandable; she hated to see him go. He could hardly blame her for that, of course, but her neediness could become somewhat annoying.

He'd been out of contact with his office for hours, almost all morning in fact, having shut off his cell phone earlier, as soon as he'd been alone with Susan. That closedown of communication nagged at him, a little. Colonel Paz didn't like it when Raoul was out of reach.

Too bad. He was entitled to a little downtime. After all, what could happen that the Colonel and company couldn't get along without him for a couple of hours?

The buzzer sounded again, an unpleasant sound suggestive of an insect being electrocuted by a bug zapper.

Susan reluctantly untangled herself from Raoul and

crossed to the desk, long legs flashing, long, lithe golden form naked except for a towel draped across her shoulders.

She leaned forward, over the desktop. A red light flashed on the communicator. The buzzer blatted again. She grabbed the phone, cutting off the buzzer in mid-blat.

She said, "What?"

A voice on the other end said quickly, "It's me, Hal. Sorry to bother you, Susan, but this is important."

Hal Dendron was no mere hireling; he was her deputy director and manager.

Susan started to say something, paused, and started listening. Hal had the authority to override Susan's version of the DO NOT DISTURB sign and the sense to know not to abuse the privilege. He wouldn't burst in unless it was something important.

He said, "I've got Mylon Sears on the other line." Hal's voice was pitched low, confidential.

Susan said, "I'm listening."

"There are some men here asking about Raoul." Hal paused, adding, "Government men."

A vein started to throb in Susan's forehead. Or perhaps it had already been throbbing, but this was the first that she noticed it. Her jaw muscles flexed, her teeth clenched.

This was the onset of a too-familiar syndrome of frustration, irritation, and rage.

It was an effort for her to keep her voice level, and even then, some strain crept in.

She said, "FBI?" The FBI had distinguished themselves, in her experience, as the most persistent pain-in-the-ass component of U.S. government harassment. She called it harassment. They called it investigation.

Hal said, "Not, not them—CTU."

Susan said, "Who? Which ones are they? There's such an alphabet soup of government organizations harassing the Initiative—FBI, NSA, Homeland Security, Treasury, SEC, you name it—that I can't tell one from the other anymore."

Hal said, "CTU, Counter Terrorist Unit. It's kind of a domestic police force for the CIA." Not pausing for a breath, or letting her get a word in edgewise, he plowed forward to get his message across. "Susan, they want to talk to Raoul and they're quite insistent about it."

She stiffened. The throbbing in her temples was turning into a pounding, forerunner of a near-future splitting headache. "What does Mylon Sears say?"

"He's stalling them but he can't hold them off much longer."

Raoul crossed to her. Instinctively he walked soft-footed, minimizing his tread, so nobody outside the room—like, say, a U.S. government spy with an ear pressed to the door—could hear him. He mouthed the words, "What is it?"

Susan said, "Hal, I'll get back to you in a minute." She put him on hold.

She turned to Raoul, said low-voiced, "More of those government pests. A couple of snoopers outside who want to see you."

"I don't want to see them," he said.

Susan looked less angry than worried. "It's not anything serious, is it, Raoul?"

"Certainly not. It's just more of the same, part of the pattern of oppression that your government routinely inflicts on all members of President Chavez's government in this country. They hate us because we're trying to help the people—the people of Venezuela and the United States."

Susan said, "It makes me ashamed of my country, Raoul."

Raoul smiled, patted her bare shoulder. "These idiots have nothing better to do than to take up my valuable time asking a lot of fool questions about plots and conspiracies that exist only inside their own heads. I have better things to attend to. Besides, this delightful interlude of ours—I wouldn't have missed it for the world, my darling—but it has put me behind schedule.

"I can't afford to lose any more time. And so, my dear, I will say farewell, and take my leave via your private exit," he concluded.

"Oh, Raoul . . ."

She opened to his embrace, yielding, molding herself to him. They kissed. Raoul gave it enough to be convincing, but not too much. He was eager to be away.

He had immunity, Caracas-issued documents attesting him as a member of the diplomatic corps. He could not be arrested, need not answer questions. But he had better things to do with his time than waste it sparring with more Washington stooges.

He came up for air first, breaking the clinch. Fingers reluctantly parting contact with Susan's golden, velvety flesh. He said, "We'll have dinner tonight."

They had both resolved to stay in town despite the storm, he to ride it out at the consulate, she "to show solidarity with the people of New Orleans" and because she had a first-class house in the Faubourg Marigny and a top-notch security staff to protect her.

She said, "Phone me as soon as you get clear, Raoul."

"I will do so."

A back door exit from Susan's private quarters had proved useful in the past and would do so again—in fact, now. He crossed to it, opening the door. Beyond lay a narrow passageway. He opened the door a crack and peeked into the hall. It was empty.

He turned, blew Susan a kiss. She blew one back to him. He eased into the hall, shutting the door behind him.

Now that he was in the corridor, he could hear voices

coming from around the corner and deeper into the main hallway. Several voices. The rhythms were ordinary, conversational. He couldn't make out what they were saying.

He went the other way, turning left toward the tall window at the end of the hall. Before he reached that, he came to a fire door. He opened it, stepping out onto an empty stair landing. No voices or sound of ascent or descent reached him. He was alone.

He went down several flights to another landing, opened a fire door, and entered a hallway. He was now several floors below the main floor of KHF offices and Susan's private retreat.

He got on an elevator and rode it all the way down, to an underground parking garage on a sublevel of the building.

The elevator car came to a halt with a slight bump, doors sliding open. Ahead lay a square-sided corridor of white-painted concrete-block walls, some lined with pipes and cables. Raoul followed it to the underground garage.

So far, so good. He'd eluded pursuit. All that remained for him to do was get in his car, exit the garage to street level, and be on his way.

He was unarmed. He never carried a gun or a weapon. That was for the likes of Colonel Paz and his bullyboys, not for a Garros. He was insulated from that side of the business, too valuable to risk for mere vulgar gunplay and strong-arm activity.

"From each according to his abilities, to each according to his needs." That was a philosophy much in favor with the new masters in Caracas. In this case, Raoul approved of the sentiment.

He headed for his car, saying to himself, "Home free."

• •

THE FOLLOWING TAKES PLACE
BETWEEN THE HOURS OF
1 P.M. AND 2 P.M.
CENTRAL DAYLIGHT TIME

• •

The offices of the Keehan Humanistics Fund occupied several upper floors of the Mega Mart building. Not the topmost floors, because the flat roof doubled as a helicopter landing pad and the KHF offices had been sited below them to buffer and muffle the chopper noise.

The main floor of the complex was the one where Susan Keehan maintained her office and adjoining suite of rooms.

The official title below her name on the brass plate mounted on her door was "Coordinator." It was a prime example of newspeak, language meant to hide and obscure rather than clarify. In other words, double talk.

According to the ideology that passed for gospel in her set, the very concept of leadership, of corporate hierarchies, titles, and chains of command, was a relic of the Neanderthal past. It was "classist," a holdover from the patriarchal hierarchy of the Bad Old Days when power was concentrated at the top, rather than the progressive, future-forward model of power sharing among equals: a pyramid rather than a circle.

She affected the title of "coordinator," the liaison between KHF and LAGO.

By any name, the reality was that she was the boss, the person in charge who called the shots. She made the decisions, and her word was final—subject, of course, to review and revision by her father, Wilmont, and her uncle, Senator Burl. They preferred not to exercise their ultimate authority openly or with a heavy hand, allowing Susan some illusion of independence.

But her key people were their people, who kept them abreast of any and all developments that might negatively impact dynastic interests.

Her office was the biggest and most luxurious, made up of a suite of rooms that included the inner sanctum that was her private retreat from executive cares and responsibilities. It had the best location, the most spectacular view, the most lavish accoutrements.

In the time-honored mode of royals and courtiers, the more important an officer of KHF, the closer that person's office was to Susan's. Proximity equals prestige. Her suite was flanked on one side by that of Hal Dendron, her top lieutenant, and on the other by that of Alma Butterworth, her executive assistant.

One area where newspeak had failed to penetrate was in the Security Division.

EXECPROTEK was a distinct and separate corporate entity that was not part of KHF.

It was placed squarely on the profit-making side of the ledger and under the direct control of Wilmont Keehan: "Daddy."

Mylon Sears was the chief of the New Orleans branch, Gene Jasper was his right hand man.

Earlier, the EXECPROTEK apparatus had managed to stall Jack Bauer and Pete Malo long enough for Raoul Garros to give them the slip.

Down on the ground-floor level, entrance to the building's main lobby was open and unhindered. Anyone could walk in, but before they could get much farther, they were halted by a long, waist-high, countertopped barrier staffed by a security squad. Those seated behind the counter wore civilian clothes, but were backed up by a team of uniformed armed guards posted discreetly (but readily available) on their flanks.

All persons who worked in the building were issued security badges with photo IDs, which they were required to show before being allowed to proceed to the elevator banks accessing the rest of the structure.

Visitors had to check in at the desk, report their business, and be cleared by the in-house parties with whom they had appointments. Only then were they issued visitors' passes and given the go-ahead to enter.

Jack Bauer and Pete Malo occupied a gray area where the lines were blurred and the ordinary rules did not apply. They were Federal agents on official business. Yet, lacking warrants or similar documents, they couldn't hard-ass their way through and barge right in.

Further complicating the mix was politics. More so than usual because of the antagonism between the Administration in Washington and the opposition party of Senator Keehan. They must be careful not to create a political fracas that the Keehan faction could exploit for propaganda purposes.

Or an international incident by leaning too hard on Raoul Garros, possessor of Venezuelan diplomatic accreditation.

Gene Jasper, second-in-command to security chief Mylon Sears, went to the ground-floor checkpoint to personally escort Jack and Pete upward to the Olympian levels of the KHF offices. Jasper was built like a pro football player and had thick, dark hair and a mustache.

A high-speed elevator whisked the trio to the cloud-piercing heights, depositing them on the main KHF floor where top management was massed.

It was some layout. The main hall seemed about the size of the nave of Westminster Abbey. It was decorated in warm earth tones, tans, beiges, and light browns, with dark brown trim.

Opposite the elevator bank was the main reception area, behind whose oversized front desk, mounted on the wall above it, was a three-dimensional KHF logo, each letter three feet high.

Office doors ranged along the walls. Interspersed between them were imitation folkloric prints alternating with stark, black-and-white Family of Man–type portrait photographs of wrinkled, ethnic peasant women, gaggles of Third World children, and suchlike.

From wires strung high above and at right angles to the long axis of the hall were colorful banners celebrating the Hearthstone Initiative and inscribed with its motto, "Warm Homes, Warm Hearts"; also a larger-than-life-sized photo print of President Hugo Chavez shaking hands with Senator Burl Keehan.

Pete Malo struck his fist against his left breast and said, "Gets you right here, doesn't it?"

Jack Bauer said, "That's heartburn, I think."

"Must've been those hot dogs I had for lunch."

* * *

Mylon Sears came out to meet them, further delaying the inevitable face-off between the CTU agents and Susan Keehan. Sears was of medium height, with broad shoulders, a barrel chest, and thick arms. Balding, he'd cut his remaining hair close to the scalp. A horseshoe-shaped patch where hair still grew looked like a band of graphite particles adhering to his shiny scalp.

He had a habit of leaning forward as he spoke, rising on the balls of his feet when he wanted to emphasize a point. The stall could not last forever, though, and presently Jack and Pete found themselves squaring off against the KHF coterie.

The blocking of the scene emphasized the confrontational nature of the meeting.

On one side stood Jack and Pete. Opposite, facing them, were Susan Keehan and her seconds: Hal Dendron, Alma Butterworth, Sears, and Jasper.

Hal Dendron, fortyish, had thinning auburn hair, curling over his ears and shirt collar. His face was soft, boyish, freckled. He wore a bow tie and a seersucker suit. His loafers looked like golf shoes.

Alma Butterworth had a pug nose and a bulldog jaw. She was short, squat, solidly built.

Susan Keehan wore a navy blazer, pale yellow silk blouse, skirt, and shoes. Her hair was still damp from the recent shower. Her demeanor and body language expressed skepticism and downright hostility.

She stood face to face with Jack and Pete, taking the fight to them. Her subordinates would have stood in front of her if they could, physically screening her, but this desire was negated by Susan's take-charge attitude. Nobody gets in front of a Keehan.

Mylon Sears handled the introductions. He was in the uncomfortable position of the man in the middle, his loyalty to his employers balanced by his knowledge of the Golden Pole massacre and the potential threat element bubbling up around the scene.

Susan was uninterested in the agents' names and barely took notice of them. All she saw was two frontline troops of The Enemy, that is, the U.S. government.

Hal Dendron, anxious, was all but wringing his hands. "I suggest we wait for Ferlin to arrive and let him do the talking." Ferlin Maybrick was KHF's chief legal counsel in New Orleans, as high-powered and effective as they come. He'd been called to the Mart but hadn't yet arrived.

Susan said, "I'm perfectly capable of speaking for myself, thank you very much. I've certainly had enough practice in dealing with government snoopers for the last six months, ever since the Initiative began. This is nothing new; it's the same old story."

Pete said, "That's what you think."

That got her attention, at least, giving her free-floating hostility a focus and allowing it to crystallize on the agents, whom she looked on with frank distaste, like a pair of particularly noxious insects that had scuttled out from under the baseboard. She was handicapped by the fact that Sears hadn't had time to brief her on the full extent of the developing situation.

Jack, playing the good cop to Pete's bad cop, said, "We'd like to see Mr. Garros as soon as possible, please. It's for his own good."

Susan said, "Where's your warrant?"

"We don't have one."

"Then you don't belong here. You're trespassing and I have every right to have you thrown out."

Mylon Sears became the focus of her discontent. She turned to him and said, "What are they doing up here? I'm surprised you let them get this far."

Sears cleared his throat. "This is an unusual situation, Susan. There are a lot of tricky angles here. This is one time when we're all working on the same side, and speed is of the essence."

Jack said, "We don't need a warrant when it comes to saving a man's life."

Susan said, "What man?"

"Your man," Jack said. "Raoul Garros."

She looked at Jack with new interest, the kind demonstrated by a scientist when a lab specimen exhibits an unusual pattern of behavior. "That's a new one."

Pete said, "You've got us all wrong, Ms. Keehan."

"I doubt that's possible," Susan said, in a tone meant to be withering. "I've played this same scene too many times."

"We're trying to protect Mr. Garros—no thanks to you."

Susan shook her head, firm knots of muscle flexing at the hinges of her jaw. "I know how the government protects people. Like the way you protect the people of Iraq."

Mylon Sears winced. Jack, irked, said, "We didn't come here to argue politics. Or play games. Garros is in danger, serious danger."

Susan said, "The only danger he's in is from you."

Jack forged ahead. "Earlier today, an attempt was made to assassinate Colonel Paz. Two of his men are dead and he's missing."

Susan tossed her head. "I don't believe you."

Pete Malo chimed in, "We wouldn't dream of asking you to take the word of a couple of Federal agents who're sworn to uphold and protect the Constitution. Try turning on a television set. The local news is full of the story. Seven people are dead."

Jack gestured at Mylon Sears. "Ask him."

Susan said, "I'm not minded to carry this farce any further."

Mylon Sears harrumphed, loud enough so that everybody looked at him, Susan included. "It's true," he said.

Susan said, "You know it for a fact? Or is it just something they said?" "They" meaning Jack and Pete.

Sears said, "It's a fact. We've confirmed it—independently."

Susan paused, hesitant, her timing thrown off. There was still plenty of fight in her, though. Plenty of stubborn opposition. She said, "What about the Colonel?"

Jack said, "He escaped, when last heard from."

Susan said, "Thank God for that!" It sounded heartfelt. Then, accusingly, "If anybody tried to assassinate him, it was probably our government."

Jack said, "It was our government that saved his life." Why bother to mention that he and Pete had been the ones who rescued Paz? She probably wouldn't believe him, anyway. Besides, he wasn't so sure anymore that rescuing Paz had been such a hot idea—but there was no choice for it, not when Paz held the potential to point the way to the Holy Grail that was spymaster Beltran.

Jack went on, "The attack on Paz may not be an isolated incident; it might be part of a series of attacks. The Venezuelan Consulate and LAGO Tower are on lockdown. Paz was the first target. Garros is a known associate of his. He may be marked for murder, too."

Susan was starting to seem a bit unsteady on her feet. "This is too utterly fantastic."

Jack said, "The sooner you trot Garros out and produce him, the safer he'll be."

She fired back, "What makes you think he's here?"

Jack pressed. "Are you saying he's not?"

Susan said, "Yes—that is, he's not here."

Jack said, "Are you sure you want to stick with that answer? Because it's a crime to lie to Federal agents in the course of an investigation."

Mylon Sears stepped in. "As far as Ms. Keehan knows, Mr. Garros is not on the premises."

Susan said, "Don't worry about protecting me. Raoul's not here."

Jack said, "Where is he? If you want to save his life, you'd better talk fast."

Susan was definite now. "He's not here. That's the truth."

"Where is he?"

Sears cautioned, "You don't have to answer that, Susan—"

"We'll sort out the legalities later," Susan said. "If Raoul really is in danger—"

"He is," Jack said.

"—then we've got to do anything we can," she said. "But if you're lying—"

Jack said, "Where is he?"

"He's gone," Susan said. "He was here earlier but he left."

"Does he know he's in danger?"

Susan was abstracted, her gaze turned inward. "No, he knows nothing about it . . . neither of us did."

Jack was openly skeptical. "The consulate didn't notify him?"

"No—I don't know. They might have. His cell was turned off . . . We were holding an important conference and he didn't want to be disturbed."

Jack let that one pass. "The consulate didn't phone, didn't try to reach him here?"

"No," Susan said. "I don't know." She turned to Alma Butterworth. "Did they?"

Alma Butterworth said, "No, they didn't, Susan."

Susan glanced at Mylon Sears, who shook his head no. Jack said, "So Garros doesn't know the score. When did he leave?"

Susan said, "Five minutes ago. Maybe more, ten."

"Where did he go?"

"I don't know. He said he had business to attend to."

Jack said, "Did he have a car and driver?"

Susan shook her head. "He doesn't have a driver. He likes to do the driving himself."

"Where's his car? Downstairs in the parking garage?"

"Yes, I suppose; I don't know—"

Jack and Pete exchanged glances. They stepped aside from the others. Pete said, "Good thing we've got Topham and Beauclerk covering the garage."

Jack was worried. "We should've heard from them by now if Garros is on the move."

Pete took out his cell, pressed some buttons, inputting a number. He held the cell to his ear. Seconds passed, ticking away, the silence unbroken. His brows knit, his face darkening. "No reply."

Jack said to Susan, "See if you can reach Garros."

She took out her cell, hands trembling. Fear made her clumsy and she misdialed, said, "Damn!" and tried again.

"No answer," she said. "His cell was off and he might have forgotten to turn it back on."

Jack said, "How'd he leave? Which way did he go?"

She indicated a passageway several doors down, to the left, away from the main banks. "There's an elevator there."

Mylon Sears said, "I'll show you." He was in motion, energetic, briskly striding forward, leaning into it. He walked flat-footed, the soles of his shoes slapping the floor tiles.

The others followed, all trooping down the main hall, turning left into the side corridor. They halted at the elevator. Jack pressed the button. The wait for the car seemed interminable, though it couldn't have been long.

A bell pinged; the doors slid open. Everybody got on, crowding the car. Jack bumped into Susan, jostling her. "Sorry, excuse me."

She glared but made no reply.

All in; the button was pressed for the underground parking garage. The elevator car descended, making no stops on its plunge to the bottom.

The Mega Mart's infrastructure extended for several levels underground. Beneath the sprawling, stepped pavilions and landscaped gardens at surface level lay an extensive underground parking garage complex. It was huge, occupying the space of a city block. A necessity for the legions of employees who drove their own vehicles to and from work.

Admittance was restricted. Nobody could just drive in out of the blue and grab a space. The underground complex had a number of ramped portals, each of which was secured by mechanized gates and tollbooths. It was monitored by security cameras, most of which were trained on the main aisles and cross passages and the entrances and exits.

There was room for several hundred vehicles.

Most of the companies housed in the Mega Mart and their employees put little credence in the concept of the five-day workweek. On Saturdays, from eight A.M. until midafternoon, it was not unusual to see the underground lot filled to anywhere from a fifth to a quarter of its full capacity.

Not today, though; not this Saturday, with Everette coming on. Here was where the truly dedicated strivers and workaholics were separated from the merely ambitious corporate worker bees and drones. They had come, even today, several score of them, their vehicles scattered around the subterranean lot.

Due to the reduced demand, and in preparation for the coming storm, all but one of the exit/entrance ramps were closed. That ramp was secured by a mechanical gate and manned by a single attendant in the tollbooth.

The express elevator touched bottom, easing to a halt. The doors opened, spilling out its carload of passengers. The riders exited on the hustle, double-timing their way through winding corridors of white-painted concrete blocks and slick gray cement floors.

In the lead were Jack Bauer, Pete Malo, and Mylon Sears. Susan Keehan raced along with them, but the three in the lead were grouped to screen her from potential threat and wouldn't let her pass them. Gene Jasper jogged alongside her, for additional security. Alma Butterworth flanked her on the other side, her short thick legs churning. Bringing up the rear was Hal Dendron, huffing and puffing.

Trouble lay ahead, the only question being how much.

Jack and Pete had a two-man CTU backup team posted in the garage to keep an eye out for Garros, to intercept and detain him should he elude the senior agents and make for his car. These agents, Topham and Beauclerk, failed to respond to Pete's repeated cell phone calls.

Raoul Garros, likewise, failed to answer the calls to his cell made by Susan Keehan.

Building security had reported that the attendant in the exit tollbooth also did not reply to their increasingly urgent queries.

The newly arrived group half-walked, half-ran as they threaded the corridors into the vast underground space.

It was a totally artificial environment made of stone and steel, lit by electric lights. Modern-day catacombs, subdivided by rows of round, upright pillars that created vanishing point perspective lines as they filed across the expanse of cement floor toward the space's far-distant opposite end.

It smelled of exhaust fumes, oil, gas, rubber, and a flinty dankness that came of being below the surface of one of the most humid cities in the world. These scents persisted despite a powerful ventilation system.

Rank has its privileges, not only aboveground but beneath it. Those at the apex of the Mega Mart organization and the businesses it housed had been assigned parking spaces that were conveniently close to the elevator banks. Not for them the inconvenience of having to traverse the cavernous space of the lot to go to and from their vehicles; they had merely to step out of the elevators and proceed to the nearby reserved area that had been set aside for them.

Naturally Susan Keehan and her upper management cadre were allotted prime parking places in this privileged compound.

As the object of Susan's affections, Raoul Garros was routinely assigned one of these coveted spots and issued a permit and sticker allowing him unrestricted access to it.

His car, a late model maroon Mercedes with diplomatic plates, was there now, neatly positioned within the painted lines of its high-status parking space amid a cluster of similarly entitled VIP vehicles.

But Garros himself was gone, nowhere to be seen.

Sprawled on the floor near the Mercedes were two bodies. They lay in plain sight, where they had fallen. No attempt had been made to cover them up. They were CTU agents Topham and Beauclerk.

Topham's head lolled at an unnatural angle, the result of a broken neck. Beauclerk's death was messier. His throat had been cut with such force that the head was almost severed from the neck.

Susan Keehan gasped, biting the back of her hand to

keep from screaming. She swayed, seemingly in danger of fainting. Gene Jasper grabbed her upper arms, steadying her. Alma Butterworth gave him a dirty look.

Jack, eyeing Beauclerk, said, "The angle of the cut and the pattern of the blood spray indicate he was attacked from behind."

Pete Malo said, "No mean feat, to sneak up on Topham. He was a good man. Beauclerk, too." His expression consisted of mingled parts of grief and rage. "It probably happened while we were wasting time on that jag-off session upstairs in the KHF offices," he said.

Mylon Sears said, "That's not necessarily the case; we don't know that for sure."

Pete said, "Give me a break and stop singing the company song."

It was a long walk across the concrete pavement to the far side of the garage, where the exit ramp lay, the only one that had been in operation this afternoon.

The ramp slanted up to street level.

Before exiting or entering, all vehicles must go through the checkpoint and gate.

Machines belonging to persons employed in the building were fixed with a plate or card similar to the automatic E-ZPass system used on certain state highways. A card with a microchip was fitted to the front of the vehicle. At the checkpoint, a monitoring device with a sensor electronically read the pass card; if valid, the gate lifted and the vehicle was allowed to proceed.

Visitors without the pass card must punch an auto-tab machine before entering, to receive a ticket stamped with date and time of entry. The gate would then lift, admitting them. If they were transacting business with one of the companies in the building, the ticket would be validated at the respective office or by the front security desk on the ground floor.

Since the sprawling subterranean site had more space than there were vehicles issued to building personnel, it also served as a public parking lot for the midtown business district, another way for Mega Mart management to maximize profits.

It also allowed entry to the public at large, with all that implies for good or ill.

In which case, the driver would present the stamped ticket at a tollbooth on the way out, where an attendant would levy charges for the time spent parked in the lot, collect the fare, and open the gate for the vehicle to exit.

Today, one sole tollbooth had been in operation. Violence had been done to the gate, a yellow-and-black striped metal pole that worked like a railroad crossing barrier, lifting when the fare was paid. The pole now lay on the ramp, crumpled and twisted and torn almost completely loose, except for a rivet or two that attached it to the gatepost.

Violence had been done to the gatekeeper, too.

The attendant now sat on the floor of the booth, his legs extended through its open doorway. He was wearing loafers, one of which had come off, leaving him with one foot shod and the other shoeless. He was wedged in the bottom of the booth, arms raised over his head and pinned in place by the narrow, upright walls.

His head was slumped forward, eyes open and staring, chin on chest, a bullet hole in the middle of his forehead.

Pete said, "Drilled him right between the horns. A young guy, couldn't be more than eighteen or nineteen."

Mylon Sears tsk-tsked, said, "I know him, I've seen him around. Lonnie, his name was. Nice kid. He worked here part-time to help pay his way through school. That's why he was working today."

Jack said, "Garros was the target. The job was probably done by some members of the same outfit that made the try on Paz. Had to be two of them at least, maybe three or more. They eliminated Topham and Beauclerk first, clearing the way to move on Garros. They might have killed him, but it's more likely they took him alive; otherwise, why not leave his body behind?

"It all went down at the opposite end of the parking garage, way to hell and gone. No shots fired, a pair of quiet kills. Three, if they did in Garros, but again, it looks more like an abduction than a murder. The kid attendant was unaware that anything had happened. His position shows that. He stayed in the booth, doing his job. The crew drives up to the gate, just like any car using the parking lot. They shoot the youngster to eliminate him as a possible witness, then crash the gate and take off.

"That how you see it, Pete?"

Pete nodded. "I'll notify Center."

• •

THE FOLLOWING TAKES PLACE
BETWEEN THE HOURS OF
2 P.M. AND 3 P.M.
CENTRAL DAYLIGHT TIME

• •

Threat assessment—that's what Mylon Sears was engaged in. Namely, the threat to his career, reputation, and continued economic and social well-being.

Now, as he stood around in the underground garage with Jack Bauer and Pete Malo, waiting for CTU reinforcements and forensics techs to arrive and do their thing, he'd already moved to secure his bread and butter.

His immediate priority was the safety of Susan Keehan. Not his top priority. His top priority was Mylon Sears and the continued care and feeding of same, at the high level to which he'd grown accustomed.

But his first action in the aftermath of discovering the bodies in the basement garage was to protect Susan.

The unknown assailants who'd abducted Raoul Garros and killed three others, including two CTU agents, were obviously no respecters of any kind of social order. He could only thank God that they'd targeted Garros and not Susan herself.

If she had been kidnapped! Well, that would have put him in quite a position in the private security industry. And with Clan Keehan.

Even so, he'd still have to scramble and do some slick damage control to get out of this with his job, reputation, and career intact.

He'd been quick to surround Susan with a hardened security cordon. Easy enough; he was in position to draw on a depth of personnel, EXECPROTEK's New Orleans offices being based right here in the Mega Mart building. He blanketed her with a half-dozen bodyguards, top protectors all, including several ex–Secret Service operatives.

For now, the safest place for her was right here, in the Mega Mart building. Hard as it was to credit, considering the crimes of violence that had already gone down here today. But it was still the safest, best-protected locale available.

It came equipped with its own small, private army of security professionals. The building was privately owned, allowing for maximum control of entrances and exits, as well as any other unorthodox or extraordinary procedures necessary to protect the heiress to the Keehan fortune.

Caution dictated that she be secured here, rather than moved to some other location, exposing her to increased risk.

The building was a self-contained, potential fortress. It was also ready to ride out the coming storm, no matter how bad it got. It had its own private generator, fuel supply, stocks of food and fresh water. It was easiest to guard Susan here, on-site. The Mart could survive any tempest, and Susan could always be airlifted out by helicopter later when the storm force had broken.

Susan was not his boss, although as a matter of form he

deferred to her in all matters not directly connected with the operation and running of the Security Division.

His boss was Brinsley S. Wolters, head of EXECPRO-TEK; Wolters's boss was Wilmont Keehan, who owned the company.

That Keehan's daughter's fiancé had been abducted and three persons killed in the building where EXECPROTEK's New Orleans branch was based was a public relations nightmare and worse; as the man in charge on the spot (he was on the spot, all right), Sears knew that one false step could put him on the chopping block.

He was a born competitor and a winner and hadn't reached his current position by folding when disaster struck; his nature was to keep fighting until the last dog died.

Some powerful cards remained on the table for him to play when it came to keeping his job and reputation intact.

Chief among these was the fact that it had been Susan's decision to obstruct, stall, and mislead CTU agents Bauer and Malo to keep them from confronting Raoul Garros.

What would have been a minor peccadillo, one that in ordinary circumstances would never have had any official comeback, had taken on a deadly seriousness due to the violence that had resulted.

In fact, it was not stretching a point to note that her delaying tactics were indirectly responsible for the deaths of Topham and Beauclerk. Not to mention the parking lot attendant. His family might have the makings of a multimillion-dollar negligence lawsuit.

Susan Keehan was vulnerable; by association, so was her father, Wilmont; and her uncle, Senator Burl Keehan. The Senator especially was the public face of the oil-for-the-poor Hearthstone Initiative; his close dealings with Venezuela's Chavez regime were already controversial in some quarters.

This debacle would be red meat to his political foes, who were legion.

Three principal Keehans, Wilmont, Susan, and the Senator, were mired deep in the mess if they didn't play their cards right. The dynasts were sacrosanct; they'd be looking for someone, anyone else to be the fall guy and take the heat for the disaster. A role Sears was determined to avoid.

He had plenty of incriminating evidence on the family, not just in this matter but in countless other Keehan dirty deals; he could and would use the threat of revealing it to get himself off the hook.

Who to hang it on? That was a toughie. It might even be necessary to put the blame where it belonged, on the homicidal abductors who'd grabbed Garros.

If only he knew who they were.

Acting on Sears's orders, bodyguards literally surrounded Susan Keehan, screening her behind a wall of solid, well-armed flesh. They escorted her to the KHF offices on top of the building.

With her went Hal Dendron and Alma Butterworth. There wasn't much either could do down here in the basement garage, where the situation required Sears's adroit interfacing with the authorities.

Besides, he didn't want them looking over his shoulder and getting too clear an idea of what he was up to. What they didn't know couldn't be used against him later.

He put Gene Jasper in charge of the squad guarding Susan. He knew Jasper would like that; he was always trying to get close to her, to make a personal connection with the heiress and develop his own direct line of communication to her instead of having to go through his boss, Sears. Yes, Jasper would welcome the chance to make himself useful and do some politicking with the boss's daughter.

That suited Sears fine; he didn't want Jasper watching him too closely, either; not at this critical time.

In addition to Susan's immediate circle of personal protectors, security was beefed up on her floor, with a troop of heavily armed trigger pullers guarding the fire doors, stairs, and elevators.

Not only would they guard her from those who might do her violence, they would also shield her from any law enforcement, national security, or media types who might want to question her.

The carnage in the underground garage was less easily resolved. For now, the bodies must lay in place, stark specimens of the violence that had been unleashed here today.

They were denied even the minimum of privacy and decency that would come from having their dead eyes closed and their faces decently covered, for fear of contaminating trace evidence or destroying vital clues.

It wasn't pretty. Mylon Sears in younger days had seen combat and worked law enforcement, but his high status in the EXECPROTEK organization had insulated him for long years from the grittier realities of the profession, such as blood and violent death.

Careerism now provided the mental numbness necessary for carrying on.

Relations with CTU were extremely delicate. Two of their own were dead, murdered, and under circumstances that boded ill for the Keehan clan. Intensifying Sears's desire to cooperate, or at least seem to be cooperating.

Still, the situation had its positives as well as its negatives. CTU wanted all other law enforcement and national security agencies kept out of the loop for as long as possible. To ensure that the Counter Terrorist Unit took the lead in tracking down and avenging the slayers of their own.

That guaranteed a degree of control and confidentiality over a volatile situation that was a media magnet.

Sears knew Pete Malo, their respective positions in the private and public security sectors here in New Orleans having fostered over the years a working relationship between the two. This time out, though, the death of Topham and Beauclerk radically altered the basic dynamics of their association, and not for the better.

Sears didn't know Jack Bauer; Bauer was a stranger to him, a variable, an unknown quantity.

It was Bauer who suggested that they open the trunk of Garros's car. "Maybe he's stuffed inside it," Jack said.

Sears vented a pious, heartfelt "Lord, let's hope not!"

Pete Malo said, "I didn't know you were so attached to Raoul."

Sears said, "I'm attached to my job. I'd like to keep it, which seems unlikely if Garros is dead."

He reached for his communicator, intending to contact the building's security center to send a man down to open the trunk. Civilian employees were always doing something like locking their keys inside their cars; the security staff had several locksmiths on duty.

Pete Malo said, "Never mind, I'll do it myself. It's quicker." He took out his pocket kit of lock-picking tools and went to work. In moments, the tumblers clicked into place, the trunk unlocked, and he lifted the lid.

Inside, there was nothing more than a spare tire. Pete said, "Now we know he's not there, at least."

Jack prowled around the area of the parking attendant's booth and gate, searching for any brass cartridge that might have been ejected by the murder gun. Finding none.

Jack noted other leads worth following up on. One such was the ticket-issuing machine at the gate at the bottom of the entrance ramp.

The killers' vehicle had not been equipped with one of the pass cards for automatic entry issued to building personnel. Otherwise they could have driven out of the garage without having to bust through the gate.

On entering, a ticket would have been issued to them. A record was kept of all such tickets. By checking the record against all other visitors' cars, the time of the killers' car's entry could be determined. This would help pinpoint the time of some of their movements. Perhaps someone in the garage or on the street at that time had seen something of value.

Surveillance cameras monitored the garage. They were automatic—the space was too vast and the building too large to allow for individualized oversight by human operators in the Mart's security command post. The camera feeds were recorded onto large spools of tape that were changed every twenty-four hours. Examination of the relevant spools might reveal significant details of the crime, its perpetrators, and their vehicle.

The getaway car was a stolen one, no doubt, and fitted with a set of plates lifted from another vehicle—standard operating procedure for professional crooks and hitters—but the motions had to be gone through anyway. Legwork and attention to detail had a way of paying off in the long run, and sometimes sooner than that.

Jack and Pete stayed on the scene until the first CTU vehicles began to arrive.

CTU Agent Ned Lauter took charge of the on-site investigation.

Jack and Pete got in their SUV and drove off.

The principals met in a conference room in the KHF offices to hold a strategy session. Present were Susan Keehan,

Mylon Sears, Gene Jasper, Hal Dendron, and Alma Butterworth. Closeted in conference.

All were grouped around a circular table. Susan stood, restless, too uneasy to sit.

Her expression was strained. The cords in her neck stood out. White-knuckled anxiety rolled through her in waves, threatening to make her physically ill. Fear alternated with rage.

Mylon Sears assumed the remote, owlish expression of a doctor about to give a patient the bad news. "I'm afraid that there's no other conclusion than that Raoul has met with foul play, that he's been abducted."

Gene Jasper hastened to put a positive spin on it, saying, "That's a good thing, Susan. That means that he's still alive. Otherwise they would have killed him in the garage and left him there with the others."

Susan shook with frustration. "'They'! Who are 'they'?"

Sears said, "No reason to trust CTU or any other government agency when it comes to Raoul and LAGO." His remark elicited plenty of head-nodding agreement around the table.

"But that doesn't necessarily mean that they're totally off-base on this one," he added.

That line was less well-received, generating scowls and frowns from the others, with the exception of Jasper, who received his boss's statement with a look of studied neutrality.

Sears forged on, bearer of bad news. "The Venezuelan official presence in this city is definitely under assault. Our own independent sources have verified the attack on Colonel Paz this morning. It left seven dead: his two bodyguards, and all five of the attackers. He's still missing, and nobody at the consulate has heard from him."

Alma Butterworth said, "Convenient."

Sears said, "How so?"

She fired back, "Dead men tell no tales. No witnesses are left behind to contradict the official story."

"You're suggesting our government is behind the slaughter?"

Alma said, "It wouldn't be the first time. We've seen what this Administration has unleashed on the people of the Middle East and Latin America."

Sears tried to gloss over the rhetoric to keep his presentation moving. "Be that as it may, even the blackest of government black ops avoids this kind of violence at home. Bad press and all that. These mass killings will generate a ton of international ill-will.

"Besides, I hardly think that even CTU would kill two of its own men to buttress a cover story," he added.

"Hmph," Alma Butterworth said, her flinty stare and tightly set mouth suggesting strong disagreement with his analysis.

Susan Keehan was showing signs of impatience, danger signs. Storm warnings. "I wouldn't put it past our government. They hate President Chavez and his populist reforms and would do anything they can to derail it."

Sears said, "How does this violence help Washington's propaganda line? It makes us look like a banana republic." He'd spoken without thinking and added quickly, "Pardon the expression."

Susan wasn't buying it. "If not us, then—who?"

Sears, hesitant, suggested, "This kind of violence is the stock in trade of drug gangs."

Susan exploded. "That's another slur on Venezuela, trying to associate it with drug trafficking! That's what Washington always does whenever it wants to smear a progressive

Third World regime, accuses it of being involved in narcotics and terrorism!"

A phone rang. Not so much of a ring tone as an electronic bleeping.

Susan started, gasping. She looked ready to jump out of her own skin. Several more ring tones sounded before she realized that their source was her own cell phone. Only a select few had access to her private number; among them, Raoul currently headed the list.

She reached into her pocket for the cell, hand shaking so much that she almost dropped it. She fumbled with it, then recovered. Meanwhile, the electronic bell tones chimed again.

She flipped open the lid of the cell and said, "Maybe it's Raoul!"

That galvanized the others at the table, causing them to lean forward in their chairs toward her, lunging, quivering like hunting dogs on point.

Bright spots of color blazed in Susan's cheeks, making her look feverish, consumptive. "Hello, Raoul! Raoul!"

A voice on the other end said, "Yes, it's me. Raoul."

Susan vented a rapid-fire torrent. A rush of words, babbling. "Oh, thank God! I've been so worried! What happened to you, Raoul? Are you all right? Where are you?"

Raoul did not immediately reply. Susan said, "Raoul? You are all right, aren't you, darling?"

He said, "Susan, please listen. This is serious." Raoul's voice was husky, cracking. He sounded like he was going to cry.

"Raoul, what is it, dear? You're frightening me—"

"Please, Susan, let me speak without your interrupting for once. It is a matter of life and death—*ugh!*"

Raoul was silenced in mid-phrase, sounding like he'd been choked off. Strangled noises gurgled in the background.

Susan called his name several times in ever more frantic desperation. "Raoul? Raoul! Raoul, speak to me! Raoul, are you there?!"

A new voice said, "I am here, but I am not Raoul."

No, the speaker was most definitely not Raoul. The voice sounded flat, mechanical, chillingly inhuman. Sexless, identifiably neither male or female. There was a quality to it that suggested that it emanated from some kind of electronic voice box, a filtering device that took human speech and digitized it, reproduced it with all traces of individuality of tone, timbre, dynamics filtered out. The distortion maximized its sinister aspect.

Susan was thrown by it; for a moment it left her speechless—for her a rare experience. The caller said, "Miss Keehan? Are you there, Miss Keehan?"

Susan recovered, finding her voice. "Who's this?"

"This is me," came the reply.

"Yes, but who are you?"

"I have Raoul Garros."

"Have him? What do you mean, you have him?"

"The role of naif ill becomes you, Miss Keehan. Especially not at a time like this, when the crisis has arrived. I have the body in question. Whether that body remains among the living or the dead is entirely up to you."

"You—you've kidnapped him!"

"Yes."

"What do you want?"

"Money. A great deal of money, that is what I want. You want Raoul. Here is a basis for negotiation."

For a flash, Susan's fear was replaced by anger. She said, "You must be crazy! Put Raoul back on!"

The caller said, "Certainly. One moment, please."

A pause was followed by a shriek of agony—Raoul's shriek. So loud and piercing was it that it was plainly audible to the others seated around the conference table. It seemed to go on forever.

When it ended, Susan, shivering, said, "What are you doing to him?"

The machine-made voice returned. "You would like to hear more?"

Susan said, "No! For God's sake, don't! Please stop! Don't hurt him!"

"We understand each other better now, eh? You do agree that the man you spoke to is Raoul Garros, no?"

"Yes—"

"You are certain of his identity, Miss Keehan? If not, I will send you some body parts as proof. A finger, or perhaps an ear. Possibly both. Or would you prefer some more, uh, intimate part of his anatomy?"

"No!"

"I am in charge, Miss Keehan. Please remember that. Or else Raoul will experience a great deal of pain. More than he has already suffered."

"No, don't! Please don't hurt him anymore!"

"Ah . . ." Even the mechanized tones of the voice distorter failed to disguise the pleasure in the caller's voice. "I have Raoul. You have one million dollars. I suggest an exchange."

Outrage colored Susan's reply: "A million dollars!"

The caller said, "It is your money, and you have a great deal of it. A mere million is no great hardship for you. Should you refuse to pay, however, Raoul will experience a great deal of hardship. Death will come to him as a blessing."

She said, "I'll pay."

"Such compassion! So very charitable of you. Raoul will be deeply grateful," the voice said. "Here is how I want the ransom money. Write this down. A single mistake will be fatal for Raoul."

A frantic interval followed as Susan got hold of a pen and notepad.

The caller said, "Listen carefully. The money must be made up of small bills, no larger than hundred-dollar bills. Old bills, which have been in circulation for twenty years. No consecutive serial numbers. Do you understand?"

Susan said, "Yes."

"Read it back to me to be sure you've got it right."

"Small bills, nothing larger than a hundred. Twenty years old. No consecutive serial numbers."

"Correct," the voice said. "Cooperate fully and without question. Make no attempt to contact the authorities. They are bunglers who will succeed only in getting Raoul killed. Messily."

The caller continued, "Stand by. I will contact you presently, within the hour, with instructions on how and where to deliver the money. Do nothing until you hear from me. Make no attempt to trace this call, or Raoul dies."

Click.

Connection terminated.

Leaving Susan shouting into a dead phone.

• •

THE FOLLOWING TAKES PLACE
BETWEEN THE HOURS OF
3 P.M. AND 4 P.M.
CENTRAL DAYLIGHT TIME

• •

Planters and Traders Mercantile Exchange,
New Orleans

Gene Jasper was saying, "It's a waste of time to have Susan go down to the vaults to get the money, Molineux. Why not just bring it up here to her? Time is of the essence."

"Yes, you've made that abundantly clear," Molineux said, sniffing. He was the president of the bank; nothing less would do when it came to dealing with Susan Keehan.

He said, "However, there are certain procedures for accessing the funds which can only be carried out by Ms. Keehan herself. She has to go through the retinal and fingerprint identification scan and fill out the magna-screen card for the on-file signature comparison."

Jasper said, "Why all the red tape? You know who she is. Everybody does. I mean, what the hell, this is a Keehan bank."

Molineux said, "The safeguards are built into the system. They're mechanized. I know Ms. Keehan, of course, but the machines don't. It's impossible to circumvent them, even for her."

Susan said, "We're wasting time now talking about it. If it has to be done that way then that's how we'll do it. Let's go, Mr. Molineux."

Mylon Sears spoke up. "You'd better let me hold your cell, Susan. Being underground might affect the phone reception, in case the kidnapper should call while you're down there."

Susan said, "You think he will? He said he'd contact us on the hour."

Sears said, "Who knows what he might get it in his head to do? I wouldn't necessarily trust the timetable of a kidnapper and killer. He might call at any time just to be unpredictable, to break up our timing and keep us off-balance. Or something could come up that could require him to contact us sooner."

Susan said, "You're right. Here's the phone, take it."

"Thank you. I'll take good care of it; don't worry."

"Don't worry!"

"You know what I mean," Sears said. "You'd better go with her, Gene. A million dollars in small bills packs a considerable weight. You carry it."

"Will do," Jasper said. "I think I can handle it." He sounded eager and made no attempt to disguise it. To stay close to Susan Keehan and make himself useful to her, especially at this time of crisis, was something he greatly desired.

Molineux said, "Shall we go?"

There was the sound of footsteps, three sets of them, as he, Susan, and Gene Jasper crossed a long marble floor. It was a big bank, a big building, with a lot of floor to be crossed.

Molineux said, "We'll ride the elevator down."

The signal had been affected by the masses of stone and metal making up the bulk of the bank's aboveground structure.

Now, as Susan, Jasper, and Molineux descended to the sub-surface vaults, with even more steel and concrete to block against the transmission, the signal began breaking up. The reception got mushy, muddy; gaps opened in the dialogue.

Noise fought with signal. There was more static than voice. Finally the voices gave way entirely to a hissing stream of white noise.

Jack Bauer said, "There goes the signal. Only temporarily— I hope."

He and Pete Malo sat in their SUV, which was parked around the corner from the Planters and Traders Mercantile Exchange building in the city's staid, old-line financial district. The area lay cross-town from where the Mega Mart building was sited.

The SUV was parked on a side street around the corner from the front of the bank building. Its windows were rolled up and the air conditioner was on. Pete sat behind the wheel, Jack in the passenger seat.

Their faces were intent, a study in concentration. Both men were hunched over a portable transceiver unit fitted into a dashboard housing and plugged into a power outlet. The idling SUV's engine supplied the power for the comm unit.

The console was roughly the size and shape of an attaché

case, its face crowded with dials, switches, and screens. Beaded telltale lights glowed green: on.

A digitized readout screen displayed real-time data measuring the strength and frequency of the signal from a bugging device that the agents were monitoring.

Earlier, back at the Mega Mart building in the KHF offices, Garros's absence and the failure of agents Topham and Beauclerk to respond to communications had alerted Jack that a crisis was at hand. He reached a quick decision to bug Susan Keehan, on the grounds that she was likeliest to receive a message from Raoul. As the group was riding down the elevator to the parking garage, Jack had accidentally-on-purpose bumped into Susan. He had done so for the purpose of planting a Flea on her, slipping the stick-on, button-sized electronic eavesdropper under the lapel of her blazer in the guise of steadying her after the collision.

That was why he and Pete had departed the underground garage as soon as possible, to activate the Flea and begin listening in. It proved to be in good working order, and once switched on, began transmitting the voices of Susan Keehan and those of her associates who were in close proximity to her.

The signal was beamed to the transceiver in the SUV, whose amplifiers boosted the feed and sent it along to the board operators of CTU Center across the river.

It was a bold thrust, potentially risky, for CTU to bug a prominent Keehan dynast. Done without a warrant, too.

Mylon Sears orchestrated regularly scheduled electronic debugging sweeps and physical searches of the Mart's KHF offices, phone lines, computers, and faxes, as well as the private, personal vehicles of Susan and her management cadre and their places of residence.

It was his business to thwart CTU and all civilian and military government agencies and any other private parties that wanted to listen into the intimate details and secret dealings of the Keehan/Chavez alliance.

One thing he hadn't been prepared for, though, was a bug being planted on Susan herself.

The Flea model was proactive, capable of evading and eluding electronic anti-bugging devices. It came with a feedback sensor that responded to beamed or wave-pulse signal probes by closing down communication while continuing to passively store up information on its microchip; later, when the detector probes had ceased, the Flea sent the stored data to home base in compressed burst transmissions.

Today's killings and abduction had left Sears with tasks more pressing and immediate than to go bug hunting. When circumstances permitted, he would order a sweep of the KHF offices where Jack and Pete had been earlier today, on the chance that they might have planted some electronic eavesdropping devices there; but the idea that anyone had the lowdown gall to stick a bug on Susan Keehan was the furthest thing from his mind.

Jack Bauer had taken the initiative of bugging Susan Keehan. He'd taken the responsibility, too. The act was audacious, pushing the envelope, but the deaths of CTU agents Topham and Beauclerk had left him in no mood for half measures and pulled punches. He'd informed Cal Randolph of his act, one that the Center Director had heartily endorsed.

When the Flea was eventually found, it would close down for good. Inside it was a micro-fuse that could either be remotely tripped by CTU board operators monitoring the feed, or that would activate itself in response to any attempts to open or tamper with it, leaving its sophisticated electronic innards a chunk of fused plastic and metal.

It had deniability, too; no one in the Keehan camp could prove it had been planted by CTU.

Having a big ear planted squarely in the midst of the KHF ruling cadre's secret conferences and strategy sessions would have been a coup enough, but the Flea really started paying off dividends when it picked up the communication between the kidnapper and Susan Keehan.

Too bad it wasn't sensitive enough to pick up the kidnapper's voice on the cell phone, but it did pick up Susan's responses and the words of those around her. Here was the hottest of hot leads toward Garros's abductors, the slayers of agents Topham and Beauclerk.

The Flea broadcast two sets of signals. One came from a transponder, beaming its location on a wavelength that could be correlated to a map grid to plot its whereabouts at any given moment. Another frequency carried the audio component, the voices and sounds within the listening device's radius of activity/receptivity.

The speaker grid of the SUV's transceiver board was switched on, allowing Jack and Pete to follow the transmission without having to don earphones. Now, though, it gave out white noise: static. Chattering voices had been replaced by pips, pops, bleeps, and hisses.

Frustration showed on the agents' faces. Jack said, "We've lost the audio, at least for now."

Pete said, "Center's operating on our feed, so if we're not getting anything, they're not, either."

Jack scanned the transceiver board. "The bug's still working, but the transmission's not getting through. I don't think it's been detected; it's probably being canceled out by interference. Which makes sense if Susan's gone underground, into the vaults beneath the bank. All that stone and steel is blocking the signal. With any luck, it'll come back when she's topside again."

He raised his gaze from the box, looking up and around.

Stiffness ached in his neck and shoulders from having sat hunched forward for so long, focused on the feed from inside the bank.

The Planters and Traders Mercantile Exchange was located in the old-line financial district.

No glittering sky towers of more recently developed commercial areas were to be found here; this was a citadel of old money. Broad boulevards were lined with rows of buildings built in the first decades of the previous century, and before. It was a place of banks, brokerages, and investment firms.

Much of the architecture dated back to the Neo-Greek Revival of the 1920s, gray-brown stone temples of money featuring domed roofs, triangular pediments, and columned porticoes. The atmosphere was reserved, serious, solemn, foursquare with respectability. Properly reverential. A district where money was taken seriously and an air of solemnity prevailed.

Structures were relatively modest in height, most of them no more than a few stories tall. Boxy and bunkerlike, they hunkered down as if to protect their considerable assets.

Staid and traditional, the area ordinarily would have been quiet and closed on a Saturday afternoon. Closed for business after twelve noon on Saturday.

Today, though, the Planters and Traders Mercantile Exchange was the site of unusual energy and activity.

That was because Susan Keehan needed to get a million dollars in a hurry.

Ransom money.

The kidnapper's nonnegotiable demands: one million dollars in cash; old, unmarked bills, nonconsecutive serial numbers. The highest denomination allowed was hundred-dollar bills; none of which could have been printed during the last twenty years, when the U.S. Treasury had begun installing monitoring strips in its currency to allow for the tracking of money-laundering and currency-smuggling schemes.

A tough assignment in any case, made still more difficult on a Saturday afternoon when the banks were closed and the city squirmed and seethed under the threat of an oncoming hurricane. A labor virtually impossible to be carried out on such short notice by anyone not a Keehan.

The dynasty, however, was in the banking business in a big way. Among its New Orleans assets was the Planters and Traders Mercantile Exchange, one of the oldest financial institutions in continuous operation on the North American continent. The name might have been old-fashioned, but the reality was that of an up-to-date, modern banking concern.

Its doors opened this day on command of Susan Keehan, and its officers from the bank president on down were in place and on point to carry out her wishes.

Thanks to the bugging device, Jack and Pete—and CTU Center—were aware of the KHF clique's strategy and tactics as soon as they were voiced.

Mylon Sears wanted to maximize Susan's safety by minimizing her personal involvement, but she was having none of it. She intended to spearhead the effort to ransom Raoul Garros and refused to be diverted from her course.

In any case, it was necessary for her to take a leading role, for there were certain key financial instruments and procedures that could only be activated by her personal participation.

Sears was forced to strike a balance between surrounding her with as much protection as possible, while at the same time keeping the security shield light, mobile, and fast-responsive.

The near-deserted streets of the financial district were

energized by an EXECPROTEK convoy consisting of several SUVs, a scout car, a tail car, and several outriders on motorcycles.

The caravan was now lined up at curbside in front of the bank building. Security guards in plainclothes were posted on the sidewalk, on the wide brownstone stairs leading up to the bank, and under its columned portico. Sears would have liked to have armed them with machine guns, but instead settled for equipping them with big-bore, semi-automatic pistols worn in shoulder holsters concealed under suit jackets.

Machine guns and shotguns were in the possession of some of the guards remaining inside the parked vehicles, however.

The heavy security presence had caused Jack and Pete to take up their listening post a good distance away, around the corner and down the street from the bank.

They were additionally handicapped by having to operate in a city depopulated by the Everette threat. Made even trickier here in the financial district, whose closed buildings and near-deserted streets hampered their ability to follow the convoy too closely. Stealth was required, demanded.

That disadvantage was counterbalanced by the bug on Susan Keehan, which kept them apprised of their quarry's plans as soon as they were conceived.

Jack and Pete were not alone; they had Center's resources to call on. For now, though, it was necessary to minimize CTU's footprint to avoid provoking Sears's suspicions.

Center provided valuable backup in the form of its ability to tap into the city's network of traffic and surveillance cameras—both private and public. Its technicians were able to hack into them and use them without permission, without their owners being any the wiser.

Minutes dragged by, while they waited for the audio signal to return. Pete said, "Here's a wild one: what if Garros faked his own kidnapping?"

Jack considered it for a while. "I'm not ruling anything out, but what would he stand to gain by it?"

"A cool million. Not bad for a day's work. He lets Susan 'ransom' him and resumes his normal life, richer by a million bucks he's got stashed away for a rainy day. Minus whatever he cuts his accomplices in for," Pete said.

Jack was doubtful. "When he marries Susan Keehan, he'll be in line for a couple of hundred million dollars. Would he risk all that for a quick score? One that leaves him with three kills hanging over his head?"

"Maybe he needs some ready cash," Pete said, shrugging. "I don't know, the kidnapping seems out of pattern somehow. The move against Paz was a hit, a murder attempt. No plan to take him alive, just to take him out. Execution stuff. But kidnapping's a money crime. The two don't jell."

Jack said, "The kills at the Mart fit with the assault on Paz. They're both cut from the same cloth. Professional. Ruthless. They look like they came from the same gang, one that plays rough.

"Maybe Paz's escape caused them to change their plans. Paz alive and gunning for you is enough to give even a hardened murder crew the shakes. So they move to Plan B, a money crime. Crime of opportunity with an element of spur-of-the-moment planning.

"As bad as Susan's got it for Raoul, I'd say they could have shaken the Keehan money tree for a lot bigger ransom: five, ten million. One million seems a little light by comparison, as if they carefully calculated just what the market would bear for a quick, short-term fix. I'd say they were in a hurry. Could be they need the money to put some distance between them and the Colonel," Jack said.

* * *

The static hissing out of the speaker grid took on a new rhythm now, an intermittent choppiness. White noise began to blat and squawk in irregular patterns, with snatches of words starting to break through. Gibberish so far, but even that was heartening, because it meant that the audio was coming back.

Words, phrases began to emerge, several different voices: " . . . not doing too badly now, we're back on schedule—make the exchange—no guarantees, can't trust—I'll carry the briefcase—Raoul's got to be all right, he's got to!"

That last voice was unmistakably Susan's.

Pete gave a thumbs-up sign. Jack said, "We're back in business."

Pete contacted Center. "We've got them, they're coming in again."

A Center operator said, "Affirmative, we read them, too. We're picking them up off your carrier signal."

There was a flurry of activity at the bank. Gene Jasper exited through the front entrance, carrying a suitcase, presumably with a million dollars inside it. He was flanked by several sidemen who escorted him down the stairs and into a waiting SUV.

At the same time, at a side door, a circle of bodyguards emerged, Susan Keehan at its center. They maneuvered her across the sidewalk and into another SUV.

The convoy moved off, arrowing down the boulevard and out of the deserted financial district.

Jack and Pete followed, from a long way off. They could afford to give them a long leash. The Keehan crowd was Flea-bitten.

· ·

THE FOLLOWING TAKES PLACE
BETWEEN THE HOURS OF
4 P.M. AND 5 P.M.
CENTRAL DAYLIGHT TIME

· ·

Supremo Hat Company, New Orleans

Felix Monatero was a worried man. This alone illustrated
the seriousness of the situation he now found himself in.
His state of anxiety was uncharacteristic. He was a lifelong,
committed revolutionary and Fidelista with the iron self-
discipline demanded of the commandante of the Supremo
spy cell. Espionage is no game for those with weak nerves.

Monatero had been a deep-cover agent for many years.
He had not been home to Cuba for more than fifteen years,
not since first establishing his assumed identity here in the
Gulf Coast. He was no comfortable resident spy attached to
the Cuban diplomatic corps, with the priceless immunity to
arrest and prosecution it conferred.

He was an illegal, subject if caught by the U.S. counterintelligence to spending many years, if not the rest of his life, in a Federal super-max prison.

He'd devoted his life to the cause. He was a bachelor, living alone. A wife and family could only be an encumbrance at best and a vulnerability at worst for one in his profession. Being a man with natural physical urges, he satisfied them in the company of prostitutes. He rarely patronized the same one more than a few times.

No one could be allowed to get too close to him emotionally. He avoided making friends with colleagues and associates and others in the profession. The time might come when operational necessity would force him to put them in danger or even sacrifice them to gain an objective. He dared not risk having his judgment clouded by the bonds of friendship, fearing it could compromise the clear-thinking objectivity required of him as commander.

He himself had killed on behalf of the cause, having personally slain a number of men and women. Some were traitors and double agents, others merely hapless types whose removal was deemed necessary by Havana.

He'd looked his victims square in the face when shooting them at point-blank range, not flinching when struck by blood spray, brain bits, and bone fragments.

In the course of his long career, he had ordered the deaths of dozens more, rarely if ever giving a second (or even first) thought about it. His peace of mind was untroubled by compunctions about having carried out his soldierly duties. A revolutionist must obey orders without question.

He was a hard man, not given to self-doubt or second thoughts. The revolution justified all.

Yet now he was a worried man. Not for himself—never for himself—but for the cause.

Seated behind the desk in his office in the showroom of the Supremo Hat Company, he chain-smoked a succession of the little brown cigarillos he affected. He was unsure if the smoking was easing his tension or increasing it.

Even here, in the matter of smoking, his revolutionary fervor came into play. Back home in Cuba, he'd enjoyed the finest cigars. Compared to them, these cigarillos were only so much dried horse droppings.

Now, of course, he couldn't smoke those fine Cubanos, not without violating his cover. His mission required that he sanitize himself from all contact with the home island. His connections would have easily allowed him to procure a steady supply of the finest Cuban cigars. But he denied himself even that little luxury, for fear of compromising his cover.

Here, Cuban cigars were contraband; their possession was a violation of U.S. law. A little thing, but attention to detail often made the difference between concealment or exposure.

It was a sacrifice, a hardship, for a man who knew and savored the finest in cigars. Yet he continued to smoke these detestable cigarillos, puffing away, filling his office with stale clouds of smoke.

His desktop ashtray was littered with cigarillo butts. One lay smoking in the ashtray, while another was wedged in the corner of his mouth. He'd set down the first for a moment and forgotten it, lighting up another and going to work on it.

He had a troubled mind. He was being tossed and gored by a two-horned dilemma. A product of the shadow world of false fronts and double identities to which he'd devoted his life.

The problem was, how far could he trust Beltran?

The Generalissimo was a fabled figure in the spy world.

Back when Monatero was a rookie, a raw recruit in communist Cuba's intelligence service, the phantom spymaster's exploits were already the stuff of legend. As Monatero rose through the ranks, earning ever-higher security clearances that allowed him entrée into the deepest secrets of Havana's spy system, his insider's knowledge had only burnished Beltran's achievements with a brighter luster.

It was a measure of the trust that Havana reposed in his fidelity and ability that Monatero had been designated as the contact for Beltran's ongoing operations in the United States. Even in the top ranks of Cuba's intelligence corps, few were aware that Beltran was still actively engaged in operations in the homeland of the counterrevolutionary Colossus of the North.

This ultrasecret professional association—his and Beltran's—had resulted on a number of occasions in Monatero's putting the Supremo cell's resources at Beltran's disposal. Due to the paramount operational principle of compartmentalization, Monatero's agents had carried out their tasks without knowing that they were performing at Beltran's behest. They were unaware of his very existence, or at least of his role as invisible puppet master pulling their strings to carry out sensitive missions for Havana.

Only Monatero, commander of the cell, was privileged to have that knowledge. And yet even he had never come face to face with Beltran. Never met him in the flesh.

Had no idea of what he looked like, or any other details of his cover or operations in the Gulf Coast, except for those few scraps of hard fact he had managed to piece together over the years in the course of carrying out Beltran's orders.

To Monatero, Beltran existed as no more than a cleverly disguised fax message, an encrypted e-mail, or, at most, a voice that came to him over the phone. Sometimes, rarely, Beltran found it necessary to initiate telephonic communication with the spy cell commander.

Such rare encounters could hardly be called conversations. They consisted of Beltran passing clarifications or special instructions that needed to be conveyed in a timely manner.

At such times, Beltran spoke through some kind of electronic distorter that not only disguised his voice, but digitized and reassembled it so that no identifiable voiceprint could be taken from it.

Voice patterns are like fingerprints and DNA, each one is individual, unique, and belongs solely to the speaker. Should Monatero's cover ever be blown, his cell penetrated or communications surveilled by NSA or the like, the opposition would be unable to sample Beltran's voiceprint for their records.

Beltran was always prepared with the recognition codes and passwords supplied to him and changed daily by Havana. These passwords and codes were his sole and singular badge of identity.

Remarkable measures, taken to protect the identity of a unique asset. They worked: the proof of their efficacy was Beltran's continuing success in the spy game, when even most of the experts were unsure whether the Generalissimo was alive or dead.

The system worked; Monatero had never thought to question it. Until now. Because Beltran had committed the Supremo cell to an extraordinary risk level based solely on his say-so.

This was how the system worked, how it had always worked, but never before had the stakes been so high.

* * *

The Supremo cell had been uninvolved in today's dawn assault on Colonel Paz.

Uninvolved was an understatement. Monatero himself had been in the dark about it.

None of his people had participated in it. Indeed, he would have appreciated some advance notice of the strike, rather than having it fall on him like a stone dropping out of the sky.

He now knew, on the basis of information gathered from some of his sources and from Beltran's subsequent actions, that the attack had been orchestrated by none other than the Generalissimo himself.

Confirmation of his darkest suspicions on that score had come thanks to Beltran's communiqués that had reached him earlier today. He had ordered Monatero to put three of the cell's best field men under his command: Rubio, Torres, and Moreno.

Specialists in violence and sudden death.

Their mission: the abduction of Raoul Garros.

Monatero had obeyed, of course—as always. As per standard operating procedure, the assignment was handled so that Monatero's men were unaware of the identity of the man for whom they would be working.

This was accomplished easily enough, the trio being equipped with special cell phones and a specific set of new recognition codes and passwords. They would never meet Beltran or know of his participation or even existence; all they knew was that they'd been assigned by Monatero to another Havana agent, a phantom figure whose identity was top secret and must not be revealed, even to them.

Their dealings with their new temporary commander would be conducted via the cell phones. They'd carried out similar missions in the past; this was nothing new to them. They knew how to follow orders.

But Monatero was appalled by the mission.

Getting into a rumble with Venezuela's Paz was regrettable but acceptable. These things happened. Monatero knew that Paz and Beltran were partners in some dirty business: drug dealing, weapons and people smuggling, murder. All for the cause of the revolution. A regrettable necessity and hazard of the profession.

Raoul Garros, however, was a whole different order of being. He was a public figure, prominently featured on society pages and the lighter side of local television news shows. He was glamorous, dashing, rich, and handsome; a playboy. Telegenic. He'd have made good copy even if not for his engagement to Susan Keehan.

But his romance with the Keehan heiress catapulted him to new heights of celebrity. Snatching him would make not only national but international headlines. Worse, Susan Keehan's uncle, the Senator, was not unfriendly to the revolution and the Cuban cause. Why risk alienating him? He and his brother, Wilmont, the girl's father, would make bad enemies.

Well, the question was academic now. The thing had been done. Monatero only hoped it could be handled without becoming public news.

Most worrisome of all, he was unsure if this was a Havana-mandated operation or if Beltran had come up with it on his own. Not only the Supremo cell but Cuba itself had been put into an extraordinary state of risk. Stratospheric, dizzying.

All on the say-so of one man: Beltran.

Yet that was how the system had been set up by Havana, Monatero's supreme masters. It was the home island spy chiefs who'd invested such extraordinary powers in the Generalissimo, their master spy. The setup had been designed for fast action, bypassing the red tape ("red," indeed) and delay associated with going through clandestine channels to get clearance from Havana.

The flaw, perhaps fatal flaw of that system was now apparent. Ultimately, it all depended on the reliability and accuracy of Beltran's judgment. And—honesty? Depth of revolutionary commitment?

Monatero, used to working in the dark, for once longed to contact his superiors in Havana. But Beltran had specifically forbidden him to take such a course, enjoining him to maintain a blackout on communications with the Cuban high command.

Ordinarily Monatero would have accepted the dictate without question. Now, though, it increased his anxiety, deepening his ever-growing suspicions of the man. He wanted validation, assurance that his chiefs back home were apprised of the situation and approved of it.

He was seriously considering disobeying orders and contacting Havana.

Yet it was his business and duty to maintain revolutionary discipline and follow orders without question. His unease was worsened by being pinned down here at the command post, waiting for Beltran's next communiqué. Whenever that came. If ever.

Beltran, the much-vaunted Generalissimo, had made three serious if not potentially fatal mistakes. At least that was how Colonel Paz saw it.

The first, and least potentially disastrous slipup, was the use of Beatriz Ortiz as part of the assault on Paz.

For Paz knew her. Beatriz had recently operated for a time in Venezuela, in the hinterlands of the Orinoco rain forest, participating in a terror campaign against the wealthy, hidebound owners of the *estancias*, the estates, the sprawling ranches and plantationlike farmlands that had been cleared out of the jungle and employed countless numbers of *campesinos*, peasants, to do the donkey work on near-starvation wages.

The land barons would never reconcile with the new Chavez regime; they were the most ultra of the ultraconservative counterrevolutionary faction.

So it was better, according to Caracas's lights, that they be done away with, liquidated, and the survivors frightened away from their holdings and into exile.

This would be accomplished by the use of radical militias and death squads, operating in-country, living off the land, and covertly supplied with food and arms by the government. The great estates could then be broken up and redistributed to the peasants, further ensuring their gratitude and dependency on President Chavez's program of twenty-first-century socialism.

It was the kind of operation that was tailor-made for the likes of Beatriz Ortiz, who specialized in revolutionary activities in agrarian and rural regions, as she had done so notably in Colombia with the FARC militia.

Paz was a confirmed urban dweller by birth and inclination; his bailiwick was the cities of Venezuela. But as a top hand in President Chavez's secret police, there was little that he didn't know about the regime's clandestine activities in town and country.

He had met Beatriz Ortiz once or twice in passing in the capital at strategy sessions for solidifying the grip of the revolution in Venezuela and exporting it to neighboring countries.

When the attack at the Golden Pole went down and he'd

spotted her taking potshots at him, he'd instantly recognized her.

Beltran's second mistake, according to the Colonel's reasoning, was in underestimating Martello Paz.

This high-and-mighty Cuban revolutionary, Fidel Castro's favorite spymaster, had disdained the Venezuelan as a johnny-come-lately to the world socialist cause, a mere secret policeman, thug, and enforcer. A useful idiot.

He had forgotten, or never taken notice of, the fact that Paz himself had run a vast and efficient spy system, one using a legion of informers, double agents, and operatives from all levels of society, from shoeshine boys in the slums to elegant hostesses in the most exclusive salons.

Paz made it his business to know about those he did business with. Beltran was no exception. Paz was a survivalist by nature and needed no encouragement to open a file on the Generalissimo and gather every fact he could about him and his New Orleans operation.

He'd unearthed vital facts about Beltran's shadow organization, including the man's own tight-knit personal cadre, as well as his association with the Supremo spy cell, which he called upon from time to time for various services as required.

Paz's spies had spotted Beatriz Ortiz coming from several meetings with Beltran; she was part of a small clique of freelance operatives that he kept insulated and independent of his Supremo cell connections.

Beltran's third, and most serious mistake, was botching the hit on Paz and leaving him alive.

In a sense, this could be regarded as an extension of his second mistake; namely, underestimating Paz.

A fatal oversight, if Paz had anything to do with it.

* * *

Beltran wasn't the only one with an organization here in New Orleans. Paz ran a formidable machine himself.

The Venezuelan Consulate and LAGO offices, with their vital shield of diplomatic immunity, both served as platforms for his spy operations. Yet even they had to be insulated from the down-and-dirty mechanics of violence and murder so necessary to maintain discipline and instill the respect that comes from fear.

Those chores were handled by an independent enforcement arm, overseen by Paz himself.

Running a death squad was old hat to him. He'd specialized in violence since boyhood days, first as an up-and-coming street gang tough, later as a police officer.

Many were the ace murder teams he'd put together and honed to perfection.

When first posted to the New Orleans consulate, he'd selected a group of his top killers from Venezuela to accompany him on his new assignment.

He played a rough game. The game was always rough when high-volume narcotics dealing was involved, and Paz was in the trade up to his eyebrows—professionally and personally.

Why, it was his patriotic chore. No government, not even an oil-rich state like Venezuela, could afford to ignore the sky-high profits generated by the drug trade. There was no such thing as having too much money.

Besides, the narcotics trade was vital in developing contacts in all layers of New Orleans society. Remarkable, how many of the city's wealthy elite craved illicit drugs.

Product was power, and Paz moved plenty of product. That required muscle and guns, and he had plenty of both of them, too.

Earlier today, from his hideout at the abandoned Jiffy

Pump gas station, Paz had set the wheels in motion to gather his death squad for action.

Why had Beltran betrayed him? For his own personal profit, no doubt. That was how Paz's mind worked. Nobody did anything unless there was something in it for him.

What was in it for Beltran? Was he simply following orders from Havana, reflecting an abrupt and murderous turn against Venezuela?

Not likely, not with all the free oil and free money they were getting from Caracas, thanks to Chavez's genuine admiration for Fidel Castro and the irresistible opportunity to stick it to Uncle Sam by siding with communist Cuba.

So where was the heat coming from? From Beltran himself?

It was possible; it was possible. Beltran was a deep player; not even his own ostensible masters in Havana could know all he was into.

He and Paz were joined at the hip in a number of illicit operations: narcotics, first and foremost; but also gunrunning; espionage and sabotage operations; smuggling of priceless pre-Colombian artifacts and relics; and contraband shipments of oil and gas.

Maybe Beltran got greedy and decided to X-out Paz and keep all the profits for himself. Maybe he'd sold out Paz to the American Mafia, New Orleans branch, a competitor in the drug trade. Or to a rival Latin American drug cartel.

Why the betrayal? Paz would ask him, should Beltran be taken alive. Not a top priority for the Colonel from Caracas.

Whatever the reason, Beltran had committed a capital crime for which there could be only one penalty.

Cross Martello Paz, and die.

Now, as evening came on, the Colonel had his murder

team in place, staked out on a rise several blocks away from the Supremo Hat Company.

There were two vehicles and eight men. The men were all stone killers; Colonel Paz being the stoniest of them all.

He scanned the building through a pair of binoculars. There were two men on the roof. They tried to keep out of sight, but the parapet was low and they couldn't help but skyline above it from time to time. A couple of others were posted around the structure at street level, on the corner, and in the parking lot at the rear of the building.

Paz lowered the field glasses. The approaching storm had brought on a premature dusk. He would unleash the strike in an hour or so, when the gloom had deepened to provide his death squad with the cover of darkness.

· ·

THE FOLLOWING TAKES PLACE
BETWEEN THE HOURS OF
5 P.M. AND 6 P.M.
CENTRAL DAYLIGHT TIME

· ·

Playsquare Day Care Center, New Orleans

An unusual gathering was massed at the Playsquare Day
Care Center, located about an eighth of a mile from City
Hall. It had been commandeered by Susan Keehan and her
EXECPROTEK contingent.

The modest neighborhood featured office buildings
tenanted mostly by mid-sized legal firms and insurance
agencies. The day care center was in a two-story building
fronting the north side of a vest pocket–sized park. Ordinarily open on Saturdays, it was closed today because of the
storm threat.

Several SUVs and dark-colored, late model cars were
parked in front of the building.

The nonprofit day care center was owned and operated
by the Keehan Humanistics Fund, one of many charitable

facilities it maintained in the city. Susan's Free Raoul Action Squad was temporarily perched at the site, using it as a staging area. A place where they could wait for final word from the kidnappers as to where and how to deliver the ransom money in exchange for Garros.

The abductor chief was impatient, eager to move fast. He'd told them during his most recent call that he'd be giving them their instructions within an hour or so, definitely no more than two hours.

The day care center had been chosen by Mylon Sears. It was centrally located with easy access to all parts of the city. A business zone on a Saturday, it would have been quiet and depopulated even if not for the hurricane warning. There weren't a lot of civilian types around to gawk and wonder about the heavy security detail.

The day care facility, a KHF asset, could be used without question. Today, now, it was deserted, save for a sole caretaker.

He liked his job and was easily persuaded to sit tight and mind his own business; one of Sears's men kept him under watch anyway, to make sure he didn't make any outside calls to his wife or friends to report the exciting news that Susan Keehan herself was in the building, thus spreading the word and attracting attention.

Susan, Sears, and the rest of the security squad sat and waited.

So, too, did Jack Bauer and Pete Malo sit and wait, in their SUV parked at the southeastern corner of the park opposite the day care center. Other CTU operatives were posted at key intersections in the area, maintaining the lowest of low profiles.

Mylon Sears was no fool; he and his men were professionals, and would be quick to detect a too-heavy presence of watchers. For the same reason, no CTU helicopters had taken to the skies above the area; that would have been another tip-off alerting Sears that he was under observation.

Yet Sears would also have been suspicious if no attempts had been made to follow him, in the aftermath of the abduction and triple murders.

Earlier when the Keehan convoy had first left the Mega Mart building, it had been tailed by a couple of unmarked CTU vehicles. Their purpose was to be discovered in the act of shadowing the convoy.

Sears, ready for the eventuality of tail cars, had roving chase cars of his own in the area. He put them to use, blocking intersections along the route, physically obstructing the shadowers with "stalled" vehicles and faked traffic jams to thwart pursuit.

Satisfied that he had eluded the tail cars, Sears continued on his way in confidence.

Jack and Pete had the Flea bugging device planted on Susan Keehan. Since Sears stayed right beside his client, they knew what he knew the moment he knew it, including the convoy's planned destinations. That enabled them to proceed to the locales in a roundabout way without being observed by EXECPROTEK spotters, first at the bank and later at the day care center.

The Flea continued to remain operational and undetected, sending a steady stream of chatter to their transceiver set.

Now, as the agents waited, a message came in from CTU Center. Since they were continually monitoring the Flea's output on the transceiver's speaker grid, they used secure, scrambled cells to maintain contact with the Center.

Jack took the call, while Pete stayed on top of the Flea stream. The Center operator said, "We have a positive ID on the driver of the Paz hit team."

The audio came in through the cell, while a corresponding video feed appeared on the SUV's dashboard monitor screen.

A photograph appeared of the dead driver, a man with a potato face, meatball nose, and jug-handle ears. The monitor went to split-screen, one window depicting a full frontal face and another a profile view.

Jack's eyes narrowed with interest; the feeling that he'd seen that face before but couldn't place had irked him, and he was intensely interested in the solution of the mystery.

The operator said, "The subject was identified by Interpol." Interpol, the international police organization based in Brussels and covering the European beat.

New images came on screen, police mug shots from the look of them, the tip-off being the row of numbers being held under the subject's face. He looked about ten years younger but still very much the same, except that the crew-cut hair was a bit thicker and darker and the lumpish face slightly less saggy and jowly.

The operator said, "He's Hermann Ost. German by birth, although he hasn't been in his home country for years, due to a number of outstanding warrants out on him for murder, attempted murder, numerous counts of violent assault, rape, illegal possession of firearms and explosives, gunrunning, racketeering and drug dealing.

"That's his criminal dossier in his homeland. He's also wanted in several other West European countries for similar offenses. But these crimes are only incidental to his main source of livelihood.

"Ost is a mercenary, a professional soldier for hire. His history is too long to go into now, but here are some of the highlights—or lowlights, depending on your point of view.

"He first enlisted in the German Army, serving for eight years and reaching the rank of top sergeant before being court-martialed and dishonorably discharged for striking an officer. Next he surfaced in Africa, serving in various mercenary legions in Rwanda and the Congo. He achieved a certain level of notoriety as part of an extermination unit working for Liberian dictator Charles Taylor. He followed that up with extensive action in the Blood Diamond conflicts in Sierra Leone.

"He headed an outfit protecting foreign oil field workers in Nigeria, until he was implicated in a scheme to kidnap and hold for ransom the same executives he was supposed to be guarding.

"Africa being too hot for him, he moved his theater of operations to the Balkans, where he worked for most of the nineties. Since then, he's plied his trade in Indonesia, Malaysia, and East Timor. Most recently, reported sightings have placed him in the Persian Gulf emirates and Lebanon."

Memory returned to Jack with a rush. Now he knew why the potato-faced killer had seemed so familiar.

Before joining CTU, Jack had been a member of the U.S. Army's elite Delta Force. He'd participated in a number of actions carried out in the Balkans, where Christian Serbia and Croatia had warred with each other and made war on predominantly Muslim Bosnia. The conflict had produced mass atrocities, mass murder, and mass graves, leaving at least one hundred thousand dead.

With the European Union and United Nations paralyzed into impotency, the United States was able to act. At the height of the madness, the Serbian leadership under Milošević made ready to escalate its program of "ethnic cleansing"—that is, genocide—against thousands of Muslims in the borderlands. Not that the Serbs were any

worse than their antagonists, just quicker off the mark to do
to their foes what their foes planned to do to them.

Someone had to cool down the conflict before it escalated
into the neighboring states of Albania, Macedonia, and beyond. Washington used Delta Force to put out the hottest
fires, sending in secret teams to assassinate key Serbian
warlords, decimate their militias, and destroy their arsenals.
These were the blackest of black ops, covert missions that
were kept secret even from allied NATO forces operating in
the region as peacekeepers.

Bosnia, too, was not without its own clandestine backers.
Legions of foreign fighters flocked to the area, militant Muslims recruited from throughout the Middle East, armed and
financed by wealthy Saudis. Their numbers were augmented
by professional soldiers who served for pay. Top pay.

Among them was Major Marc Vollard, a mercenary
commander who organized and led a wickedly effective
counterforce to the Serb militias.

One can't be too picky in wartime. On several occasions,
Jack's Delta Force team had found it expedient to work in
conjunction with Vollard, using his troops as auxiliaries for
backup and support.

Once the Serbian fire had been damped down, however,
Washington turned a hard eye on its erstwhile ally. Vollard
was amoral, pragmatic, and ruthlessly efficient.

When the Serbs massacred a Bosnian village, he massacred two Serbian villages. By the standards of international
law, he was as much of a war criminal as any who'd ever
been dragged before a court of justice in the Hague.

One attribute of a successful mercenary is to know when
to get out of town. His sixth sense for survival operating at
full bore, Vollard abruptly ceased operations in the area and
vanished, departing for parts unknown.

That suited Washington, which preferred that its temporary alliance of convenience with the mercenary major be filed and forgotten, never to see the light of day.

Jack told the operator, "Let me talk to Cal Randolph."

After a pause, Cal came on the line. "What is it, Jack?"

Jack said, "Now I remember where I've seen Ost before. Fifteen years ago, in the Balkans, he was a top noncom with Major Marc Vollard's mercenary legion. He was part of Vollard's leadership cadre, the inner circle who follows Vollard from hot spot to hot spot, serving as his core support system."

Cal said, "Interesting. I can see where Ost ties in with Dixie Lee, they're both gunrunners on the same political wavelength. But where do they fit in with a brainy Maoist shooter like Beatriz Ortiz? Or, for that matter, the Generalissimo, Beltran?"

Jack said, "I don't know—yet—but I'll tell you this. If Ost is on the scene, Vollard can't be too far away."

"We'll run a trace on Vollard and see what comes up," Cal said. "Oh, and Jack—one more thing."

"Shoot."

"Susan Keehan's compromised in this business— Topham's and Beauclerk's death ensured that. That doesn't mean that her uncle, Senator Keehan, can't do us a lot of damage if things go sour on this ransom deal."

"We'll rig it so we don't make our move until the exchange is made, Cal. But it could go sour anyway, if Sears drops the ball or the kidnappers do something stupid."

"Then CTU will be in the clear. Just so long as we have deniability."

Jack said, "We'll be careful."

Cal said, "Good. I'll get back to you as soon as we've got something on Vollard." Cal signed off; the Center operator did likewise.

A sultry blast of wind blew up from the south, whipping up all kinds of dirt and chaff, sending old newspapers swirling and spinning in midair. A trash can was knocked over and blown into the street, where it rolled around on its side in several half circles before another booming gust came up, picked it up bodily, and tossed it ten feet farther down the road

Jack and Pete looked at each other. Jack said, "Storm's rising."

. . . .

THE FOLLOWING TAKES PLACE
BETWEEN THE HOURS OF
6 P.M. AND 7 P.M.
CENTRAL DAYLIGHT TIME

. . . .

Supremo Hat Company, New Orleans

Fear, real fear, is a physical thing, born not of the mind but
of the body.

At its most extreme, it can cause death. Death by fright
is no myth, but a reality, as the victim's heart bursts under
supreme shock. A few notches down, it can induce paralysis
or the loss of intimate bodily functions. Slightly lower on
the scale, it can induce waves of nausea, cotton-dry mouth,
loss of feeling in the extremities, and a drop in body tem-
perature that is popularly known by the expression, "blood
runs cold."

It was this last group of symptoms that now afflicted Felix Monatero as he sat at his desk in his showroom office,
staring at the monitor screen of a laptop and not seeing it,
his awareness limited to a sick-making body terror.

He'd just received a Triple-AAA urgent communiqué from Havana, a missive that was at a level so far above top secret that it could only be classified as cosmic.

His masters back on the home island were in a state of near-hysteria, one that could not be disguised by the officialese in which their urgent message was couched.

Decrypted, it boiled down to one frantic query: What is going on in New Orleans?

Elaborations on the theme included questions as to whether Monatero had lost his mind or merely turned traitor. Was he trying to start a war between Cuba and Venezuela by his attack on that friend of the revolution and trusted Chavez hatchet man, Colonel Paz? Or for that matter, with the United States? Trust the gringos to find a way to exploit the street violence into a casus belli, a cause for war, to unleash their long-held dream of stamping out by force the Fidelista revolution!

The big picture had emerged from the fog of deception, and it wasn't pretty. Monatero had been played. Havana had never ordered the assassination attempt on Paz, was in fact totally in the dark about the motivation and meaning of the assault.

They blamed Monatero for the debacle, unaware that it was their favorite, Beltran the Generalissimo, who deserved all the blame.

Havana had yet to learn the worst of it, that Beltran had used a trio of Supremo cell action men to kidnap Raoul Garros. Monatero shuddered to think of the reaction that would follow when they discovered that bit of bad news.

It was all clear to him now—too late—that his suspicions had been right from the start. Beltran had gone into business for himself. Who knew? Maybe he'd gone even over to the arch-villains in Washington, selling out to them as part of a plot against Cuba.

He might easily have burned the Supremo cell, exposing it to his new paymasters, whoever they were. Which meant that the site was no longer even partially secure, but subject at any moment to raids by Federal agents.

The revelation of supreme treachery had temporarily caused Monatero to go into brain lock, the gears of his mind jamming and stalling.

Now, as the initial shock wore off, his mind started to unfreeze, thoughts and schemes beginning to percolate through his stunned psyche.

The end was not yet; it was not too late. All was not lost. There was still time for him to contact his three enforcers, Rubio, Torres, and Moreno, and alert them to Beltran's betrayal. They could free Raoul Garros, short-circuiting the plot and minimizing the worst of the damage.

Havana would be informed that Beltran had gone rogue, using his extraordinary position in the spy hierarchy to bend and warp the Supremo cell to his own sinister purposes, and that Monatero and the rest of his people were blameless.

Then the Supremo cell must shut down, destroying all potentially incriminating hardware, software, and documents, while the personnel scattered in all directions, each of them finding a hole to hide in to thwart the hunters that were sure to follow.

All this must be done, and quickly—but first Rubio, the leader of the action trio, must be contacted immediately to abort the mission and free Garros.

Monatero reached into the breast pocket of his jacket, clawing out the cell phone that would put him in touch with Rubio. His hands shook, causing him to fumble with the cell, nearly dropping it.

Recovering, he got a good hold on it and lifted the lid to initiate communication—

The world blew up in his face.

* * *

Colonel Paz divided his death squad into two groups. The first included him, Carrancha, Vasco, and Aguilar. The second was headed by his lieutenant, Fierro, sided by Septiembre, Sancho, and Ramon.

Paz and his group rode in the Explorer he'd had stashed in the Jiffy Pump safe house; the machine was armored and fitted with bulletproof glass. Fierro's group was in a second SUV, one lacking such hardened extras. Rank has its privileges.

The Explorer was driven by Vasco, a former taxi driver in Caracas, whose mad whirl of heedless, anarchic traffic was good training for a getaway car driver.

Paz wore a bulletproof vest and was armed with a Kalashnikov assault rifle complete with grenade launcher, plus a pair of pistols stuck in the hip pockets of his pants. He rode shotgun, sitting in the front passenger seat; Carrancha and Aguilar were in the backseat.

The second SUV was driven by Septiembre, he of the sad eyes and mournful face.

Fierro had declined the option of riding in the front passenger seat, relegating it to Ramon. With the vehicle unarmored, the backseat was perhaps marginally safer than the front. Fierro rode in the rear, along with Sancho.

All death squad members were heavily armed with assault rifles, machine pistols, and shotguns, as well as a multiplicity of handguns. Paz and Fierro, the respective leaders of their squads, were also each equipped with several hand grenades.

The vehicles stood idling on a side street, screened from the direct sightlines of the Supremo Hat Company building.

Now Paz gave the go-ahead hand signal, the two SUVs rounding a corner and entering the square opposite the

Supremo site. Engines roared; wheels spun, burning rubber, as the murder machines lurched forward, charging the building.

Closing in on the site, the SUVs parted company, Paz's vehicle hurtling toward the front of the hat company building, the other whipping around toward the rear.

A Supremo sentry was posted on the corner in front of the building, armed with a couple of handguns hidden under his jacket. Looking like any other ordinary idler, standing there loafing and smoking a cigarette, he looked up to see the Explorer coming at him. His mouth fell open, the cigarette clinging to his lower lip. He pulled a pair of handguns out of the waistband of his pants.

Paz shouted, "Get him!"

Vasco wrestled the steering wheel to one side, swerving the vehicle to put the sentry directly in its path. The sentry did some fancy high-stepping to try to get out of the way, but the Explorer clipped him with its right front fender.

A booming impact sent a shudder through the SUV, the sentry flying off into the air like he'd been dropkicked. The arc of his trajectory was interrupted by a lamppost; he flopped to the base of it, motionless.

There was a double bump as first the Explorer's front wheels and then the rear wheels hopped the curb as it plowed across the concrete apron fronting the building.

Vasco stomped the brake, slamming the vehicle to a halt. He and Paz were wearing seat belts; Carrancha and Aguilar were not, and the sudden stop bounced them around in the backseat.

Paz flung open his door and lunged sideways, in such a hurry to get into the fight that he'd forgotten to unfasten his seat belt, which caught him up short. Cursing, he hit the release, shrugged out of the harness, and hit the sidewalk with both feet at the same time, dropping into a crouch and bringing up the Kalash. The Kalash was fitted on the underside of the barrel with a loaded grenade launcher.

On the roof of the building, two riflemen popped up, showing themselves above the waist-high parapet, scrambling to draw a bead on Paz.

Paz beat them to the punch and let fly, lofting the grenade in a high arc that sent it plopping on the rooftop behind the riflemen.

It exploded in a booming fireball that filled the roof with red light, heat, and smoke.

A fragmentation grenade, it sieved the riflemen with shrapnel, the concussion picking up one of them and tossing him off the roof, to land with a splattery thud on the sidewalk in front of the building. The other staggered around for a few steps before flopping down out of sight behind the parapet.

On Paz's right, the second SUV had crashed through the locked gates of the chain-link fence surrounding the parking lot. They flew open as the vehicle bulled through.

A couple of armed men ran out from behind the back of the building into the lot, opening fire with handguns at the oncoming SUV.

Ramon leaned out of the passenger side front window, firing a machine pistol.

Sancho stuck his assault rifle barrel out of the left side window behind the driver's seat, shooting at the Supremo gunmen. He had a better line of fire on them than Ramon, since they were on the left side of the vehicle.

Incoming rounds racketed against the front of the SUV, punching into the grille, headlights, and engine block. The SUV kept on coming.

A shot tore a hole through the top of the middle of the

windshield, passing so close to Septiembre that he could feel it whizzing past his head.

Sancho squeezed off some bursts but missed his targets; he held down the trigger and burned off one continuous rapid-fire blast. That took down one of the gunmen, and then the SUV was rounding the corner of the back of the building.

The second gunman broke to the right of the vehicle, running for cover and instead running into gunfire from Ramon's machine pistol.

The SUV slewed around on the gravel and loose dirt of the lot, the wheels on its left side lifting off the ground, threatening for a breathless instant to overturn the top-heavy machine.

They touched ground again, the machine skidding to a stop in a plume of pebbles and dirt clouds. It stood broadside at right angles to the loading platform.

For a few beats, the vehicle was hidden behind a curtain of dust. By the same token, the back of the building was obscured, too. The sectioned metal door of the loading dock bay was raised and thrown open.

Winds blew, dispersing the dust cloud. The murk cleared, revealing a machine gun just inside the loading bay. A .50-caliber machine gun, mounted on a tripod, manned by two defenders.

The gunner sat with crossed legs behind the weapon, gripping the twin rear handles with both hands, his thumb poised over the firing button. The other stood on one knee beside him, holding the cartridge belt lightly in his open hands. His job was to feed the belt steadily into the machine gun, avoiding snags.

Fierro, sitting on the right side of the backseat, flung back the sliding door and threw himself out of the SUV before the firing began. He hit the dirt, belly-crawling behind the right rear wheel for cover.

The others in the vehicle lacked his hair-trigger reflexes. They sat frozen in place for the split-second before the gunner opened fire.

The machine gun streamed big-caliber, high-velocity slugs into the SUV, making a sound like a jackhammer tearing up pavement.

It tore up the SUV, ventilating it at high speed, sieving it with rounds that tore through its shell like it was so much cardboard. Septiembre, Sancho, and Ramon were shot to pieces.

The machine gunner was an enthusiast. Standard doctrine stated that the weapon should be fired in a succession of short quick bursts, but he was having none of that. He held down the firing stud, loosing a continuous blast of bullets, swiveling the machine gun back and forth on its tripod, working over the SUV like he was spraying it with a fire hose.

Peppering it with hundreds of rounds in less than a minute. In that time, the gun barrel turned red-hot.

Fierro lay flat and at right angles to the right rear wheel, hugging the ground, eating dirt. The machine gunner was shooting high, the rounds passing harmlessly over Fierro's prone form. The SUV rattled and rocked on its chassis like it was throwing a piston rod.

The sideman handling the cartridge belt feed got so excited by the havoc wrought by the machine gun that he got careless and allowed the belt to get twisted. Causing the weapon to jam. There was a sudden silence as it ceased to operate.

That was what Fierro was waiting for. He had a couple of grenades stowed in the side pockets of his utility vest. Rising, he took out a grenade, pulled the pin, and counted

to three before tossing it overhand at the open bay door.
Throwing himself flat on the ground as soon as the grenade
left his hand.

The machine gunner and sideman could see the grenade
coming at them, fat and sassy. It hit the floor a few feet in
front of them, then blew.

In front of the building, Aguilar and Carrancha had piled
out of the Explorer, weapons in hand. Paz stood on one
knee, fitting a grenade into the launcher sleeve below the
barrel of the Kalash.

Aguilar moved up beside him on his left, only to step into
a burst fired from inside the building. He wore no flak jacket
and the gunfire chopped him in the middle, spraying Paz
with blood spatter.

Joaquin, the big Supremo bodyguard, stood framed in
the open front door, working a leveled assault rifle. Standing there outlined in the doorway, he made a sweet target
for Carrancha, who returned fire.

Joaquin jackknifed, falling back into the interior and out
of sight.

Paz shouted, "The window!"

Carrancha's big, bearish form dropped into a crouch as
he poured some slugs into the hat company's big plate-glass
display window. It came apart, glass shards falling like
sheets of ice.

Paz fired a grenade through the hole where the window
had been, into the showroom. The blast was satisfyingly
spectacular.

Around back, Fierro reached into the rear of the SUV, grabbing a sawed-off riot shotgun from the floor where he'd
left it.

It was his personal weapon—it cleared out a room with

authority. It was fully loaded and there were more twelve-gauge shotgun shells stuffed in the front pockets of his vest. Along with another grenade in a side pocket.

The shotgun seemed to have survived the fusillade intact and unharmed but he checked it to make sure. It worked fine.

He caught a glimpse of Septiembre, Ramon, and Sancho. They looked like they been put through the human equivalent of a paper shredder.

Smoke poured out of the loading platform's open bay door. Fierro slipped around the rear of the SUV, charging the platform from the side, out of the direct line of fire of anyone who might still be left in the back of the building.

On the left side of the platform was a flight of stone steps. He climbed them, flattening his back against the wall to the side of the open bay door.

He peeked around the corner, inside. Just beyond the opening, there was a mess on the floor that had been the machine gunner and his sideman.

Fierro stuck a little more of his head around the wall edge, craning for a view.

Someone inside shot at him, the rounds tearing off pieces of concrete and spraying his face with stinging stone chips.

He ducked back, covering. The shots had come from deeper inside the space. He dug a shotgun shell out of his pocket and tossed it into the building, drawing another blast of gunfire.

Now he had a better idea of where the shooter was. He pulled the pin on a grenade and lobbed it in, underhand, in the appropriate direction.

A blast boomed, red and white light flashing out of a roiling smoke cloud.

Fierro rushed inside, moving off to one side, taking cover

behind a head-high stack of wooden pallets. Waiting for the smoke to clear before continuing with the cleanup.

The showroom was a shambles of smoky wreckage. Overhead light fixtures swung at the end of loose wires dangling from the ceiling; clouds of plaster, sawdust, and straw hung in mid-air.

Colonel Paz prowled around, holding a leveled pistol at waist height, looking for Beltran. The big killing was done, and for close-in work, a pistol was better than a rifle.

The Supremo defenders were dead, all but one or two of them in the back of the building who were only critically wounded. Carrancha and Fierro were finishing them off, delivering the coup de grâce of a bullet through the brain.

Vasco was outside, guarding the Explorer and keeping watch.

Not much mopping needed to be done in the showroom area. Joaquin lay just inside the front entrance, where he'd been cut down. Mrs. Ybarra lay sprawled nearby.

She'd been standing in front of the display window when Carrancha had shot it out.

Slugs had stitched her across the middle, nearly cutting her in half.

Paz went through the reception area, into the front office. Smoke clouds drifted across his field of vision, obscuring his view. Holes gaped in ceiling and walls, revealing broken wooden latticework and cratered plaster.

The body of a man lay facedown on the floor. His hair was white and his head was turned away from Paz, hiding his face.

Paz got excited: was this his man?

He crossed to him. The body lay so his hands were in plain sight, empty of any weapons. Paz still couldn't see his face. He toed the body, wedging a booted foot under it and flipping it over, so that it rolled over on its back and came to a rest faceup.

Disappointment. It wasn't Beltran after all. The hair had fooled Paz. What he thought was the white hair of age was an illusion, caused by a powdery covering of plaster dust that had fallen from the cracked and riven ceiling.

The other groaned, closed eyes fluttering open. Blinking.

Paz said, "Not dead yet? I can fix that . . ."

The other's glazed eyes came into focus, fastening on the man who stood above him, arm at his side, pointing a big-bore pistol barrel at his head.

He gasped, "*El Colonello.*" The Colonel.

Paz grinned, his ego tickled as always by any sign of recognition that comported with his inflated idea of his own status. Especially by one who could be considered a colleague, a fellow professional in the field. Not professional enough, though, or their positions would be reversed, with Paz flat on his back on the floor and the other holding the gun.

He said, "You know me, eh? I know you, too, Monatero."

Earlier during the fracas, a grenade blast had picked up Monatero and bounced him off a wall. The wall was hard and he was soft and now he was all broken up inside. There wasn't much of him left, and what there was, was fading fast.

Paz said, "Surprised? You shouldn't be. I know many things. I know you're the boss of this outfit—you were."

Monatero found he could speak if he spoke slowly and carefully, his lips shaping each word. "So . . . Beltran didn't get you."

"I'm the one who does the getting."

"You can't kill me, I'm already dead. Thanks to him."

"That's all right, I'll finish the job," Paz said.

Monatero smiled, allowing himself a whisper of a chuckle. Anything stronger would finish him off. Paz was half puzzled, half amused. "What's so funny? Tell me the joke, so I can laugh, too."

Monatero said, "Beltran's killed me . . . and yet, I've never even met the man."

Paz frowned, waving the gun barrel like a chiding finger. "Don't lie. It's a sin to go to your Maker with a lie on your soul."

Monatero's voice was a husky whisper, as remote and distant as if it already emanated from the tomb. "No lie, it's the truth. I've never met Beltran face to face, never seen him. His identity's a mystery to me. I've only talked to him over the phone. I didn't have a need to know, wasn't important enough."

Paz said, "A dying man shouldn't play games."

"No games."

"You really don't know who he is?"

"No. Not even now, at the end."

"That is funny," Paz said, grinning.

Monatero was sinking fast, but he had more to get in. He took a new tack. "Garros—Garros . . ."

Paz said, "What about him?"

"It's not too late. You can save him."

Paz snorted. "Save him? From what? Too much wine, women, and song?"

Monatero nodded, as if to himself. "Then you don't know. He's been kidnapped. Beltran's got him."

Paz said, "I think maybe you've gone off your head."

"You must listen."

"Must I?"

"Yes. For the sake of your country. And mine." Sparks

blazed up behind Monatero's fast-glazing eyes. "For the revolution!"

Paz was unimpressed. "That fancy talk's too much for me. I'm a simple man."

Monatero said, "Do you want Beltran to make a fool of you?"

"No one makes a fool of Martello Paz!"

"Beltran's a traitor. He went off on his own. Havana had nothing to do with the attack on you. All Beltran's doing."

"Why?"

"Perhaps because he knew you'd kill him for holding Garros for ransom. A million-dollar ransom."

Paz rubbed his chin, thoughtful. Off his head or not, Monatero was making sense. "A million dollars is a lot of money."

Monatero said, "On my dying breath, I swear to you that Cuba had nothing to do with it."

Paz shrugged. "Sure, sure, but what about the money? The million dollars?"

A glint of shrewdness came into Monatero's eyes. "You don't want Beltran to have it."

"I want Beltran dead!"

"I can tell you how to get him."

Paz went down on one knee beside Monatero, wanting to believe, the knowledge of that want making him cautious. He said, "You don't know who Beltran is, never met him, but you can tell me how to find him. How is that?"

Monatero said, "He's using my men to trade Garros for the ransom. My men! But I know where the exchange is going to be made."

Paz said, "Where?"

Monatero told him. Paz said, "If true, I'll send word to Caracas that Beltran went off on his own and Havana had nothing to do with the plot. You have my word on that."

Monatero said, "You believe me, then."

"I'll believe you when I've got Beltran looking down the barrel of my gun."

"You will, if you act quickly."

Paz said, "One good turn deserves another. Now I'll do you a favor. This is funny—you know who Beltran is, you've known all the time."

Monatero said, "No, no."

"Yes. You know him but you don't know him. It all makes sense to me now and it will to you, too, when I tell you who he is."

Paz told him Beltran's true identity, who he really was. Monatero looked like a sleeper trying to awaken from a nightmare and failing. "No . . . it can't be! *Him*—Beltran?"

Paz nodded. "That's right."

The sheer, outrageous audacity of the revelation struck Monatero as funny. The funniest thing in the world. Too bad the joke was on him.

Or almost. It would be even funnier when Beltran found himself cheated of a million-dollar ransom and, with luck, face to face with Paz, thanks to what Monatero had told him.

Monatero laughed out loud. The effort was too much for him, snapping some vital thread inside him, the one that held him to life. He coughed, choking, blood coming out of his mouth.

He shuddered and died.

Paz went into the showroom, stuck his head in the door to the back of the building, and called for Fierro and Carrancha. He said, "All done?"

Fierro nodded. "All done. None left alive."

Paz said, "Here, too. Let's go."

The three of them piled out the front door. Vasco saw

them coming and jumped behind the wheel of the SUV. The trio hurried toward it.

Gunfire blasted, hitting Carrancha in the back, ripping through him.

Paz and Fierro ducked, crouching, looking around in all directions for the shooter. More gunfire followed, coming from above, ripping up the pavement a few feet away from them.

Fierro spotted the shooter first. It was a rifleman on the roof, the one who hadn't fallen to the ground. Mortally wounded by the grenade, he still had enough left to try and take out the enemy before they made their getaway.

Fierro tagged him with a shotgun blast in the chest and head, knocking him backward out of sight.

Carrancha lay on the ground, bleeding from several bullet holes in the back, arms and legs thrashing, gasping for gurgling breath.

Fierro said, "Of all the filthy luck—"

Paz said, "We can't leave any wounded behind. He would do the same for me; I would expect no less."

Carrancha saw what was coming and raised a hand, pawing empty air, pleading, "No—no, don't!"

Paz shot him, putting a bullet in the back of his head.

Paz and Fierro hopped into the Explorer. Vasco drove off almost before they were entirely inside, putting distance between them and what was left of the Supremo Hat Company.

Paz reached inside his shirt, squeezing the talisman of Saint Barbara. Breathing a silent prayer of thanks to the dark spirit that was his guardian angel.

. . . .

THE FOLLOWING TAKES PLACE
BETWEEN THE HOURS OF
7 P.M. AND 8 P.M.
CENTRAL DAYLIGHT TIME

. . . .

Sad Hill, New Orleans

The site of the swap was a footbridge spanning the Long
Canal in Sad Hill, a forlorn patch of lowlands south of East
New Orleans. East New Orleans was one of the most impoverished neighborhoods in the city. Sad Hill was a few
notches below that.

Named for Governor Huey Long, who'd had it dug in the
early 1930s, the canal was part of an intricate system of wa-
terways and pumping stations designed to prevent flooding.
It ran roughly north-south through Sad Hill.

Its east bank was a weedy field sloping to a low rise. Its
sole distinguishing feature was a knoll on which was sited
an ancient cemetery, Our Lady of Sorrows, which had given
the area the name of Sad Hill. The graveyard had been
abandoned close to a century ago.

Beyond it, farther east, the rise topped out into a ridge-line running parallel to the canal. It had been cleared and flattened and now served as a power trail, along which ran a row of steel pylons carrying high-tension electric wires. The towers were placed high enough to avoid being swept away by floodwaters.

Linking the east and west banks was a footbridge with a cast-iron framework and a wooden plank bed. It was old, but its antique construction had survived Katrina better than other newer, more modern spans.

On the west side of the bridge was a deserted neighbor-hood, a tract of ramshackle huts and burned-out ruins. The few paved roads were veined with cracks, out of which grew waist-high weeds. Most of the cross streets were dirt tracks.

The canal, like so many others, had failed under Katrina, leaving Sad Hill part of the eighty percent of New Orleans that had been flooded by the storm. The residents who'd evacuated it had never returned.

Since then, a number of houses had been burned down by vandals; the charred remains stood in place, no effort hav-ing been made by the city to clear them away. Many stand-ing houses bore spray-painted Xs and other symbols left by searchers in the immediate aftermath of Katrina, signs indicating whether any dead bodies were left in the houses, and if so, how many. The dead had been carted away then, only to be replaced more recently by others, victims of gang killings and random murders.

The site was so blighted that even the teen gangs who haunted New Orleans's phantom zones had forsaken it, ex-cept as a body dump.

Such was Sad Hill. Blighted, blasted, and abandoned, an ideal spot for shady dealings best conducted beyond the eyes of the law, or for that matter, those of any other witnesses.

* * *

Not long ago, within the last hour, the kidnap gang chief had resumed contact with Mylon Sears, naming Sad Hill as the site where the ransom swap would be made. He didn't give Sears much time to get there, either. Fast-fast-fast, that was how the deal had to go down.

Sears had told him, "We'll get there as quick as we can without breaking any speed laws that might attract police attention."

The abductor said, "No police, or Garros dies."

"I get the message."

"Hirelings like you need things repeated to drive them home into your pea brains," the abductor said, breaking off communication.

The EXECPROTEK crew waiting at the day care center hopped into their vehicles and drove cross-town for some miles before arriving at Sad Hill.

Now, Susan Keehan and her Sears-led security squad were on the west bank of the canal, where they'd been told to wait for final word on swapping a million dollars in ransom money for Raoul Garros.

The hour of exchange was at hand. The convoy of a half-dozen SUVs and outrider cars was parked in the middle of a cross-street in the tract of abandoned houses. Not as many reinforcements as Sears would have liked, but enough to repel any possible attack.

Susan had insisted on coming along. There was no way around it; it was easier for Sears to give in than to try and fight it. Otherwise she'd have tried to fire him and replace him with someone more amenable to taking her orders, requiring Sears to invoke the authority of Wilmont Keehan to back him up; a diversion that would have eaten up precious time and created a dangerous distraction.

Better to have her along where he knew where she was

and could exert some control over her contacts with the outside world, preventing her from throwing a wild glitch into the situation by going outside the closed circle of in-house channels.

Susan was allowed to be present under strict conditions; she was to remain in a bulletproof, armored SUV surrounded by a cordon of armed guards. They were in the midst of the tract houses, which served as a barrier screening them from potential snipers on the far side of the bank. In case the kidnap plot turned out to be an elaborate ruse to make Susan herself the target for abduction or even assassination.

Stranger things had happened in the world of the ultrarich; Sears recalled the chain of mysterious deaths in the Niarchos/Onassis feud of the great Greek shipping tycoons.

Sears refused to let Susan leave the protective cocoon of the armored SUV. To keep her company (and to keep an eye on her), he had Gene Jasper beside her, figuratively and by now literally holding her hand.

She seemed to take comfort in the presence of the big, good-looking security specialist; Jasper was feeling no pain from the assignment, either. He knew the score: not Susan but Wilmont Keehan was their boss; no harm must come to a single hair of her head. With Jasper covering Susan, Sears had one less distraction to worry about.

To be on the safe side, though, Sears had put a guard on the guard, also posting Ernie Bannerman in the Keehan limo as a precaution in case Jasper proved unable to resist Susan's blandishments, financial or otherwise. Bannerman was a middle-aged, hard-nosed, old ex-cop with a one-track mind who knew how to follow Sears's orders.

Sears sent out a detail of several men to search the vacant houses in the immediate vicinity, to make sure that no ambushers or spotters lurked in hiding. None of them much liked having to poke around in the garbage-strewn rattraps, but they did what they had to do. The buildings came up clean—of potential threats, that is.

Sears posted a sentry to keep an eye out for cops, too. All he needed was for some zealous NOPD officers to come snooping around to investigate suspicious doings in Sad Hill. Luckily, storm-related duties kept the city police far from the locale.

Sears and a squad of five hard-core protectors from the EXECPROTEK roster were grouped near the footbridge under a cypress tree hung with Spanish moss. Winds blew, ruffling the dank black canal waters, agitating the tree branches.

Sears reflected sourly that the kidnappers had chosen their site well. The footbridge was too narrow to allow the passage of a motor vehicle, thwarting any possible pursuit from that direction. The tract of deserted houses was set far enough back from the canal to leave a belt of open ground between it and the footbridge, forestalling a buildup of backup forces for an ambush or counterattack.

Presumably the kidnappers were somewhere on the east bank, but if so, Sears was damned if he could tell where they were; the area seemed deserted.

He stared at his cell phone with irritation. He couldn't call the kidnap gang chief, he could only wait for the kidnap gang chief to call him. He'd had a devil of a time keeping the all-important contact cell away from Susan, finally convincing her of the necessity of his having possession of it for immediate handling of all fast-breaking developments.

With Susan on the line, she'd have wound up agreeing to anything, pledging five, ten, twenty, a hundred million dollars if that's what the kidnapper demanded for Raoul's safe return.

The kidnapper himself kept changing cells, using a different one for each call to ensure their untraceability.

Sears looked across the canal at the cemetery on the knoll. A more mournful sight would have been hard to find, even in New Orleans, lately a showcase for so many scenes of devastation and destruction.

The city was famous for its aboveground cemeteries; persistent floods cause bodies buried below ground to rise from their graves and float away. The dead are generally interred in aboveground mausoleums.

Our Lady of Sorrows had seen its peak a century and a half ago. It had been on the decline back in the late nineteenth century; it had been closed in the 1920s. The remains were removed from their crumbling mausoleums and reburied elsewhere. It was a necropolis gone to seed, the remains of ruined stone tombs, catafalques, and monuments peeking out from a tangle of weeds and scrub brush.

Sears's downbeat reflections were suddenly interrupted by the jangling of the cell phone. His nerves were so taut that he found himself catching his breath for an instant at the sound of it. But only for an instant. Now that he was in action, trained reflexes took over; he was all business.

He hauled it out of his pocket and answered it. "Yes!"

The kidnapper said, "You have the money." Not a question, a statement, delivered in the mechanical tones of the electronic voice changer. Somehow, that flat, denatured mechanical intonation was more hateful to Sears than would have been the leering, preening tones of a crook who knows he's holding the whip hand.

Sears said, "Where's Garros?"

The kidnapper said, "Where a million dollars will allow him to resume his interrupted life."

"Let's make the exchange, then."

"Soon, soon," the kidnapper soothed. "One more point:

Miss Keehan will deliver the ransom money personally."

Sears had been more than half-expecting something like that, some new quantum jump in escalating demands to demonstrate the kidnapper's control of the situation. Susan would have done it, too, in a heartbeat, but Sears was having none of it. He said, "Not a chance."

The kidnapper said, "I suggest you talk it over with Miss Keehan. She may have a different perspective on it, especially when she hears her fiancé screaming during the removal of certain vital body parts."

Sears hung tough. "Nothing to talk about. It's a non-starter."

The abductor came back strong: "Then Garros dies."

Sears fired back, "So does your shot at a million-dollar ransom. No way in hell that Miss Keehan is going to take part in this exchange. I'll never agree to it. She can't fire me, I'm not working for her, I'm working for her father. He'd have my head if I agreed to that.

"Don't overplay your hand. Wilmont Keehan's not that crazy about Garros to start with. If something happens to him, he'll be able to control his grief. She can always get another fiancé, he can't get another daughter."

The abductor said, "This is no bluff."

Sears said, "You can chop him up on a live webcast for all I care; that's nothing compared to what Mr. Keehan would do to me if I put his daughter in harm's way. It's a deal breaker, so don't even bother mentioning it again. I'll restrain her by force if necessary, rather than let her take the risk.

"You've played it like a pro up to now; the money's almost in your hands, don't blow it at the last minute by trying to get cute."

The abductor paused, as if thinking about it. Finally he said, "I take your point." Like he was magnanimously ceding some major concession.

He added, "You make the exchange instead."

"Me?"

"Yes, you, Mr. Sears. You hand over the money and make the exchange."

"Done," Sears said, without hesitation.

The kidnapper said, "If anything goes wrong, you'll be the one to pay the consequences."

"Fine."

"You—and Garros," the kidnapper said. "Remember, no tricks. If I don't like the look of things at the exchange, Garros dies. If there's interference from the police or FBI, Garros dies."

Sears said, "No outsiders have been notified. We don't want those bunglers around any more than you do."

The other went on as if he hadn't heard him. "Any suspicious persons or vehicles in the area, Garros dies. Any helicopters or low-lying planes, he dies."

Sears said, "We want Garros alive, that's all."

The kidnapper said, "You'll get him, as long as you follow orders. When I tell you, take the money and bring it to the middle of the bridge. You, alone. Keep your cell ready for further instructions."

He broke contact.

Sears was doing it the hard way: no gun, not even a flak jacket. His jacket was off and he was in his shirtsleeves. Characteristically he still had his tie on, and it wasn't loosened, either.

He was doing it to allay the abductors' fears of a double cross. He told his men, "I want to show them I'm unarmed and that there's no tricks. Don't want to panic them at the last minute. But if they try to pull a fast one on us, shoot them."

He had a couple of sharpshooters posted around under cover, too, as a last resort.

His only sideman in the open was Deauville, an A–1 trigger puller. A clean-shaven face of hard planes and angles, with the cold-eyed, alert gaze of the hunter. He wore a gun in a shoulder holster.

Sears said, "Here goes nothing."

Deauville said, "One million is a lot of nothing."

That it was. Heavy, too. Sears held the briefcase with the money at his side, his other hand holding the cell phone to his ear.

He and Deauville stood at the west end of the footbridge, facing the other side. The opposite, east end of the bridge remained empty.

There was a pause, a long one, by Sears's reckoning, but then he was in no position for objective timekeeping.

Then, across the canal, higher up on the slope, there was a stir of motion in the graveyard. Three figures stepped out from behind the standing wall of a collapsed tomb, moving into view.

All three had hidden faces: two masked, the third hooded. The masked men wore dark baseball caps pulled low over their faces and knotted bandanas covering them below the eyes. One was of medium height, athletic build; the other was a head taller, a big, heavyweight bruiser. They flanked a third man who stood wedged between them.

A black hood covered the head of the man in the middle. Opaque, impenetrable, it had no holes for eyes, nose, or mouth.

He wore the clothes that Raoul Garros had worn earlier today, when last seen at the Mega Mart building. They seemed much the worse for wear; the once-dapper lightweight suit was rumpled, filthy, torn at the knees and elbows. The captive's tie was loose and unknotted, his shirt torn open. His hands were tied behind his back. He was weak at the knees and unsteady at his feet, which were bare.

The masked man on his left, the behemoth, held him by the upper arm, supporting him. His other hand held a gun to the side of the hooded man's head.

The masked man on the captive's right held a cell phone to his ear, as though listening to instructions.

Sears guessed that neither masked man was in charge; they were henchmen, taking orders from their chief, who must be hidden somewhere nearby, where he could watch the scene as it developed.

The trio approached the far side of the bridge. The hooded captive shuffled along, uncertain, stumbling. The big masked man gripped him one-handed, half-carrying, half-dragging him, all the while holding the gun to his head.

Sears's men, hidden off-scene, had their guns trained on the masked men; Sears suspected that the abductors had several hidden gunmen keeping him in their sights.

The mechanized voice of the kidnap band's chief came rasping through Sears's cell.

He said, "Here is how we will proceed, Mr. Sears. One of my men will go midway to the bridge. He will lay down a bag and withdraw. You will go there with the briefcase and empty the money into the bag. That will ensure that you are not passing any extras along with the money, such as dye packs or tracking devices."

Sears said, "I'm not."

The chief said, "Do as you're told."

"All right."

"Remain standing there with the money bag. My man will cross the bridge with Garros, meeting you at the middle. You will give him the bag, he will give you Garros. You will take Garros to your side of the bridge. Our transaction will be concluded."

Sears said, "Not so fast."

The chief said, "This is a very bad time for you to be making any conditions—a bad time for you and Garros."

Sears said, "If it is Garros. Take off his hood and show me his face."

"You are in no position to make demands—"

"Like hell! We're not buying a pig in a poke. I have to be sure it's Garros and not some ringer you're trying to pass off as the real thing."

Was that a chuckle at the other end? "You are a suspicious man, Mr. Sears. However, I suppose if I were in your position I would do the same thing. Very well."

A pause on Sears's end of the cell, presumably while the chief passed along the word.

The henchman holding a cell received his instructions. He pulled the hood off, unmasking the captive.

It was Raoul Garros. His hair was disheveled, his face was bruised and cut, and his eyes bulged over two strips of duct tape that had been pasted in an X-shape across his mouth. He was unused to the light and squeezed his eyes shut against it. He sagged, knees folding.

The other henchman, the big man, pressed the gun barrel hard against the underside of Garros's jaw, exerting a steadying effect.

The kidnap chief came back on the cell. "Satisfied, Mr. Sears?"

Sears said, "Let's get to it. And no tricks."

"The same applies to you."

The masked man holding the cell put his gun away, sticking it in the top of his waistband. He set foot on the bridge, carrying an empty knapsack. He halted at the midpoint of the bridge, set the knapsack down on the wooden plank bed, and went back to the east side of the bridge.

The chief said, "Now you, Mr. Sears."

Sears said, "Wait a minute. I'm unarmed." Holding his arms out from his sides—briefcase in one hand, cell in the other—he did a slow 360-degree turn to show that he carried no weapon.

He got back on the cell. "Tell your man to leave his gun behind."

The chief said, "He does not need a gun. At the first sign of treachery, he will snap Garros's neck like a twig."

More cross-talk followed between the off-scene chief and his henchmen. The big masked man, the behemoth, made a show of handing his gun to his partner. He grabbed Garros by the neck with one big hand, giving it a little squeeze. Garros's eyes popped open, bulging, as if about to start from his head.

Sears said in an aside to Deauville, "Here's where I start earning my salary." He took a deep breath, exhaled, and started walking, a briefcase full of money in hand.

Across the bridge, the more modest-sized masked man, the one not holding Garros by the neck, held a gun pointed at Sears. Sears wondered how many other guns were being leveled at him, by gunmen he couldn't see.

Unconsciously squaring his shoulders, he went toward the center of the bridge. Walking not too fast, not too slow, his movements deliberate. He halted at the span's midpoint, the empty knapsack at his feet.

He went down on one knee. This wasn't the kind of operation he could carry out standing up, trying to juggle the briefcase with one hand and the knapsack with the other.

He set the briefcase down on the planks, facing the

masked men. Opened the lid, holding the attaché case so
those on the opposite bank could see the stacked money
packs lining the inside of the case to the rim.

Setting the briefcase down on the bridge, he began trans-
ferring the cash into the knapsack, feeding packets into the
bag's open mouth. Continuing until the briefcase was empty
and the knapsack full.

Done, he lifted the briefcase, turning it upside down and
shaking it to show that it held no more money.

He could have tossed it over the handrail into the water but decided against it. Too much violent motion might
spook the other side. He closed the briefcase, leaving it on
the planks. Gripped the knapsack by one of the straps and
rose, standing up.

With a sideswipe of his foot, he half-kicked, half-slid the
briefcase across the planks and over the edge, into the water. It raised a splash. It didn't sink but floated downstream
on the slow, idling current.

The masked behemoth holding Garros by the neck
started forward, bringing the captive along with him. Garros staggered along like a drunkard. He looked ghastly.
Under his tan, his skin was taut, sallow. Shiny with sweat.
Cold sweat.

Sears wondered if he looked any better; he could feel
some of that cold sweat rolling off himself, too.

Captor and captive neared the midpoint of the bridge.
Where Sears waited.

A red bandana covered the kidnapper's face below the
eyes, like an old-time Western bad man. He was so close
that Sears could see his thick, bushy eyebrows that almost
but not quite met over the bridge of his wide, flat nose. His
eyes were dark brown, a warm chestnut color.

He halted within arm's-reach of Sears, holding out his
free hand, the one that wasn't holding Garros by the neck.

Sears handed him the knapsack by the strap. The other hooked it with a pawlike hand and released Garros, giving him a hard shove forward. Garros stumbled, getting tangled up in his own bare feet.

Sears caught him to keep him from falling. Garros stank, a rank smell of fear and stale sweat wafting off him.

Sears gave him a quick once-over, pat-down frisk, checking to make sure that he hadn't been wired with hidden explosives that would have turned him into a human bomb. That would have been a cute trick, an added refinement in the theory and practice of terror.

He found none. This wasn't about terror, it was about crime and profit. Ransom money.

The masked man turned, holding the knapsack by the strap, and walked away, unhurried, ambling along.

Sears turned toward the west end of the footbridge, feeling like he had a big bull's-eye drawn right between his shoulder blades. Garros stumbled, almost falling, and for an instant Sears thought the other was going to faint. He said, "Buck up, Mr. Garros, you're almost there."

Garros replied, saying something, the duct tape sealing his mouth making his words a garbled muddle.

Sears did not run, but hustled Garros across the bridge as quickly as he dared, expecting at every second a bullet to come crashing into him. His pace did not slacken when he'd reached the end of the span and the wooden planks gave way to ground beneath his feet. He did not look back.

Deauville stood waiting. Beyond him, in the middle ground, were other members of the security squad. All were standing in place, motionless, a frozen tableau; as if time stood still.

Came a blast. Several blasts, in a series of flat, crumping booms. Concussion. Pressure waves.

Sears and Garros were swept forward by an invisible hand, hurling them forward for several paces before knocking them to the ground.

Smoke, noise, heat, and fire rose in a fiery column where the bridge had been. Debris rained down, pelting the scenery.

Sears raised himself on hands and knees, reversing position to see what had happened. The footbridge no longer spanned the canal, it wasn't there anymore. The middle of it had been blown up and the two ends had collapsed into the canal.

Water fell, splashing, raining down rank canal water.

Hissing sounds now began issuing from the east side of the canal. Not falling water, but something else—smoke bombs.

On the opposite side of the canal, the weedy slope, knoll, and graveyard all became obscure through an everexpanding pall of thickening smoke. Not from the blast that had destroyed the bridge but from a point centered in the cemetery.

Smoke clouds increased. Brown, black, gray. Billowing, streaming, screening the canal's east bank with a pall of darkness.

Sears could guess what had happened. The kidnappers had blown the bridge to foil any foot pursuit from that direction. It had been done with neatness and dispatch. A nice pro job of demolition, wiring explosive charges to the main support beams and blowing them via remote-controlled detonation. More a case of collapsing the bridge than blowing it up, though the blast had shoved the center span skyward.

The demolitions were not the source of the ever-growing smokescreen rapidly fogging the east bank. That had been caused by several smoke bombs.

The murky clouds were thickest in the graveyard area;

that's where the smoke bombs must have been set. To cover the escape of the kidnappers.

The dull, fading echoes of the bridge blast were now crosscut by several high-pitched whining sounds, like the buzzing of motorized mosquitoes.

Unless he missed his guess, Sears reckoned that the buzzing blats were the sound of motorcycles being used by the masked men to make their escape. Dirt bikes probably; quick, lightweight, with fat, knobby tires designed for off-road riding. Ideal for the rugged terrain. Easily hidden and handled.

The smoke bombs were added insurance, covering the getaway, screening the fugitives from the guns of Sears's men. Helpful in case a helicopter should suddenly show up, too. A clever ruse.

Raoul Garros was battered, bruised, scared half out of his wits, terrorized—but alive. Susan Keehan had gotten her fiancé back.

The kidnappers had gotten away with a million dollars in ransom money.

As far as Sears was concerned, the other side had gotten the better of the deal.

• •

THE FOLLOWING TAKES PLACE
BETWEEN THE HOURS OF
8 P.M. AND 9 P.M.
CENTRAL DAYLIGHT TIME

• •

Sad Hill, New Orleans

Not two men but three—Rubio, Torres, and Moreno—
handled the Garros ransom exchange. They were the trio
of action men supplied earlier by Supremo cell commander
Monatero in response to Beltran's demand for top enforcers
to carry out his plans. His plans, not Havana's—a vital fact
unknown to Monatero until it was too late.

Rubio was the leader, the ramrod of the team; Torres, the
muscle; and Moreno, the all-around utility man.

Rubio was the one who'd been in contact with and taking
his orders from Beltran by cell during the exchange. Torres,
a bull of a man, had "escorted" Garros across the footbridge
and picked up the money. Moreno had been held in reserve,
lurking unseen in the graveyard, covering the footbridge
with an assault rifle.

Overseeing all, directing the action, was the phantom plotter and puppet master, Beltran.

He, the Generalissimo, had conceived the kidnap plot; it was he who'd spoken to Sears throughout every step of the way, giving him his instructions. Just as he'd given the Supremo action men their instructions.

Both Sears and the trio, and for that matter, Monatero, knew him solely as a voice over a phone, an unseen and intangible presence hovering over all. Sears and the EXECPROTEK contingent had obeyed him because he had Garros; the Supremo trio had obeyed him because their boss, Monatero, had told them to do so.

During the ransom exchange, Beltran had overseen the action, safely hidden in his observation post in the brush at the west side of the ridgetop power trail, overlooking the canal area below.

He was comfortably nestled in a hollow, concealed by a clump of bushes. He had several cell phones, one for communicating with Rubio and another for Sears; a pair of binoculars, and a semi-automatic pistol with several spare clips of ammo tucked in his pocket. Not neglecting minimal creature comforts, he also had a plastic bottle of water and several candy bars.

All had gone according to plan. Garros had been swapped for the ransom, the footbridge had been blown, the smoke bombs detonated. Three dirt bikes hidden in the graveyard had been started up and mounted by the action men, now beginning their climb up the east slope to the power trail. Hidden from the guns of Sears's men by the smokescreen.

Time for Beltran to get moving. He started into motion when the bridge blew, well before the motorbikes had started up.

In a sense, for him this was the hardest part of the plan,

because it required him to move fast, and at his age, that just wasn't a strong suit anymore. But he could handle it.

The power trail was long but not wide, about thirty yards across.

This was the part that Beltran liked the least, not only because of the demanding physical activity, but also because it required him to expose himself in the open, however briefly.

The hour was late, dusk was at hand, deepened by the gloom spread by the low, overcast sky.

Utility company maintenance crews kept the power trail cleared of weeds and brush; a dirt road ran along its length. Beltran didn't run, didn't jog, but hustled along in a kind of quick time, bent low, making a beeline across the trail toward an opening in the bushes lining the far side of the trail.

Overhead, high-tension lines hummed, buzzed, spat, and crackled. Winds blew, rattling the wires against the condensers that linked them from tower to tower.

The mosquito whine of the motorbikes loudened, nearing. Beltran did not look back. Reaching the far side of the trail, he ducked through a gap in the wall of foliage. The gap stood at the head of a dirt path leading down the side of the slope through the brush.

Beltran forced himself to slow down. That's all he needed, to trip and fall and maybe break something right in advance of the oncoming motorbikes. They sounded very loud, very near.

Beltran went down the dirt path in a controlled slide. About a third of the way down, on his right, a white plastic sack of the kind used for carrying groceries was stuck in the branches of a bush.

It looked like it might have been blown there by the wind,

but he'd placed it there earlier, spearing it through the twigs to hold it in place and make sure that it was not blown away by the rising winds.

It was a marker, a signpost. Behind the bushes lay a game trail, hemmed in on all sides by scrub brush. Beltran ducked into it, holding his arms in front of his face to keep from being scratched by twigs and branches as he made his way deeper into it.

Several paces within lay a small clearing. He ducked down below some waist-high branches and crawled on hands and knees into this hiding place. He was drenched with sweat, his clothes soaked through; his heart hammered and colored spots flickered before his eyes. Gratefully he sat down, panting.

He reached under some bushes, groping for and finding the package he'd left there earlier. It was a rifle inside a gun-carrying case, a form-fitting plastic sheath.

He unzipped it, hauling the rifle out of the shroud. It was a high-powered deer rifle with a telescopic sight. He sat on the ground with his legs crossed, laying the rifle across the tops of his thighs. While he panted for breath, trying to recover.

A gap in the greenery surrounding him gave him a view of his surroundings. The east side of the power trail embankment was a gentle slope tilting downward for about thirty yards before leveling out on the paved lot of a mini-mall.

The mini-mall's main feature was a Kwik-Up Konvenience store whose rear faced the bottom of the slope. Behind the back of the building stood several Dumpsters and a pile of wooden pallets. To the right could be seen part of the parking lot, crowded by a fair amount of vehicles. People were doing their prestorm stocking up on food, water, flashlights, batteries, portable radios, and so on.

Standing atop a twenty-foot-pole, shaking and swaying in the wind, was a marquee reading KWIK-UP KONVENIENCE STORE.

The building fronted a highway that ran north-south, parallel to the power trail.

The strip was lined on both sides by big-box stores, discount appliance centers, fast-food joints, car stereo installers, and the like.

Apart from the vagaries of operational details, Beltran's master plan had only one potential flaw, but that was a big one: namely, that Rubio, Torres, and Moreno might decide to go into business for themselves and abscond with the ransom money.

The rifle and sniper's nest was his insurance against their going rogue. Their honesty was about to be put to the test. Beltran waited for their arrival; he would not have long to wait.

The sound of motorbikes was very near, a jarring physical presence. They were almost upon him. Should they fail the test, he was prepared to deal with the contingency.

Beltran's gut feeling was that there was little likelihood of that happening; by all accounts, the three men were dedicated soldiers of the revolution whose loyalty had never been called into question. Of course, his masters in Havana had reposed a similar confidence in him, and look what had happened.

Spymasters are a dangerous breed. Both to their foes and to those for whom they work. Their business is to ferret out secrets; they can't help but find out the way things really operate. Everyone's dirty little secrets, especially those of the high and mighty.

Making the spymasters potentially the most dangerous

threat to those who employ them. What keeps them in check is the nature of the job itself. Secrets are their business, currency, and pleasure.

Beltran was no exception to the occupational hazard of his profession, that too much knowledge is a dangerous thing. Once, long ago, he'd actually believed in the revolution.

He could look back on that period with amused tolerance; it was like a child believing in Santa Claus. Beltran had never believed in Santa Claus, or the saints, either. But he had once believed in the revolution. That naïveté had died early.

One didn't have to be a spymaster, not even back in the days of his youth, to realize that the revolution was a lie. Without the massive influx of aid, material and financial, from the old Soviet Union, the Cuban socialist regime would have gone bust virtually overnight.

By the time the Soviet Union had itself failed, swept up in the dustbin of history, Cuba's Fidelista regime had already consolidated its police state apparatus to such an extent that its overthrow was a virtual impossibility. For one thing, the majority of the populace subsisted on a near-starvation diet that kept them too weak to resist the police state whose control reached into every level of Cuban society.

Beltran had long moved past that, into a higher realm of awareness. His professional duties had kept him out of Cuba for most of his life; in all honesty, he preferred it that way. The creature comforts of the arch-capitalist American state where he was posted far transcended the economy of scarcity and privation on the home island.

For long years now, decades, his true devotion had been reserved for skullduggery itself, intrigue, the clandestine. The spy game was his true love; the cause itself was immaterial. Ridiculous, really, if one gave it a moment's thought.

He'd carved out a special niche for himself, one allowing him extraordinary freedom of movement, open comm lines to the top of the leadership, and the authority to commandeer vast resources of the state and the spy service. His virtually unique position of trust had offered him limitless opportunities to feather his own nest.

Why had he gone into business for himself? Why not?

Age was the main reason. Time was overtaking him. He'd lasted longer than most, but no one lasted forever. Retirement beckoned. A tricky proposition, for one in his profession. At his rarefied level.

The best-case option was that his masters would put him out to pasture somewhere in Cuba, under close surveillance, to make sure he didn't get gabby in the manner of senile old duffers who were best put to sleep. Which was no option at all, as far as he was concerned.

He'd banked away a fair-sized fortune over the years. Cuba's illicit drug trade with the United States generated mountains of money. He oversaw the Gulf Coast part of the operation. It had been child's play to divert masses of cash into his offshore and Swiss bank accounts—he had both. What he'd come to think of as his retirement fund.

To enjoy it, he had to be somewhere other than Cuba, out from under the watchful eyes of the police state. He'd been looking to make a break for some time. To close out accounts by making one last big score before jumping down the rabbit hole and closing it behind him.

Then, as if in answer to his prayers, along came Vollard. Major Marc Vollard, of mercenary infamy. The go-between had been Dixie Lee, killer and gunrunner. He was scum, but useful scum, whose connections in the extremist militia movement included sympathizers in important positions in U.S. military arsenals and National Guard armories.

Dixie Lee had come to Beltran's notice through the Generalissimo's dealings in the drug trade. One could never have too many weapons, especially not in the narcotics business. Guns and bombs were much-valued currency, and Dixie Lee was a dependable supplier of both.

Beltran made it a practice to know as much as he could about the people with whom he did business. In recent months, it had come to his attention that Dixie Lee had a new client. A rich and powerful one, whose needs had come to monopolize more and more of the gunrunner's professional attentions.

Beltran's business was finding out secret things and he went to work, putting his network of informants and contacts on the case. They first fastened on the new player's associates.

Most of them were outsiders, real outsiders. Not gringos but Europeans, or at least of European origin, although their résumés reflected extensive acquaintance with the battlefields of Africa, Asia, and the Middle East.

Beltran had had excellent contacts with the old Soviet spy system, contacts that were largely carried through into the new era of the Russian Federation as the KGB morphed into the new FSB. Different initials, similar functions. From these contacts, he was able to identity the new gang in town.

They were a band of professional mercenaries, Dogs of War, whose leader was Major Marc Vollard.

The laws of physics hold true for the spy world as elsewhere; every action produces an opposite and equal reaction. Beltran's probe of Vollard's operation had triggered a counterprobe by Vollard. Contact.

A prickly mating dance followed, operating first through emissaries, ultimately resulting in Beltran and Vollard holding an exploratory meeting in search of common ground.

Already each of them had enough on the other to put them in bad with the U.S. government. They also shared this in common, that both of their respective operations were hostile to Washington: all its interests and all it represented.

Here was the basis for a frank and full exchange of ideas. Both men were professionals with an eye on the main chance: what's in it for them?

The answer: a great deal of money.

Vollard was a man with a plan. Not a man alone. His sponsors were very highly placed in Saudi Arabia, with every possibility of rising even higher, should their master plan work out.

Beltran was in position to foil that plan or facilitate it. If he foiled it, Vollard would hit back hard, initiating the destruction of Beltran's Gulf Coast network, if not Beltran himself.

Beltran liked the plan. Despite his own acquisitive instincts, he retained enough of the old revolutionary snobbery to despise Washington and the current Administration.

A side benefit was that it would also put a hurting on Caracas and the Chavez regime.

Venezuela's oil wealth had put communist Cuba in the position of being a poor relation. This would knock some of the cockiness out of them.

The newfound Cuba/Venezuela alliance had forced Beltran to work closely with Colonel Paz here in New Orleans for the last six months. He'd had a bellyful of Paz, of his thuggish ways, massive conceit, vulgarity, and rudeness. That alone would have convinced Beltran to seal his deal with Vollard.

The huge payday that awaited successful completion of the mission didn't hurt, either.

The plan required a fall guy. A patsy. Its Saudi backers had tagged Caracas for the role. Venezuela was closely allied with Iran, the Saudis' arch-nemesis. Caracas and Tehran dominated OPEC, throwing their weight around, trying to take over the world oil market.

Vollard's strike would be engineered to make it look like Venezuela's handiwork.

That would push Washington's buttons. The Administration was already sore at the socialist regime, the Hearthstone Initiative's free-oil-for-the-U.S.-poor being only the latest Chavez finger stuck in Washington's eye. It would jump at the chance to hang one on Venezuela.

The frameup required the planting of the dead body of Colonel Paz at the scene of destruction, in a place where even the bumbling Yanquis couldn't fail to find it.

That was Beltran's bit. It made sense. He was close to Paz, professionally speaking, and therefore in the best possible position to betray him. He knew Paz's comings and goings, friends and associates, watering holes and hideaways. Knew his routine, his pattern.

Beltran had set up the hit. The plan was to liquidate Paz when he emerged from his girlfriend's apartment in the early morning hours and eliminate his bodyguards at the same time. Quietly. The bodies would be loaded into the utility truck and taken away.

His limo would be stolen for future disposal at some optimally incriminating spot, preferably linking it to a few more major crimes.

The corpses of Paz and the bodyguards would be delivered to Vollard's riverfront base at Pelican Pier, where they'd be put on ice—literally packed in ice coolers to retard the signs of dissolution, decay, and rigor and throw off the timetable of any medical examiner seeking to establish the time of death.

At zero hour, they'd be taken to the scene of destruction and planted there for the Americans to find, clinching the case for Venezuelan involvement in a massive terror strike.

* * *

Such was the plan, anyway, as devised by Beltran.

He'd supplied some of the personnel, including two Cuban shooters illegally in the United States, and one of his most valuable players, Beatriz Ortiz. Her revolutionary fervor was impeccable. All Beltran had had to do was feed her a line about Havana's wanting Paz hit for counterrevolutionary activities, and she was ready to go. The Generalissimo planned to have her killed upon completion of the Paz job; she was a dangerous fanatic who knew too much about his operation and had to go.

Vollard liked to keep an eye on things and his hand in all mission-related activities, and had put his top noncom, Hermann Ost, in on the job to make sure it was carried out properly. That hadn't worked out so well.

Vollard and Beltran had both agreed on including Dixie Lee in the hit. A hometown boy, he knew the turf and could do the talking if the team ran into any interference from citizens or the law. He, too, was slated for demolition post-Paz; Vollard and Beltran would both feel easier when the volatile gunrunner with the long prison record was permanently silenced.

All Beltran's intricately laid schemes went out the window, however, when the hit went sour. Not having been there, he was unable to conceive of how the team had made such a botch of things. He'd underestimated Paz, a quick and cunning killer. And he was unaware that CTU had become involved, in the persons of Jack Bauer and Pete Malo, who'd helped polish off the hitters and by so doing allowed Paz to escape.

He knew this, though: now he was in danger of being made the patsy, the fall guy.

No less than his masters in Havana, his new partner, Vollard, demanded results. Never mind that his top kick Ost had been present; it was Beltran who'd failed to deliver on his promises.

That was how Vollard would see it, and how he'd tell it to his Saudi backers.

Beltran knew that, because that's the way he would have handled it himself.

Paz knew nothing of Vollard and his master plan; he knew Beltran, and the presence of Beatriz and the Cubans would set him on Beltran's trail. Not to mention alerting Havana to the spymaster's double dealing. Once his bosses started scrutinizing Beltran's doings, he'd zoom straight to the top of their priority kill list. Assuming Paz didn't get him first.

It was then that Beltran demonstrated a flexibility of mind rarely possessed by men half his age, the ability to make a 180-degree turn and reverse field to salvage what he could of a situation that had gone sour.

He'd routinely surveilled not only Paz but other key members of the Venezuelan infrastructure, overt and covert, in New Orleans. One target of opportunity now immediately stood out: Raoul Garros.

Scion of an oligarchic clan closely tied to Chavez, Garros had proved a particularly useful tool for the new regime. He was young, handsome, charming, educated, spoke several languages fluently, and had a first-class education and grounding in business.

He was also an opportunist of the first rank, with a talent for backstabbing and a total lack of scruples when it came to betraying former friends and associates of questionable loyalty to the new President and his much-touted brand of "twenty-first-century socialism."

Garros was the urbane face of the new regime, seemingly embodying the best of the old and new orders. He was a key executive in LAGO's corporate hierarchy in New Orleans.

It was no accident that his post at the state oil company had thrown him in close contact with Susan Keehan by way of the Hearthstone Initiative.

That was the brainchild of the strategists of Chavez's military-intelligence clique back in Caracas. A simple plan: put lady-killer Raoul in close proximity with rich, available Susan Keehan and let nature take its course.

Now they were engaged to be married. An enviable alliance for both families: clan Garros would be plugged into one of America's richest families, one whose wealth was matched by its political clout; while the Keehans would have a son-in-law who was a pillar of the new establishment in Venezuela, giving them entrée into that country's oil wealth.

Which provided Beltran with a chance for a quick score. Grab Garros and hold him for ransom.

The Keehan woman was besotted. She would pay. Thanks to her family connections, she had the ability to get hold of a good deal of money fast. That was vital, because with Vollard and Paz coming after him, Beltran would have to move fast to get out of this with a whole skin.

Beltran had the organization to pull it off—for a limited time only, because the botched Paz hit and its repercussions would soon be heard in Havana. His bosses would move quickly to curtail his extraordinary powers and freedom of movement. He had to complete the kidnapping and ransoming fast.

Beltran had mobilized the Supremo cell for the operation. Political kidnappings were nothing new in their line of work. His Havana-decreed authority and autonomy served him well; Monatero assumed as a matter of course that he was carrying out the directives of Cuba's Maximum Leader.

Beltran's network routinely kept tabs on Garros as well

as other leading members of the consulate and LAGO, so it was easy to locate him at the Mega Mart building. Raoul's lifestyle also facilitated the snatch. He relied on his solid-gold cover and credentials, rarely if ever traveling with bodyguards, complaining that they cramped his style. Knowing that they all reported back on his doings to Paz.

Involving Supremo was a further cutout, covering Beltran's tracks and further muddying the waters. At this point, nothing would serve his purposes better than a good, hot shooting war between Paz's death squad and the Cuban spy cell. Chaos was his friend and would aid him in making his getaway.

By the time the gun smoke had cleared and the body count had been toted up, he'd be long gone with a cool million in untraceable cash. Operating cash. A nice fund to keep him going until he'd reached a safe place from which to access those other millions he'd salted away in offshore and Swiss banking accounts.

He'd picked Supremo's ace action squad for the job, the team of Rubio, Torres, and Moreno. He'd used them in the past to great effect, always operating as a shadowy presence who communicated with them solely by phone.

This was a business of compartmentalization. All they knew or needed to know was what their boss, Monatero, had told them: that they'd been chosen for an important job by a top secret operative and to follow his orders to the letter.

Beltran had been careful to make sure that the trio maintained silence and isolation once they'd come under his sway, ordering them not to contact Supremo until told otherwise. They figured it was just good tradecraft, insulating and securing their home base against possible repercussions if something went wrong.

They made the snatch, abducting Garros from the Mega Mart underground parking garage.

Rubio and Torres handled the strong-arm chores while Moreno drove the getaway car. The abduction had required more than muscle; it needed wet work. The presence of the two CTU agents in the parking garage presented a complicating factor. The American agents' focus was on Garros and the elevator door from which he'd emerge, diverting their attention from the killers until it was too late.

Rubio had used a knife on one; Torres, light-footed for a big man, had dispatched the other by hand, sneaking up behind him and breaking his neck.

They'd braced Garros when he emerged from the elevator, Torres putting a sleeper hold on him while Rubio relieved him of his gun, billfold, and cell phone. The sleeper hold had caused Garros to black out from lack of oxygen. They'd covered his head with a black hood, tied his hands behind his back, and tossed him into the trunk of their car.

The car had rolled up to the exit ramp gate, where the attendant manned a booth. Rubio had shot him; Moreno had crashed through the gate and driven away. From then on, they'd been on the move, receiving updated instructions from Beltran.

Beltran had contacted Susan Keehan to deliver his demands. He'd used an oral appliance, a portable electronic voice box that fit over his mouth, reproducing his words in digitized tones and also altering his distinctive voiceprint so it could not be used to identify him.

The Keehan wealth and power had worked in Beltran's favor to facilitate the plot. She had the ability to get the money fast, even on a Saturday when the banks were closed and the city was bracing for a storm.

Her EXECPROTEK staffers had also done their bit for Beltran, however inadvertently or unwillingly; their mission was to carry out the wishes of their employer and get the captive back alive and unharmed, not to make arrests and crack the case. They'd no more contact the police or FBI than he would.

As for CTU, they were the odd man out, the last in the game and the last to know what was going on, Beltran told himself. Keehan political clout could keep them at arm's length and out of the loop. Let them get on the trail of Paz and the Supremo cell, for all he cared; it would buy him precious time to complete his task and make his getaway.

Years of living and operating in New Orleans had worked to his advantage; he knew the terrain. The Long Canal foot-bridge was a site he'd marked down long ago as useful for a future operation; there would never be a better time than now to use it.

Rubio, Torres, and Moreno, and their captive, had transferred to a panel van for the final phase of the ransom exchange. The van had three motorcycles, dirt bikes, in the rear.

Moreno had driven up on the power trail; along it was a dirt road used by the utility company for their roving repair trucks. The captive, hooded and with his hands tied, was hauled out of the van and hustled downhill by Rubio and Torres, into the graveyard. Torres remained behind to keep watch over the captive while Rubio slogged back up the hill.

A ramp was lowered from the rear of the van and the first dirt bike rolled down to the ground. Rubio rode it downhill to the cemetery, then walked back up the hill and repeated the process with a second bike. He and Torres stayed in the cemetery with Garros.

Moreno drove the van along the power trail to a crossroads, where another dirt road took him down the east side of the embankment. He drove to the Kwik-Up, parked the van in the lot, and rode the third bike up the dirt path behind the convenience store, up to the power trail and down again to the cemetery.

The power trail was a popular site for dirt bikers, and the activity going on around it attracted no attention from random passersby in the parking lot or along the highway.

Rubio was the demolitions man. He'd fastened explosive charges to the underside of the footbridge and rigged the smoke bombs in and around the cemetery.

All the munitions were rigged with remote-controlled detonators.

With everything ready for the exchange, and the trio safely emplaced in the cemetery, Beltran had arrived, parking his vehicle in the Kwik-Up lot. He located the getaway van, knelt down beside it as if examining the undercarriage, busied himself there for several minutes, rose, and returned to his own vehicle.

He took out the rifle in its carrying sheath, toting it casually under an arm; the power trail was also popular with target shooters and varmint hunters, and in a state where guns were a way of life, he was unlikely to attract undue attention. All the same, he'd waited until the lot was empty of any pedestrians or shoppers who might notice him before getting out of his machine and crossing to the back of the Kwik-Up.

Going around to the rear of the building, he'd climbed the dirt path most of the way up, stopping when he saw a likely spot for his sniper's nest. He'd squirmed through the bushes, finding a spot that afforded him a clear firing line on the back of the building and the getaway van parked in the lot.

Leaving the sheathed rifle hidden under some bushes,

he'd emerged on the dirt path, sticking an empty Kwik-Up white plastic bag on a branch to serve as a marker so he'd easily find the site.

He'd climbed to the top of the power trail, crossing to the other, west side, where he'd found himself a hollow in the bushes with a good vantage point on the cemetery and canal area. Settling into the nest, he'd run a routine comm check with Rubio, giving him a last-minute briefing and instructions.

After that, there was nothing to do but wait for the Keehan crowd to arrive with the money.

Now the ransom had been collected and the plan was moving into its final, terminal phase.

The dirt bikes were almost upon him, causing Beltran to involuntarily tense up. In the short time since arriving at his sniper's nest, he'd managed to recover his breath, and his heart rate had slowed to something like normal. The sputtering blat of the nearing motorcycles caused his heartbeat to speed up again.

They were here; they had arrived. The drone of their engines was offset by the sound of breaking branches as the first bike entered the gap and started down the dirt path on the east slope of the embankment.

Beltran turned his head toward the path, which was mostly hidden behind a screen of brush. The first bike flashed downhill past him, a blur of motion barely ten feet away.

Beltran could even hear the jouncing of the suspension springs over the motor noise.

The second bike followed, only a length or two behind. Turning his head away from the trail, Beltran looked down through the gap in the brush.

The first bike reached the bottom of the hill and pulled over to the side, idling.

Rubio was the rider, the knapsack slung across his back. He was barefaced, the bandana pulled down around his neck.

Beltran raised the rifle, shouldering it, pointing it downhill.

The second bike reached the bottom of the slope; its rider, Moreno. He, too, had uncovered his face.

Where was Torres? Beltran could hear him but not see him. He'd fallen well behind the other two. Not surprising, Beltran told himself. Torres was a big man and not particularly comfortable on the small, quick dirt bike.

After a pause, Torres came downhill, bouncing and sliding to a halt at the bottom of the slope.

Moreno went on ahead, riding his bike out from behind the building, around the corner, and into the lot, rolling to a halt at the rear of the van. He set the kickstand down and climbed off, opening the van's rear door and sliding the ramp to the pavement.

Rubio was the object of Beltran's obsessive interest. What would he do, how would he play it? Beltran sighted the scoped rifle's crosshairs on the back of Rubio's skull.

Rubio dismounted, swinging his legs off the bike. Crossing to the nearest Dumpster, the one closest to the corner of the building, he slipped out of the knapsack, shrugging it clear of his shoulders.

He lifted the lid of the Dumpster, dropping the knapsack with the money inside. He gently lowered the lid, went to his dirt bike, and saddled up.

Torres had sat there idling, waiting for Rubio. The big man looked ridiculous on the small bike, like a circus bear riding a tricycle. Rubio and Torres rode their bikes to the rear of the van, where Moreno had already loaded his bike into the back of the box.

Not bothering to dismount, Rubio rode his bike up the ramp and into the rear of the panel van.

Torres had had enough of motorbikes. Dismounting, he picked up his machine bodily and tossed it into the back of the truck. He wrestled the ramp free and slid it up to his partners, who wrestled it into place in the box.

Torres slammed the rear door shut and jogged around to the right front passenger side. Moreno was already in the front seat, starting up the engine. A blue-gray cloud of smoke jetted from the exhaust pipe in the rear.

Beltran had already set down the rifle. He now held a re-mote-controlled detonator, armed and ready. It was similar to the one used by Rubio to explode the blast charges under the bridge and the smoke bombs in the cemetery.

The van pulled out of the lot, turning right and starting southbound along the highway. Fastened to its underside was a charge of explosives that Beltran had fixed there ear-lier, when he'd first arrived at the Kwik-Up.

This was a matter of nice timing. If the van got too far away, the detonator might not work. But he didn't want the van too close to the Kwik-Up, either, for fear that that might block his own escape.

Beltran watched the van roll southbound, his finger poised over the red button. The machine was about a hun-dred yards down the road when he pushed the button, trig-gering the explosives wired beneath the van.

He might have been a trifle overzealous in the amount of explosives he'd used; the blast was tremendous.

The van disappeared in a blinding flash of white light. Disintegrating, its pieces fountaining skyward, it geysered upward in a roaring column, a pillar of smoke and fire.

A mighty crumping boom reverberated along the strip, the concussion blowing out plate-glass windows in stores on either side of the highway near where the van had been.

Beltran, a fastidious man, used a handkerchief to wipe down the rifle, removing all fingerprints. He left the weapon

behind, hidden under some bushes. Before, it would have attracted little if any attention, but now a man with a rifle even
in its case shrouding would likely catch the eye of some of
the many who were rushing out of stores on all sides to see
what the blast was all about.

Beltran pushed his way through the bushes to the dirt
path and descended the hill. Down the road, the crumpled
shell of the van was the center of a smoky, oily blaze whose
scarlet tongues of flame stood out dramatically against the
lowering darkness of the stormy night.

Cars were stopped in the middle of the road in all directions. People were running across the lot for a better view.

No one, absolutely no one, had eyes for the rear of the
Kwik-Up building. Beltran lifted the Dumpster lid, a stench
of garbage rising to meet him. Reaching in, he got hold of a
shoulder strap and hauled out the knapsack.

What was it the old Roman emperor—was it Domitian?—
had said?

"Money has no smell."

Chuckling to himself, Beltran went the long way around
the back of the building, emerging around the corner of
the north side. He crossed the lot to where his vehicle was
parked. Standing facing the driver's side door, he reached
for his key when he heard a scuffle of shoe leather on the
pavement behind him.

A voice said, "Hello, amigo."

Even before turning around to meet his destiny, Beltran
knew without a doubt to whom that voice belonged:

Colonel Paz.

. . . .

THE FOLLOWING TAKES PLACE
BETWEEN THE HOURS OF
9 P.M. AND 10 P.M.
CENTRAL DAYLIGHT TIME

. . . .

Kwik-Up Mini-Mall, New Orleans

Jack Bauer and Pete Malo sat in their SUV in the Kwik-Up parking lot. Pete said, "Looks like our plans to tail the kidnappers back to Beltran just went up in smoke."

The blast that had obliterated the getaway van was still echoing up and down the highway. A CTU Center team was still covering the mini-mall parking lot. The stakeout would continue.

Jack said, "Beltran wouldn't have blown up the money along with his stooges. They became expendable only after they passed the money to him."

He went on, "Our people had the kidnappers under observation from the moment they left the cemetery. We've been here in the lot, waiting for them. One of them went to the van immediately. The other two stayed behind the building for about a minute, minute and a half, before they went to the van."

Pete nodded, encouraging him to go on. "True."

Jack said, "Our spotters on the power trail reported that the trio had a bagful of ransom money when they started downhill. We know that they didn't have it when they came out from behind the back of the building. Somewhere during that time, they got rid of it. We know that they didn't stop to talk with anybody in the lot. They went directly to the van, got into it, and drove away."

Pete said, "And then—blooey!"

"Beltran pressed the button on them. It had to be him and nobody else," Jack said. "But back to the ransom money. That million dollars. They had it coming downhill and didn't have it a minute later when they went to the van. What happened to it?

"Either they handed it off to somebody or they left it in a dead drop for pickup later. Knowing Beltran's history of a penchant for anonymity, I'd opt for the latter."

Pete said, "Sure, but where is he? We can't go around detaining every old geezer in the lot, holding them for questioning."

Jack said, "Our spotter up on the hill reports that there's nobody behind the building now. We haven't seen anybody come out from there since the kidnappers showed. Let's sit tight for a while and see what happens."

The SUV was parked where the CTU agents had clear sightlines of the front and sides of the Kwik-Up store. They looked around in a 360-degree circle, slowly scanning the scene, seeking any odd or off-pattern detail.

Traffic was stopped in both directions in the highway. Backed up. From a distance, sirens sounded and emergency lights flashed as police cars and fire trucks approached the scene.

Some civilian vehicles were turning into the lots of the stores lining the road, searching for a way out of the ever-worsening jam. A couple of cars and vans pulled off the road into the Kwik-Up lot, mostly so their occupants could park and get out and see what was happening.

A short, slight, white-haired man ambled across the lot toward the store. Pete said, "Check out that old dude."

The man in question was a contrarian. Foot traffic in the lot moved away from the store and toward the highway, as people crowded, massed, and craned to get a better look at the blazing wreckage of the van.

The white-haired man moved in the opposite direction, his back turned on the scene of devastation. His gaze was fastened straight ahead, looking neither to the left nor the right. Nearing the storefront, he did not enter but instead angled off to the right and kept on going, rounding the corner and vanishing from view.

Jack said, "Bingo."

Pete leaned forward, on the edge of his seat. "He fits the demographic. Beltran would have to be a fairly ripe old age, seventy years old if not more."

A minute later, a voice broke in on the CTU comm net, coming through the dashboard speaker grid. "Hathaway here." Hathaway was the spotter up on the power trail, keeping watch on the east side of the embankment.

He said, "We've got something. A guy just came around to the back of the building."

Jack spoke into the hand mic. "Affirmative, we saw him, too."

Hathaway said, "I've got cover on the ridgetop. I can see him, but he can't see me."

"What's he doing?"

"Walking toward the south end of the building." After

a pause, Hathaway said, "He went to the Dumpsters. Now he's lifting the lid of one of them."

Pete said, "This could be it."

Hathaway went on, "He's taking something out—looks like a bag—a knapsack. The ransom money is in a knapsack, we know that from watching the swap go down on the footbridge." He sounded excited.

Jack used the comm net to alert the other team members posted in and around the lot. "Get ready, but nobody move until I give the signal."

Hathaway said, "Now he's going back the way he came. With the knapsack. He's going to the north end of the building—he's turned the corner—now he's heading toward the lot."

Jack and Pete were already suited up in bulletproof Kevlar vests, having donned them earlier in the night, as the Garros ransom swap neared. Now, as a standard precaution before going into action, they once more checked their handguns.

The old man reappeared from behind the corner of the Kwik-Up, emerging into view, carrying a hefty knapsack by the strap, so that it hung down by his side.

Pete said, "What do you think?"

Jack said, "Let's take him."

Pete broke into the comm net: "This is it. We're moving in." He and Jack got out of the SUV.

Their person of interest was short, thin, birdlike, with a shock of white hair and a clean-shaven face. He was darkly tanned, with dark eyes. He wore a loose fitting white guayabera short-sleeved shirt, khaki pants, rubber-soled boat shoes. Straight-backed, spry, he moved with an energetic stride.

He crossed to his vehicle, a beat-up old food vendor's truck, with a front cab and a quilted metal box behind. Mounted atop the cab was a mini-sized loudspeaker.

Jack and Pete separated as they closed in, approaching the suspect from the side, maneuvering to take him in a pincer movement.

Someone else got there first.

The food truck was parked in a row of parked cars that was at right angles to the highway. About seven or eight vehicles away, toward the roadside, an SUV stood idling.

A man got out of the front passenger side, walked around the front of the SUV and down an aisle at the head of the row toward the store.

The newcomer was a few paces ahead of Jack and Pete. He came abreast of the old man as the latter stood on the driver's side of the food truck, opening the cab door.

At that moment, a car came rolling down the lane, cruising, trolling for a parking space. Temporarily blocking Jack and Pete and barring their progress, but not before they got a good look at the newcomer's face.

"Paz!"

Several moments earlier, Colonel Paz had watched Beltran go behind the back of the Kwik-Up building. Yes, the white-haired old man was indeed the Generalissimo. Unlike the CTU agents, Paz knew Beltran and recognized him immediately.

Paz sat in the SUV's front passenger seat, Vasco was behind the wheel, and Fierro was in the back. Paz said, "I've got some business to take care of."

He reflexively reached for his Saint Barbara medallion to give it a squeeze, only to receive a shock. It was missing.

His heart lurched in his chest. He experienced a sensation not unlike grabbing for one's wallet and finding it's not there. A sensation multiplied tenfold.

He cursed under his breath. He felt around his bull neck, stubby fingers encountering the thin but tough length of chain from which the medallion hung. He hauled it out from under the top of his bulletproof vest, only to come up with the chain and no medallion. The catch of the chain had broken, allowing the medallion to slip free of it.

Paz swore again, sticking his fingers inside the top of the bulletproof vest—a tight fit—groping around for the medallion, not finding it. When had he seen it last?

He knew he'd had it when leaving the slaughter site of the hat company building, because he'd made obeisance to it then. It might have fallen off then. Perhaps his handling of it then had been what caused the chain to snap.

The medallion could have dropped off before he got into the Explorer to make his getaway. Or since. It might be trapped in his clothes even now, pinned between the vest and his flesh. If it was there, he couldn't feel it, though.

Which might mean nothing, because the flak jacket was heavy and hot and he was tired from a long day of being on the boil, seething with kill-lust since surviving the predawn ambush.

Think! Back at Supremo, after ritualistically squeezing the medallion, he hadn't gone far, not more than a dozen paces before getting into the van. Maybe it had fallen out of the bottom of the vest, into the top of his pants.

He felt around his waistband, running his fingers along the inside of it. No luck.

Spreading his meaty thighs, he felt around the seat cushion for it.

Nothing—*nada*.

Vasco glanced curiously at him. Fierro leaned forward, said, "A problem?"

Paz broke into a sweat. Fighting to keep his voice calm, neutral, he said, "Turn on the light."

Vasco switched on the overhead dome light, illuminating the front cab. Paz raised up out of his seat, squirming, looking at the seat cushion and the floor mat at his feet. No medallion.

Vasco said, "What is it, *jefe*?"

Paz spoke through clenched teeth. "I lost something—my religious medal." He opened the door, stepping out carefully, ears alert for any ringing noise of the medallion falling to the pavement. Hearing none.

Standing outside the Explorer, he reached around the seat, under the seat cushion where it met the vertical backrest. Coming up blank.

He ducked down, squatting as he peered at the floor. It was too dark to see under the seat. He ran his fingers over the mat and reached under the seat. Results nil.

Fierro had been keeping watch over the storefront and now he stirred. "The old one is coming back."

Paz swore again. He'd told the others nothing of his plans. He was not in the habit of explaining himself, figuring it made him look weak. Vasco and Fierro knew nothing of Beltran, who he was or what his role was in the chain of events that had led them to the Supremo killing ground.

They did know that Paz was highly interested in the oldster in the food truck, that he'd evinced great satisfaction upon sighting him, satisfaction of the kind that betokened nothing good to the object of that interest.

Fierro said, "He's carrying something, looks like a bag. Wonder what's in it?"

His voice sounded innocent enough, but Paz still gave him a suspicious side glance. No mention of the million-dollar ransom money had crossed his lips; he feared to lead his henchmen into temptation. That size sum—in cash, no less—could engender greed sufficient to overcome their fear. Especially in Fierro, a bold and unprincipled rogue and conscienceless killer. Too much like Paz for Paz himself to ever fully trust the other. But he needed Fierro; he did good work.

No more time could be spared by Paz for searching for the lost medallion, he had to get about his work. It was an ill omen, though. He'd had the piece for many years; it was his good luck charm, his talisman.

He mentally damned himself for being a superstitious old woman. If he didn't get moving, and quick, he risked losing Beltran. That must never be.

He straightened up, said, "Wait here. I've got to go kill a man and then I'll be right back."

He went around the front of the Explorer, padding light-footed along the aisle at the head of the row of parked cars. He hauled a pistol, a flat, big-caliber semi-automatic, out of his right hip pocket.

He caught fresh sight of Beltran, from up close, feeling the old familiar sensation of bloodlust rising in him. A good feeling.

Monatero had steered him right, he told himself. The Supremo cell commander hadn't known who Beltran was, who he really and truly was, not until Paz had told him. But he'd known the operational details of the kidnap exchange.

Beltran had ordered Rubio, Torres, and Moreno to maintain comm silence and not contact the Supremo home base. He hadn't said anything about home base contacting them, though.

His doubts mounting as the day wore on, Monatero had finally given in to his fears and phoned Rubio's cell late in the day to find out what was happening. Rubio had briefed him on developments, including where and how the ransom swap was set to go down.

Monatero had learned that the Kwik-Up mini-mall off the highway was the staging area for the Garros exchange at Sad Hill. He'd told Paz, and the tip was a good one.

* * *

Paz walked soft, but at the last instant, eagerness for the kill had caused him to speed up as he closed in on Beltran.

The sound of his footfalls might have betrayed his approach, or perhaps Beltran had sensed something at the last: impending doom casting its shadow before it.

Paz said, "Hello, amigo."

Beltran turned, face to face with Paz. Beltran, Havana's ace spymaster, the deep cover legend whom Monatero had known only as Tio Rico.

Uncle Rico, aged, amiable, ineffectual vendor of snack treats from a beat-up old food truck.

Paz loomed, standing up close to Beltran, separated from him only by the length of the gun barrel whose muzzle he held jammed into the other's middle. With his free hand, Paz relieved the oldster of the burden of the knapsack, gripping it by the shoulder strap and taking it away from him.

It was heavy, bulging at the seams. A million dollars! Not bad for a day's work.

The rest went quickly, in a businesslike manner. Beltran wasted not a breath on appeals, pleas, or last words.

Paz made no final speeches, no taunts, no exit lines. Having said hello to Beltran, all that remained for Paz to do was to say goodbye to him.

"Adios, amigo," he said, pulling the trigger. He fired several times, blowing out most of Beltran's middle, muzzle flashes underlighting his face to showcase its gleeful, mask-like cast.

Having the gun wedged up tight against Beltran's flesh served as a kind of silencer, muffling to some extent the sound of the blasts. Beltran stood there in place, thrashing and thumping against the truck door as Paz unloaded into him.

A round ripped through him and the door into the cab, setting off the computerized musical ditty that the food vendor had played through the roof-mounted loudspeaker to announce his approach and peddle his wares.

The tune was the same one that had played earlier today, when he'd showed up at snack time at the Supremo Hat Company:

"La Cucaracha."

It was on a short loop and now kept replaying itself, again and again, its piping notes shrilling through the parking lot.

Paz stepped back from Beltran, who slid down the side of the door, sitting down on the pavement and slumping forward, head bowed, as if bowing down to his slayer. A distinctive touch; Paz liked it.

He started to move, intending to circle around the front of the food truck and return to the Explorer the way he came.

People in the lot had heard the shots, but the amplified strain of "La Cucaracha," repeated again and again, defused the threat and made it seem like nothing more than a food vendor's ill-timed advertisement for himself.

Stepping off, Paz felt something slipping out from under his bulletproof vest, falling to the pavement at his feet. Light glinted off the object: his Saint Barbara medallion.

It hadn't escaped him after all! It had been stuck somewhere under the vest and finally worked itself loose during the shooting.

Total satisfaction spread through Paz, suffusing him from head to toe with its warmth. The talisman's loss had worried him more than he dared admit; finding it again filled him with a surge of good feeling, almost equal to what he'd felt pumping slugs into Beltran's belly.

He leaned forward from the waist to pick it up, setting down the knapsack on the pavement and releasing for an instant his grip on the knapsack to retrieve the medallion.

A shout came, loud enough to be heard over the refrain

of "La Cucaracha," which continued its idiotic, monotone blaring over the loudspeaker.

"Martello Paz!"

Jack Bauer stood behind Paz, no more than six feet away, gun in hand. Paz half-rose, whirling, swinging the gun around.

Jack shot him twice in the head. Ordinarily he wasn't a headhunter, going for the body shot, the safest and most reliable course in a gunfight. Odds were that Paz was wearing a bulletproof vest, though. This was one time that a head shot trumped a body shot.

One-two, the double tap, surest way to inflict instant death. Kill the brain and the reflexes crash, including those of a trigger finger.

In the Explorer, Vasco and Fierro suddenly found themselves confronted by CTU agents who popped up on both sides of the vehicle, sticking riot shotguns through the open windows into their faces.

"Freeze!"

Fierro moved.

A shotgun blast filled the cab interior. As did much of Fierro's head, blown off at point-blank range.

Vasco froze and stayed that way. Not moving even after a CTU man had frisk-patted him down, relieving him of his handgun and ordering him to get out of the cab.

He had to shout to be heard over "La Cucaracha."

Vasco remained in place, clutching the steering wheel. Until his fingers were pried open and he was hauled out of his seat and thrown facedown to the pavement and handcuffed.

Jack stood with his arm hanging down at his side, smoking gun barrel pointed at the pavement.

Pete Malo reached across the food truck's rooftop, grabbing a handful of wires leading into the loudspeaker and yanking them out. Cutting off "La Cucaracha" in mid-note.

Blessed silence.

Pete moved up beside Jack, said, "You took a chance there, calling him out."

Jack's ears were still ringing, not so much from the gunfire as from the music. He said, "I wanted him to turn around so I could shoot him from the front instead of from behind. Looks better that way for the record. Less like an execution."

Pete said, "No working that diplomatic status to get off scot-free and board the next plane for Venezuela, not for him. There's no diplomatic immunity from a couple of bullets in the head."

He gave Jack a quick side glance. "I guess you had it figured that way."

Jack shrugged, his silence committing him to nothing.

Pete indicated the white-haired oldster. "So that's the legendary Beltran. Too bad we couldn't take him alive."

Jack said, "Paz had other plans."

Reflected light from an overhead lamppost glinted off a metallic object on the pavement a few inches away from Paz's open, grasping hand.

Jack picked it up, held it to the light. About the size of a silver dollar, it was a rough-edged, silvery medallion stamped on one side with the image of a haloed woman in a long dress, holding a fistful of lightning bolts.

Pete said, "What's that?"

Jack said, "I don't know. It must have meant something to Paz, though. He was reaching for it when I called him out."

"A good luck piece, maybe."

"Not for him."

Jack eyed the medallion, turning it over in his hand, unsure of what to do with it. An odd trinket, yet it didn't seem right, somehow, to toss it away. Might turn out to be evidence, or a clue, though he didn't see just how yet. He pocketed it; he'd decide what to do with it later.

• •

THE FOLLOWING TAKES PLACE
BETWEEN THE HOURS OF
10 P.M. AND 11 P.M.
CENTRAL DAYLIGHT TIME

• •

Belle Reve Street, New Orleans

*"Vikki Valence, this is the police. Come on out of the front
door, now."*

Belle Reve was a side street down by the riverside. At the
waterfront end of it, at right angles to it, stood a waist-high
guardrail, its horizontal post painted in black-and-white
stripes. Beyond it lay an embankment sloping down for
about twenty yards before ending at the shoreline. The river
was a choppy black mirror reflecting the landward lights.

Belle Reve was a cul-de-sac, dead-ending on the waterfront. A quiet little street, lined on either side by a few
bungalow-type houses. Not the low-rent district, but nothing fancy, either. Far from it.

And far from quiet, too, with an unmarked police car
parked in front of it, facing it, with Sergeant Floyd Dooley

speaking through the car's public address system. His partner, Buck Buttrick, stood on the passenger side of the car,
leaning a hip against the front fender.

The car, a late model, dark-colored Crown Victoria sedan, stood at right angles to the curbside, its high-beam
headlights pointed at the front of the house, bathing it in
white light.

Nearby, parked along the curbside, was the SUV that
Jack Bauer and Pete Malo had been using. Its engine was
off, its lights dark. Jack and Pete were nowhere to be seen.

The one-story house was raised on support poles, leaving
about eighteen inches of crawl space between the bottom
floor planks of the house and the sandy ground below. The
front windows were curtained and the house was dark inside, no lights showing.

Floyd Dooley stood on the driver's side of the sedan.
The door was open, and stretching out from where it was
plugged into the dashboard was a long, coiled cable wire,
at the end of which was a microphone clutched in the lawman's hand.

Dooley spoke in a normal, conversational tone into the
mic, his words being amplified through the loudspeaker of
the car's PA system.

He said, *"Come on, now, Miss Vikki, let's have no more
foolishness. This is Sergeant Dooley speaking. You know me."*

Inside the house, Vikki Valence stood to one side of the
front window, flattened against the wall. The high-beam
headlights shone through the window curtains, illuminating
much of the interior, leaving dark squares and patches in the
areas where the light did not reach.

Vikki was sweating. Much of the look of a trapped animal showed on her face, a contorted mask of fear. Her hair
was a tangled mess, strands falling across her face. A sweat-
soaked black dress clung to her body.

She held a butcher knife in one hand, clutching it with the blade pointed downward. It was the only weapon she could find in the house and she'd kept it close to her for most of the long hours of the day and night she'd spent hiding out. She wasn't about to let it go now.

"You know me."

She knew him, all right. Knew that Dooley and his partner, Buttrick, were the two crookedest cops on Bourbon Street. Making them two of the crookedest cops in New Orleans, which qualified them as contenders for the title of crookedest cops in the world.

She had no doubt that they'd sell her to Marty Paz, or Beltran, or whoever made them the best offer. She had no intention of finding out their intentions.

Dooley's voice came over the PA system: *"Miss Vikki, Miss Vikki, come on out now, you hear?"*

It was starting to rain, that rain which the storm clouds had been promising all day but which had been so long delayed. It fell in big, fat drops that made plopping noises as they struck the Crown Victoria and the crown of Dooley's soft, small-brimmed fishing hat.

Vikki got down on her hands and knees, crawling away in the opposite direction from the front door. It wasn't so easy to crawl holding the butcher knife but she managed it.

The front room was a kind of living room, with two armchairs and a couch that pulled out to become a bed. It was folded up now. She crawled into the back room, which was much larger, a studio space. The rear wall had a set of French doors that opened onto an outdoor wooden deck. Now they were closed.

The space was an artist's studio, smelling of paint and turpentine and canvas. A wooden easel stood in the middle of the floor space, a square of stretched, framed canvas mounted on it.

Outside, the pace of the rainfall was quickening. Rain-drops rustled the leaves of the small, shrublike trees in the front yard and made silver streaks where they fell in the path of the headlight beams.

Dooley said, *"You are purely trying my patience, Miss Vikki. It's raining and I ain't gonna stand out here much longer getting wet."*

Vikki crawled behind a head-high partition, which screened her from the headlights shining into the house. She got ready to make her break. Not wanting to give herself away by the clip-clop of her sandals on the wooden deck, she took them off.

Holding them by the ankle straps in one hand, and the butcher knife in the other, she tip-toed barefoot to the French doors, keeping the partition between her and the headlights to avoid casting shadows.

She reached for the door handle with the hand hold-ing the sandals by the straps, not wanting to let go of the butcher knife for a second. Holding her breath, she turned the handle, easing the door open to the width it took for her to slip through it, stepping outside onto the deck.

Raindrops pattered on the deck planks. The backyard was dark, except where the headlights shone through the house and through the section of the French doors that wasn't screened by the partition.

She planned to make a run for it, climbing over the back fence into a neighbor's backyard, and making her way away from Belle Reve Street.

It was good to be out of the house where she'd been cooped up for most of the day and night, the thick, humid air of the oncoming storm feeling positively fresh and re-freshing after the atmosphere inside the house.

A shadowy figure stepped around the corner of the house

on her right, looming into view. He said her name, "Vikki Valence."

A little shriek escaped her as she reflexively raised the butcher knife high.

A deck plank creaked behind her, and before she could react, a strong hand reached around her to clench the wrist that held the knife. A strong arm encircled her wasp waist, lifting her up and raising her bare feet off the ground.

The man who stood behind her, holding her, gave her wrist a little twist in a direction in which it wasn't designed to go. Gasping, white-faced, she let go of the knife, which fell clattering to the deck planking.

The man holding her said, "Easy does it, Miss Valence. We're CTU. You contacted us, remember? Well, here we are."

The speaker was Jack Bauer; the other figure, the one at the far end of the deck, was Pete Malo.

She said, "I'll scream—"

Jack said, "Save your voice for talking. You're going to be doing a lot of it, because we want to know all about your friend Colonel Paz and his friend Beltran." No point in telling her they were both dead, not yet.

Vikki stopped struggling, not that her squirmings were getting her anywhere. Jack's calm, conversational tone convinced her that she was dealing with the real thing, a government man. Hoodlums and hard guys of the Bourbon Street variety that she was used to dealing with rarely bothered to be polite.

Jack set her down on her feet, keeping his grip on her wrist. "Don't run. Where would you go to, anyhow?"

She said, "Don't turn me over to Dooley and Buttrick—"

Pete Malo stepped up, said, "You belong to CTU now." He bent down, picking up the butcher knife. "Nice."

Vikki said, "I was only going to use it in self-defense."

Pete said, "Let's all go inside, hmm?"

Vikki started to struggle again, but Jack held her wrist in a police-style come-along, controlling her movements. She said, "No—no, not inside—"

Jack said, "Why not?"

Pete told her, "Don't get frantic, Vikki."

"I don't want to go back in there!"

Pete said, "I do. I'm getting wet out here."

He opened one of the French doors wide, crossing the threshold and stepping inside, halting almost immediately. "Uh-oh," he said.

He padded around in the studio area lit by the headlights' glare, finding a wall switch and flipping it on, turning on an overhead light.

Jack followed, escorting Vikki inside. His nostrils caught a whiff of decay, a stench of corruption. He knew that smell.

Pete said, "We don't want to leave our police friends out in the rain." He crossed the studio into the front room, opening the front door and standing in the doorway. "Come on in, men."

Dooley and Buttrick hurried across the front yard, up the three front stairs and inside, eager to be out of the rain, now falling somewhat steadily. As soon as he stepped inside, Dooley made a face, nostrils crinkling in disgust. Buttrick said, "What up and died in here?"

Pete said, "Guess."

He turned and went into the studio, the two cops following.

An easel was positioned to take advantage of the natural light that would come shining through the French doors in daytime. Mounted on the easel was a half-finished painting of a nude female. Not Vikki, but some other femme, one who presumably didn't figure in the case, but—who knew for sure?

The draftsmanship was adequate but the enthusiasm unmistakable. The technique identified the artist as the painter of the life-sized nude portrait of Vikki that hung above her bed in the apartment over the Golden Pole club.

The wooden floor was marked with red stains that weren't paint. Bloodstains.

Off to one side of the room, against the wall, was a man-sized object wrapped in canvas. Jack, Pete, Dooley, and Buttrick all stood there silently for a moment, looking at it.

Vikki said, "I didn't do it!"

Jack absently patted her shoulder. "You've held up fine so far, don't get hysterical now."

He crossed to the big bundle, crouching down beside it. He peeled the canvas back from the head area, unmasking it down to the neck.

The corpse was that of a middle-aged man with a roosterlike shock of black hair and a long, bony face. He had a mustache and a scruffy three-day beard. A single bullet hole had been drilled through the middle of his forehead. His eyebrows were lifted, as if in surprise at being dead.

Dooley sidled up alongside, peering down at the body. "Yep. That's him, all right. That's that artist fellow, Marcel."

Jack rose, straightening up. As the others were doing, he turned his gaze on Vikki. She said, "I didn't do it, I swear!"

He said, "Who did?"

"I don't know! Maybe Marty, or some of Beltran's people!"

"You'd better tell us all about it."

Pete said, "Tell us outside, in the car. We could all use some fresh air."

They all sat in the SUV, which was roomier than the Crown Victoria. Jack had the idea that Vikki would be more forthcoming in the CTU vehicle than she would be in the police car. Possession being nine-tenths of ownership. She was CTU's now.

That was okay with Dooley and Buttrick. They didn't care who had possession of Vikki, as long as they got credit for her discovery. This was going to make them the fair-haired boys of the NOPD. Which was fine with Jack and Pete.

The vital lead had been furnished earlier that night by Dorinda, the busty, brunette exotic dancer second-billed after Vikki on the Golden Pole lineup. Being detained for questioning at CTU Center since early morning had helped concentrate Dorinda's recollection. She finally volunteered information about a male friend of Vikki's, some "crazy artist" who hung around on the fringes of the star dancer's orbit.

Dorinda had barely remembered him because he was a down-at-the-heels bohemian type who didn't have much money, making him a less than negligible figure in her eyes. After being questioned and cross-questioned about Vikki's associates by CTU interrogators, Dorinda had at last re-called the artist.

All she knew of his name was that it was "Alan, Alan something." One item that stood out in her memory was that he was always trying to get the dancers to pose in the nude for him, so he could paint their pictures.

She claimed she wasn't interested: "Honey, I could never sit still that long."

But Vikki's narcissism had overcome her fidgetiness, according to Dorinda, long enough for Alan to paint her portrait, "in the altogether." Armed with that clue, CTU investigators had examined Vikki's portrait in her apartment, signed by the artist, "A. Marcel."

They were in the process of checking with gallery own-ers and art dealers to track down his name and address right around the time that Dooley and Buttrick had showed up at the Kwik-Up mini-mall in the aftermath of the van bombing and shootout.

That was a little off their bailiwick, which was generally centered around the strip joints and dives of Bourbon Street, but the events of the day, starting with the Golden Pole massacre, had quickened their interest in the fast-developing big picture. And its promise of big publicity for those who played their cards right.

Nothing if not live-wire opportunists, they had hastened to the scene when the police dispatcher began broadcasting a general alert about the action at the Kwik-Up.

There, as Colonel Paz and Hector Beltran were being carried away dead on stretchers, the two cops had encountered Jack and Pete.

Dooley said, "Whoo-whee! You boys are sure cutting a swath through town, I don't mind telling you."

The CTU agents let that pass without comment. Word had just reached them from Center about one "A. Marcel," and Pete gave the lawmen a quick sketch of the artist's background and asked them if they'd ever heard of him.

Dooley said, "Now that you mention it, that does ring a bell." He knew all the characters on Bourbon Street; he didn't know Marcel's name, but he did have a vague recollection of a painter who hung around on the fringes of the Golden Pole and other like establishments, who was always trying to hustle the girls into posing nude for him.

"That's his come-on," Dooley said. "Hell, once he's got 'em in his place with their clothes off, he's more than half-way there, eh?"

He didn't know where Marcel lived, but he knew someone who knew someone who did; a short time later, the Crown Victoria was pulling up in front of the Belle Reve address, with the SUV containing Jack and Pete right behind.

Dooley had used the police vehicle's public address system to call out Vikki because, as he put it, "it beats walking in there without knowing if she's half out of her head and has a gun or whatever."

He had no objection to Jack and Pete taking the lead in that department, however.

Vikki Valence indeed had been there, and she now told her story.

Some people are police buffs, civilian amateurs with a fascination with the world of cops and their doings. Al Marcel's interest was politics. He'd painted Vikki in the nude when she'd first started going out with Raoul Garros. During the sessions when she modeled for him, she'd gossiped about Raoul and his friends and associates and their doings. Marcel hung on her every word and encouraged her to tell him more.

Later, when Raoul passed her along to Marty Paz, she'd had to be more circumspect in her meetings with Marcel. Paz was the jealous type. His busy schedule at the consulate and at LAGO left her with a lot of free time on her hands, especially in the daytime. She managed to keep on meeting regularly with Marcel for coffee and drinks in little, out-of-the-way places that high rollers like Garros and Paz wouldn't be caught dead in. She kept Marcel entertained with plenty of gossip about the comings and goings of her rich, powerful Venezuelan "friends."

A couple of times, Paz had used her apartment to meet with an older man, a white-haired old gentleman. He gave her money to go shopping so that she'd be out of the apartment during those meetings. That was fine with her; she wasn't interested in his boring deal making and mysterious meetings and whatnot.

Once or twice, Paz had slipped up, and while talking to

his bodyguards when Vikki was in earshot had mentioned the old fellow's name: "Beltran."

The name meant nothing to her, but Marcel had been very excited when she'd mentioned it. He wanted to know everything about this Beltran, when he met Paz and for how long, was he alone or was someone with him; no detail was too minute for Marcel when it came to this Paz.

The way he carried on, Vikki suspected that Beltran was a lot more than the polite, gentlemanly old geezer she'd taken him for, which now piqued her interest in him, too. She could never really come up with much, though, because Paz's meetings with Beltran were few and far between, and he made sure she was out of the apartment during their conclaves.

Only recently, in the last week or so, a change had come over Marcel. He wasn't his usual breezy self; he was a worried man. Scared. The change in his demeanor threw a scare into her, too.

The last time they'd met for coffee—on Thursday, only forty-eight hours ago—Marcel had been a frightened man indeed. He was a mess, with dark rings under his eyes, nervous, jumpy, constantly looking over his shoulder and giving a start each time a stranger entered the little coffee shop where they were meeting. He sat at a rear table, facing the door.

He warned her that she was in danger, too, due to her closeness to Paz, that "sinister forces" were closing in on the Colonel, and if she wasn't careful, she might be caught up in events that were about to overtake him, events with dire and possibly even fatal consequences.

He refused to say more than that, telling her that she was better off not knowing and what she didn't know couldn't hurt her. He did hand her a matchbook with a name and telephone number written on the inside of the cover.

The name was a set of initials unknown to her: CTU.

She'd heard of the FBI and CIA, of course, but never of CTU. Not that she followed current affairs much; her interest in the news extended to what headliners were playing at what clubs.

Marcel didn't go into any long explanations, merely telling her that CTU was a U.S. government agency, like the Department of Homeland Security, only tougher—much tougher, was the impression she got. If something happened to him, Marcel, or to Paz, or if she ever felt herself in danger, she should call the telephone number he'd written down, the number of CTU's public hotline.

She should call and be sure to mention the name Beltran. On that point, he was very specific. That name was a key sure to unlock their interest, and they would move quickly to secure her safety.

She asked Marcel what he meant by something happening to him or Paz, but he wouldn't elaborate. He'd cut the meeting short and made a hurried exit, scurrying away, scuttling down the sidewalk with his head down and his shoulders hunched, as if awaiting a blow.

He'd put the fear in her, and she couldn't shake it. Worried, she'd gone to his place on Belle Reve Street the following day, on Friday afternoon, determined to find out what it was all about.

What she found instead was a corpse—his. He lay sprawled on his studio floor with a bullet hole in his head. No question about whether life lingered in him; he couldn't have been any deader. Terrified, afraid now for her own life, she got out of there fast.

She was in a panic, not thinking straight. She walked around in a daze for several hours, in shock. Not until twilight approached, and with it the remembrance that she had a show to put on tonight, that her performance was imminent, did she return to some sense of herself.

She'd used a pay phone to call the CTU hotline and pass on her message. Then she'd gone back to her usual haunts, to her apartment over the Golden Pole, trying to fake a semblance of normality that would see her through until CTU agents came to pick her up and take her to safety.

It was torture, mental torture, for her to go through the motions of doing her act for several sets on Friday night going into Saturday morning. As was his custom, Marty Paz had come to see her last set and then accompany her upstairs to her apartment for an erotic tryst.

She didn't know if he'd had Marcel killed, even done the job himself, or if he was merely an innocent party—innocent in the matter of the death of Al Marcel, that is. Marty Paz could be charming, even courtly, in his way, but innocent he could never be; he was a carnivore born and bred—a dangerous man, capable of extreme violence. Vikki knew the type; she'd seen enough of them in her years of working the exotic dancer circuit, and the milieu of vice, hoodlums, and gangsters in which it flourished.

It had been an ordeal of a different sort for her to "entertain" Colonel Paz early that Saturday morning in the amatory fashion to which he was accustomed; as with her striptease act, which she'd performed flawlessly earlier that night, once again professionalism came to her rescue, as she did what came naturally. The Colonel certainly seemed no different than usual in his manner or attitudes, giving no sign that he suspected her of anything or intended to do her harm.

Dawn was breaking that Saturday morning, when he'd finished dressing, given her a goodbye kiss, picked up the briefcase that he habitually carried with him and took everywhere he went, and exited her apartment, going downstairs and into Fairview Street—only to step into a whirlwind of violence, gunfire, and mass murder.

Vikki had already been poised to run, and even before the last gunshots had stopped echoing, she'd thrown on some clothes, grabbed her bag, and slipped down the backstairs and out the rear exit of the building.

She was on the lam. Luckily she knew Bourbon Street and the French Quarter inside-out, knew all the back alleys and cellar clubs and shortcuts. She knew better than to take a cab or hire a car, since the drivers were required to keep records of the destinations of their passengers. She avoided the buses and streetcars for similar reasons.

She managed to put some distance between herself and the Golden Pole before ducking into an after-hours club, one where the action was still going strong when the sun was coming up. She'd managed to persuade a passing acquaintance to give her a ride to the riverfront. She had him drop her off several blocks away from Belle Reve Street, parting from him with promises of showing him "a real good time" the next time they met.

She went to the one place she was sure was safe: Marcel's house. He was already dead; the killers, whoever they were, wouldn't be back. She'd lay low there, contacting CTU and waiting until they came to pick her up and take her to safety.

It was pretty grim there, in the murder house. She couldn't bear to look at Marcel's corpse, so she'd rolled it up in a sheet of canvas, covering it up and pushing it across the floor to the far side of the studio.

Her plan to contact CTU for help hit a potentially fatal snag when she reached into her bag for her cell phone and found it wasn't there. Frantic, she turned the bag upside down, emptying its contents on the floor. No cell. She must have lost it sometime this morning during her wild flight from the Golden Pole as she ran through alleys, climbed fences, and squirmed under guardrails to make her escape.

Marcel had a cell, she knew; she'd seen him use it. She

searched the bungalow, looking for it, but couldn't find it. She forced herself to examine the corpse, turning out the dead man's pockets in search of a cell. No luck. She became aware that another searcher had been through the place before her. Cabinet drawers showed signs of having been ransacked; pillows and cushions had been slashed open and the mattress stripped of its bed coverings and overturned. No doubt the culprit was Marcel's killer. Maybe he'd taken the cell.

There was no landline telephone on the premises. Vikki was pinned in place for lack of a phone. She didn't dare show herself on the street in daylight to use a pay phone. She was afraid to stir from her hiding place, despite the macabre presence of Marcel's dead body.

Who to trust? Not the police; she didn't trust them not to sell her out. Whatever was behind all this killing, it was something big. The Syndicate maybe, or major narcotics traffickers, or even something political. Whoever was big enough to unleash the violence outside the Golden Pole was big enough to reach inside police headquarters, put a hand on Vikki Valence, and place her among the missing.

She told herself that she'd make a move when it got dark, that she'd have a better chance of getting away then. But she couldn't summon the resolve to make the jump. Bad as the Marcel death house was, it was better than whatever unknown fate awaited her on the streets.

She sat around in a kind of shocked stupor, trying to summon up the will to make a move. Then the decision had been made for her, with the arrival of Dooley and Buttrick, and with them, CTU agents Bauer and Malo.

That was her story, the gist of it anyway. No doubt there was plenty more good intelligence to be gotten from her, but that was a job for the full-time interrogators at CTU Center across the river.

Floyd Dooley said, "You can believe what she says about the NOPD being full of crooks and double-crossers. Except for me and Buck. You can trust us; we're your boys."

Jack had contacted CTU Center early on, to let them know Vikki had been found. He and Pete got her story during the twenty minutes or so while they were waiting for a detail to arrive at Belle Reve to take her to Center for debriefing.

The CTU vehicle arrived, Vikki being transferred to their custody. One of the agents was Hathaway, a field man who'd earlier been the spotter on the Sad Hill power trail, monitoring the progress of the kidnappers from the cemetery to the Kwik-Up parking lot and the blast that would ultimately send their remains to another cemetery.

Hathaway took Jack aside for a private word. "Quite a party at Center! Not only are those two other dancers from the Golden Pole, Francine and Dorinda, down there, but so is Raoul Garros and Susan Keehan, too. And now Vikki Valence!" He smacked his lips.

Jack said, "I know that Garros was going to be picked up by our people as soon as he was released by the kidnappers, but what's Susan Keehan doing down there?"

"Raising holy hell," Hathaway said, showing every evidence of having enjoyed the spectacle. "Sears balked at turning Garros over to our guys, until someone dropped a word in his ear about Susan Keehan being liable for obstruction of justice charges for helping Garros get away from us at the Mega Mart. Sears played ball after that. Garros hollered about diplomatic immunity, but we said we were taking him into protective custody to make sure nothing else happened to him before he was deported for acts of espionage against the United States of America."

"How did Susan horn in?"

"Oh, she insisted she be allowed to accompany him, to make sure that his rights weren't violated. Cal Randolph said okay, why not? She might spill something without even realizing it, something we could use," Hathaway said.

He went on, "The Flea on Susan has been neutralized. The abort switch was thrown, turning it into a piece of plastic and metal junk."

Hathaway got confidential, lowering his voice. "You should have seen what happened at Center when Susan came face to face with Raoul's former gal pal, Dorinda! Dorinda wasn't shy about letting Susan know that she and Garros were more than, er, just friends, if you know what I mean."

Jack said, straight-faced, "I do, but does Susan?"

Hathaway said, "If she didn't, she does now. Let's put it this way: if I were Raoul, I wouldn't go setting that wedding date anytime too soon!"

• •

THE FOLLOWING TAKES PLACE
BETWEEN THE HOURS OF
11 P.M. AND 12 A.M.
CENTRAL DAYLIGHT TIME

• •

Pelican Pier, New Orleans

"Al Marcel" was more than just a woman-chasing painter
with a penchant for international politics.

Inputting his name and facial photographs taken from his
dead body, CTU Center analysts were able to make a quick
identification of the mystery man. His name was not Alan
but Alain—Alain Marcel. If, indeed, that was his real name
and not just another cover identity he had assumed while
working in the United States.

A native of France, Marcel was revealed to be an under-
cover agent for French intelligence, on assignment in New
Orleans.

France maintains strong political, economic, and military ties with a number of its former colonies, including the
tiny South American nation that used to be called French

Guyana. Guyana borders Venezuela, and with the advent of Hugo Chavez and his aggressively expansionist socialist regime, he'd been leaning hard on his neighbors, particularly Colombia and Guyana.

In his office at Élysée Palace in Paris, the newly installed, centrist French president had noted Chavez's belligerent moves toward Guyana with anger and alarm.

He'd tasked his spy service to keep close tabs on Chavez and his creatures, gathering intelligence about their present activities and future plans.

One member of that effort was the man named Alain Marcel. Marcel had been posted to New Orleans, assigned to monitor the activities of Colonel Paz at the Venezuelan Consulate and Raoul Garros at the state-owned LAGO oil company offices in the Crescent City. Paz and Garros both were major womanizers, giving Marcel a wedge to gather information on their doings.

Posing as a painter, Marcel had insinuated himself into the bohemian world of the French Quarter, that demimonde where the art world intersects the world of dancers, prostitutes, dives, and cafés.

His painterly skills were adequate for the task, while his personal charm and good looks were more fitted for success in penetrating the society of showgirls and exotic dancers frequented by Paz and Garros.

Striking up an acquaintance with Vikki Valence—which wasn't hard, since she had a yen for personable, good-looking men—Marcel had managed to collect a good deal of intelligence first on Garros, and then, after the Venezuelan playboy had tired of Vikki, on her next boyfriend.

The Venezuelans in New Orleans were Marcel's primary target, but while on assignment, he'd been informed by liaison with French intelligence that Major Marc Vollard had surfaced in New Orleans.

The French were highly interested in Vollard, whose mercenary activities had crossed some of their operations in their former African colonies. They kept a detailed dossier on him, continually updating it. They definitely wanted to get their hands on him, first for a lengthy period of interrogation to squeeze him dry of everything he knew about the sponsors and details of his past operations, and then to quietly liquidate them so he would trouble them no more.

Marcel had been tasked to keep an eye out for Vollard and his associates and find out everything he could about them. His assignment had come to fruition unexpectedly early, when he'd discovered that certain members of Vollard's permanent leadership cadre, such as Hermann Ost, had been meeting with communist Cuban spymaster Hector Beltran.

More, Vollard's men had been tailing Paz, clocking his movements. Marcel knew what that meant: they were building a profile of his pattern and routine, preparatory to assassinating him.

Paris was interested in Beltran, as any intelligence service would be, but it was Vollard whom they really wanted to get their hands on.

Marcel had pushed perhaps too hard, for in the final week leading up to Bloody Saturday and the Golden Pole massacre, he'd come to the notice of Vollard and his crew.

Instead of tailing the mercenaries, they were tailing him, closing in on him.

On Thursday he'd met with Vikki Valence to warn her as best he could of the danger encompassing Paz and all those in his orbit. She was part of his assignment, but he cared for her, too, in his way, and he didn't want to see any harm come to her. He told her as much as he dared, without breaking his cover or revealing his ties to French intelligence.

That was why he'd steered her to CTU. Washington and

communist Cuba had been mortal foes since Castro first came to power and revealed his Marxist-Leninist ties back in 1960. The mention of Beltran's involvement in the Paz/ Vollard affair was sure to prod Washington into quick action, and CTU was its most effective, fast-moving domestic action and enforcement arm.

Not long after he warned Vikki, Vollard's killers had caught up with Marcel at the Belle Reve riverfront bungalow, putting a quick end to him. They took his cell phone, address book, and any documents or letters that might supply some new intelligence.

Now, armed with the knowledge of Marcel's ties to Paris, CTU Center Director Cal Randolph moved quickly to contact the man he knew was French intelligence's top agent in New Orleans.

This individual, a resident agent assigned to the French Consulate in the Crescent City, was known to Cal solely as Monsieur Armand.

Contacting him personally on a secure, scrambled phone line, Cal had succinctly laid out the background of Marcel's death, and how it tied into the events of the day: the Golden Pole massacre, the Garros abduction and ransoming, the Supremo Hat Company slaughter, and the carnage at the Kwik-Up parking lot and environs.

Monsieur Armand, expressing sorrow and regret at Marcel's death, thanked Cal for providing him with the information and vowed full cooperation. He arranged for his people to immediately send all their computer files on Vollard, especially his New Orleans activities, to CTU Center. Center analysts sent a copy of the files to headquarters in Washington, D.C., for deconstruction, permutation, and combination of the data by CTU's linked national net of supercomputers.

Monsieur Armand was able to provide Cal Randolph

with one last, intriguing clue: during the final days of his life, Marcel had focused a good part of his attention at a site at Pelican Pier on the New Orleans waterfront.

Since Marcel was no painter of seascapes, there was every possibility that he'd scented some kind of link between Vollard and the site.

That was why Jack Bauer and Pete Malo now found themselves sheltering in the recessed doorway of a warehouse building adjacent the site on Pelican Pier, scanning the suspect site to see what they could see.

The answer was, literally, not much. The rain was really coming down now, a continuous, high-volume downpour whipped into greater frenzy by ever-mounting winds from the oncoming storm. It was as if those ominous, low-hanging clouds that had roofed New Orleans from morning to night had suddenly had their bellies ripped open, releasing a torrential rainfall.

Slanting sheets and curtains of rainfall now obscured their view of Pelican Pier.

Something was afoot there, to be sure. A lot of activity was centered on a barge that was berthed to a floating dock on the downriver side of the long pier.

There was movement, too, around the warehouse with corrugated tin siding that sat at the middle of the pier, its rear edging the upriver side of the wharf, leaving an open space in front where a number of SUVs were massed and where men were seen going in and out of the building, loading bundles into the vehicles.

There wasn't much that could be made of that, though. The doings could have been nothing more than the usual activity associated with a civilian, law-abiding, dockside operation. A closer look was required.

The downpour that restricted visibility was now their

ally, helping to shield Jack and Pete as they made their sur-
reptitious approach toward the pier.

Earlier observation, even through heavy rainfall, had revealed the presence of a number of video surveillance cameras mounted at key points along the landward end of the pier,
which was sealed off by a gated metal fence and watchmen.

The building where Jack and Pete sheltered was upriver
of the pier; abandoning the doorway where they sheltered,
they moved out on foot. The waterfront was on the north,
left bank of the river.

The optimum angle of approach toward Pelican Pier
seemed to be on the west corner of its landward side. The
chain-link fence barring entry to the pier crossed the foot of
it at right angles, turning at the front corners to provide wings
extending for seven or eight feet along the edge of the pier.

The top of the fence in all directions was strung with spiraled loops of razored concertina wire; no climber could
get through that, so there would be no scaling the fence and
going over the top.

Jack and Pete made their way to the west corner at the
front of the pier. No video cameras were in evidence at the
edge of the fence.

The agents came in low, crouched almost double, scurrying toward their goal.

An inch of water covered the street bordering the pier,
sloshing and splashing underfoot as Jack and Pete crossed
to the corner. Gusty winds coming in off the river battered
them, trying to knock them down. Reaching the corner of
the fence, they hunkered down.

Jack's lightweight, waterproof nylon Windbreaker
jacket and Pete's supposedly water-resistant raincoat were
no match for the downpour; the two of them were already
soaked to the skin.

The next part was the chanciest. To get on the pier, they'd

have to climb across the wing extension of the fence that did a ninety-degree turn at its front corner, extending for ten feet back along the pier's edge.

It was a metal chain-link fence, affording handholds. Even so, it was a long drop down, and once fallen in the turbulent waters surging around the pilings upholding the pier, the strongest swimmer could expect nothing more than a quick death by drowning.

Jack said, "Here goes nothing." Leaning around the fence corner post, he reached inward to the wing of the fence, grabbing two tight handholds of the chain links, wrapping his fingers around them.

Holding on for dear life, he swung outward, his feet leaving the curbed edge of the pavement. He now clung spiderlike to the fence wing; below lay surging river water, boiling and furious.

The fence was wet and rain-slick, winds slammed him, trying to knock him off his perch. Maintaining a death grip with his left hand, Jack reached sideways with his right, hooking his fingers into the interstices of the fence.

His right handhold secure, he released his left hand and moved it toward him, riverward. There were no footholds; the fence links were too small for that. Jack had to proceed by upper body strength alone.

He repeated the process, working his way crosswise along the fence, narrowing the gap toward the corner post anchoring it to the pier. His hands ached; the pain in his shoulder joints was intense. Rain battered the top of his head, sluicing down his face, getting into his eyes. He kept tossing his head to clear the water from his orbs.

Creeping spiderlike along the fence, he reached its end, swinging his feet around the corner post and planting them firmly on the pier. He was now inside the fence of this suspect dockside facility.

His hands were stiff claws; he flexed them, opening and closing them to restore circulation and feeling to them. When he was ready, he signaled Pete to make the crossing.

Pete hooked his hands into the fence links and swung out into empty air, over the river water twenty-five feet below. He followed the same agonizing course as Jack had; when he reached the corner post, Jack reached out to give him a hand, gripping his arm to help him swing to safety inside the fence.

They both now crouched down, huddling in the corner before making their next move. Pete panted, gasping. When he'd recovered his breath, he said, "A safe desk job in Center doesn't look so bad now!"

Now they moved riverward, closing on the barnlike structure that stood in the middle of the pier. Scattered along the pier's west side were a number of boxy containers and stacked wooden pallets, providing welcome cover as they advanced toward the building.

The building was a simple construction, a big, looming, barnlike structure with high walls and a peaked roof. Its long walls were parallel with the sides of the pier.

The roof was made of tin; the noise made by the rain falling on it was slightly terrific. Runoff water showered down from the eaves.

Jack and Pete sheltered in the lee of the building, below a row of ground-floor windows. The sills were set at shoulder height; the windows were made of panes of glass set in gridded metal framework. The frames were flaky with corrosion and rust; the panes were opaque with grime.

The window closest to the pier's edge seemed like the likeliest choice to open on an obscure and deserted corner of the building; the CTU agents targeted it as their avenue of entry.

Pete shucked off his raincoat, wrapping folds of cloth

around his right hand to protect it. He then palm-heeled the windowpane in the lower right corner of the frame.

It popped out, falling inward.

Here was where the downpour was working for them; the sound of the glass falling inside and breaking would never be overheard over the rattle of rainfall drumming on the echoing tin roof.

Jack peeked inside through the gap. As they'd guessed, the window lay in a dark corner of the shedlike structure. The interior was vast, gloomy, cavernous, the dimness broken by a series of floodlights hanging overhead on wires suspended from a rafter beam that ran along the building's central axis.

It was an old building, filled with a lot of old junk, stacked piles of metal truss braces long since gone to rust, massive blocky mounds wrapped in greasy, age-darkened tarpaulins, worktables and benches that hadn't been put to use in decades.

The real action was going on in the center of the space, where a knot of men were loading bundles of material into the backs of several SUVs that were parked inside. The long west wall was broken by an open bay door; floodlights mounted outside the bay and atop it threw cones of light onto the pier, illuminating slanted lines of rain that sliced through the glow.

Still, there was nothing about the activity to suggest whether it was lawful business or illicit doings; Jack and Pete needed a closer look.

Jack hooked his hands together, giving Pete a boost so he could reach up inside the empty square where the pane of glass had been. Pete's hand was still wrapped in the folds of the raincoat, protecting it. Groping around at the top of the window, he located a catch; he turned it, unlocking the window.

He stepped down from Jack's knitted hands, planting both feet on the pier. Hinge-mounted to the frame along its upper end, the window swung open and inward as Pete exerted pressure against it, easing it open until the space was wide enough to accommodate the passage of a man.

The dark corner on which the window opened was hemmed in by some wooden packing boxes stacked to the left of the frame; beyond the corner of the stack, a view opened to the center of the building, where the loading of the SUVs continued uninterrupted, the handlers seemingly oblivious of the activity at the far end of the structure.

Pete unwrapped the raincoat bundled around his arm, letting it fall to the pier. Jack was in better shape, so he gave Pete a boost up, allowing the older agent to enter first.

Pete wriggled headfirst through the opening, squirming down the side of the wall to the floor. He kicked his feet clear and tumbled to the concrete floor, moving into the square of shadow cast by the pile of packing cases. Rising, he motioned to Jack that the coast was clear.

Jack gripped the lower end of the frame, chinning himself up and over the opening and going through headfirst, slipping noiselessly to the floor. He was just gathering his feet under him when moving shadows fell across him and Pete.

Three men stepped out from behind the stacked packing cases, where they must have been lurking. Backlit by the lights on the center of the building, they were shadowy forms, their faces hidden. Reflected light glinted on the guns in their hands, guns leveled on Jack and Pete.

One said, "Hold it!"

Pete made a try, throwing himself to one side and grabbing for the gun worn in a holstered side clip at his hip. His piece hadn't even cleared the holster when a shot rang out, a muzzle flare spearing from the gun barrel of the shooter, the man in the middle.

Pete toppled, dead weight slamming to the concrete floor. He rolled into the light, his upturned face revealing a hole in the center of his forehead.

Jack stayed in place, keeping his empty hands clear of his body. Pete had reached against a drawn gun, an impossible try. Just as Colonel Paz had tried to go against Jack when the latter had the drop on him. Paz had had a gun in his hand, and he still hadn't had a chance. Pete's hand was empty, making the odds against success even more astronomical.

Possibly he'd gambled that he could take a few hits to the body and still return fire, giving Jack a fighting chance to go for his gun. But the gunman standing in the center of the trio was too good; a dead shot, he'd drilled Pete squarely through the middle of the forehead. And that with a hip shot made while Pete was in motion, too; the killer was an ace marksman.

The shooter stepped forward, a line of gun smoke curling from the barrel of his gun. Turning to one side to face Jack, he moved so that his face was partly in the light.

He was young, in his mid-twenties, dark hair slicked back straight from the top of his forehead and worn long in the back, curling over his collar. Clean-shaven, with chiseled features, he had bright blue eyes that stood against a deep tan.

Smiling with his lips, he said, "You want some, too?"

Jack stayed in place, motionless.

The shooter took a step forward, toward Jack. He said, "A snoopy guy, eh? This is what happens to snoopy guys."

He slammed the flat of his pistol against the side of Jack's face.

Jack dropped, all going black.

. . . .

THE FOLLOWING TAKES PLACE
BETWEEN THE HOURS OF
12 A.M. AND 1 A.M.
CENTRAL DAYLIGHT TIME

. . . .

Pelican Pier, New Orleans

Jack came to. He was soaked, dripping. Blood?

No, it was water, a bucketful of water that had just been dashed in his face by a hulking goon who stood looming over him.

Jack was sitting up, in a straight-backed, roller-mounted swivel chair. Damned near antique, by the looks of it; it was made not of steel and plastic, but of old brown wood, nicked and scarred.

His hands were secured behind his back. He could barely feel them; they were lumps of meat. He tried to wriggle his fingers to see if he could; they responded, producing agonizing sensations that wrung a groan from him.

A voice said, "Don't bother shamming; I know you're awake." A familiar voice, crisp, well-modulated, slightly accented. The speaker had to speak loud to be heard from the rain drumming on the rooftop.

Jack's eyes came into focus; he looked around. He was in a different part of the building, a corner square that had been partitioned off into a sizable office space.

The partitions were ten feet tall; the top had not been roofed over but left open.

Overhead, a cable dangled down from a rafter beam, terminating in a half-shaded lamp suspended about ten feet above the floor.

The partitions were old, too, made of age-darkened wood; starting at shoulder height, their upper halves were made of frosted, translucent glass, no doubt to let some light into the space.

There was a rectangular wooden desk, as dark and scarred as the partition walls; it contrasted with the layout of computer towers and monitor screens arrayed on the desktop. Some filing cabinets stood in the corners where partition walls met.

The office space had no door, only a door-shaped opening that served as an entryway, set in a partition opposite the rear wall, one of the walls of the building. The office looked like it dated back to the 1950s; the high-tech equipment assembled there was brand-new.

To one side of the entryway stood an old wooden table; atop it were a number of glass cases, terrarium-style, each containing its own set of nasty nature specimens.

One case held a mess of wriggling coral snakes, brightly colored with their bands of red, black, and yellow. They were incredibly venomous; a bite could easily kill a full-grown man. Another held several water moccasins, entwined among one another—black snakes, the inside of whose mouths showed white when they bared their long, curved, poison-dripping fangs, a distinguishing mark that had given rise to their nickname of cottonmouths. A third was stocked with foot-long black centipedes, each of whose bite could make a human limb blacken and swell to elephantine proportions; a fourth was chock-full of tarantulas, black and hairy eight-leggers with bodies the size of silver dollars.

A set of two-legged venomous creatures stood grouped around the chair where Jack sat. Two were known to him: Major Marc Vollard and Rex de Groot, one of Vollard's lieutenants.

The third was the blue-eyed, bronze-tanned shooter who'd killed Pete Malo.

De Groot held the bucket, which he'd just emptied into Jack's face to bring him around.

Vollard was of medium height, compactly made, well-knit. His spade-shaped face showed long green eyes, a snub nose, and a pointy chin. His upper lip was so thin as to be almost nonexistent; above it he wore a neatly trimmed pencil mustache, iron-gray.

He was outfitted in a safari jacket, light blue T-shirt, khaki pants worn tucked into the tops of a pair of combat boots. A thin, lightweight red scarf knotted around his neck added a flash of color. A black patent leather Sam Browne belt was fitted around his torso, holding a holstered sidearm at his hip.

De Groot was big, fleshy, built like an old-time wrestler from pre-steroid days, with sloping shoulders and thick arms, a barrel chest and a big gut. A mop of unruly, silver-gray hair covered his ears and the back of his collar, framing a ruddy, jowly, thick-featured face. He was outfitted in hunter's camouflage-style fatigues; a gun belt worn below his sagging gut held a holstered, long-barreled .44 magnum revolver.

The third member of the trio, the ace gunman, was slim,

straight, and athletic, with a swimmer's build; long-limbed and lean-torsoed. He wore a shoulder holster; the gun holstered under his arm was the weapon that had killed Pete Malo.

Vollard's eyes turned up at the corners, giving them a merry aspect; he smiled thinly with his lips. He said, "Of all the people in the world, it had to be you who found me, Jack. Truly, it is a small world after all."

Jack remained silent, eyes in motion, scanning the room, looking for something, anything he could turn to his advantage. Nothing suggested itself on that score.

Vollard went on, "I'm sure you're wondering where you slipped up, so allow me to enlighten you on that score. Every door and window in the place is covered by electric eye beams. When you and your associate entered, you triggered a silent alarm.

"By the way, I didn't recognize your partner. Ex-partner, I should say. No familiar face from the good old days in the Balkans, not like you and me. Who was he?"

Jack said nothing. Vollard's smile widened, showing his teeth. White, gleaming, they were beautifully capped and bleached.

He said, "Standard doctrine: say nothing to your captors. The slightest word or reply holds the danger of loosening the tongue; once you start talking, it's hard to stop."

The ace gunman said, "The other was a brave man; at least he died fighting. Not like this coward."

Vollard shook his head. "No, Arno, make no mistake. Jack doesn't lack for bravery; he's smart enough to know the futility of throwing away his life to no purpose. Stay alive as long as you can; there's always the chance that circumstances will change in your favor, or that fate will take a hand and deliver a last-minute reprieve from the gallows. Where there's life, there's hope. That's the cruel hoax of it all."

The left side of Jack's face, where Arno had pistol-whipped him with the flat of the gun, was swollen and numb. Jack worked his jaws around, trying to estimate the damage. He switched tactics, abandoning the silent treatment. He said, "What's the plan, Vollard? Where do you figure in all this—"

De Groot stepped forward, delivering a vicious backhand to Jack's face that sent him rocking backward, nearly knocking him out of the chair. The impact caused the roller-mounted chair to glide backward for several feet before bouncing up against a wall.

De Groot said, "That's *Major* Vollard to you, scum!"

Vollard tsk-tsked. "Control yourself, Lieutenant, there's no need for that now. At least, not yet. No need to stand on formality; Jack and I go way back, as you may recall."

De Groot said, "Bah! We should have killed him back in the Balkans!"

Vollard said, "Here he is now, so it's all worked out for the best after all. What's the plan? I don't mind telling you, Jack; you're a dead man, and dead men tell no tales. Besides, frankly, it's rare that I get the chance to converse with someone who has the mentality to appreciate my genius."

Jack spat some blood out of his mouth. "Like that botched hit on Paz?"

De Groot raised a heavy hand to deliver another blow, but a sharp look from Vollard was enough to freeze him in his tracks.

Indicating with a tilt of his head the glass boxes full of spiders, snakes, and centipedes, Jack said, "I see you've brought your relatives along for the mission, Major."

That was enough to set off de Groot again; forestalling

him, Vollard said, "He's just trying to bait you, Rex. Anger you so that you forget yourself and give him a quick death."

De Groot said, "No chance of that." The thought seemed to cheer him. His face was red and swollen, as though he wore a collar several sizes too small; he was wearing an open-neck shirt.

Vollard gestured toward the glass boxes and said, "How do you like my little menagerie, Jack? Nature itself has always been my school. One can only admire the purity and perfection of these single-purpose predators, evolved over the ages into a murderous symmetry of form and function. I find inspiration in such creatures of destruction."

Arno, perhaps not liking that crack about Vollard's lack of opportunity to converse with someone with the mentality to appreciate him, scowled. "He's stalling for time, to keep himself alive a little longer," he said.

Vollard said, "Can you blame him? Let him go to hell knowing the full extent of the disaster that's about to befall the 'good old U.S.A.'; his last thoughts will be devoted to contemplating the catastrophe and regretting his inability to prevent it."

He turned to Jack. "As for the failure of the assassination attempt on Colonel Paz, that was Beltran's responsibility. I assure you that if I had been handling it, the results would have been quite different."

Jack shrugged, the movement sent renewed agony shooting through his bound hands. He fought to keep his face expressionless, but there was nothing he could do about the cold sweat beading up on his pale face. Fighting to keep his tone casual, he said, "So what's the master plan, genius?"

Vollard warmed to the subject. "You'll appreciate this, Jack. Within a few short hours, New Orleans is about to go out of business as America's primary locale for receiving imported oil. Operation Petro Surge—of which you've no

doubt heard, with your high level of security clearance—
will be over before it's begun.

"Simply put, we are going to smash New Orleans. The
Petroleum Receiving Point will be turned into an inferno,
and the Mississippi River Bridge will be sunk at the same
time, ensuring that the port will be closed to all traffic for
months to come—years, considering how you Yanks seem
to have lost the ability to repair your crumbling infrastructure, or even keep it from falling apart of its own accord.

"We're just going to give it a good, hard push in that
direction."

Imported oil doesn't unload itself; it has to be unloaded. The
petro-laden supertankers come to port in the United States,
completing their long transoceanic trips from the Persian
Gulf—or for that matter, Venezuela's Maracaibo Bay. Their
leviathan dimensions, as long as several football fields put
together, require specialized receiving facilities.

The Port of New Orleans is the nation's number one des-
tination for such massive shipments of imported oil. Its primary facility is the Petroleum Receiving Point.

Located several miles downriver from the Mississippi
River Bridge, the PRP, or Point, is located on a spit of land
that thrusts out for a fifth of a mile from the mainland into
the harbor.

It holds an intricate maritime infrastructure designed to
handle the docking of supertankers and the emptying of
their vast stocks of oil, through a network of pumps and
pipelines extending along the point to the mainland, where
a sprawling field of titanic oil storage tanks and petroleum
processing plants and refineries awaits.

Scattered in different places in the harbor and upriver are
a handful of similar sites, though of far lesser magnitude,
but the PRP was the Big One, the league leader, handling

the most traffic and processing the greatest volume of imported crude, the equivalent of hundreds of millions of barrels of oil per year.

Making it a big, fat target for destruction by Major Marc Vollard and his mercenary squad. Unlike his Saudi backers, Vollard was apolitical, a true mercenary. He went where the money was.

It just so happened that the money, the real money, now lay in the oil-rich Middle East. Dogmatic to the ultimate degree on doctrinal points of faith, the radical fundamentalist imams, mullahs, and their acolytes in the ruling class were pragmatic enough when it came to launching a hammer blow at the Great Satan, U.S.A.

The destruction of New Orleans's Petroleum Receiving Point would be a hammer blow indeed. With the PRP down for the months required to make even the most minimal repairs, the flow of imported oil would be checked at the moment it was needed most. Right at the height of what Washington planners called Operation Petro Surge and the Saudi royals called Cloak of Night.

By any name, both the White House and the current power holders in the House of Saud were counting on the successful delivery of that oil. With it, Washington could continue to maintain its guardianship of the vital sea-lanes in the Persian Gulf and protect the kingdom from Iranian aggression.

If the PRP were out of commission, all those oil-filled supertankers would have no place to go. Oh, there were other port facilities in the United States, but none of them had the massive infrastructure needed to process, store, refine, and distribute the Petro Surge oil influx.

They were already backed up and unable to process their current quota.

Oil was the nation's lifeblood, yet the politicians had dithered year after year, building no new refineries and leaving the ones in operation virtually defenseless against sabotage and terror strikes.

America was wide open for a sucker punch, and Major Marc Vollard was about to deliver it.

The target itself allowed him to make a maxi-strike with minimal forces. The silvery globes that were oil storage tanks massed on the mainland at the PRP were giant incendiary devices just waiting for a pyro with a pack of matches.

No great amount of explosives was needed to touch them off; it would take only the blocks of C–4 and Semtex plastic explosives and a handful of thermite bombs that his twelve-man merc squad could tote in on their backs.

The explosives would be placed at carefully plotted nodal points on the oil storage tank farm grid where they could do the most damage. Once they were planted, the bombs' mechanical timing devices would be set, allowing the merc force to make its getaway.

The plastic explosives would rupture and breach the shells; if they didn't touch off the massive stores of oil, the thermite bombs surely would.

The tanks would become a massive string of firebombs, each blast touching off similar explosions in nearby tanks that hadn't been mined; they in turn would set off other tanks, until the entire field was a blazing inferno, a literal Hell on Earth.

That was the Big Hit, the major component, but the strike was designed to be a one-two punch. The second half was the destruction of the Mississippi River Bridge.

Downed, it would block virtually all major river traffic, barring the route to all but the lightest of small craft vessels. That would prevent upriver refineries from taking up any of the slack from the downed PRP.

More, it would present a major headache in its own right, impeding repairs to the PRP and adding extra months to a rebuilding effort that was sure to take a year if not more. The recent Minnesota bridge collapse had shown the kind of damage such an event could do in the way of impeding river traffic.

The Mississippi River Bridge downfall would make that one look sick by comparison.

Vollard handled most of that operation, obtaining the barge now berthed at Pelican Pier, stocking it with explosives and rigging it for its last voyage. He'd handled every part of it but the recruitment of the actual boat handlers.

It was a suicide run, and that was out of Vollard's line; such strikes were for fanatics, true believers, not mercenaries. Mercs were true believers only in money, and expected to live to enjoy their hard-won loot.

The actual kamikaze run itself would be handled by Ahmed and Rashid, a pair of Yemenite boat pilots who'd been supplied by his Saudi backers, Prince Tariq serving as go-between. The Yemeni mariners were skilled boat handlers, having captained vessels in the Persian Gulf, Arabian Sea, and Red Sea.

They craved holy martyrdom; money to them was just so much trash; their goal was beyond: Paradise.

That element had been a bit tricky, since the purpose of using mercenaries to carry out the strike was to go outside the usual box and use personnel generally not subject to the scrutiny that American authorities focused on the usual suspects from the Middle East.

The Yemenis had flown to Mexico and then been smuggled into New Orleans by boat. Vollard had installed numerous safeguards and double-checks along the way; he was satisfied that they had come in under the radar.

All was now ready to go, and tonight was the night.

* * *

Vollard didn't bother going into any detail; he told Jack only that the PRP and the Mississippi River Bridge were targets. Jack was a professional who knew the score, he could figure out the details and fill in the blanks in the short time left for him to live.

Vollard couldn't resist one parting shot, though, a final turn of the knife. He said, "Operation Petro Surge will never happen again; an incredible opportunity that will be lost to America forever. The prime mover and shaker of the surge, Minister Fedallah, will be assassinated at a council meeting in a few hours by another would-be martyr on a pathway to Paradise. With Fedallah gone, the surge will cease to exist.

"Who knows? Perhaps future historians will date the beginning of the final downfall of the American empire from this night.

"Take that thought to hell with you, Jack. And now, I bid you not au revoir, but . . . goodbye."

Vollard turned to Rex de Groot. "You can have him now. You know what to do. Make him talk—though I doubt he has much to offer—and kill him. Make it quick; if CTU was really closing in, they'd be here in force already. The fact that they sent just two agents shows it was more of a recon job.

"Still, no point in lingering here longer than we have to. When the agents don't report, CTU might move in. We'll accelerate the timetable, launching the boat and moving out now, ahead of schedule."

Vollard turned, with parade ground snap, and exited the office, Arno trailing after him. Leaving Jack alone with de Groot.

· ·

THE FOLLOWING TAKES PLACE
BETWEEN THE HOURS OF
1 A.M. AND 2 A.M.
CENTRAL DAYLIGHT TIME

· ·

A man entered the partitioned office. Short, stocky, middle-aged, he had a headful of iron-gray, curly hair; bushy eyebrows; and a short, gray-white beard.

De Groot glanced at him, said, "What do you want, Silva?"

Silva said, "I want to be in on the fun." He smiled, a broad, sloppy, loose-mouthed smile with a gleam of drool in the corners.

"Don't you have something better to do?"

Silva shrugged. "The SUVs are all loaded up, the barge is ready to cast off, the chores are all done. Besides, what's better than torturing a Yanqui spy?"

De Groot snickered. "You might be of some use at that. Come over here and give me a hand. I need him standing up."

He and Silva flanked Jack, sitting in the chair. De Groot was on Jack's left, Silva on his right. De Groot leaned down, sticking his face in Jack's, breathing on him. His breath was hot.

De Groot said, "Let's see how tough you are when you've got a black centipede biting you on the scrotum." He nodded toward the glass boxes, which were on his side of the room. He turned to Silva. "Help me lift him up."

They each hooked a hand under Jack's bound arms, hauling him out of the chair and up on his feet. De Groot said, "Take down his pants—"

Jack stomped down hard with his heel on top of Silva's foot, breaking some bones. Silva screamed, letting go of him. Jack lurched to the side, dropping a shoulder and slamming it into de Groot's midsection, knocking the air out of him and knocking him off balance. Jack lunged hard to the side, shoving de Groot into the wooden table and ramming him so hard against the glass boxes that they broke. Jack pushed back and away from him, regaining his balance on both feet.

De Groot fell back, feet off the floor, half-leaning, half-falling against the table, groping for its edges for support. A coral snake slithered quick as a shot out of its tank, sinking its fangs into his meaty forearm.

A big, fat cottonmouth suddenly uncoiled, lunging, battening on de Groot's neck and chomping down on it.

The coral snake had started him hollering, but the cottonmouth really drove him into paroxysms of agony and fear. He flopped around, knocking already shattered glass boxes to the floor. He grabbed with both hands at the cottonmouth, which clung to his neck, his hands missing hold as the black snake writhed and flailed, not letting go.

Silva had stumbled off to one side, hobbling and cursing, leaning against a partition and holding on to it for support, favoring the leg with the broken foot.

Jack came at him, intent, inexorable. Closing on Silva, he lashed out with a side kick, driving the outside edge of his foot into the other's kneecap. The kick was so hard that Jack felt the impact all the way up to his hipbone.

Silva's kneecap might not have been broken, but it wasn't any good anymore. He flopped to the floor in breathless agony, too pained to scream.

Jack popped a front snap-kick at Silva's head, the ball of his foot taking Silva in the point of his chin. Silva's head jerked back, recoiling on the top of his spinal column.

He fell back.

Jack stomped Silva's upturned throat, then stood on it, putting all his weight on it and grinding his foot there until he heard something snap.

De Groot lay spasming on the other side of the floor, his face swollen purple-black, eyes popping and saliva foaming at the corners of his mouth.

Jack raised a leg, using it to sweep the desktop clean of its stacked computers and monitors, sending them crashing to the floor.

He sat on the edge of the desk and leaned back until his back was flat on the desktop, almost passing out when he put his weight on his bound hands. Lifting his legs, he rocked back some more, raising his rear off the desktop, weight resting on his shoulders. He folded his legs, doubling them, knees touching his chin as he dragged his bound hands out from under them, pulling them in front of him and clearing them past his shoes.

His hands were in front of him now. They'd been bound together with a section of baling wire whose ends had been twisted together to hold him in place. They were almost as purple-black as de Groot's face. The circulation was not entirely cut off; he still had some movement in his fingers, though he could barely feel them.

He rocked forward, planting his feet on the floor and standing up. He could have used that big .44 holstered on de Groot's waist, but was not minded to dispute possession of it with the cottonmouths and coral snakes swarming all over him.

De Groot lay on his back, mouth gaping, jaws stretched to the breaking point. A black centipede twelve inches long wriggled off the tabletop, falling onto his upturned face and slithering inside his mouth.

From the time Jack had been pulled out of the chair by Silva and de Groot, little more than sixty seconds had passed.

Jack made for the opening in the partition, stepping lively to avoid the snakes slithering across the floor. He darted through it, into the open, the high-ceilinged, barnlike space of the building.

He now saw that the office section was at the opposite end of the building from where he and Pete had entered. He'd gotten a break; the drumming of rainfall on the tin roof, the noise of SUV engines and barge motors, all had helped cover up some of the racket generated by his escape.

Behind him, through the open bay door, he saw an SUV roll past, moving landward, its driver oblivious to anything happening in the warehouse. Nearby, at the riverward end of the building, stood a closed exit door. Jack stumbled to it, reaching out toward it with his two swollen, inert hands.

Footsteps sounded on the other side of the door, the doorknob rattling. Someone was coming in from outside.

Thinking fast, Jack pressed his hands against his chest, tearing open the front breast pocket of his shirt and fastening his fingers on the Saint Barbara medallion that Colonel Paz had been reaching for when he died, and that Jack had picked up out of curiosity.

Jack's thick fingers fumbled for it, freeing it from the torn pocket. It fell a few feet in front of the door, glinting with reflected light.

The door swung inward, opening. Jack dodged to one side of the door, flattening against the wall.

Arno entered, bareheaded, his face and shoulders soaked with water but not a hair out of place. He entered quickly, a man wanting to get in out of the rain. Crossing the threshold, he stepped inside, halting when he caught sight of the coinlike medallion on the floor, all shiny and gleaming.

Murmuring with interest, he leaned forward and bent to pick it up. Holding it up to the light, he eyed it appreciatively, turning it this way and that. He slipped it into his front pants pocket.

While Arno's hands were at his sides, Jack made his move. He'd seen Arno's lightninglike gun work and wanted to catch him at the moment of optimum vulnerability.

Jack hooked his hands over Arno's head and around his neck, yanking them inward. The nail-like point where the twin strands of the baling wire were entwined caught Arno in the hollow of his throat.

Jack pulled him closer, tighter, abruptly pivoting to the side, putting everything he had into it. Snapping Arno's neck.

He dragged Arno's body to the side, into the shadows behind a wall of the office partition. He fumbled Arno's pistol out of his shoulder holster, able to accomplish the task only by pressing his pawlike, swollen hands together against the gun butt. Arno had left the safety strap of the holster open and unsnapped, no doubt to facilitate his fast draw.

The gun wasn't much good to Jack in his present condition, but it was better than nothing. An idea came to him.

Going to the door, he opened it a crack and peeked outside, peering through a silvery curtain of slanting rain. No one else was in his field of view.

Returning to Arno, he stooped down, getting one of the dead man's feet wedged under an arm. He dragged the body to the door, opening it and backing out into the rain-swept pier.

The wind and rain felt good, washing over him and bringing a rush of renewed energy. He dragged Arno to the upriver edge of the pier. He pulled the gun from the top of his pants, clutching it between both hands. His thumb felt so numb and lifeless that he had to look to see where it was in order to release the safety on the pistol.

He fired several shots into the air, then shouted in his best imitation of Arno's voice, "Here he is! I got him!"

Footsteps pounded around the corner of the building, voices shouting.

Jack shrieked, then kicked Arno's body over the side into the water. It raised a big splash. He stepped behind some containers, gun in hand, waiting.

Five or six of Vollard's men dashed out on the end of the pier, guns drawn, looking in all directions. One said, "I heard a splash!"

He went to the edge of the pier, looking downward into the dark, swirling waters. Oblongs of light from lamps on the pier fell on the water, illuminating Arno's body for an instant as it bobbed around in the eddying current, pinned for an instant against a piling.

Then it came free, and was sucked down and under and out of sight.

Vollard exited through the back door, joining the others where they stood in the rain at the end of the pier, staring down into black water. Less than a dozen paces away, Jack huddled behind a container box, holding the gun.

Vollard said, "Idiots! The American killed de Groot and Silva and escaped."

One of the men said, "No, sir, he didn't. Arno got him. They both went over the side."

Vollard said, "Are you sure?"

Another said, "I heard them go over and saw the splash!"

A third said, "Me, too, Major."

Vollard said, "Nobody could survive that, no matter how strong a swimmer they are. They've both drowned."

Somebody swore and said, "Of all the rotten luck! Three of our best, dead—"

Vollard shrugged, resuming command. "Hazards of war. Forget it. Their shares go into the common pot to be divided up among you men. All it means is that your shares got bigger."

That cheered up the others. Vollard said, "We've tarried here long enough. Let's move out."

They went away, rounding the corner of the building and going landward along the pier. The riverward end was empty of all but Jack. He slumped down, sitting on the planks with his legs stretched out, back propped up against the container box.

The wire binding his wrists was a problem. It was tied tight and had cut deep. His wrists were bleeding, but the blood wasn't enough for him to work his hand free of the wires. The splice resisted his efforts to undo it. There was no way he could get a grip on it.

He jammed the end of the splice into a thin, slitted gap in a flange of the metal container box. He started working it back and forth, hoping to weaken the resistance of the wires enough to break them. It was hard work, a devil of a job.

While he was doing it, he became distantly aware of the sound of engines starting up, motors chugging away. He redoubled his efforts. He became discouraged; it seemed he was making no headway at all.

Suddenly he felt a flash of heat stab into his hands near the base of the splice. The metal was weakening, giving way. He worked it back and forth some more and it came apart, strands of wire falling away from his hands.

His hands felt like they were in another country. Jack dropped to his knees, head sinking down until his forehead touched the planks. Water pooled there; it was cool and refreshing.

He straightened up, shaking his head, trying to clear it. He worked the last of the strands off his wrists. The flesh was scored, banded, and cut, blood-slick. There was a lot of blood, and for a moment he was afraid he'd cut a vein or artery or something. That would be all he needed.

There was no blood flow, no gushing, so he guessed he was intact after all. He wrestled himself back up to his feet, hanging on to the container for support.

His hands tingled, sensation returning to them. After a moment, the pain became so great that it wrung tears from his eyes. He blinked them away. All he wanted was to get enough feeling back in his hands so he could work Arno's gun properly and shoot some people.

He couldn't wait forever, though. The clock was ticking. He slumped against the short end of the building with his shoulder, leaning on it for support as he moved forward, step by step, toward the downriver side of the pier.

Something large and whalelike lumbered away from the pier, into the mainstream of the river. It was the barge, dirty gray clouds of exhaust spewing from the stacks, resisting the efforts of wind and rain to break them apart. As soon as they were dispersed, new ones spewed from the smokestacks to take their place. The barge was on its way.

Jack glanced landward. At the far end of the pier, two red dots that were taillights winked for an instant and vanished, as the last SUV in a three-vehicle column turned right and drove away, eastbound on River Road.

Vollard's mercenary force was gone, moved out, leaving the pier deserted.

Jack pointed himself landward and stumbled forward. The opposite end seemed impossibly distant. Memory came to him of some of the forced marches he'd been on in the Army. What you did was put one foot in front of the other and keep on going until you got where you were going. It was as good a system as any.

At the ends of his arms, his hands throbbed like a pair of twin beating hearts. After a while, he found he could open and close them. It was agony, but at least they were working. He kept on doing it; it gave him something to occupy himself with while he slogged through wind and rain.

By the time he neared the front gate, his hands worked well enough so that he could hold a gun in them. He came on toward the lighted guardhouse, ready to blast the first thing that moved.

It was empty, abandoned. The gates hung open, swinging free, senselessly bashing themselves against the fence each time the wind blew a fresh gust.

He went through the open gate, across a paved strip, nearly falling when he stepped off a curb that he hadn't seen. The gutters ran high with water, swirling over his feet and around his ankles.

River Road was deserted; he hadn't seen a car or truck pass along it in the time he'd made his way across the pier. Across the street, in the mouth of a side street that met River Road at right angles, stood a parked car.

Now its lights flashed on, pinning him in its headlights. Throwing up his left arm to shield his eyes against the glare, Jack dropped into a combat crouch, leveling his gun.

An amplified voice came blaring across the street from the car's roof-mounted loudspeaker:

"Hold up, Jack! Don't shoot! It's us—Dooley and Buttrick!"

Jack didn't know whether to laugh or cry. Hostiles or friendlies? If the two Bourbon Street cops had wanted to, they could have shot him down like a dog before he could have reacted. On that evidence, they were friendly. Jack stuck the gun in the top of his pants and moved toward them.

Dooley and Buttrick got out of the car, meeting him halfway. Jack staggered and they grabbed him, holding him upright. Dooley said, "Whoo-whee, what happened to you?"

Jack replied with a question of his own: "What're you doing here?"

Dooley said, "You and Pete have been kicking up such a fuss that we figured we'd tag along and see what happened, just for the fun of it. We tailed you here from Belle Reve Street. You been gone so long inside there, we was starting to get worried."

Buttrick said, "Hey, where's Pete?"

"Dead," Jack said. "They killed him."

Dooley's face took on the aspect of a mournful basset hound. "That's a shame, a damned shame."

Buttrick said, "You look half kilt yourself, Jack."

Jack said, "This is important. I've got to contact CTU. The police radio in your car—"

Dooley shook his head. "Ain't no good in this kind of weather, Jack; the storm's got the reception breaking up all to pieces. Can't get through to headquarters or nothing."

"You've got to get me to a phone, it's a matter of life and death—"

Buttrick said, "We got us a couple of satellite phones in the car."

Jack started. "What? You do?"

"Sure 'nuff. We found that out last time in Katrina. Radio wasn't no good, cell phones didn't work worth a good damn, but satellite phones worked just fine throughout," Buttrick said.

Jack was having trouble processing it. "You've got satellite phones? With you?"

Dooley said, "Right here in the car. You want to use it?"

"Hell, yes!"

Dooley said, "Like I said, Jack: we're your boys!"

1 2 3 4 5 6 7 8 9
10 11 12 13 14 15 16 17
18 19 20 21 **22** 23 24

. . . .

THE FOLLOWING TAKES PLACE
BETWEEN THE HOURS OF
2 A.M. AND 3 A.M.
CENTRAL DAYLIGHT TIME

. . . .

*A quarter mile upstream from
the Mississippi River Bridge, New Orleans area*

Not even the wind and rain of the rising storm could hide
the lights strung along the Mississippi River Bridge as the
suicide barge plowed downstream toward it. The river was
choppy, slowing the barge's forward progress.

The barge wallowed amid dark and turbid waters, chugging along, leaving a dirty-white, V-shaped trail in its wake.

In the deckhouse, Ahmed and Rashid were in near-
transports of ecstasy as the bridge loomed in their view, its
lights glimmering hazily, a string of pearls seen through a
gauzy veil.

Paradise was only moments away.

Plowing upstream were three boats, two Harbor Patrol
launches and a Coast Guard cruiser. The launches were

armed with machine guns; the cruiser had a deck gun and machine guns.

The three vessels were between the barge and the bridge, racing to intercept the kamikaze craft. They knew what they were dealing with, having been briefed in full by CTU's Cal Randolph about the explosives-laden barge. They advanced in a kind of crescent shape, wide and shallow, with the two launches at the ends and the cruiser in the center.

The barge kept on coming, ignoring radioed demands that it immediately alter its course. It was equally heedless of the same commands delivered by loudspeakers. It neared the point of no return, when the interceptors must act.

The Harbor Patrol launches fired machine-gun rounds with tracers across its bow, to no avail.

The Coast Guard cruiser upped the ante with an artillery shell from its forward-mounted deck gun. The first shell was in the nature of a warning shot; the succeeding shells were in deadly earnest. The third shell tagged the barge.

A flash, as of lightning; a booming blast, as of a thunderclap; and the barge exploded, disintegrating with such force that pieces of it fell on the shores of both sides of the river.

A crater opened in the black water where the barge had been, the mouth of a funneling underwater whirlpool. In a very short time, the whirlpool contracted, closing in on itself, shrinking from a crater, to a dimple, to nothing at all.

Ministry of the Interior Substation,
Riyadh, Saudi Arabia
10:27 A.M., local time

The ground-floor lobby of the building where the council of twelve met was T-shaped, with a vertical bar extending from the tinted, glass-walled front entrance to the double doors of the council chamber; and the horizontal bar of the T formed by a long corridor that stretched along the front wall of the chamber, its branches extending on both sides to other wings of the structure.

The session of the conclave was scheduled for ten-thirty; at that time, the double doors would be unsealed and opened, allowing the members entry to the conference room.

Now the council members were gathered in the front lobby, along with their administrative assistants, staff members, and other members of their various entourages.

When the meeting convened, admittance to the conference room was reserved strictly for the council members; their followers must wait outside during the closed session meeting.

Among those milling about in the lobby were council members Imam Omar, Prince Tariq, and Prince Hassani. Omar and Tariq and their assorted hangers-on were grouped close together; Hassani stood off by himself, way over on the opposite side of the lobby.

Imam Omar's face was all aglow, as usual, perhaps even more so, as he greeted a succession of dignitaries, smiling and waving, his face cherubic behind its thatching of long, wiry, ash-gray beard.

Prince Tariq was clad in Western garb today, a custom-tailored Savile Row shirt and expensive, hand-tooled Italian shoes, a leather portfolio with a gold clasp tucked under one arm. He smiled often, but tightly, and seemed preoccupied.

Prince Hassani was garbed in the traditional white robes and headdress of the desert tribes; his garments were spotless, immaculate. His gaze was distant, as if fixed on otherworldly matters; his smile was beatific, radiant in its boundless compassion.

A stir went through the crowd as Minister Fedallah approached, striding along the right-hand branch of the horizontal bar of the T, closing on the conference room. Now that he was here, the conference must surely start.

Fedallah wore the dress khaki uniform and peaked cap of a commander of the Ministry's Special Section; his shoulder boards were studded with gold stars, his cap trimmed with gold braid. He walked along in military manner, as if on parade, arms and legs swinging with clockwork precision and timing. His eyes were alert, his face utterly expressionless.

He was flanked by two bodyguards, who marched in step alongside him. A minor breach of protocol, this, since their standard practice was to march a pace behind and to the side of him, a measure of respect that delineated that he was the leader, they the followers.

Also, a sharp-eyed observer might have detected that the flaps of their holstered sidearms were unbuttoned, allowing for speedier access to the weapons.

Fedallah's arrival produced a second stir in the crowd, a most unusual one, as one of the assembled in the lobby suddenly darted forward, rudely shouldering aside his fellows in a brazen attempt to rush to the fore.

Even more startling, the offender was Prince Hassani, ordinarily self-effacing to the point of near-invisibility.

Reaching into the folds of the oversized sleeves of his robe, he pulled out a big-caliber, semi-automatic pistol. Crying out, "Allah Akbar!," his weapon leveled, he rushed toward Minister Fedallah.

With equal and surprising suddenness, the conference doors burst outward and open, revealing a squad of Fedallah's Special Section gunmen, elite marksmen chosen for their dead-accurate skill with handguns. Their guns were out and ready; when the doors flew open, they opened fire, blasting away.

Prince Hassani was caught square in the fusillade, shot through the body a dozen times in the blink of an eye. He whirled and spun in a dervish dance, slugs ripping through him.

Panic and complete chaos seized the civilians massed in the lobby. They scrambled for cover, darting to the sides, throwing themselves to the floor, some shouting, some screaming.

Prince Tariq went into a crouch on the floor, dropping his portfolio, covering his head with his arms as the shooting continued, a concentrated blast of furious firepower that filled the lobby with noise, gun smoke, and bullets.

Then it was over.

Tariq drew a breath and was surprised to find himself doing so; he'd felt sure that the bullets would find him and rip him out of this world and into the next—a transition that, unlike Hassani, he had not the slightest desire to undergo.

Hassani had found his destiny. He lay sprawled on the marbled floor in the contorted posture of violent death, shot to pieces, blood from many bullet holes staining and overspreading, from head to toe, his once linen-white robes.

He was not the only casualty. Somehow, during the shooting, Imam Omar had fallen to several stray bullets—about a dozen or so. Any one of which would have been fatal. The Smiling Cleric would smile no more.

"A terrible accident," Minister Fedallah said, allowing himself a rare smile, all the more chilling for the genuine pleasure it displayed.

He, too, had received a timely warning from CTU, an urgent message warning of an imminent assassination attempt. Not that gratitude for his narrow escape had altered his opinion of the unbelievers one iota.

They were dogs, these Americans, that he still believed; but at least this one time, their barking had proved useful.

. . . .

THE FOLLOWING TAKES PLACE
BETWEEN THE HOURS OF
3 A.M. AND 4 A.M.
CENTRAL DAYLIGHT TIME

. . . .

Petroleum Receiving Point, New Orleans

Departing the Pelican Pier base in a hurry, Vollard had directed the three-vehicle convoy containing his twelve-man
mercenary force to a remote, little-traveled underpass beneath a railroad bridge, a mile or two away from the PRP.

He wanted the storm to reach a greater fury before he
struck, providing maximum chaos and confusion to allow
him to successfully complete his mission. Yet not so much
so as to interfere with his getaway; his, and his troops.

Hurricane Everette did not affect his mission plan greatly;
he'd always planned to approach by land. His primary target
was the vast field of oil storage tanks and the web of pumps
and pipelines enmeshing it. The target area was at the foot
of the Point, solidly on the mainland.

The storm would not affect the explosives, either. The

bombs would be triggered by automatic timing devices, rather than by remote, radio-controlled detonators.

Now, two hours after leaving Pelican Pier, Vollard gave the order to attack. The time had come; the strike was on. The force was on the move, closing in on their objective.

His twelve-man force was divided into three SUVs. The tall-sided vehicles had a high center of gravity that made them particularly susceptible to being blown over by powerful blasts of wind. But the SUVs were roomy, with space enough for four or more fully equipped troops, complete with weapons, gear, and field packs of explosives.

The winds hadn't reached gale force yet; with any luck, the bombs would be planted and the mission completed well in advance of the storm's peak.

Vollard rode in the front passenger seat of the lead vehicle. Rainwater sluiced nonstop across the windshield, side and rear windows; it was like driving through a car wash several miles long. Water streamed along the gutters, pooling in the low spots in the road. No real flooding yet. The SUVs' raised carriages helped, minimizing the danger of drowned, stalled engines.

The three-vehicle convoy cruised the riverfront, coming up to the Point. An impressive sight, this technopolis, one that not even the deluge could wholly subdue.

Looming up against the black backdrop of the river, it looked like a lunar colony out of a science fiction dream.

Rows of oil storage tanks, giant silvery cylinders and globes, were laid out on a grid of avenues and side streets. The tank farm was wrapped in a web of multilevel platforms, catwalks, valve hubs and clusters, junction boxes and pipelines. Avenues were lined with rows of streetlamps; the tanks themselves were bathed by floodlights.

The downpour screened the scene, veiling it, dimming the lights, making them hazy, glowing blurs. Blacktopped rainy streets shimmered with wavy bars and bands of re-flected light.

The Point was approached by a broad thoroughfare, a four-lane avenue leading up to the main gate. The entrance was secured by several guardhouses manned by a squadron of security police.

Vollard could have taken them out by main force, but why bother? It was less risky to avoid them than to elimi-nate them. Why force the front door when it was so easy to enter by the side?

Intelligence precedes attack. Vollard had made a study of the site, photographing it from various angles, clocking the routines of patrols and shift changes, gaming a variety of mission plans at the Pelican Pier base to map out the opti-mum angle of attack.

The Point was on the north side, left bank of the river. River Road highway ran east-west along the shoreline. The massive complex was on the south side of the road. A ten-foot-high chain-link fence bordered the property, walling it off from the mainland.

West of the fence lay a football-sized field that served as a dumping ground for the Point. The final resting place for obsolete hardware and old junk that was less expensive to leave in place to rust and rot, rather than to recycle it or have it carted away.

It was heaped high with sections of pipe eight feet in diameter; old wooden electric cable spools; mounds of V-shaped metal brackets and X-shaped support metal braces; piles of rubble consisting of broken-up pavement and concrete; and similar castoffs.

The dump was fenced in and gated, not so much to dis-courage thieves, who were uninterested in the rubbish, as it was to keep out kids, who'd think it a great playground, where they could break their fool bones and necks, and their parents could then sue the company for big bucks.

It was unguarded, even by junkyard dogs; it was unlit. It was perfect for Vollard's plan.

Now the three-vehicle column pulled off River Road, turning right onto a gravel road leading up the dump yard gate. The machines turned off their headlights, leaving on their parking lights.

One of Vollard's men got out and used a bolt cutter to snip open the padlocked chain securing the gate. He opened it wide and the SUVs drove in.

A dirt road led inward to the depths of the dump, mounds of rubble rising on all sides. The bleary glow of the PRP complex's lights underlit the bottoms of low-hanging clouds sweeping in northward from the river.

The SUVs halted deep in the dump site. Eastward, beyond the fence and inside the Point complex, stood a vast lot filled with big rig trailers and container boxes. The trailers were empty; the truck cabs were parked elsewhere, in a more secure motor pool.

Directly south of the container lot stood the tank farm, the tract of oil storage tanks that was the target for tonight.

Vollard and his men were outfitted for the weather in waterproof ponchos.

The rain slickers were worn over their field packs, similar to knapsacks but more heavy-duty, laid out on a lightweight, tubular aluminum frame allowing the bearer to carry weighty loads. Those packs were filled with blocks of plastic explosives, detonators, and thermite bombs.

A macabre but effective touch, the mercs' assault rifles were weatherproofed by latex condoms covering the barrel muzzles to prevent water getting inside them. The troops also toted green khaki satchels with shoulder straps, containing spare clips of ammunition and grenades.

The relentless rain rendered night-vision goggles useless; it was impossible to see through lenses ceaselessly soaked by nonstop rain. High winds would have ripped them off their faces, too. So they had to forgo them.

Most of them carried commando knives worn in hip sheaths, in case any old-fashioned throat slitting was required.

A couple of mercs began working on the chain-link fence with bolt cutters, opening up a gap big enough for several of them to pass through abreast.

Vollard wasted no time on inspirational speeches, saying only, "Time to earn our pay."

Through the gap in the fence they filed, twelve mercs plus their leader. Vollard was first through the gap; he led from the front. Always.

Now they were in the geometric gridded maze of truck box containers, acres of them. Rain drummed on the rooftops of empty containers, setting an unholy racket rising up on all sides. Water sheeted down the sides of the big boxes; rivulets streamed through the gravel lot.

The force followed an east-west aisle eastward. They had not gone far, when Vollard noticed on his right in a cross street a big yellow bulldozer. It had not been there on the most recent recon mission performed by his scouts the day before.

What of it? There was always plenty of movement around an industrial site.

Typical of the Americans to leave a valuable piece of construction equipment out in the middle of a hurricane; childish, extravagantly wasteful. Shrugging, he thought no more about it.

The containers were laid out in a grid. On the north-south lanes, the south view opened on the tank farm. Rows of cylindrical oil storage tanks, looking like round silver pegs driven into the earth.

The tanks would be mined in hexagonal cluster patterns, with each central, mined tank igniting the adjacent tanks, blowing them up; they in turn would blow up their neighbors, and so on, until the whole field went up like a string of firecrackers.

In a sense, the bombs themselves were a kind of detonator, trigger mechanisms that would unleash the incredibly greater potential energy of each tankful of oil.

The storm would only increase its fury. Oil and water don't mix. Drenching rains would do nothing to suppress the conflagration, but only help spread it. High winds, rather than snuffing it out, would fan it to greater fury, like a stream of oxygen fueling an acetylene torch.

When they blew, the devastation would be awesome. Spectacular.

The sound of a motor engine starting up nearby was explosive in its loudness and surprise shock value. It gave Vollard a start, and the rest of his team, too.

Nothing should be in operation at this time. Vollard was already unslinging his assault rifle out from under his poncho. Around him, his men were dropping into combat crouches. Unlimbering their weapons, they tried to look in all directions at once.

The engine noise loudened, rising to a roar that outshouted the howling winds. It came from behind him, lumbering around the corner of a container and into view.

The bulldozer.

The mighty machine lurched forward, its Caterpillar treads turning, grinding up turf, sending thick gobs of mud flying. Gears shifting and grinding, engine torquing into higher RPMs, the dozer entered the east-west corridor behind the file of mercs.

The corridor formed by rows of container boxes laid end to end was like a chute: a cattle chute. The kind that cattle are herded down on their way to the slaughterhouse.

The bulldozer advanced, coming on, picking up speed. Inexorable juggernaut.

Some of the mercs broke and ran eastward along the corridor, others had the presence of mind to open fire on the oncoming machine.

More and additional motors went into action, whining and grinding as they lifted the bulldozer's front blade, providing cover for the driver and his passenger in the open cab.

Bullets turned into lead smears as they struck the massive, concave blade, striking sparks, ricocheting, making no headway against its heavy-duty metal.

The corridor between the parked containers was just wide enough to allow the bulldozer to pass through with a foot or two of clearance on either side. Not enough for a man to pass through.

The mercs were shooting at the bulldozer; now the dozer opened fire on the mercs.

Back when he was in his teens, and during summer semester breaks during college, Jack Bauer had worked construction. It had served him well then and continued to do so in his present line of work. Being a construction worker was good cover at home and abroad, anywhere where big projects were afoot.

Jack was a pretty fair heavy-equipment operator. Now he was doing a better than fair job of driving the bulldozer down the corridor at the mercs.

His hands and wrists still hurt like hell. He'd had them patched up by CTU medics, passing on the painkillers to keep his reflexes sharp and his mind clear. He'd popped a few energizer pills, amphetamines, to keep him amped up for the big finish.

Wearing wrist-length work gloves to protect his hands, he double-shifted, working the floor-mounted stick shifts.

The cab was surrounded with four vertical poles holding a square-shaped metal roof over the driver's seat. It was open on all four sides, but the raised blade served as a bulletproof shield.

Jack did not ride alone. Hathaway was with him, manning a .50-caliber machine gun that had been rigged in the cab, wired into place over the top of the hood.

They both wore strips of white cloth knotted in place above the elbows of their left arms. A means to instantly identify CTU personnel from the enemy. A lot of bullets were going to be flying, and CTU wanted to lose no men to friendly fire.

Hathaway cut loose with the machine gun, laying down a line of fire that tore up the turf several feet away from the mercs at the rear of the file.

That did it. Vollard's troops broke and ran for the open space at the opposite end of the corridor.

The bulldozer kept on coming, treads tearing up turf, machine-gun muzzle flashing fiery spear blades. The corridor was a chute with no way out on the sides.

Vollard realized that the machine-gun fire wasn't ripping into the men, it was nipping at their heels, setting them running. Herding them!

One of the mercs in the rear of the file tripped and fell, sprawling face-first in the mud. He got his hands and knees under him and started to rise just as the bulldozer was upon him.

The dozer rolled over him, grinding him flat under its

treads. He made not so much as a bump in the machine's forward progress.

The mercs were stampeding now, running toward what looked like safety at the far end. Before they were even halfway there, a big-rig tractor-trailer truck rolled into view, crossing the opposite end at right angles, blocking it and closing off the exit.

Turning the corridor into a box.

A kill box. The trap had closed and the endgame was opening.

Stretched out prone on top of the container boxes on both sides of the chute was a squad of CTU marksmen. Sharpshooters.

They wore rain hats and ponchos, their weapons wrapped in waterproof sheaths until now, when they were brought into play. With the terrible patience of hunters, they'd lain in wait for a long hour in the rain, since spotters had first announced the arrival of Vollard's men.

Now they opened fire, shooting down at the merc force. The opening crack of the fusillade was so synchronized that it sounded like a single thunderclap.

No battle this, but a firing squad. Each sharpshooter sighting down on a man and bagging him. Taking him down with a head shot. Less messy that way. No one wanted to touch off a grenade or thermite bomb.

At this close range, they couldn't miss.

No prisoners. No quarter.

Instead of fleeing, Vollard rushed the bulldozer. Grenade in hand, he pulled the pin, counting three.

Hathaway saw him, swung the machine-gun muzzle in his direction.

Vollard tossed the grenade at the bulldozer, lobbing it in over the top of the raised blade.

Jack dove sideways out of the cab, diving for the dirt. Splashing facedown in soft mud with only several inches of clearance between him and the outside of the tread.

The dozer kept on rolling.

The grenade dropped to the floor of the cab. Hathaway readied to jump—the grenade blew. The blast jarred something in the dozer, causing it to stall out.

Deeper into the chute, the firing squad continued, cutting down the mercs. Like hailstorm flattening a wheat field.

There was a flash of quick, catlike movement as Vollard raised himself from the mud, shucking off his field pack.

Getting his feet under him, he charged the stalled bulldozer, using the now-motionless tread as a stepping stone, vaulting himself up to the blade. He grabbed the top of the blade with both hands, chinning himself up, hauling himself by main force up and over the blade.

Ignoring the smoking, shredded heap that was Hathaway curled on the riddled cab floor, Vollard scrambled across the top of the driver's seat and out the back of the open-topped cab, dropping to the ground behind the machine.

Jack, momentarily stunned by the concussion of the blast but unharmed, looked up in time to see Vollard scramble up and away.

Rising, turning sideways, he sidestepped through the space between the stalled dozer and the container box and took out after Vollard.

Vollard had a good head start. He headed back the way he came, toward the gap in the fence to the dump yard. Checking his advance when he saw flashlight beams and vehicle headlights inside the fence.

CTU was already there, cutting off that avenue of escape.

He glanced left, right. To the right lay a long stretch of open ground between him and River Road, plus a fence bordering the perimeter of the property.

To the left, closer, about thirty yards away, was a metal tower about a hundred feet high. It was shaped something like an oxygen tank, long and slender, with lots of knoblike appurtenances on top of it. Wrapped at the base with a web-work tracery of stairs and platforms.

The tower was an outpost of the tank farm. If he could make it there, he stood a damned good chance of evading pursuit and perhaps extricating himself to safety through the maze. These calculations were performed at lightning speed.

Vollard shifted left, running toward the tower. He serpentined, not proceeding in a direct straight line, but dodging, bobbing, weaving.

Jack saw him and took after him.

Some CTU agents armed with assault rifles emerged from the dump, through the hole in the fence and into the PRP grounds. One of them saw what looked like two figures fleeing south across an open field toward the tank farm.

He shouldered his rifle, drawing a bead on Jack's back—then saw the strip of white cloth hanging from his target's left arm, the CTU identifying tag.

He swung the rifle toward the other fugitive, the one in the lead. That one was too far away for the rifleman to make out whether he wore the white cloth strip.

Rain was falling so heavily that it brought down visibility to a minimum; the rifleman had barely, just barely, seen Jack's identifying strip of cloth in time.

Not knowing whether the man in the lead was CTU, the rifleman decided not to risk a shot.

Thanks to Jack's warning earlier via the satellite phone in Dooley and Buttrick's car, CTU had managed to forestall Vollard's planned onslaught in all three theaters: the suicide

barge on the river, the hit try on Minister Fedallah in Riyadh, and the merc force's assault on the tank farm.

CTU had had two SWAT teams on the scene at the PRP,
plus some mobile, auxiliary roving backup squads. Spotters
were posted at selected vantage points, their sightlines covering 180 degrees on the landward side. Even with visibility
reduced to a minimum by wind and rain, they had seen the
three-vehicle convoy coming eastbound on River Road.

The invaders had chosen the stealth approach, one that
would take them through the dump yard into the truck container lot.

Jack, seeing a bulldozer parked nearby, had the idea of
herding Vollard's team right where CTU wanted them. He
and Hathaway had climbed up into the dozer's open cab,
mounting the machine gun to the left of the driver's seat.

A squad of CTU sharpshooters, ace marksmen all,
climbed up on top of the container boxes that formed a
corridor from the edge of the dumping grounds to the tank
farm. It got pretty hairy up there at times when the wind
gusted, threatening to blow them off the rooftops.

Vollard's force had cut a breach in the fence and filed
across open ground to the near end formed by the corridor
between two lines of parked trucks. It was a logical choice,
providing as it did the best cover against being seen by observers and allowing a close approach to the tank farm.

As soon as the last merc bringing up the rear had followed the others into the corridor, Jack fired up the engine.
Using both hands to work the floor-mounted gear switches,
opening the throttle, he'd maneuvered the dozer behind
Vollard's men, coming at them.

Hathaway had deliberately aimed the machine gun for
the ground just short of the invaders, not wanting to risk
tagging one of the bombs they were carrying and triggering

an uncontrollable, unpredictable blast that might endanger defenders as well as attackers.

Bulldozer and machine-gun fire had herded the merc force deeper into the corridor.

The idea was to put them square in a crossfire of CTU sharpshooters, deadly marksmen who could pick their shots and neutralize the enemy with precise head and body shots that would avoid hitting the munitions they carried in their field packs. The corridor was a kill box.

CTU sharpshooters fired with deadly accuracy, decimating the enemy force. There was still a risk of a stray slug tagging a munitions pack and setting off a blast. A hot round would have no effect on the plastic explosives blocks; it was the detonators and mostly the thermite bombs that were the big threat.

Jack planned to cut off the snake's head, but he hadn't reckoned on the cat-quickness of Vollard. The merc man had gone up and over the bulldozer, getting clear of the chute and making his break.

Jack recovered quickly, taking off after him. The chase was on.

Vollard ran toward the tower, the outlying rampart of the tank farm; Jack following. Here in the open, beyond the shelter afforded by parked trucks and the solidity of the bulldozer cab, the full force of wind and rain made itself felt.

Winds blew in from the south, coming across the river and sweeping north, whipping driving rains before it. Some of its force was broken by the tank farm that stood between it and the running men. Wind funneled through the gaps between the oil storage tanks, creating a venturi effect that magnified their force.

As soon as Jack was in the open, the wind hit him like

an invisible force field, fighting him. He leaned forward, almost double, charging head-down into the torrent.

He still wore the work gloves to protect his aching hands. Time enough to pull them off when the shooting started.

Vollard reached the first barrier, a bundle of waist-high, horizontal pipes that stretched across the field at right angles. It was supported on a stand that kept the bottom of it a foot or so above ground level; the space was too small to duck under, he had to go over the top.

He bellied across the uppermost pipe, flopping down on the other side. Rising, for the first time since beginning his flight he dared to look back. He saw a figure about a dozen yards away, closing on him.

He failed to recognize the newcomer, but the strip of white cloth tied to the other's upper arm was a sure cue that it wasn't one of his men. Behind the pursuer, a couple of dozen yards back, several more figures were making for the tank farm.

Vollard drew his pistol, holding it in a two-handed grip, bracing it against the top of the pipe to steady it. He blasted a couple of shots at the lead pursuer.

Windborne rain reduced visibility; even at these close quarters, his target was a blur. The figure fell forward, flattening facedown on the ground. Vollard exulted; he'd tagged his man!

Then the other fired from a prone position, a round angling past Vollard's head.

Jack had peeled off the gloves and pulled his gun. The time to start shooting was now. He'd placed his return fire very carefully, aiming it upward at a high angle that would pass harmlessly through the gaps between the storage tanks. He had no desire to accidentally put a bullet into a pipeline or tank and possibly trigger the very blast he'd labored body and soul to prevent.

The shot served its purpose, goosing Vollard into motion. The merc turned and ran; Jack jumped up, following.

Jack angled to the left instead of continuing straight-on, to avoid approaching from the direction in which Vollard had last seen him, using the element of surprise to avoid running into a bullet. He threw himself over the pipeline, coming down on the other side.

He saw Vollard climbing a metal stairway that led to the first level of platforms and catwalks. Appraising the situation, thinking quickly, Jack continued on his leftward tangent, closing on a second metal staircase about fifty feet left of the one Vollard was mounting.

Jack was winded, panting for breath. He was in good condition, but in the last few hours he'd been knocked unconscious and beaten. Merely making the dash from the dozer across open ground in the face of storm-force winds and rain to the tank farm had required a supreme physical effort.

Taking several deep breaths, he gripped the stairway's metal railing and started climbing. Rainwater cascaded over the stairs, trying to tear his feet out from under him and trip him up.

He reached the top of the stairs, where a platform stood, the hub of a network of catwalks radiating out in several directions. To his right, he saw Vollard come back into view; the merc leader was stymied, boxed in.

Jack's quick scan of the framework of platforms, stairs, and walkways had indicated that the tower platform was a dead end, off by itself and isolated from the rest of the framework. He'd guessed right. Vollard was cut off. Jack blocked his only access to the network of metal webwork binding and linking towers and tanks, pumping stations and pipeline hubs.

Vollard had hoped to lose himself and elude his pursuers in the intricate, multileveled tangle. To do so now, he'd have to come through Jack. Let him try!

Jack refused to let Vollard take the initiative and make the next move. He made it first, starting along the catwalk toward the tower where Vollard lurked. Winds buffeted him, slamming into him with body-blow force.

Shots sounded, Vollard firing at Jack.

The storm was impartial, taking no sides. The same winds that sought to tear Jack loose from the catwalk also slammed Vollard, knocking off his aim, making it impossible for him to draw an accurate bead on Jack.

His bullets went wild. The closest he came was a round that spanged the steel safety railing of the catwalk; metal sang and shivered, generating an impact that Jack could feel up to the elbow of the arm whose hand clutched that rail. It didn't do his sore hand any good, either.

He kept on coming, closing in, holding his fire, waiting for a clean firing line for a killing shot.

Perhaps Vollard had emptied his clip; he stopped shooting and dodged around the platform that skirted the tower, disappearing around the curve. The platform was an apron that made a 360-degree ring around the tower; Vollard had vanished on the far side, the one facing riverward.

Jack stepped onto the platform, crouched almost double, gun arm stuck out in front of him, free hand clutching the rail. No tanks or other obstructions stood between him and the terrific force of northbound winds.

He decided on a quick change-up, abandoning the safety rail at the outer edge of the platform and darting inward, flattening himself against the curving metal wall of the tower. Hugging it to keep from being windblown across the platform.

He reversed position, so that not his front but his back was now flattened against the tower. Sidestepping, he edged around the tower toward the windward side.

As he rounded the curve that put him in the direct path of the storm, the wind became an ally, pushing him back against the tower and helping to hold him in place. He inched farther along, looking up.

On the windward side, a vertical metal-rung ladder was bolted to the side of the tower, rising straight up for sixty or seventy feet before accessing an upper platform level.

Vollard clung midway up, his free arm hooked through a rung to hold him in place, gun hand pointed downward at the platform below. He'd expected his pursuer to come along the outer rim of the platform, where the safety rail provided some protection against being blown away. Instead, Jack had come along the inner rim, back flattened to the curving tower wall.

A flash of motion glimpsed in the corner of his eye alerted Vollard that the showdown had come.

He and Jack opened fire, Jack's first shot coming perhaps a split-second before Vollard's, both squeezing off a rapid-fire burst of rounds.

Vollard, caught unaware by his foe's unexpected change of position, missed his target, his rounds sailing clear of Jack and hammering the floor of the platform beyond him.

Jack fired straight up along the ladder, pumping slugs into Vollard hanging fifty feet above him. Emptying his clip into the other.

Vollard's hold broke; he pitched forward, falling free.

A streaming, screaming blast of wind caught him in mid-air, swiping him to the side. The wind screamed. Vollard was silent, no sound escaping him as he took the big dive.

His trajectory caused him to hit the catwalk rail, thudding

against it with an impact that Jack felt through the soles of his shoes right up to his knees.

Vollard bounced off, cartwheeling into space and dropping another twenty-five feet before slamming into the ground below. With a thud that was clearly audible to Jack, even above the winds.

Jack reloaded before starting down. It was a matter of routine. Vollard was done. The steel safety rail he'd struck on the way down was bowed and crumpled.

Jack climbed down to solid ground, fighting wind and rain to cross to Vollard, who lay in a heap near where a T-shaped pipeline rose out of a concrete platform.

Crouching down beside the body, Jack turned him faceup. His bullets had tagged Vollard in a leg, the belly, and on his left side under his arm, drilling him through the chest. Vollard's open eyes lay unblinking as rain pelted his face.

A CTU agent came up beside Jack. He put his mouth close to Jack's ear and spoke loudly to be heard over the storm. He said, "Which one is that?"

Jack's thoughts were not of Vollard, but of those who'd been lost along the way, men like Pete Malo, Hathaway, Topham, and Beauclerk; real patriots who'd risked all and sacrificed all, not for personal gain, for money, but for that most intangible thing of all: an ideal, a dream of freedom and a hope that the nation might perhaps, at its best, embody that ideal.

Thinking that Jack hadn't heard him, the agent said, "Who was he?"

Jack said, "Who was he? Nobody, just a hired gun.

"Now retired," he added.

1 2 3 4 5 6 7 8 9
10 11 12 13 14 15 16 17
18 19 20 21 22 23 **24**

. . . .

THE FOLLOWING TAKES PLACE
BETWEEN THE HOURS OF
4 A.M. AND 5 A.M.
CENTRAL DAYLIGHT TIME

. . . .

Hurricane Everette never did make landfall at New Orleans or even the Gulf Coast. At the last moment, it changed course, veering on a path that ultimately sent it crashing full-force into Cuba.

CTU arranged for Havana and Caracas to learn enough select details of the Paz/Beltran affair to cause a serious breach in the alliance between their two countries.

Society pages bannered the forthcoming nuptials of Susan Keehan. The bridegroom: Gene Jasper, a security expert who was leaving EXECPROTEK for a seat on the board of several Keehan-owned corporations.

Floyd Dooley and Buck Buttrick became nationally famous as "Hero Cops Who Thwarted a Terror Plot." Their ghostwritten autobiography spent several months on the best-seller list and was optioned by a Hollywood studio to become a major motion picture, which was never made. Dooley went on to run for the post of Louisiana Parish sheriff; narrowly defeated, he went on to become a front man, spokesperson, and greeter for New Orleans's newest and most lavish gambling casino. His partner, Buck Buttrick, became the host of a popular fishing show on an outdoors-oriented cable TV network.

A week or so after Hurricane Everette, a body washed up on the shores of the Mississippi River. It was identified as that of Arno Puce, Corsican gunman and member of Vollard's mercenary force. Among the contents of his pockets was found a medallion bearing the likeness of Saint Barbara. It quietly became the property of a young assistant at the parish morgue, who palmed it when nobody was looking and took it home. He figured it might be some kind of good luck piece.

In Saudi Arabia, the Rub' al-Khali, the Empty Quarter, is a bleak wasteland so forbidding, so unremittingly hostile to human life, that even the most hardened, desert-dwelling Bedouin tribes give it a wide berth on their wanderings.

Not long after the failed assassination attempt on Minister Fedallah, an air-conditioned Cadillac car was driven deep into the Quarter, as far as it would go before its gas tank registered empty. It stood inert in the middle of a sun-blasted flat, several hundred miles from the nearest human habitation.

Its occupants were two members of Fedallah's Special Section and Prince Tariq.

The pair of escorts treated Tariq with the impersonal politeness of the executioners that they were.

Presently, the vault of white-hot sky was broken by a flyspeck, a blur of motion that resolved itself into a helicopter that closed on the site where the Cadillac stood.

It touched down long enough to pick up the two Special Section men before lifting off, leaving Tariq marooned in the middle of a desert hell without so much as a drop of water.

Fedallah had neutralized the threat posed by the Prince, and the Prince himself, while still obeying the prohibition that his royal blood not be shed.

Before twenty-four hours had passed, Tariq had truly experienced the "mouthful of sand" that Fedallah had once promised as the fate of those who defied the will of His Majesty, Supreme Master of the House of Saud.

At the end, his brains boiling in the cauldron of his skull, Tariq realized to the full the truth of the old saying:

If you strike against the king, strike hard!

HE SAVED THE WORLD.
WE SAVED THE BEST FOR DVD.

24

24 SEASON 6 ON DVD
DECEMBER 4TH

Includes The Complete Sixth Season – Plus Deleted Scenes,
Commentaries, Featurettes, Season Seven Preview & More